It Does Not Die

Maitreyi Devi

# The Author

Daughter of the eminent philosopher Surendranath Das Gupta, Maitreyi Devi was born in September 1914. Her first book of verse appeared when she was sixteen, with a preface by Rabindranath Tagore. She was a devoted disciple of Tagore who accepted her invitation to stay with her family, more than once, in her home in the mountains, near Darjeeling. Her notes and diaries of that period were organised into a Tagore Memoir (in Bengali) renowned in Bengali literature as *Maung-pu te Rabindranath*. This book was published soon after Tagore's death, and was later translated into English by her as *Tagore by Fireside*. In 1955 she visited Switzerland and Russia; in 1961, the Tagore Centenary year, she was invited to Bulgaria, Hungary, G. D. R. and Russia. In 1973 she lectured at various universities in the U. S. and, in 1975, toured Europe on invitation. She founded the Council for the Promotion of Communal Harmony in 1965, and has established two boarding schools for destitute children, one in Dacca, the other in a village near Calcutta. Closely associated with the Gandhi Peace Foundation and the Quaker Society of Friends. Vice-President of the All-India Women's Co-ordinating Council. She passed away in 1991. Publications include 4 volumes of poetry in Bengali; 8 books on Tagore in Bengali and English; 4 books of travel, philosophy, and social reform; and 3 collections, edited by her, on Tagore, Gandhi, and secular-minded Bangla Desh writers. Her English writings have appeared under the name Maitraye Devi, the phonetic rendering of Maitreyi Devi, which is the correct transliteration (used in this book).

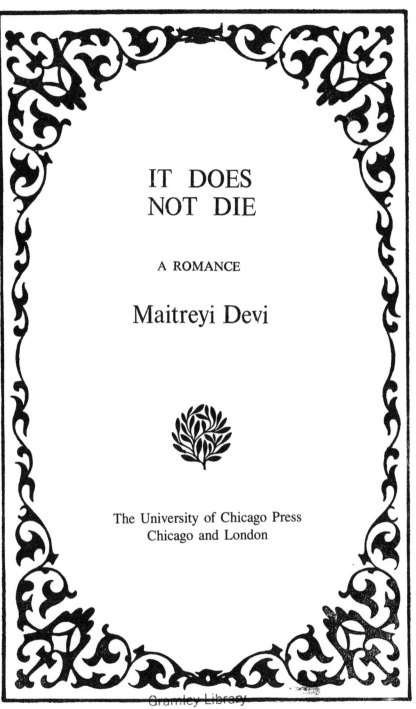

# IT DOES
# NOT DIE

## A ROMANCE

## Maitreyi Devi

The University of Chicago Press
Chicago and London

This work originally appeared in Bengali under the title *Na Hanyate,* published in 1974 by Manisha Granthalaya. The author's English translation first appeared in 1976 under the imprint of Writers Workshop, published by P. Lal in Calcutta. Writers Workshop brought out a new printing in 1992; it is this edition which we have offset, correcting only a few typographical errors. The author's heirs have requested that idiosyncrasies in diction or grammar not be changed, in order to preserve Maitreyi Devi's English-language version of her story.

The University of Chicago Press, Chicago 60637
The University of Chicago Press, Ltd., London
© 1976 Maitreyi Devi
All rights reserved. Originally published 1976
University of Chicago Press Edition 1994
Printed in the United States of America

01 00 99 98 97 96 95 94     6 5 4 3 2 1


ISBN 0-226-14363-5

Library of Congress Cataloging-in-Publication Data

Maitraye Devi, 1914–
    [Na hanyate. English]
    It does not die : a romance / Maitreyi Devi.
        p.   cm.
    I. Title.
PK1718.M24244A26   1994
891'.4436—dc20                                               93-38599
                                                             CIP


♾ The paper used in this publication meets the minimum requirements of the American National Standard for Information Sciences—Permanence of Paper for Printed Library Materials, ANSI Z39.48-1984.

## Dedication

an offering
at the temple
of Mahākāl

ajo nityah śāśvato'yam purāno na  hanyate hanyamāne śarīre
*Unborn, eternal, everlasting, primeval, it does not die*
*when the body dies.*

BHAGAVAD GITA Canto Two Sloka 20

# Contents

# Book One

1ST SEPTEMBER 1972. MY BIRTHDAY. MY DEAR FRIENDS, Goutami and Parbati—you were the ones so keen to celebrate it, but you never knew that this evening, in the middle of the music, recitations and laughter in the room, I was constantly drifting away. The tide of time was turbulent, it touched me and carried me away, not forward, towards the future, but backwards—deep into the past.

It is midnight, it may be two o'clock. I am standing alone on the verandah. From where I am I cannot see the full sky. The half of the Great Bear like an eternal question mark looks down on me—questions, questions. Why did *this* question come back to me crossing over so many decades? Sometimes I used to ask myself why did such a thing, which had no consequence, happen to me? Now I see it had no beginning and no end. The stars are bright, they have witnessed the ordeals of countless persons, just as they are watching me to-day. The sky attracts my whole being. I feel I am not here, yet I am very much here. Can I ever go away anywhere else? This is my world. In the bedroom my husband is sleeping peacefully. What confidence he has in me! He does not know me well, yet how he loves me. I am his all-in-all, but he must have felt the same is not true for me; but he has no regrets, nor have I. My life is full.

Whatever I could offer to this world I feel I have offered. I feel I have known the glory of a supreme love, a love that became worship, a love that threw an upward flame. I have found a completeness, a fulfilment by offering to my Guru all that was best in me. Why then, from yesterday, has my life changed so?

What tormenting discontent ruffles the hot sands of
the Sahara and threatens to cover my fertile, green and
beautiful world! I know that under the cover everything
is as it was. I am still as fixed in the unconscious mind of
my sleeping husband as I ever was, and my little grandson,
who is now asleep nestling near his parents, will run downstairs
in the morning and embrace me as usual. My world still is
the same—tender, lively, green. Yet I am afraid, for I feel
the heat of a molten lava that threatens to engulf it. No, not
lava. It may be molten gold. I know I do not want to reject
it, because there is joy in it. I remember the poem "When
everything becomes ash, something remains unconsumable"—it
is that something, it is the unconsumable remnant. Yet, for
the last two days, what agony! I ask myself : What is it?
Is it the inscrutable yearning Kalidasa describes in *Sakuntala*—
"Seeing a beautiful object or hearing a beautiful sound, even
happy persons become restless; may be they remember a
forgotten love from another life."

No, I am not talking of another life—it is not past life,
it happened only the other day—only forty-two years ago.
I have stepped forty-two years backwards. For us human
beings it is a long period, but how small it is in eternity!
Time is not anchored anywhere. It has no front, back or
sides. Time does not rise and set. Only to express me the
Infinite becomes finite. Suddenly today it has wiped off the
boundary of fortytwo years round me. And I have entered
eternity, I have no future or past. I stand with one foot
in 1972 and another in 1930.

It happened on the morning of 1st September 1972. The
day before, an old friend, Gopal, phoned me after many
years.

He asked, "Amrita, do you remember Mircea Euclid?"
"Yes, a little," I hesitated. "Why do you ask?"
"One of his friends has turned up. Euclid was your
father's student. Since your father is no more, he wants to
meet you," Gopal replied, almost casually.

A spark of joy flared up for a second. On the other end of the telephone Gopal was getting impatient. "Why are you silent? Shall I bring him to you now?" "No, no." I stopped a little, fumbling for words. "I'll go to him tomorrow. Give me his address." It was raining from the morning. I was lucky to get a taxi and reach in time. Why do I go? I asked myself. Why should I be so keen for news of a person who does not even reply to my letters? Plain curiosity. I satisfied myself. Nothing wrong in enquiring about a person you knew once. To be truthful, I must admit I dressed up a little, as any woman would. I had put on an attractive sari, yet standing before the mirror I felt sorry for my looks. Time wipes away all that was once held precious. It is a great destroyer, it shatters and wears out everything. Does time only make everything old? Does it not also make any thing new? Yes, my body is old, but my mind? The mind that is eager for news of Mircea Euclid now is young. It too is a creation of time. Once in my young days I wrote a poem:

The time that was behind
comes in front,
her face unveiled, wearing star studded silk.
Who gave her dress and ornaments?
How comes the show of this temporary wealth?
In the touchless flow of time
in its formless motion
who grows flowers?
Forms take shape every moment
from the ocean of emptiness
and fall on the shoreless shore.
Waves break in an illusion of death.

When I wrote this poem I did not know that what was over could return, what was old could become new, or that the conception of old and new itself is an illusion. Sitting in the speeding car, I laughed at myself. Why did I dress up, why need I be sorry about my looks? I shall not meet Mircea. I am meeting only a stranger from his country.

The door was open. He had a tan, not the usual white
complexion of a European. He was of medium height.
He stood up to receive me, said "I am Sergui Sebastian",
and, stretching out his hand, he clasped my right palm and
reverentially imprinted a kiss on it. At this familiar gesture
the long forgotten days of my youth struggled to return.
"Are you Amrita?" he asked. I knew that this foreigner
was looking through me at another Amrita. The admiration
and surprise conveyed in that simple question could not
possibly be inspired by this Amrita, whose hair has greyed
and face has lined. He was watching me with fixed eyes; his
vision penetrating me had gone very far. I knew he was
gazing at the Amrita of 1930.

"Do you know me?" I asked calmly.

The man smiled    "Everyone in my country knows you.
You are the heroine of a fairytale."

"Why?   Because of Euclid's book?"

"Yes, his book told us of you.   He wanted to marry you,
but your father did not agree.   You a Hindu and he a
Christian."

"Nonsense," I retorted.

"You mean it's not true?"   Sergui was visibly taken
aback at my vehemence.

"What has Hindu or Christian got to do with it?   It was
all his vanity.   His pride was hurt, nothing else."

Both of us sat in silence for a while, then I spoke.   "It is
today fortytwo years since Mircea left; off and on I have heard
about the book, named after me, but I never asked anyone
about the contents of that book.   Is it a story, or a book of
poems, or a dissertation?   I never cared to enquire.   Today
I ask you, tell me, what is in that book?"

I asked this question, smiling casually.   I congratulated
myself on the ease with which I did it.   How simply I could
ask now; why did I not do so for so many years?   She was
certainly another Amrita.   What have I to do with the Amrita
of fortytwo years ago, the heroine of that book?   Am I

responsible for her deeds?  Can her Karma devolve on me
any more?  I have heard that after twelve years even a
murderer is not convicted.  Why should I be ashamed then?
But I know the answer already.  Because I am a moralist.
I judge myself severely—I do not condone any weakness.
My friends never tell me about their lapses.  I remain on a
high pedestal of honour.  Whenever I have remembered
Mircea I have frowned at myself.  How could all that happen
at all?  How could I have yielded?  Once a sense of deep
shame and guilt made me send his memory down into the
depth of the subconscious.  Yet today how easily I talk . . . .

Sergui said, "It is an autobiographical novel.  Do you
know," he continued with enthusiasm, "that reading that book
we knew Calcutta, we knew Indian society, Indian life—the
people of our country were thrilled.  The book reads like a
tragedy.  His suffering, his agony fall through that book like
droplets of blood."  Sergui does not speak English well;
haltingly he begins to narrate the story.

I remember the familiar names.  They knock at my heart;
slowly one by one shutters open to reveal a little of the room
closed so long ago.  Inside the room is darkness, yet I know
all that is there.  I am tempted to enter it, but hesitate with
apprehension.

"Sergui, please tell me the truth.  What does that book
say about me?"  I pleaded, smiling a little, and then in his
continental pronunciation, making the English "t" sound soft,
he said, "First she loved a tree."  The words fell like a
moonbeam on my heart.  A lamp of memory sparkled.
"True," I said, "true indeed; tell me more, is there anything
in that book I should be ashamed of?"

With his eyes lowered Sergui stammered, "He has
written that you used to visit him at night."

"Scandalous!  Believe me, Sergui, that is not true!"
I almost shouted.

"Yes, yes," Sergui consoled me, "that is evident.  "He
has not been able to describe you, so he had to say you came

in darkness. He had no other way," Sergui went on. I felt
helpless: I am prepared to accept an unpleasant truth but
why should I be the victim of an unpleasant lie?

Extinguishing the cigarette in the ashtray, he said,
"Forgive me, I told you everything, I had to tell the truth."

"Tell me, Sergui, what need was there to use my name?
Isn't it almost libel?" I asked sharply.

"He was not able to get away from the magic of your
name. What agony he was passing through then; if you read
the book, you will be in tears."

"But why had he to write lies? I never came to him at
night. Why this slander?"

"Fantasy. He took shelter in the world of fantasy.
That was the only way left to him to escape from the
suffering—even now he has not forgotten you," Sergui spoke
almost to please me.

"What an excuse for lying! If he really was so much in
love, why did he run away at one snubbing from my father?
Had he no duty towards me? Have you ever known of such
cowardice?"

"Haven't I?" Sergui smiled. "History is full of such
instances. You were then a young girl of sixteen, he was a
young man of twenty three. What a pity your father spoilt
your life." His voice melted in sympathy.

I was astonished. What is this man saying? "Sergui,
how much do you know of life? Who can spoil my life? My
life is rich. I have built up an ideal home. I live happily,
surrounded by children and grandchildren. So many persons
love and respect me. Granted the unbounded affection of
my Master, about whom Mircea was a so jealous, I have
experienced an ecstasy that is beyond the world of mind and
words. Can there be any room left for that twentythree year
old boy in my fifty-eight year old life?" I was very excited,
an artery in my temple began to throb. I feared a stroke.

With an apologetic smile Sergui sat watching me. "No,
no, your life has not been spoilt. But it could have been

different."

"Oh yes, it could have been different, but that's all."
Trying to change the topic he said, "I have your first volume
of poems with me"—he pronounced the title of the Bengali
book haltingly. "After Mircea left his country, I found this
book in his library."

"Tell me what the book looks like."

"Bound in blue cloth, hard cover, a floral design imprinted
in gold in the middle "

Absolutely correct. How far away those dead days
seemed now. "How could you know it was my book?"
I asked, smiling.

"On the last blank page of the book, running from the
left hand side to the inside back cover you have written in an
unsteady hand . . . "Mircea, Mircea, I have told my mother
that you have kissed me only on my forehead'." Sergui had
not fiinished, when my blood began to quiver. A weird
sensation tingled in the soles of my feet. I was sitting on a
low divan, my feet pressed firmly on the floor; but suddenly
I was lifted up. I soared, I remained hanging in a void
without support. My feet were no more on the ground, the
room had no roof. Yes, I know I was staring at Sergui,
he was smiling a little, so was I, and a strong sensation ran
through my body. I was turned into a drop of quicksilver,
unable to remain steady. I was transported to the verandah
of our Bhowanipur house. The black and white slabs of the
floor are placed like a chess board—I am stooping over its
smooth glossy surface. I am holding the book—yes, that is
me—of course it's me. In a moment, inside me the tears of
that morning returned gushing like a river in spate. How am
I conversing with this stranger, I asked myself. I knew my
arm was placed on the arm of the sofa, yet I felt the smooth
cool touch of the stony floor under it—Khoka is standing
before me, I can see his toes with dirty nails, and the end of
his shabby *dhoti* is brushing the floor—this is a morning—
maybe it is the morning of the 20th September 1930. On the

18th Mircea had left.  Khoka is talking to me.  I can hear
him perfectly—"Ru, write quickly"; then making a ridiculous
grimace, he whispers, "Spies are everywhere".  Though what
he says is true Khoka makes fun even of serious matters.
    Khoka was not a relative.  But he was like a brother.
My grandmother adopted his mother and married her off.
We called her Aunt Kutti.  Aunt Kutti had eighteen children,
so theirs was an everlasting penury.  Khoka and his sister
Shanti were our dependent poor relations.  Though both
of them were our friends, and we were playmates, yet they got
no real respect; such is the lot of all dependents, they receive
generosity, but no regard.  Even Mircea did not like Khoka,
but that was for another reason—it was just that Khoka made
me laugh.  He could talk of the littlest things with such
gesticulations that our sides split with laughter.  Mircea did
not understand half of what he said, so he sulked.  Once I
hung up a new curtain on the library door.  It was my hobby
to change curtains now and then. Khoka entered the room—
he pulled the curtain, as if with great difficulty, as if he was
unable to enter.  The more I laughed at his gestures, the
more sullen grew Mircea.  "What is that man doing?"
    "Just fooling—he says I change curtains too often—when
I have my own home I will hang so many curtains on each
door that visitors will get exhausted pulling them aside one
after another.  He is mimicking the efforts of someone trying
to enter my house—but why are you glum?"
    "Tell me, what's the inner meaning of it all?"
    "No inner meaning, just an innocent joke."
    That was Mircea—always searching for inner meanings
"How can you like that man?  He is a buffoon."  What a
pity, today he has to depend on Khoka.  Who else can talk
to him about me except Khoka?
    "Write quickly, dear Ru," Khoka whispered.  "If uncle
finds me here he will be furious.  Maybe he will turn me
out of the house."
    I am trying to write.  I find no words—I am gripped

by fear. What will happen, I think, if Mircea tells the truth?
He knows I seldom lie. I know he also does not—but I am
lying now—I am doing it for him, I want to save him. I
realise how it is not always bad to lie. What an idea! How
could I even think like this? As mother says, one wrong
leads to another, one lie follows another, and truth can never
catch up with lies. How could I stoop so low? What will
my Master say? Did I not promise to keep my face up
towards the Sun? Did I not promise to myself that I shall for
ever be pure, untouched by sin? I have failed. I can see
myself opening the book and writing on it. My hand is
shaking, the words are dancing, the line is going awry—I sit
watching the scene. As if from the depth of a profound
darkness my sixteen-year old body is glimmering out on the
screen—my hair is dishevelled—I have not combed it for three
days, for three days I have taken no food except fruit juice,
I shall never eat again. I shall cut my hair off. I shall tear
off the border of my sari.

Mother should be taught a lesson. When her mother,
my *didima*, comes, she will have to tell her, because she will
surely ask, "What has happened to Ru?" I know what
granny will say to herself—"This girl has become *svayamvara*,
she can no more be married to anyone else." But she will
never dare speak out a word because of father. So many
persons remain intimidated by just one man.

So I am writing to Mircea that he must not admit to more.
Will he understand? I cannot write much now, my English
seems to have been exhausted—words escape me.

Suddenly I was woken up by Sergui's remark, "Mircea
shows his age much more than you." Sergui has not realised
that I was not listening. What did I see for so long? Where
is Khoka? He is an old wornout man, living somewhere
in Kalighat. Did that marble floor arrive here on a magic
carpet? Oh what a wonder! As the song says: "I saw you
with the light of my eyes outside me, when there was light.

Now when darkness covers, I will see you within me." Can
one see without light? Is there any other wave than lightwave
for sight? I am an atheist; rather, an agnostic ; but am I now
starting to believe in the supernatural? Because just now, in
one moment of time or beyond time, something happened
which is not memory, not a recollection of the past, an actual
transference from one time into another. I was transported
to the morning of 20th September 1930. I felt the smooth
cool surface of this marble floor—my eyes were heavy with
incessant crying—I was hungry because of three days of
fasting—I hesitated at the spelling of *forehead*—would it
need an "e"? I find no words to describe fully this flashing
experience of the past. 1972 fused with 1930.

I was talking with ease with Sergui, yet I was shivering
inside, shaking like a leaf in danger, when attacked by a storm.
I cannot trust myself any more. I am here now, maybe, at
the next moment, I won't be here at all. I am sure it will
happen again—I will drift backwards in time. I know that
time does not rise or set, it has no beginning or end, yet I am
afraid of my new experience. I am afraid to enter the
unknown world of infinity.

Today's experience has been devastating. It has
unsettled all my old beliefs. Who will save me now? I began
to seek help from the same person who is worshipped now,
as in 1939—"Do not leave me, master, come back to my heart.
I have nothing else in my life—I never had. Covering my
past, present and future, your presence is a constant festival.
I have missed nothing. I have no paucity. Will a stranger
ruin my peace to-day by trifling talk? Will the light of my
polestar die out? Will I fall?"

At the time of departure Sergui again kissed my hand ;
again a sharp sensation rose from the soles of my feet—I
controlled myself with difficulty—this is Gol Park, this is 1972.
In 1930 this place was a jungle. I tried to re-assure myself.
Holding the door-handle of the car, I kept on reminding

myself this was an Ambassador taxi and not a Chevrolet limousine. But it was impossible to be steady. My world was revolving, revolving on its axis—it was spinning and thrusting forward what was once left behind.

Our first car was a Chevrolet—comfortable and high, no one wants that kind now—but to us it was a beauty. Mircea would offer his arm to help me out of the car.

"Do I need help to get down from this little height?"

"Our custom. One must help a lady out of the car and must kiss her hand while greeting or taking leave."

"Custom?"

"Yes. One would be considered uncivilised if one failed to do so. Have you no such custom?"

"No. Only while greeting elders one has to touch their feet and then touch one's own forehead ; this is a sign of takingthe dust from the feet of the elders to show respect—this is *pranam.* The seniors then bless the juniors by touching their heads. And one does *namaskar* to one's equal—that is, folds palms and touches one's forehead—this is reciprocated. But no one cares to do it anymore. They teach etiquette at Thakur Bari. Rabi Thakur teaches at his Santiniketan School all the rules of good manners. Students there greet each other with folded palms. But they are laughed at by others outside Santiniketan. They say it's Rabindrik, that is, too elegant."

"Will that one do everything for you?" Mircea asked, vexed.

"Yes, yes, that one man fills our sky with stars, gives words in our mouths, and kindles love in our minds." I recited a poem, "My sky blooms stars at night, and forests blossom flowers in the morning, because he is there—"

Astounded, Mircea Euclid looked at me intently. "What did you say? How can you speak like that about another human being? I don't understand you."

"Who cares?"

When I returned, I found my daughter-in-law Lekha

waiting for me. "Where did you suddenly go away? You
forgot your engagement with Khagen Babu— he waited so
long."

I am scared of this girl. She is very sharp and is always
hanging around me. She might suspect something. I shall
have to be careful. I asked her about Khagen Babu and
other matters. I heard her replies with apparent attention
and with a smile on my lips. But it was difficult to maintain
calm. Fears well up continuously. I am shaking inside.
This won't do. So I laugh a little —inconsistent laughter.
She is talking about my birthday celebrations —I feign curiosity
but I have no wish to hear of it. I do not know how, within a
few hours, the perspective of my life can change so. My
friends will celebrate my birthday, but I do not care for it any
more. What will I gain by their fond reverence? Can they
give me peace? In the unrippling smooth pool of my life
Sergui has thrown a pebble. The circles now keep on
widening. I know this will not end easily—the hope of peace
has now gone far. Work, social service, duty to the nation—
let them go to hell. I want nothing, nothing—only take me
back, take me back, back to 1930. I want to see him again.
Mircea ! Mircea! I raised my hand and found Lekha watching
me intently. "Ma, are your eyes hurting again? I must get
your drops."

I have successfully passed the perils of the birthday
evening. Indeed, I have creditably hidden my thoughts.
I have put on a new sari, recited poems eloquently and have
listened to music played for me. Had my agitation showed
people would have thought I was suffering from Parkinson's
disease.

I have been standing on the verandah since midnight.
Dawn is breaking. The stars have renounced the sky. In
this house we have no approach to the terrace. I miss the
full sky. The first evening we went up to the terrace Mircea
was amazed.

"Do you know in our country we have no terraces?"

"How odd—how do you see the stars and the sun?"

"Only astronomers watch sun and stars.  Common folk don't care."

"Here people begin their day by revering the sun."

"Do you?"

"I have my 'Sun' both inside and outside of me.  It makes no difference—morning or night.  I am always worshipful."  Mircea watched me with searching eyes.

"Explain what you mean."  And then urgently : "You must."

"No, I won't; you won't understand."

His face clouded.  "You are humiliating me.  I am not such a fool.  You must tell me who your sun is."

"My *Guru*, because he shows me this beautiful world."

"Does he show only himself or other things as well?"

"I see everything by his light."

"For example?"

"For example, you."  My eyes twinkled in fun.  Mircea was pleased at this remark.

"Will you read Whitman with me this evening?"

"No, I don't like Whitman.  So dry.  I'd rather read Shelley.  *The Sensitive Plant*."

I should go to bed now.  I have so many duties tomorrow—specially the seminar – why should I stand dreaming about what happened in the remote past?  Who is that Amrita and where is that Mircea? If we meet now we won't even recognise each other.

Days pass, but I am unable to keep myself steady in the present—constantly I go back to the Bhowanipur house, to 1930.

I do not remember the exact date or month when Mircea first came to our house, or when I first met him.  My father is a very learned man.  In fact, a versatile genius.  Only six years before he had been a lecturer in a college in a provincial town of East Bengal.  Though he had only recently come to Calcutta, he had, within a small time, reached the

height of fame.    He is well-known for his erudition and feared
by many because of it.    His scholarship is aggressive; he can
easily reduce a person in argument to shambles; he is very
fond of this game.    Yet he has a hypnotic charm.    People
cling to him.    His students are devoted to him and will go to
any length to support him.    He also loves them.    But that is
a different kind of love, there is no sympathy in it.    He loves
them for his own sake, not theirs.    For example, he loves me
not for me so much as for himself.    "Look at my girl, isn't
she pretty?    What a jewel she is!    She speaks fluent English,
writes good poetry, she is my daughter, isn't she?"    My father
is full of me, yet I know if I dare go against him the littlest
bit he won't hesitate to crush me ruthlessly.    My likes and
dislikes are immaterial.    I have to be happy at his command.

But my mother is quite the opposite.    She was exquisitely
beautiful in 1930; tall and erect, she moved like a shaft of
moonbeam in our house.    Father was proud of her beauty, but
mother never cared.    She took no pains to dress up, her toilet
was very simple.    She never cared for her own pleasure or
comfort.    Her only wish was to keep father happy, and father
kept her fully busy in that work.    Specially, whenever he
happened to be a little out of sorts, he made such a song and
dance about it that mother remained constantly worried about
her husband's health.    Mother was very fond of Vaishnava
poetry.    She often recited two lines of Radha.

The desire to please one's own senses is lust,
The desire to please Krishna's is love.

She was forever eager to please not only her husband, but
every one around her.    She carried in her heart kindness and
love like a bowl full of nectar.

Those were days when many foreigners visited us.    Our
house hummed with scholarly discussions on literary and
philosophical problems.    Of the constant visitors, I remember,
most, Stella Kramrisch and Professor Tucci.    Professor Tucci
looked almost like a student.    A lock of obstinate hair constantly
fell on his young face, he intermittently pushed it back with

a jerk of his hand. His lovely wife always wore a pearl
necklace. Professor Tucci knew twelve languages and spoke
fluent Bengali. Because of these visitors our ways began
changing; gradually we were getting westernised. This was
possible because my *thakuma* grandmother, my father's
mother, had died a year ago. Or it could never have happened.
I remember an incident clearly when in 1927 father purchased
a large mahogany dining table. Wide-eyed she gazed at it, for
some time; the movement of the golden rosary stopped between
her fingers. "Do you intend to eat on it? Well, you could
sleep on it—it is almost a bed!" she exclaimed disapprovingly.
Then knowing it was useless to object she sighed and said,
"Exception can be made of a large piece of wood." But she
completely shunned the dining room. Her disapproval of the
western style of eating was total. When she saw the cutlery,
she said in alarm, "Why do you need so many instruments to
eat?" In a vindictive mood she even wished that some diner
would get his tongue pierced by the fork and thus learn a
lesson. But we young ones liked the change. As I advanced
from childhood to girlhood to youth, I came in contact with
the great personalities of Bengal. Their ways and manners,
their house furnishings and style of life were very different
from what we saw in the provincial town of East Bengal.
In those days the word "elite" was much used, just as now
we have "bourgeoisie". But there is a touch of bellicosity in
"bourgeoisie", a quality of vendetta. "Elite" was not like
that. Another much used expression was "cream of Calcutta".
(But now the cream gets continually mixed with milk, or
rather with water.) The greatest personality of this high
society was the Poet, Rabi Thakur, or Rabi Babu, as he was
addressed then. My father regularly took me to him from
the age of thirteen, hoping to inspire my poetic talents
to the full. Father saw such philosophic ideas reflected
in my poems that he was certain in due time I would be
either a great philosopher or a great poet. I have succeeded
in destroying his hopes thoroughly on this score. Father

took me to the Poet so that I could show him my poems but
I spent the time reciting his own poems to him. The Poet
loved to hear his poetry recited by me and sometimes to
encourage me he would say, "You recite my poems better than
I do." I knew this was not true; he said it to please me.
Yet my heart welled up in supreme satisfaction. I thought:
*I receive so much from him, it is a benediction just to be near
him, but I have nothing to offer him in exchange, except this
little diversion.* So even though I felt extremely shy in front
of his towering personality, and my voice choked and I found
no words, yet I was never too shy to recite his poems. Once
I went on reciting by heart the long poems of the "Jeevan
Devata" series, one by one. He sat smiling till I had finished;
looking at me affectionately, he asked, "Do you understand
these poems?"

"Yes, yes, absolutely," I replied confidently and then
went on, in one breath, giving him the inner meanings of
*Sonar Tari, Kautukamayee* and *Hriday Jamuna* exactly as I
had heard from father. It was a thorough philosophical
discourse. Smiling, he stopped me in the middle. I know
now how comical the high philosophy sounded, coming from
a wisp of a girl of fourteen. He said, "Enough, enough:
carry on reading. You will understand all at the right time
yourself. The chirping of birds has some meaning in the
life of the world, but they do not know it, and it is not
necessary that they should. Go on reciting, at your pleasure.
Philosophical explanations by others will be of no use to you."

A Russian scholar used to visit us at this time. I think
it was Bogdanov. All the foreign scholars who visited
Santiniketan came to meet father too and were entertained
by him. They were seekers of truth. I bravely joined in
their learned discussions. An atmosphere of erudition hung
around us like a pervasive mist and a young person like me
could hardly see anything beyond it. Yet I thoroughly enjoyed
being mystified by looking at this world through the veil of
inaccessible, unattainable thoughts. And seeping through

that mist, sunlight fell on me and kept me warm and awake.
On the one side I felt the living presence of a great personality,
and the beauty of his creative powers, and on the other
a searching enquiry about the absolute, the enquiry that
remained forever unanswered, played light and shade over my
eager, young and vivacious mind.

Our home was different from the homes of our relatives
and friends and I appeared inscrutable to my fellow students.
They teased me because I always had a faraway look and
immediate things escaped me. In our time boys and girls
rarely met. We were, of course, not in purdah. Though
my mother seldom talked to father's friends, she was free
with his students. I, of course, felt no restriction. In the
provincial town of Chittagong, my mother sat behind the
bamboo curtain and joined silently in the literary discussions
that my father had with his colleagues in the library room.
She would send *pan* and cold drinks to entertain the guests,
from her unseen quarters. But after we came to the great
city of Calcutta, all such restrictions were totally discarded.
Mother never veiled her face any more. She wore shoes—an
act that affected *thakuma's* sense of piety and vexed her
greatly. I visited boys' colleges also, accompanied and
encouraged by father, to recite poetry on different occasions.
No other girl had done such a thing at that time. This was
a rebellious act both for father and me. But, of course,
I seldom spoke with the boys—an unseen veil covered our
faces. We hesitated to talk with men. If any of my father's
students walked with him up to the car, deep in conversation
with him, I would follow them, my eyes lowered, looking at
the ground silently. It would not occur to me to join them,
though I was at ease with senior men. We were strange
creatures - it was not that I did not want to talk and I was
certain the other party was also dying to—then why didn't we?
No one stopped us. Yet we could not. Before the masculine
presence, especially before young men, barring of course
relatives, we froze. So did the boys. Purdah affected both

men and women.  The effect of a taboo coming through the
ages persisted obstinately.  To-day it would seem absurd if
we said that we never realised why this taboo was imposed,
what was the underlying meaning of it all.  In higher middle
class families like ours, sex remained completely hidden.
Nobody talked about it, no books dealing even remotely with
sex were allowed.  We never saw any expression of sex, leave
alone outrageous acts of necking or kissing.  We never saw
men and women hold hands.  We could guess, a little
indirectly, about the existence of an unseen hidden world, but
we knew practically nothing about the real facts.  Novels
were selected by our elders for us.  Some novels by
distinguished authors were forbidden.  Of these I specially
remember three.  The first was by Bankim Chandra, *Krishna
Kanta's Will*.  In it a widow seduces a married man, a most
despicable thing to do, for widow marriage was illegal and so
was divorce.  The second was also by the same author.  *Bisha
Briksha (The Poison Tree)*.  Here also a child-widow, an
innocent orphan, falls in love with her protector, a married
man, and ultimately commits suicide.  Rabi Thakur's
*Chokher Bali (Dust in the Eye)* was also a forbidden book.
This was again a tale of a young widow who is seduced by
her married cousin-in-law, after which she rejects him.  But
we were allowed to read his *Nouka Dubi (The Wreck)*.  It
told the story of a bride who, after a shipwreck, mistook
another man for her husband and loved him.  But when she
discovered that he was not her husband, she left him and went
in search of the man to whom she had been lawfully married;
after many vicissitudes she found him.  This book stressed the
Hindu ideal of marriage, where the image of the husband
and the marriage vows are important, not love for a particular
person.

I ate the forbidden fruit.  I tore the cover of *The Wreck*,
hid *Chokher Bali* in it, and quietly read it.  I never understood
why the book was considered objectionable.  Though I
hesitated to converse with father's Indian students, I was free

with his foreign students.  Father allowed me complete
freedom on this score.

Around this time a Russian couple came to Calcutta.
They gave some "magic show" performances at the Globe
Theatre.  All of Calcutta was talking about it.  Father said,
"Let us go and watch the jugglers."  The lady was very
elegant.  She wore a long black silk dress that touched the
floor: she bound her eyes with a black scarf.  She stood
blindfolded in the middle of the stage, exuding a mysterious
sipirituality.  She asked the audience to put her questions,
but without speaking them out.  A man from the audience
would stand up and remain silent; her goodlooking young
husband would walk down among the spectators and feel the
pulse of the mute questioner.  Then the lady would shout
out from the stage both the unspoken questions and their
answers.  For example, she would say, "You ask how many
sticks you have in your match box?  Well, count—there are
fifty."  "You ask whether or not your wife is faithful to
you?  She is, but you are not."  The hall would explode
into boisterous laughter, to the great discomfiture of the poor
questioner.  Father said, "This witch is dangerous, we must
test her."  So he contacted the couple.  In those days, that
is, from the 19th century up to the middle of the twentieth,
especially in the late twenties and early thirties, the higher
middle class hesitated to show credulity.  They were
"rational" not "superstitious."  Gradually the pendulum is
swinging back—even westernised people now have become
more obscurantist than they were in our time.  The conjuror's
trick is now classed as yogic powers.  Frustrated affluent
people to-day have become prone towards the supernatural.
So charlatans increase, to feed the demand.  Even scientists
are no less credulous than ordinary people, or men than
women.  But in our young days the educated were not ready
to accept supernatural occurrences without test.  Father had
a hunch that they had planted their own stooges among the
audience.  So I said, "Why don't you ask her yourself?"

"Goodness, how dare I?   Who knows what that witch may
blurt out."

At the tea party a few distinguished persons turned up,
mostly professors and writers.   The entertaining game went on
over tea.   The man felt the pulse and the lady revealed the
unspoken question.   When my turn came I decided to cheat
her.   I would think something in Bengali, and fool her.   So
I said to myself, "What is the title of my last poem?"   The
lady fumbled but ultimately stammered out the correct word
in incorrect pronunciation.   *"Bhogapatra"*—"The Cup of
Pleasure".   A young professor remarked, "Simple thought-
reading."   Father snubbed him, "As if that explains
everything."

One day we went to an Italian opera with this couple,
at the Empire Theatre.   My parents and I.   Our ears were
then not trained to appreciate western music.   Some described
it as the howling of jackals and the barking of dogs.
Now-a-days with radios, transistors, radiograms and cassette-
players one can hear Beethoven or jazz played anywhere, even
in the slums.   This would have been unthinkable then.
Western music was only for those who had had the privilege of
getting western education for two or three generations, those
who were described as *ingabangas*, the Anglo-Bengalis.   In
their drawing-rooms young, marriageable girls played pianos
with nervous fingers to please their would-be in-laws, while
their proud parents sat watching.   Naturally I did not relish
Italian opera.   I would not admit it, for it gave me a grand
feeling—I felt grown-up—it was glorious to pretend to be a
connoisseur and not look a fool.   I sat watching the opera
without concentration, my mind drifting away as it invariably
did.   Then suddenly in the darkness of the room the Russian
gentleman, who was sitting next to me, slid his right arm over
my shoulders and drew me towards him.   Though our
ignorance in these matters was great, yet we could act
"rightly".   I shook his hand off with a jerk, but it sprang
back again like an automatic object.   Though agitated,

I quickly thought out a way.   I could not make a scene
here or seek my parents' help.   So I stooped, took off the
*nagrai* from my right foot and placed it on his knee.   "I shall
beat you with my sandal" I whispered.   The spring worked
in the opposite direction—he moved his hand away as quickly
as he had put it.   Coming home, when I described the
incident to my mother, she became cross with my father —
why must we allow all these nasty Europeans into the house?
But father was quietly amused.   He knew the Western world
well and said to mother, "Amrita will be meeting men of different
natures and ways—she will have to go out in the world—
she must learn to mix with people.   She will not stay at home
like you.   Why, if she exerts herself a little, she will one day
become another Sarojini Naidu."   But what shocked me and
mother most was that father was not rude to the "wizards".
He did not even cancel the engagement we had made with
Rabi Thakur for them.   Previously I had described to the
Poet their strange powers and he was eager to meet them.
He was not a credulous man; on the contrary, he was
extremely rational, but his spirit of enquiry was limitless.
According to him, it was more scientific to enquire into unusual
matters than to reject them outright.   So a day was fixed
when father and I would take them to him.   "Baba, I won't
go with them.   He is a dirty man."   "Why, *ma*?   Everything
had been fixed, what will the poet think if you stay back?
You have to meet various people in different situations and
I am certain you will always act rightly.   With your strength
of mind, commonsense and goodness, you can face the
challenges of life properly.   Should you hide in a hole because
there are bad people around?"

Next day father and I took the Russian couple to the Poet.
The three of them waited in the parlour.   I can still see that
parlour—arranged in purely Indian style—all the divans and
sofas were low, very unusual in the thirties—the cushions
were made of soft Japanese mat.   Rabi Thakur gave much
thought to house decoration.   Among Indians he was certainly

a master in this line; but in which line was he not a master?
I went up to the second floor, to the study to announce our
arrival. He was waiting for us. Seeing me he stood up
smiling, "Let us go and meet the enchantress". We
came down by the spiral staircase. As he entered the room
they stood up, awe-struck at his magnificent bearing. A few
words of politeness were exchanged; the Russian lady
blindfolded herself with a piece of blue silk. Her husband
felt his pulse. But the lady said nothing. One could see her
struggle, as if with some unseen enemy. but she could say
nothing. Rabi Thakur did not want to embarrass them but was
only curious to get at the mystery behind it all. "Shall I write
out my questions?" he asked helpfully. She woke up as if
from a dream, and said in a husky voice, "Yes, that may
help." He wrote out the questions and kept the piece of paper
inside the book he was holding. Yet she could say nothing.
Little drops of perspiration collected on her forehead. She
stood up and started pacing in the room. "There is a wall
before me, there is a wall before me . . ." Then increasing
her pace she came out in the verandah. "I can see nothing,
nothing," she cried and, leaving her stunned husband behind,
she ran out of the house. He followed her. How the sight
of a Sahib and Mem running helter-skelter through the
crowded streets of Chitpur must have left the bewildered
shopkeepers wide-eyed and grinning! I tried to imagine it and
began to laugh. Irritated, father got up. "Wait here," he
told me, "I'll get them home." The Poet remarked banteringly
about the credulity of the father-and-daughter team. "What
more can be expected of professors?" he laughed. Father was
also unhappy. He felt a little small that she could tell his
mind but not Rabindranath Thakur's. Thus ended the
Russian tale.

As far as I can remember, during this time Mircea used to
visit father. But I had not noticed him. One afternoon,
father was at his desk and, opposite his table, facing father, sat
Mircea. Father had called me in to introduce him to me.

"This is my daughter," and turning towards me, "Here is
my student Mircea Euclid." Mircea stood up. I noticed he
wore spectacles with thick lenses, his hair was thin, he had a
square face, broad forehead, high cheek bones and very
sensitive lips. I like this habit of Westerners—they stand up
to greet a woman. Our boys never care. They stay put, with
legs crossed, and take no notice of you at all, or are atrociously
servile. "Mircea is not satisfied with his present place. So I
have invited him to stay with us. Arrange a room for him,"
Father told me. For a second my heart sank. I spoke
hesitatingly, 'Baba, why must we have an Englishman stay
with us?" Father was surprised at my objection. A little
piqued, he replied cautiously in Bengali, "He is not an
Englishman, Ru—he belongs to a small country of Europe.
But even if he was, so what? Is that what you have been
taught so long?" I glanced fully at Mircea Euclid. Not an
Englishman. His complexion is white, but his hair is not
reddish –it is black and brushed backwards, what we called
"Albert-fashion". He fixed his eyes on me for a moment
and then looked away. My objection was not really against
any particular Englishman; I preferred to say it like that as
I thought it would sound "nicer".

At that time, because of frequent visits by foreigners,
and also because of our connection with the "elite", which
steadily grew, a change came over the furnishing and interior
decoration of our modest home. Father and I would visit
a large auction-house, Egbert Andrews, and purchase furniture
off and on. The brass work of Delhi and Kanpur I polished
myself. I polished the door knobs, brass handles, and the
bolts. These things were and still are totally neglected
in middle-class Indian homes. It was an extremely painstaking
job to keep a half-westernised, half-orthodox house like ours
tidy the way I wished. On the one hand there were too many
people in our house and, apart from that, our relatives from
the country side would descend in big batches, now and then,
with or without notice. Some came for treatment, some for

ablutions in the Ganga during the eclipse or the solstice, some
again to offer special puja to the Goddess Kali of Kalighat.
My mother would never refuse anyone.  If sick persons came
to consult doctors, she would attend to them like a trained
nurse.  My mother came from a Brahmo family and did not
go to Kalighat, or bathe in the Ganga, but if a religious minded
relative came from our village, she would send her every day
to Kalighat for worship and would order pitchers filled with
Ganga-water brought in our Chevrolet.  Mother's door
remained for ever open to everyone.  But it was I who had
to suffer.  Only recently had I been fortunate to get a separate
room, for me alone.  No, not quite alone—Shanti and my
younger sister Sabi slept with me at night—but the room was
mine.  I had "arranged" the room with low furniture.  I had
even cut short the legs of an old Victorian bed to make it
look what they called "Oriental".  I disliked clutter.  There
were very few things in the room.  An almost bare room; the
floor of marble alternate black-and-white slabs, like a chess
board—smooth and polished.  My room was always fragrant
with incense and flowers.  Everyone felt that it was more
than a living room, it was a temple, the deity of the temple
being a photograph on the front wall.  A bust of Rabi Thakur,
wearing a velvet cap.  A strange picture: whichever direction
you moved, the eyes followed you.  The eyes looked straight
into me.  My friend Gopal, who knew about photography,
explained to me that pictures come out like that if one looks
into the lens.  But I never believed him.  It seemed to me
that the picture kept a constant vigil over me.  I loved my
room, it was my own mysterious world.  But whenever
village relatives turned up, I had to vacate it because it was
the only spare room in the house.  They would wipe their
hands on the curtains, mess about the newly-washed walls and
door-knobs, make them dirty and greasy, splash water on my
smooth, polished table, and soil the divan by squatting on it;
and. after making havoc of my efforts at house-decoration,
they would content themselves with a dip in the holy Ganga

at the auspicious moment and then repair homewards happily,
Then I had to wash and scrub and begin the spit-and-polish
operation all over again. Mother did not mind. She was not
concerned about such "superficial" matters—to her only human
beings were important. To hurt a person for such insignificant
things would be unthinkable to her. It did not matter to her
if the linen got soiled or the walls were stained. It did to me.

I liked to read poetry sitting in a properly decorated,
tidy, and clean room. I also liked to hear the stories of our
freedom struggle from my uncle – the fight that was then
blazing around us, yet left us unscorched. Uncle Mantu was
my father's cousin. He lived with us and was educated by
father. He was a nationalist. His elder brother had been
jailed. I was very proud of the fact and narrated to my school
friends, with earnestness, all the stories of his adventures.
But father never encouraged our patriotic zeal. He
continuously minimised the exploits of the anarchists and
snubbed us when we eulogised their sacrifices. When I look
back to-day I realise what a myth we had created—that the
whole nation rose against the British. Most of the educated
and the affluent never thought that the British Empire could
really disintegrate or even wished it would. I had often heard
people say "Hah, can they drive the British away in this
fashion?" Of course they did not suggest any alternative plan.
The selfless acts of the anarchists excited the imagination of
young people like us, as did the non-violent and soul-lifting
movement of the Dandi March when, stick in hand, lean and
weak Gandhi led his followers to the ocean to break the Salt
Law. Though surrounded by the sea, India was not allowed
to produce salt. Salt had to be imported. Gandhi flouted
the unjust law imposed by a foreign and unsympathetic
Goverment. Because of father's disapproval we could take no
part in the country-wide enthusiasm that nevertheless stirred
us to the depths. But we did what we could. We gave up
the use of foreign goods totally. So my remark was quite
appropriate—"Why must we invite an Englishman to stay with

us?" The real reason for my objection was more selfish than
nationalistic—I was worried that I might be asked to vacate
my room again for this stranger.   Father reassured me on that
point.   He could live in the front room on the ground floor.
We could partition the room and Mantu could share the room
with Mircea.   In the front portion Mantu lived till he married
and then it was used as a waiting room for visitors.   Mircea
Euclid lived in the back portion, nearer to the interior.

That evening father gave me *Nationalism*, a study by
Rabindranath.   "Read this book," he said.   "Are all the
English people our enemies? A day will come when patriotism
will be considered a crime."

That night I read through the book casually, but it went
completely over my head.   Just like father: he always gave
me books that were beyond my reach.   I also liked to read
books that continuously played hide and seek with me.   The
vision of a veiled and unattainable world was the inspiration
of my poetry.

Everything was arranged within a few days.   Partitioning
did not make the room too unspacious.   We furnished it very
simply.   A single bed, a writing table, a chair and a cane sofa,
that was about all.   A standing lamp with a large white lamp-
shade was placed in the middle near the writing table.   After
a few days Mircea Euclid rented a piano.

At the breakfast table father discussed various topics.
Once father suggested that both of us should study Sanskrit
together.   "It doesn't help to begin your study of Sanskrit
with *riju patha* (elementary lessons).   That's boring, you
must start with an enjoyable book."   So the next day we
began our studies together—with Kalidas's *Sakuntala*.   I
cannot now guess how the orthodox people of those days
viewed this—a Bengali girl and a European boy sitting
together on a mat, on the floor, was indeed a very rare sight.
I had noticed jealousy in the eyes of father's Bengali students,
mistrust and foreboding in the elderly ladies, and amusement
in the eyes of my friends.   But my parents accepted Euclid

wholeheartedly and gradually he became one of us.

During our lessons I would spread the mat for us purposely, because I knew he was keen to sit on the floor with me. He wanted to be one with us, and also liked the novelty. Father sat on a sofa between us. Mircea scrutinized all the details of our customs and ways and always looked for "inner meanings".

Mother said, "Euclid is a good boy. Gentle, quiet and humble. Why do you call me Mrs. Sen, Euclid? Why not 'Ma'?"

After that Mircea always addressed her as "Ma". He later told me that in their country no one would dare address such a young person as "Ma". She would be annoyed. How old was my mother then? Not more than thirty-two or thirty-three. But with the red-bordered sari framing her face, a vermillion spot on her smooth forehead, and the soles of her feet bordered with red *alta*, she looked exquisitely beautiful, just the image of a mother. Who cared for her age, she was ageless. I told Mircea that his must be an odd country, where women felt annoyed at being addressed as "mother".

Often, after breakfast, one by one, the others would leave the table, but we would sit talking; then getting up we would stand near the library door and continue our discussions for hours. No one took any notice of us. My father's library of about seven thousand books was scattered in three different rooms. That's where our discussions went on. Sometimes while coming down the stairs, father would see us, but he did not object. Had I been talking with Milu or Gopal for so long, he would scold me severely for wasting my time. But with Mircea Euclid it was different. With him, I suppose, only high philosophy could be "suspected".

I was coming down the stairs—Mircea stopped me in the middle—"I hear you wrote a philosophical poem yesterday?" he asked me, his eyes twinkling. "Yes," I said gravely. My father was very enthusiastic about this poem. There was a line in it, "When time will lose its hours and moments",

which pleased him enormously. He said that there was a
profound philosophical question in it, or rather the question
itself was the philosophy. Two years before, when I was
only fourteen, one evening, sitting on the seashore at Puri.
I had an eerie feeling. I actually felt the evening turn into
morning at one and the same moment. Time lost its
dimensions for a while. I wrote a poem that day: "Allow me
to float away, where my dream goes"; then I described that
place. "It is a place of nothingness, there everything ends,
no hope, no speech, no voice, no sound, no traveller
shuffles on an empty path, no birth, no death, no time,
no night, no day and no morning breaks on that void."

Father said, "Ru's enquiry into the nature of Time is almost
scriptural." I was proud of father's overwhelming praise.
But when he said, "Write a poem on this theme", and gave
me an idea to develop into a poem, my elation collapsed like a
punctured balloon. My poem soared no more, it became a bird
with broken wings, and dropped to the ground. That was
why I was not happy with my poem Bhogapatra!

Mircea smiled and said banteringly, "How can a little
girl like you write philosophical poems?"

"I am not a little girl, and I am a philosopher—that is,
a seer".

"Yes?" He raised his eyebrows, obviously amused.

"Of course, one who sees, or aspires to see reality, is a
seer, and I am longing to see."

"All right, read your poem to me." I followed him into
his room. Since a few days I had been entering his room.
No one had objected, yet I hesitated. Why? I never knew.
Nonchalantly, I sat on the cane sofa; he sat exactly opposite
to me on the bed, with his back to the wall of the partition.
In between us was the writing table. "Now read your
philosophical poem." "No. I shall recite from Rabi Thakur's
latest book. Did you know he has dedicated the book to
me? I shall read out what he wrote in the dedication."
Mircea was startled. "He dedicated the book to you?"

"Is it impossible? Can't he do it?" I was laughing to myself—he had swallowed every word! No doubt he will find out later from Mantu. Ah, let him. I began to recite eloquently. "Have you heard my message? And accepted it? I do not know your name, yet to you I offer the wealth of my contemplation." I translated haltingly, searching for words. It is not difficult to guess how the translation must have turned out. But Mircea was not worried about the fidelity of the translation—he sat there, deeply troubled. I got up to leave.

"Why did he write, 'I do not know your name'?" he asked. He guessed I was up to some mischief.

I said, "That part is most secret."

All this confused Mircea Euclid. There was of course the language difficulty, but more difficult were our mannerisms, our patterns of thought, our allusions and so forth. He mistook one thing for another. The unknown world was like a snare. As he groped to find its meaning, his stare became intense and his voice quivered. The song says "The uncatchable being will not be caught. Yet she will leave behind her enchantment." Was any enchantment entering into all this? Who could know?

The *malati* creeper swung in the embrace of the *piyal* tree. There was a narrow corridor in front of Mircea's room that led to the entrance. To the east of the corridor was the yard—a few steps down. Our dining room was approachable both from the yard and also from the landing where the corridor ended. My room was exactly above Mircea's. There was a verandah in front of my room and on the ground floor corresponding to it was also a verandah which led to the street. At the eastern corner of the verandah was a *madhavi* creeper which had climbed up to the balcony. The plant was perennially in bloom. A mixture of red and white blossoms hung in bunches—they exuded perfume all day and night. I liked to sway that creeper when passing his room. I took refuge under it; I knew he would come out, because surely he had seen me pass.

I was not certain that I waited for him because I did not
want to be certain.  Yet I was all ears.  Why was he not
coming out?  Had he not noticed me?  What should I do?
Should I hum a tune or mumble a poem . . . .  No; bad.
This shouldn't be.  I mustn't do anything immoral.  I must be
a philosopher—a philosopher has to be truthful.  A seeker of
truth should never hide anything.  I was holding the creeper,
my heart pounding a little with hope and fear.  Just then,
I heard steps approaching on the street.  With an awful
shuffie of sandals Sri M. came up the stairs.  Sri M. was a
brother-in-law of my aunt.  I knew his aspirations.  I spoke
with him freely because he was more or less a relative.  Taken
aback at finding me right near the entrance he said, "So here
you are.  Namaskar."

"Namaskar," I answered briefly.

"I am going to England next month."

"Good news."

"God knows how long it will take to get the degree."

"If you apply yourself seriously, it shouldn't take long."

"I don't know.  I doubt if I shall be able to concentrate."

"Oh no," I said to myself, "now he will begin his sticky
adulations."  These endless pestering flatterers disgusted me.
Milu and I made fun of them.  But today I was nervous.
If Mircea came out and found us here he would surely frown.
Who knows what he would surmise?  My worst fears became
true.  Parting the curtain, he put his head out, glanced at us,
and immediately withdrew.  This was really bad manners.
Awful!  What would Sri M. think?  Such a nuisance!  I
became impatient.  "Why don't you go upstairs to Ma?
Why stand here?  You'll get tired "

"Are you not tired standing here?  Or are you waiting
for someone and I am in the way?"  Sri M. trudged inside
the house grudgingly.  He was markedly wounded—shot in
the heart, as it were.

Tears came to my eyes.  Why need I worry about them?

What was it to me if they were happy or hurt? Have I got
nothing else to think about? How long is it since I was last in
Santiniketan? I will have no peace till I am there.   At the
Santiniketan ashram under the spreading *chatim* tree there was
a marble tablet erected by Maharshi Debendra Nath Thakur,
Rabindranath's saintly father.   On it he had inscribed two
lines: "He is the peace of my soul.   He is the comfort of my
life."   Maharshi Thakur had faith in God, Who was his
comfort.   But I have no faith.   Once father was giving me
the arguments of the theists in favour of the existence of God.
The mechanics of the body, specially the hammer and anvil
placed inside the ear, is certainly the proof of a mind—a
superior mind, otherwise who made them? The creation itself
is proof of a Creator.   The arguments were convincing but
could arguments alone make Him the comfort of one's life.
Who soothed the eye, Whose presence made the air and water
sweet? That's what the Vedas say.   The honeyed breeze is
blowing, the rivers are flowing honey—*om madhu bata rtayate,
madhuksharanti sindhava*.   But why did I think of funeral
hymns? Maybe the lines were chanted at funerals, but I felt
them to be a hymn of love.

I remembered an evening in the mansion on Store Road.
We went to a musical soirée.   The elite of Calcutta had come
to listen to the famous composer-singer Atulprasad.   He was
singing "You are honey.   You are honey.   You are the
fountain and ocean of honey, you are the *bandhu* of my heart."
He was referring to God.   With the Vaishnava poets Srikrishna
is God, so is Radha.   Both are *bandhu* (darling).   Everyone
sat with eyes closed, some had tears rolling down their cheeks.
Why? Could they see God? Rubbish! I know them well.   They
may belong to the elite, but most of them were big liars
and braggarts.   As far as I could guess, God loved humility
and had nothing to do with liars.   And Milu? Didn't I know
her? God was nowhere near her or me. . . . His voice is moving;
what feeling he pours into the songs! But I do not want to
see his face, so I close my eyes. . . . The music flows like the

sacred Ganga. The music changes its quality—it is transferred
from the ear to the eye. It is no more sound-wave, it has
become light-wave, and behind my closed eyelids another world
reveals itself. I see a low-roofed verandah and at the corner
a creeper with blue flowers hanging in bunches—*nilmani* in
Bengali, wistaria in English. I see someone stooping over a
table, writing—on his curly white hair sunbeams have thrown a
halo. He is writing and humming a tune. That song is
certainly different from the one I am listening to now—but in
my mind both blend into one—"you are honey—you are
honey—in fire, wind and water cascades of honey flow gurgling
*madhuram madhuram.*" Why did I ever forget this scene? For
me, no one else, only one human being, can be the source of
peace and comfort. I feel a trepidation. Am I breaking a
promise? Am I moving away from an allegiance? What is
that promise? I don't know.

Now, just look at the way Mircea behaves! Sri M. has
gone—yet he is not coming out. I will never enter his room
again. I must keep this promise at least, I really must, even
if I have to break totally with him. Carelessly I pick a bunch
of flowers from the *madhavi* creeper, and as I pass the corridor,
I see him through the curtain. He is reclining on the bed with
his back to the partition. I push the curtain a little and throw
the flower at him. I walk away with quick steps. I hear his
voice, tender and soft, calling me from the back: "Amrita,
Amrita, Amrita. . . ."

"Ma, ma, ma"—the voice floated in as if from beyond
the ocean, or across the cosmos. I woke up to find my son
standing before me. My hand was on the telephone. I was
reclining in a large armchair. "Ma, ma, why are you not
picking up the receiver?" With great difficulty I tried to pick
it up; my hand was numb, my mind vacant. Could one cross
such distances in so short a time? My body certainly remained
here in this chair, but I entered *Mahakala*, infinite time, time
that had no beginning, no end—to that point where the sun
does not shine and stars are not seen. This separation of body

and soul, to be present at two different points in time
simultaneously, hurts physically. I am exhausted. My son is
thirty years old. He is not a child. Who knows what he
might have surmised? But he has taken after his father. He
would ask me nothing if I did not talk. Slowly he left the
room. I sat staring at his receding figure. Lekha came and
took the receiver from me. She talked to the person: "Ma
has gone to bed"—and took down his number. Now I could
follow everything. I should have talked with that man. But
Lekha is tactful. I must not try to speak. I may sound
irrelevant. Putting down the receiver she came to me. "Ma,
please let me help you to bed"; then, haltingly, "you must tell
someone what has happened. You really must." I looked
up at her lovely young face and said, "There is nothing to tell."
Then I muttered to myself:

> Uncovering his breast—
> I would like to see if the heart still lives there.
> This body so perishable
> holds within it the wealth
> of an immortal, undecaying entity,
> which sings and marches
> to an impossible tune.
> I am still listening to its song
> whom no weapon can pierce
> nor fire burn.
> I shall see him once again
> beyond the sea of tears.

Impossible, impossible; but life is full of such unexpected
possibilities. How can all these come back after so many years
with so much poignancy, with such rawness? Lekha stooped
over me, straining her ears, "Ma, what are you muttering—with
your eyes shut? Are you chanting a mantra?"

"A poem, a poem." I felt like writing a poem after
many years—

> Stretching my arms out wildly
> to touch that intangible life,
> let me go to this wedding so far away.
> There Mahakala presides,

breaking and tearing all that is useless,
he holds up the lamp of free life
and marks the bride's forehead
with a spark of fire. . . .
I must go where the bridal night
waits unwavering
with the steadfast devotion
of someone's love. . . .

Now I realise why for quite some time a longing to go to
some faraway place had been growing in me. I constantly
yearned to go somewhere, and now, at this moment, I wanted
to get out of this verandah and go floating across the sky.
Lekha says, "Go to bed, ma." I sing, "Let us go, let us go, let
us go", drumming the floor with my feet, and laugh. So does
Lekha, and she completes the tune: "To bed, to bed."

The night is profound. But my husband is awake. Sergui
came in September, today October begins. After fully one
month he has realised that I am not here, as it were. It is
not his way to enquire, unless I tell him myself what my
troubles are. We have now been married thirty-eight years;
our life together has been without conflict. He certainly must
have felt that though I am a homebound housewife, a good
part of me stretches beyond that which is unknown to him.
But this never worried him as he only knows how to give and
not how to demand. I must not keep him in the dark. I must
tell him something. But what is there to tell? How can I tell
him about the book after so many years? And especially such
a book. Now I begin my quarrel with Mircea. Why did
you not write the truth, Mircea? Was not truth enough? Did
you write for financial gain? Yes, you did—that is the way of
the West—books sell if they deal with lust, not love. I am
ready to accept the truth, but why should I accept the burden
of a lie? I feel hot in the face and go and splash water on
myself under the tap.

This last one month I have not slept a single night. The
fire of anger is burning and along with it are burning many
other things, my honour, my good name. I talk to Mircea:

"How could you make me naked before the world – your book has run into twenty editions—is this love?" Though I have not yet read the book, what I have heard has stunned me. Who will translate that book to me? I silently agonise. I try to visualise his face, I see only a figure half reclined with the feet stretched. I can see those feet encased in sandals, white like the feathers of a crane. I get up from bed and stand near the window. My restless mind longs to wander out of the window to go crossing the ocean of time, leaving behind all that I hold dear—my fame, duty, obligation—"Mircea, I want to see you once again."

I asked my father, "Shouldn't we go and see Rabi Thakur once before he leaves for his foreign trip?" "Certainly, Ru," he replied, "Euclid also wants to go." So father wrote seeking the permission of the Poet. Prompt came the reply: "Your request granted, come with your daughter and disciple."

During the visit we stayed at the old double-storied guest house. It was decided that the three of us would go to see him in the morning. Mircea and I had walked out early. We strolled about the tennis court, waiting for father. But father was late. Maybe he had met the distinguished professor Kshitimohan Sen and had started a discussion on the cult of the Bauls. It was good if he had. We were not sorry for this delay—what a beautiful beginning of the day—the air around us was fragrant—I was talking twenty to the dozen. Santiniketan had put its arms around us both. We swung in the embrace of its deep blue sky.

Father came—"Let us go."

I said, 'I shall go later. I must meet my friends." I would not go with them. I wanted to talk to him alone. I had many things to tell him that I could not say before them. I was not going to meet any friend: I had no friends here. I came for a very short time, why should I waste those precious moments running after acquaintances? I had only one friend here, and that one person equalled a hundred, or was it only a hundred? After visiting Rabi Thakur father took Mircea

to the library. He wanted to see the *punthis*. He had an
unquenchable thirst for knowledge. Father was immensely
happy with his student. In father's museum we two were
good exhibits.

The Poet was sitting near the large, open window,
reclining on an armchair, looking out. I crept in stealthily
and laid a bunch of flowers near his feet. Turning back he
smiled—then he spread out his hand for the flowers—"Give
them to me." He was watching me intently, a little meaningful
smile hovered over his lips—"So? What was all that chatter
with the Sahib? You talked a lot, didn't you? A fountain of
words! I have told the Sahib to ignore a good bit of what a
woman says. I saw as much talking as promenading!"

"How could you see?" I asked timidly.

"Did you want me not to see? Then you should have been
more careful."

I realised then that the compound came fully into view
through the window.

"I feel angry now!" I said blushing.

"Make up your mind which kind of anger." He used the
word *raga*.

Picking up the end of my sari he said in his captivating
voice, "Is this Nilambari?" And then hummed a song about
Radha composed by himself, "Bedeck yourself with a graceful
blue sari, your heart covered with flowers of love." I was
blushing; my heart kept on pounding. I liked the joke but it
also hurt. With my head bent and eyes closed I remained
silent. He caught my braided hair and pulling it made me lift
my face. I kept my eyes shut. I dared not look at him.
Drop by drop warm tears rolled down my cheeks. He released
my hair. "Oh no, why are you crying?" I forget all that I
wanted to tell him, I hopelessly searched for words. Then,
oblivious of all, I laid my face on his knee. He placed
his kind hand over my head to allay my fears, he smoothed
my hair. As I fell into what must have been an
all-encompassing beatitute I heard his gentle voice. "Amrita,

you are too young to trouble your mind with so much. It is not good for your mental health. Keep your mind clear and quiet like the waters of a deep lake, as transparent as a crow's eye. The bottom of the lake is deep, below the water is still. There is no need to stir it now and make it turbulent. Then on that untroubled soul, shadows of the events of this world will cast themselves—but be at peace with yourself. Accept everything calmly, accept the truth in good grace. There is an exquisite creeper of beauty in you, its root will go deep down and on the surface it will bloom flowers—just wait . . . now get up, let's see . . . how is that young *chatim* tree of yours?" "We do not live in that house any more." There was a *chatim* tree in our previous house. I wrote a poem on that tree, addressing it as a friend. Rabi Thakur enjoyed all this childish play, but Mircea was taken aback by this. He called it "pantheism". I did not know what pantheism was. "Will not the ground below you, write down the story of love between a girl and a tree?"—this line disturbed him He could not believe that this was no "ism" but just soaring poetic fancy.

When I returned to the Guest House, I found father wild with anger. He scolded me fiercely because I was late. But actually there was no harm in my being late. We did not miss a train, no one was imperilled—yet he suddenly flared up. Father, when angry, lost all sense of balance. He rebuked me so severely that I was thoroughly humiliated and distraught. So was Mircea. He watched my discomfiture with hurt eyes. In the music of the morning was struck a discord. Father was without a peer in breaking a rhythm or striking a wrong chord in a melody Had he been in the heavenly court of Indra he would certainly have been banished many times and sent down to earth as a penalty, but this was not the court of heaven. This was father's own family—so everyone had to submit to him with patience.

On the return journey to Calcutta, in the train, father continuously spoke against Santiniketan, and indeed against

Rabi Thakur. He said, "This institution won't stay. It will
disintegrate as soon as Rabi Thakur is gone." Mircea
listened silently and sometimes endorsed him. Father
continued to speak out his disapproval of the Poet; gradually
he left the Poet and talked of the poetry. He began to
criticise his works; and specially under-rated the poem "India's
Prayer": he mentioned some words that were "totally
unsuitable" in poetry. Maybe he was right. But I did not
at that time want to get into an argument about the literary
merits of Thakur's poems. Resting my head on the window
of the compartment I sat lost in reverie—the wheels of the
train in a rhythmic beat —dhak-dhak-dhak-dhak—it drums a
tune, the wheels can speak, they can sing. A song is coming
to my mind—"A distant person has come near, he stands
silently, concealed behind the darkness" . . . At that time we
had little opportunity to listen to Rabi Thakur's songs, or
Rabindra-Sangeet as they are called. There were not many
proficient singers in Calcutta. So if on occasion we came
across a song of his, the music and message of it would wring
our hearts and bring tears to our eyes. This particular song
I had heard only a week ago from Professor Kalidas Nag.
His voice was very melodious. I visited his house often,
because his family was very close to Rabi Thakur and I could
talk with them about him. That day I was late talking, so
Kalidas-babu offered to take me home. As we were crossing
the Ramesh Mitra Park, the only little patch of green in the
whole of Bhawanipore, I heard him hum this tune—  "On his
neck hangs the garland steeped with the pain of separation,
it gives out the undying fragrance of a secret union . . ." The
music lingered in my ears . . . I sing the line—"Some distant
person has come near", the wheels of the train sing the next
line-- "he stands concealed", dhak . . . dhak . . . dhak . . .
dhak . . .

 Father got up to go to the washroom. Mircea came and
stood behind me.

 "Amrita."

"Yes?"

"Look at me, please."

I turned round and glanced up towards him. He stared intently into my eyes—so did I. We remained enchanted and fixed. I see him now exactly as I did at that moment. He is holding the leather strap attached to the upper berth and, stooping down, he is looking into my eyes. After a while both of us burst into laughter. Father came out. "What are you talking about?" he asked.

"I was trying to recollect the words of a song", and then I recited the lines. "Baba, please explain to Euclid the meaning of it all."

"Why, can't you do it?" father said, trying to enthuse me. Then he went on elucidating the song: "On his breast hangs the garland steeped in the pain of separation, it has the undying fragrance of a secret union."

"Now, on one side the song mentions pangs of separation, on the other, the joy of a secret union." He proceeded, "The two are contradictory thoughts—separation and union, yet it is only these contradictories that can reveal the whole, the full, the infinite." Father elaborated on the use of contradictories in Thakur's writings. Father was now full of Rabi Thakur, his former disapproval completely vanished – he was eloquent about the relation and interplay of finite and infinite in Thakur's writings.

But this was the second time that day he broke the rhythm. What need, I said to myself, was there for so much dissertation? The moment Mircea looked into my eyes I realised the "togetherness" of separation and union and its infinite yearnings. At that moment I smelt the perfume of that unseen garland on his neck.

I do not now remember, exactly, how many months after he came to stay with us this happened, but once Mircea did something outrageous. Father was sitting at the head of the dining-table and mother was at the other end. In the middle Mircea and I sat facing each other. It was dinner time. He

slowly stretched his feet and touched mine, while discussing
abstruse philosophy with father.   Startled, I pulled my feet
back.   I tried to persuade myself that it was accidental.

I looked up at him, a bit scared.   A tremor ran through
my body and an absurd thought flashed within me, *What will I
do when this person is gone?*   And suddenly I felt very desolate
and forlorn.

When everyone left I spoke to him severely, "Was it
accidental?   I do not think so."

"No, it was not," he replied calmly.

"What impertinence!   What audacity!   Suppose you had
touched father, then?"

"Phew!   I would have at once done *pronam*."

"How would you have known?"

"Ha, ha," he threw his head back, laughing.   "Could
I not tell your feet from your father's?"   And then with total
nonchalance he stretched his feet again and pressed them on
mine.

It happened forty-two years ago.   A wonder!   A wonder
indeed—I am sitting at that dining table.   I see him, yes,
I see him.   He wearing a shirt with two front buttons open—I
can see a part of his  chest all so white—his hands are resting
on the table, but he does not dare to touch mine.   I try hard
to pull away my feet but it is impossible; I do not have the
strength.   Is it immoral?   Sinful?   What should I do?
Mother had told me, "Never touch a man other than your kin.
You may fall ill if you do."   Certainly she spoke the truth.
I am exhausted, blood shoots through my veins.   Yet he
won't remove his feet, they are planted on mine firmly, even
now, here, exactly here.

A cool hand touched my forehead.   I woke up, as if
from a slumber through the ages.   My daughter-in-law is
standing near me; she says softly, "Ma, have you no one to
confide in?   Can't you talk to your sister, daughter, or to
your friends, of your troubles?"

In 1930, the battle for freedom was at its height, both

violent and nonviolent. Some troubles were constantly
brewing at the Presidency College. Once the students
determined to do some bloodletting. Stapleton was then the
Principal of the College. Though my father and Stapleton
were usually at loggerheads, that day father saved his life.
A student was hit in the police-firing and his comrades
resolved to "mingle his blood" with Stapleton's. When the
slogan "We want Stapleton's blood!" echoed through the
corridors, father offered to mediate. He promised to take
him out of the crowd to safety, if Stapleton would agree to
offer an apology to the wounded student. To this he readily
agreed. But no sooner was he out of the crowd than he changed
his mind. Sitting safely in the car this Englishman proclaimed
"I will now go home and apologise later." Father ordered
the driver to stop the car, but Stapleton would not let him.
As father was struggling to get down, Stapleton hung on to
his coat. Helpless, father shook off his coat and got down
in his shirt-sleeves. Of course Stapleton had to apologise
later. Father described Stapleton's discomfiture, especially
the ridiculous sight of his hanging on to father's coat, in great
detail and with appropriate gestures. It made us all
split our sides with laughter. Mircea at once decided that
he must go to see the Revolution. Next morning he slipped
out of the house. The day passed but there was no sign of
him. Mother was extremely worried—she felt the
responsibility of someone else's son's safety hanging heavy
on her. When Mantu was about to inform the police, the
prodigal returned, his hair dishevelled, covered with dust,
disappoinment written all over his face. He had gone to all
the places where "picketing" was going on. He had walked
through the lanes and by-lanes of Calcutta in search of
adventure, but nothing calamitous had befallen him.
Someone threw an empty clay pot of sweet curd but
unfortunately that too missed him. No incident had happened
to give him an opportunity to brag at home. He was
bothered to think what his explanation would be when people

in his country would question him, "Where did you hide
yourself when the Revolution broke out in India?"

He was worried how he would make his people believe
that he really was in India.   He was the first one from his
country to visit this strange land.   There was another worry:
he was not getting sufficiently tanned.   So, one morning,
he went quietly up to the terrace and, spreading a mat, he
lay flat on the floor, covering his face with a towel.   The
tropical sun scorched him so that he had blisters all over his
body.   Young people can be very cruel—this became a
matter of mirth for us.   I don't think I was particularly
sympathetic, but mother was deeply troubled.   "This boy is
getting wild," she said   She did not know how to handle
a naughty child from Europe, especially as her means of
communication was so poor.   Mother brought Chandsi
ointment and Mantu applied it to his back.   Mother
supervised the operation as she went on rebuking mildly—
Mantu translated her admonitions into English.

Later father met Mircea.   "Look, Euclid," he spoke
earnestly, "the moment your people see you, they will know
you were in India.   India will speak through you whenever
you open your month.   The most important thing is the
change that will come over you.   You can get tanned
anywhere in the tropics, but your real transformation will
come through your studies.   And Revolution?   You need not
run from pillar to post to catch up with Revolution!
Revolution is going on everywhere in India.   Tear-gas,
picketing and lathi charges are not as important as the fact
that you are living in our family, as one of us; this itself is a
revolution.   Would it have been possible in my parents'
home?   Then my wife would have veiled her face before you.
And Amrita, who is now reciting poems in a boys' college,
what would have happened to her?   By this time she would
have been behind the curtains in her father-in-law's house,
kept under the constant vigil of an over-critical mother-in-law.
She would have remained tied only to housework.   Were

you in my parents' home, the plates you used would be kept
separate. If you touched anyone's food, it would be polluted,
you would be treated as an untouchable, in a hugely complicated
network of prejudice. Compared to that a revolution is
going on right here in this house itself, even now."

A big literary conference had been convened. This was
the first time I would be reading a paper before an august
body. The subject of my talk was "Where resides beauty?"
Is it outside us or within the human mind? There was no
need to make it an abstruse problem. Beauty cannot be an
objective thing; only human beings can see beauty. It is the
blue *kohl* painted in their eyes, rather in their minds, that
makes things look beautiful.

However I worked hard to write this paper. Father was
critical about many of my points—so I kept on writing and
re-writing. Ultimately I was able to build up something that
I thought could face the test. Rabi Thakur was to have
presided over this gathering, but he was not able to come. He
had fallen ill in Hyderabad. Father said this would create
some unpleasantness, for he would be severely criticised for
not keeping his appointment. None in this country hesitated
to run Thakur down. I was surprised to notice that the same
people who were so eager to meet him and would melt in
reverence in his presence, would artfully talk against him behind
his back. Father also suffered from this ambivalence. Father
had read his voluminous works thoroughly, his attraction for
Rabi Thakur was limitless. He constantly discussed his
poetry, philosophy, and the supreme quality of his genius.
Yet a stream of unending criticism flowed continuously,
specially meant for my ears. As if I was responsible for all
his lapses! So it happened at the conference. We had to listen
to many far from dignified remarks about the Poet. I was
sad, though I had reason enough to be elated. I had never
read a paper before such a large gathering. I had of course
for a long time been reciting poetry—which I had done at the
Senate Hall too. That day, at the conference, I was the

youngest literary figure and the eldest was an octogenerian
lady—Mankumari Basu, neice of Madhusudan Datta.  She
wore the borderless white sari of a widow and stood on the
dais barefoot.  What a stupendous difference between two
ages!  "Mircea should see this to realise the implication of a
revolution!" I thought.

Returning home I found him sitting alone in a pensive
mood.  He had no relative, no friends, except us.  So I
suggested to him to come upstairs to the verandah for a chat.

"Why are you so sad?" he asked abruptly.

I did not know that my answer would make him sadder.
I related all that had happened at the conference and how
Rabi Thakur was berated for no fault of his.  Stopping me in
the middle he suddenly said, "How can a little girl like you
love an old man of seventy so much? Absurd!"

I flushed with anger.  "Why? Does a person become
unworthy of love just because he's old?"

He was more disturbed than I was and spoke agitatedly,
"Let me tell you, Amrita, either you do not know yourself,
or you are cheating yourself, because you have no courage to
face the truth, or you know everything and are just lying."

I felt extremely exhausted and said, "Mircea, I have a
headache, will you please go now."

Father said, "Learn a little French from Mircea.  One is
not fully accomplished unless one learns French."  Father is
determined to make my accomplishments as thorough as
possible.  Anadi Dastidar gives me private lessons in music,
Ramen Chakraborty also does that in painting.  A Goanese
teacher teaches me the violin.  Such a huge to-do over
accomplishments hangs heavy on me!  I do not like to learn
anything.  I have no perseverance.  I like to sit on the
window-sill, book in hand, and let my mind float to a distant
land.  However, it was decided that Mircea would learn
Bengali from me, and I French from him.  We start with
good resolution to study, but our lessons do not progress.

Why? Who knows why? We sit in his room—a standing
lamp with a large white shade glows between us. Evening
matures into night—I read poems from *Balaka*—he loves to
hear them. Am I capable of translating those poems into a
foreign language? But he has understood one poem and
liked it very much. The poem says, "You have bestowed
music on the bird so it can throat out a song, but it does not
give anything more. But you have given me only a voice, so
I return you more when I sing."

Man is never satisfied with all that he has received as
gifts. He is a creator himself—his mission is to transform
his sorrow into bliss. I read this poem but I am not old
enough to realise its significance. Yet I now gradually feel
that pain and bliss can blend together.

Some days we read together as late as eleven o'clock
at night. Neither father nor mother objects. Yet I feel
a hesitancy, a queer uneasiness, I don't know why—maybe
I think people may talk. I had noticed curiosity in the
eyes of the servants and a sharpness in the eyes of my
eleven-year old little sister. Sabi is a sweet girl but her
constant complaint is that no one loves her, everyone loves
*didi*, that is me. Now she feels Mircea is also joining that
party, so she says, "I'll teach Euclid-da." That is good.
Mircea might learn a little more from her than he is doing
from me. Our mutual lessons are not advancing too well.

Sometimes we take lessons in Sanskrit, also from my
tutor Gourmohan Ghosh. Mircea is learning by heart all
the declensions—he will certainly out-do me. He has
preseverance, I have none.

In our joint-family many persons lived together. Some
of them were not our near relatives, yet we were never
conscious of this fact. Each one was as good as the other.
Among them all, my uncle Mantu loved me the most.
When we studied with our teacher he sometimes came and
joined us, not for study but just to chat, or tease. He teased
our teacher incessantly. One morning my tutor Gourmohan

arrived, freshly bathed and with a sandal paste mark on his
forehead.  He was looking very pious after an ablution
in the sacred Ganga.   Uncle came in haste and knelt down
beside him; then, folding his hands together as if in prayer,
he began to speak in mock-meekness, "O revered teacher,
I am a sinner, let me have a little dust from your feet", and
he stooped to touch Gourmohan's feet.   Greatly embarrassed
and annoyed, Gourmohan pulled his feet away.   "Stop it,
Srishbabu, what childish pranks!"   "Oh sir, won't you save
a sinner?"   Mantu asked piteously.   The two of us burst
into laughter at his theatrical manner.   My boisterous laughter
was, according to what they used to say, very "unlady-like".
So when I went upstairs my aunt frowned at me.   She had
come yesterday and would be staying with us for a day or
two.   But from the very time of her arrival I had seen
suspicion in her eyes.   It was extremely annoying.   She
looked at me severely.

   "Why all that guffawing with that highfalutin Sahib?"
she sneered.   I was also insolent, "What Sahib—has he no
name?"   "Name!   Don't get cheeky with me!   Narenbabu
(meaning my father) has turned your head with too much
pampering."

   I let her say what she liked.   I did not want to enter
into arguments with her.   It was safer to make a quick exit.

   The passage in front of Mircea's room led to a verandah,
as I had described before.   On that verandah wall is a
letter-box.   The postman delivers the letters there—the box
remains locked.   I keep the key.   I go many times a day to
open that box to pick up letters.   There are fixed times when
then the post comes, so there is no need to open the box too
many times.   But I cannot restrain myself.   Many times
during the day I tell myself, Why not go and see if there is
a letter in the box?   Especially during mid-day when the whole
household is quiet, having a siesta—though no one in our
house actually sleeps during the day, they all read—I feel

tempted to look for letters. I know why I go. I have brains ;
I am capable of knowing myself. How can I hoodwink
myself? Though Mircea had said I am either a fool or a liar,
I knew none of these is true. To-day I feel an urge to go
and look into the letter box. There is a fight going on inside
me, the fight between good and evil as described by Bankim
Chandra. The good part of my mind says, "Never, you are
not going for letters. You want to meet Mircea downstairs."
The bad part, the liar, says, "Why not? A letter might have
come." I get up and put the bar on the door. I am
determined to save myself from myself. I open *Mahua* and
sitting on the bed I start to read a poem loudly:
    You are going to a pilgrimage to a distant temple.
    I am a tree, I spread my shadow to kiss the ground you tread.
    O pilgrim, I share some part of your penance.
    In your worship I add my flowers and incense.
    I shall remain at the roadside as a witness to your journey.
    But this poem is not meant for me; it is for my mother.
Mother is like that spreading tree. She had spread a cool
shadow over my father's path, to take away his fatigue. She
wanted nothing for herself, she kept him encircled by the
warmth of her love, untiring service and constant sacrifice of
all personal comforts. Mother's life is sublime, yet I do not
want to be like her. I do not care for her way of life. The
poem *Sabala (Strong Woman)* speaks of my aspirations.
I shall build my own destiny. What strength! I have no
strength, no power, no intellect. I feel defeated. Suddenly
I feel like crying. Throwing myself on the bed I begin to
cry, "Give me strength, O, do give me strength: Make my
mind powerful, so that I can accept all the tasks you give me,
so that I can endure the fiery troubles of the world." The
song goes on repeating itself in my mind. I question myself,
"What is meant by worldly troubles? I feel a blaze over my
my mind and body, is it that? Then let it be, I like that
warmth—I like that heat." "Touch my heart with the
touchstone of fire and make my life pure, through suffering."
    Like a sleepwalker I did not know when I had walked

downstairs and reached the passage.  I found Mircea standing
before the door and the curtain lifted with his hand.  He
asked me, "Any letters?"

"No. I'm desolate."

"Whose letter were you expecting?

"An unknown person's."

"But who?"

"I do not know and that's why the expectation is sweeter."
(I was talking of the play *The Post Office*.)

He did not understand.  He looked puzzled.

What will happen—I asked myself—if I had to live with
this person all my life?  Half my thoughts will remain
unspoken and I shall have to consult the dictionary far too
often.  But what an absurd thought—foolish indeed.  How
can I live with him all my life?  He will go away after a few
days.  I will also get married and leave.  But to whom will
I be married?  I can think of no one with whom I would like
to live all my life.

"Won't you come inside, Amrita?  I have a book for
you—*Hunger* by Knut Hamsun."  This was the first time
he gave me a present.  I took the book from his hand. he
had written my name on it, and another word in French
"*Amitie*".

I am standing, so is he—I don't have the courage to
sit down—who knows why—and he won't sit till I do so.
I have opened the piano cover and am standing with my back
towards him.  Am I waiting for something strange to happen?
He is standing very near me but has not touched me.  He
could have kept his hand on my shoulder, but he has not
done so.  There is a little empty space between him and me.
We are standing, silent and numb.  I feel his presence in my
whole body.  I can feel his touch in my mind.  Strange!  The
void is not empty, it is filled with ether—I of course do not
know what ether is, yet it must be that which is connecting
us with an invisible hand.  Around me the atmosphere is
filled with the fragrance of his breath.  "The fragrant breeze

blows over the tired evening flower and fills its limbs with a
disembodied embrace"

Someone calls from upstairs: "Ru, Ru."

"Coming, mother."

Mircea is twenty-three, I am sixteen. But both of
us are a bit too serious for our age. So father calls me
"Jyestha-tata", "big uncle". But who is turning me into a big
uncle? Who but father himself? And he is making Mircea also
another big uncle. They always talk of *ashtanga yoga.* And
everyone in this house is a little pundit on Tantra. When
uncle discusses with him the mysteries of Tantra, I get
impatient. I know boys and girls of our age take life more
lightly. I had a great desire to become a pundit once but now
I am not that eager. Especially when I find Mircea's
earnestness growing so fast. No sooner do we meet than he
starts teaching me world literature. He told me a fantastic
tale yesterday. A man was being hanged. He used to love a
girl. At the moment when the noose was fixed around his
neck he thought about the girl. After many months, the girl
got married. She gave birth to a child, and the child looked
like her lover, who was not its father. I could not make head
or tail of this fantastic story. I want to chat on ordinary
topics. Why doesn't he flatter me a little like others? But he
would never praise me. On the contrary, he really made me
cross one day when he said, "Do you think you are very
beautiful?"

"Why should I think so? Others do."

"Who others?"

"Let us go out in the street. You will see how people
stare at me."

"Oh, that is only natural, because they seldom get an
opportunity to see a girl. In this country the streets are
completely empty of women. Do you know what a European
notices most on his first visit? It's the absence of women
everywhere. They wonder—are there no women in this
country?"

"But why? Women move about in brougham phaeton
carriages and those who have cars drive in them.  Must ladies
tramp around the street?"

"They do so in other countries."

"Let them.  Can't you make out whether I am dark or
fair? Are father, me, Sabi, Milu, all the same to you? Do I
even resemble Jharu?"

"I can't tell."

"All right, that's enough."  I get up, haughtily, to leave.

"Please, please sit down.  Let me look at you carefully so
that I can make a distinction."  I grimace angrily.  He needs
a microscope to find out if I am pretty!

"Sit down, Amrita.  I do not want to see your outside—I
want to see your soul."

Now I begin to fume: Big uncle may begin a discourse
on the relation between *Jivatma* and *Paramatma*.  So I
hurriedly leave, disappointed and heartbroken.

I am scrutinising myself in a standing mirror.  I really
cannot be certain whether I am beautiful or not.  I am
wavering in doubt.  All the defects show up.  Milu comes in
and asks with surprise, "What are you gazing at so intently?"

"Look, Milu, in this great sub-continent of ours there are
so many varieties of dress—why do we always wear the sari
in the same style? We can easily dress differently for a change?"

Milu says "Truly, the *ghagra* of Rajputana is beautiful.
The Maratha style of wearing a sari is also attractive."

For some time Milu and I have been making new designs
for jewellery.  In those days these were generally weak
imitations of western designs, neither beautiful nor artistic.
About two generations before us, artistic tastes changed for
the worse.

The work of artistic revival started in the House of the
Thakurs.  In interior decoration as well as in ornaments they
searched for old designs instead of cheap western imitations.
This was called Oriental Art.  Stella Kramrisch was a
connoisseur in this field.  Milu and I were two novices, yet we

also copied designs from ancient styles, still used by village
women.  Gold designs and the silver filigree of Orissa
especially caught our fancy.  How inexpensive gold was then!
At that time silver was never used by the upper class—only
villagers, labourers and farmers' wives would wear silver
ornaments.  Yes, there was a class distinction in ornaments of
gold and silver.  But we de-classed ourselves and wore silver.
Later it came to be high fashion.

That day we decided to dress up like Oriya girls.  We
made the sari shorter and covered ourselves with silver
jewellery.  My mother had a *sinthi* - something like a tiara.  It
is now out of style.  A *sinthi* has three parts, one goes straight
up covering the parting of the hair in the middle and the two
other parts branch out on the two sides of the head.  From
the centre part a locket hangs out on the forehead.  On her
wedding day mother wore a *sinthi*  Father's eyes never tired
of seeing her in it and the memory of it lingered for so long
that he remained forever attached to that particular piece of
jewellery.  But mother would not wear it any more.  So father
was very happy if on any pretext he could make me wear it.

That day I wore the *sinthi*.  I had put on an Orissa sari
of gorgeous saffron and used *kadamba* flowers for ear-rings.
I had brushed my face with the fragrant pollen of *kadamba*
flowers—so did Milu.  We did not use toilet soap any more
because we had renounced all foreign goods.  We were used
to Hazeline vanishing cream and talcum powder, but these
also we touched no more.  That was the season for *kadamba*
pollen, but this flower was only an annual, it would not last
long.

"Dear Ru, it has been a good idea to give up soap.
Your complexion has improved by using lentil paste."

"Shut up," I blurted out angrily, to the great surprise
of my devoted friend.  "Don't talk rubbish," I continued.
"You should never speak about my looks, I'll get wrong ideas."

"Is that so?" she replied, a little puzzled.  "We may
not use powder, but why can't we brush a little *alta* on our

lips to brighten them up? *Alta* is not foreign."

"Oh dear Milu, I have no courage, no courage," I said as
I concentrated on fixing the *sinthi* in the middle. I was
reciting from *Meghaduta.* "Dear Milu, our dress would be
complete if we find a lotus."

"What will you do with a lotus?"

"Not an ordinary lotus, I want a *lila-kamal*" (the lotus with
a long stalk that the maidens of Kalidasa's age held playfully in
one hand when they met their lovers). "Brides have a *lila-kamal*
in one hand and young *kunda* flowers stuck in their hair. They
make their faces pale with the pollen of *lodhra.* In the knot
of their hair they hang *kurubak* in their graceful ears they
place *siris* blossom. In the middle partings of their hair
are *neepa* flowers that blossom at your advent, O cloud."

"What flower is *kurubak*?" asked Milu confused with
so much Sanskrit thrust on her. "Is it the *bak* flower?"

"Tch, tch, is that possible? *Bak* is edible, it tastes
nice, my friend—can one write poetry on a flower like that?"

"Why? Why can't a flower be mentioned in poetry just
because it is eaten?"

"Why don't you read the arguments going on in *Bichitra*
monthly between Rabi Thakur and Sarat Chandra? He says
utility goods cannot be the subject of art."

"Is that so? Why, all flowers have some utility."

"For example?"

"To blossom into fruit, my dear—just as you are a young
girl, a flower . . ." before she could finish our cousin Arun
entered; he was both a cousin and friend. Loved by
everybody, he with his flute. Swinging his flute like a little
baton he stood transfixed, observing our dress and make-up.
"What's up, where are you going?"

"Why? Can't we be a little beautiful at home?"

"Of course you can; but tell me, where resides beauty?"

He was quoting the title of my paper. Then he went
round and round me scrutinising all the details of the finery
from all sides. "Hmm, she has put on a *sinthi?*" Then he

hummed a song from Thakur's *Vaisnava* poems where Radha
requests her friends to dress her up—"Bedeck me with a pearl
necklace, put a *sinthi* on my forehead.   Tie up the tresses
of hair dangling to my knees with champak garlands."

Singing and traipsing, he suddenly pulled the bun tied
loosely on my head and a shower of India ink fell on my
shoulders like a cascade over a valley.   Just at that moment
the three of us chanced to look into the mirror.   Our eyes met
speechless, we stood bewildered.   I told myself, "Do not
worry, little girl, Big-Uncle has been teasing you."

I enter into the events of 1930 one by one—I do not
know how I can do it.   How the scenes of a lost drama pass
before my closed eyes like scenes from a cinema!   Could
I have written like this twenty years ago?   Never.   If I could,
then my whole life would have changed.   For so long I did
not know that through my whole life a tragedy was being
written, slowly and steadily, in invisible ink, in an unspoken
language and in an unheard voice.   Gone now are fortytwo
years of my life!

All that time these scenes were shut up—locked and
sealed with lac.   Sometimes, when tossed about in the
vicissitudes of life, I have felt the pressure of some hidden
sorrow in me.   But that morning just one word from Sergui—
"Mircea, Mircea, Mircea, I have told my mother that you have
kissed me only on my forehead"—a lie uttered by a frightened
child, became a golden key, it opened the door of that
inaccessible cave—through that open door Bhairava has
come out—I can hear the foot steps of Mahakal.   Nataraj is
dancing with one foot in the past and another in the present.
He is dancing—trap-trap-trap-trap—waves of laughter and
tears are rising and falling, the emeralds and diamonds of
my experience are lying scattered all over—the vehemence
of his foot-falls crushed my ribs—what unbearable agony!

Nataraj, stop your dance!   Stand with your feet together,
become Krishna holding conch-shell, chakra, mace,
and lotus in your spreading four hands, O remover of all

distress! Or come in the form of Vamana and keep your
third foot on my head—crush it—let me melt under your feet,
O Krishna. Can't you become merciful Buddha, purifier of
sins, remover of darkness? Soothe my burning heart.
O Kesava, just as you once became Buddha when your heart
melted in pity, seeing the animal sacrifice. Release me,
release me, wipe out this illusion—I do not want to see him
any more. I want to wake up in my everyday life, in my
beautiful home, in the minds of my nearest ones . . .

There he is, stooping over the gas ring, boiling coffee.
The gas ring is on one side of the dining room. Jharu is
standing before the kitchen door. Jharu is our cook, plump,
very dark; curly hair sprouts like a forest on his chest—he
literally looks like a gorilla—he will not put on a shirt—he
refuses to get civilized. He is holding out the sugar pot.
Mircea likes the coffee to be frothy. He must have coffee
after each meal. I can see him. He has taken out the
handkerchief from his pocket and covered the handle of the
saucepan with it to protect his hand. Jharu is following him.
On his fair face, on the black rims of his spectacles drops
of water have formed from the vapour of the hot coffee.

Mircea now sits on the dining chair and places the cup
on the table.

> Vapours rise from the steaming coffee
> And moisten the black rims of
>               Your spectacles,
> That morning remains waiting
> Somewhere in the limitless blue.

On our way to the library we began to quarrel again and
it ended at the verandah upstairs, when we sat down for
cataloguing. Mircea asked, "So? You won't speak?"

"No, if you behave like that, I shall never talk to you;
why should you bother anyway? I am not a nice person."

"Have I said that?"

"I am cruel, heartless. I don't even know manners.
If that is not bad, what is?"

"Why did you behave like that yesterday?"

"What did I do?"

"You and Milu went away hand in hand and shoulder to shoulder with Arun, but if I stand near you, you at once move away."

"How silly, Mircea, he is our relative—you are not a relative."

I remembered mother's advice, when I was a little girl, about twelve years ago, before I had started to wear saris. A relative of mother used to visit us often. He was much older than mother. I do not know how old he was, because children can never guess the age of their elders. He had pleasant manners and was a well-wisher of the family. Everyone liked him. Our house echoed with laughter the moment he entered. He used to make me sit on his knees and tell absurd tales. I was a small girl in a frock, so no one objected. But then suddenly he started a funny game— sliding his fat hand inside my frock he would touch my freshly budding breasts. At first, I did not realise what he was after. The second day I told mother. Shocked and scandalized, she exclaimed, "Oh, he hasn't changed then, even after marriage—I shall never allow that *haramjada* to enter my house." Mother never used slang or words of abuse. In our house no one could utter a vulgar word for fear of mother. I have heard in other houses people easily using such words as *haramjada* or *sala* but they were never uttered in our house. We shuddered when such vulgarities hit our ears. This was the first time I heard mother use such a terrible word. She was so angry that she could not find any other word to express her indignation. Mother told me, "Ru, if anyone does such a thing to you, at once come and tell me, dear. You must never allow any man even if he is a very near relation, ever to touch you. It is very bad for a girl to be touched by a man—it can do great harm—she can get sick, her health can break down, she may even die." I could not fully trust her words so I asked, "But why should she die?"

"I cannot go into all the details, but you must obey me
and do exactly as I tell you.   A girl has to be very careful."
Mother is right—I told myself—some people do really behave
funnily.   As I was growing up I saw greedy looks even in the
eyes of distinguished men.   So lecherous they made me sick.
For example Kamal-babu, he was so educated, he was one of
those who were considered cultured, "elite".   He was an admirer
of Rabi Thakur and had got by heart many of his poems.
Yet he would tease me the moment I was alone.   One day
I was busy sweeping the visitors' room with my sari tucked
round me and with a broom in hand (I was never satisfied
with the servant's work).   Kamal-babu entered and seeing me
busy in menial work began to recite a poem by Rabi Thakur.
Addressed to woman, the poem says: "O woman, you can
double the glory of a king by the touch of your hand, yet your
greatness and glory are such that with the same beautiful hands
you brush the dust in your own home. . . ." No sooner is a
poem recited than my mind starts dancing, so I joined him,
reciting loudly the lines that follow—when suddenly Kamal-
babu embraced me from the back.   Startled by this surprise
attack, I forcibly freed myself and ran away.   I felt as if a
viper was about to sting me.   When I told mother she said,
"Only fancy *panjabi* and *nagrai* do not make a gentleman."

I now realise better what mother had been saying:
I know there is an unknown unseen secret world about which
I have no clear idea.   A sense of sin is growing in me.   She
is right.   I shouldn't have allowed Arun also to place his hand
on my shoulder; he is like a brother, but he is not a brother.
I stood thinking all these thoughts when suddenly I looked up
and saw Mircea watching me with a fixed stare.   Saying
"Forgive me, forgive me", he took both my palms in his hand
and kissed them.   I stood silent, quiet as a painted picture.

He did not release my hands—my two tender palms were
getting crushed in his, he was pressing them with his lips—
infinite time possessed us—for how long did we stand? Who

knows how long? I was trying to free my hands but was unable
to do so. I looked up and began to pray. To whom was I
praying? Only to myself. Oh, save me, save me from myself!
Yet I did not want to run away. I wanted to have his arms
round me. But he had not pulled me towards him at all—
there was much space between us—he thought I was trying to
escape. "O stop it, Mircea, stop it. You have crushed my
hand. You have killed me." He raised his face, 1 staring at
him in wonder. I did not want to get away from him. Bells
began to tinkle in my veins—this was certainly not like getting
ill—a butterfly seemed to have opened its wings on both my
sides—I could easily fly now. Mircea again put his face down
on my hands. The sky came down on earth—the sun-glazed
blue sky fell on the ground below—it remained motionless,
weighed down with the load of a kiss.

That night was magnificent. The moonbeams creating a
mosaic of light and shade had turned that street of Calcutta
into Indrapuri—a paradise. I am standing on the verandah—
the clock strikes one, two, ding-dong. The moon walks across
the sky. So does Orion, the Kalpurush. I am standing alone
leaning on the railing. I have not braided my hair, so its loose
ends are in disarray. On the wall I see my silhouette. I am
watching it. Like Narcissus I remain spellbound by my own
shadow. I gaze at the shadow of my slender body wrapped
in the magic of the moonlight and I wonder -- what is the mind
which resides in that body? I am forever in search of it—
Mircea says he wants to see my soul. Sankara had said that
except for the Supreme Soul everything was an illusion, like that
shadow. But that shadow is also not an illusion and that
*madhabi* creeper swinging beside it is also real. This night,
with all these together, is a reality, a complete lustrous reality.
1 feel happy—an ineffable bliss fills me. I once heard the
phrase, "to float in the ocean of joy"; now I realise what it
means. My mind itself has become one with the moonlight,
like the *somapayees*. I have drunk the intoxicating juice, the
essence of the moon—I am floating on the *akashganga*, the

sacred Ganga of the sky.  In one hand I hold the lamp of
stars, on my neck twinkles a necklace of stars—watch that
burning capella Brahmahriday, that is the vermilion spot on my
forehead.  On my feet jingle the bells of stars—tink, tink, tink,
tink—no, no, these are not the sounds of bells—this is a piano.
Mircea is playing in his room.  I am sure he will keep playing
deep into the night—just like me, he won't be able to sleep.
I know what he wants—the curtain is moving slowly and I
am getting a glimpse of the unknown mysterious world.  I
had an unwavering faith in my mother's words but now I am
not so sure—I am certain there is no sin in all this.  If there
was, I would have surely known.  Have I not many times
recognised attacking vipers?  This is a garden of light, or
a lotus-lake or, as the poet has said, the lake of beauty.
Whenever I think anything deeply, poetry rushes into my
mind and as soon as I think of poems, I remember the
poet.  How long I have not seen him, but I feel no grief over
that, isn't that wrong of me?  Am I breaking a promise?  Am I
going away from truth?  Did I, some morning—looking up to
the sun—take a vow—"Let all my love flow towards you, my
master.  I shall never allow anyone, or anything, to become
dearer than you."  Am I moving away from truth?
   Since a few days this question perturbed me intermittently.
Today I know the answer.  The answer has reached me
climbing on the steps of joy.  Can anyone fall away from
truth?  It is truth that supports everything.  All the strings
of my mind are tuned to his music—he is the player—it is he
who is playing this melody in me—it is he who has raised this
wave of music in my body and mind.  I am entering into this
wonderland through his songs.  Somewhere he has written,
"When I look at this world through your music only then can
I know it, everything becomes familiar."  He wrote this
about God.  I am thinking about a man—I am a little girl—
for me God is not necessary—a human being is enough.
   Inside the room Santi is waiting for me, half asleep.
She calls me drowsily, "Won't you come to bed, Ru?"

"Yes, I am coming " In my room my eleven-year old
sister Sabi and Shanti sleep. Shanti is sleeping on the floor—
I and my sister will sleep on my bed. Sometimes I also sleep
on the floor, on a mat. I like it. Sabi is asleep. I sit
beside her and pull the sheet over her. On her pretty, little
face, framed by locks of soft curly hair, moonlight is shining.
How heavenly she looks with her guiltless innocent face
bathed in light! Can a person be fully innocent at any time?
Or are we all born with the seed of evil in us, I ask myself.
This morning when we were coming out of the library room
I had noticed a sharpness in her bright beautiful eyes. I got
goose-pimples as I remembered it, and an unknown foreboding
made my ocean of joy tumultuous. I pressed my palms
together and tried to pray—I did not know to whom to pray.
The human ear is capable of grasping only waves of sound—
these do not go very far—is there any ear which can grasp
everything which is far yet near? Who are you who have
given a touchstone in my master's hand to awake me? Who
are you who have made this river of joy flow—if there is any
such entity, I beg you, give me the treasure I am seeking.
Do not turn me away empty-handed. My eyes are getting
heavy with sleep. Mircea made a small bruise on my
hand—I am nursing it softly with the other palm, but it is
gradually growing bigger and bigger and spreading over my
heart—I see myself fallen on the ground, wounded; and
Mircea is gone.

For the last few days we have been busy cataloguing
father's books. Father told me that if Mircea could give some
time, the two of us could make a list of his books. Father had
a large library. Some six or seven thousand books. There
was a big box with small square chambers. and the cards were
ready. Every day we sat together for four hours, at least,
in the morning, and did this work, and then in the afternoon
all of us went out for a drive. Every day, for at least seven
to eight hours, we were together, yet the little time in the

midday that I passed upstairs seemed unbearable to me.
It seemed I was getting bound to him with an invisibe cord.
Could this tie break?   If it did, I would too.   But I never
told him this.   I gave him no opportunity to know my mind.
So he was unsure.   He really was given no scope to have
faith in me.

Whenever we were together we talked about books or
some poem or other.   I had read *Hunger* but I did not like it.
I was never able to tell him why.   The reason was that a
scene in it had filled my mind with both disgust and curiosity.
Besides, the "hunger" of someone who remains without
food, day in and day out—how could I know what that could
mean to a person?   I never knew how it felt to be hungry—
mother was always there with good food.   I could never eat
enough to satisfy her.   Maybe there was some other hunger
of the body, but I was not yet oppressed by it.   That world
was still unknown to me.   And about the hunger of the mind,
I really was totally ignorant.   In beauty, colour and fragrance,
the world of the mind around me remained full.   So I told
him, "I do not like this book," and pushed it towards him.
He said, "Let me see", and then stretching his hand, as if
to get the book, he got me instead.   Putting his arm round
my waist he pulled me towards him.   In an instant, propelled
by the prejudice and taboo of ages—even though I was
holding him with my left arm—I . . . well . . . I am ashamed
to mention it even now . . . I slapped him on his white cheek,
my fingers making five pink marks.   Shocked beyond
measure, he watched me with stern eyes.   Holding my wrist
strongly, he said in an undertone, "How dare you hit me?"

"What else can I do?"

"Do you know, in our country if a girl does this to a man,
it would be considered a deep insult.   It is called jilting."

"But this is not your country."

"All right.   I shall go away tomorrow and never come
back."   Fear spread like fire in me, drying up my soul.   What
shall I do, I told myself, if he really goes away?   "Forgive

me, Mircea. I did not do it purposely."

"Oh, what do you mean?" He was even more surprised.
He did not know who goaded me to this unexpected rudeness.
It is our custom, our social habits, our ideas of modesty and
chastity taught over thousands of years that lifted the hand of
a robot. "I am telling you the truth, Mircea." I said, gulping
my tears. "It is not me, just my hand that misbehaved so."

It did not take long to clear up the situation. I was
repentant, thoroughly repentant. My attitude was: if he does
it again I will not repeat my action. But he had become
careful, cautious. Indeed he was treating me like a fragile
object and would not dare touch me any more.

We made peace. I pondered hard to find a solution.
Since he wants me so much, I shall have to find a way. My
idea about the relation between man and woman was very
hazy indeed. But gradually the fog was getting clear and I
was getting to know more and more, not consciously but
intuitively. When the sun's rays fall on the flower and make
its petals open it does not know that it is obeying an order
coming from some unknown quarter for the purpose of
bearing fruit. So love, bright and warm and lustrous love,
like the sunbeam itself, entered my body and made it eager
and ecstatic.

Yet I did not know in which direction it was moving me.
Indian women have come to have fixed ideas about bodily
purity. I was certainly not free from that. For example, they
can love no one but their husbands; if anyone does otherwise,
it is considered a most degrading act. Yet there are some
women who fall for men other than their husbands. In
Sanskrit there are some "technical" terms for them, such as
*svairini*. . . . I think of a character from a novel of Sarat
Chandra, in which a young wife of an old, ailing husband tells
her lover, "The thirst that can make a man scoop water from
a gutter and drink it—I had such a thirst." I see that she had
some kind of affinity with that hungry man in Knut Hamsun's
book, for this cannot surely mean thirst for water. However

poor they may be, they certainly had a tap in their house.
As I sat revolving all this in my mind, a song entered,
murmuring, "I have thirst in my eyes and the thirst swells
up in my breast." No one can speak of other people's minds
as beautifully as Rabi Thakur. Conflict of good and evil
continually shakes my whole being, yet I have formed certain
ideas about chastity. Which parts of the body are sinful to
touch—for example, every day when we sat at the dining table,
he puts his feet on mine—can this be sin? Impossible—it
cannot be a sin to touch another's feet—so my argument
goes—it cannot be sinful to touch hands either. We shake
hands with everyone—mother shakes hands with Professor
Tucci—is that immoral? So one day I told him in the library,
"Mircea, you can take my hand"—and I spread out my arm
towards him. He caught it with both his hands—I realised
then why an arm is compared with the stalk of a lotus, because
over the stalk the palm blooms like a flower. But his hand
over mine looked very white indeed. I watched with jealous
eyes. He caught my arm with his two hungry hands and kept
his head and face on it. From my shoulder to the palm I felt
his lips moving—slowly my hand got separated from my body,
or the hand became all of me. All my senses concentrated
there and my whole being began to pulsate there. I did not
know for how long he held my palm on his breast. His breast,
his neck I felt on my elbow, and his face over my shoulder.
He was unsteady, he was constantly moving—gradually my
hand got transformed, it no more remained an object of flesh
and blood, all solid matter disappeared from it. It turned
into lightning and flashed in the limitless sky. All the atoms
and molecules in it got loosened—they rotated and danced—
revolving like the planets and constellations—"planets, stars,
the moon and the sun flurried in their own motion"—I stood
motionless, my eyes shut and tears streaming down my
cheeks—"Mircea, Mircea, Mircea: what is this, what is this?"

My pillow is soaked with tears, I am not in the library
of our Bhowanipore house. I am in bed, in my Ballygunge

home. Yet how strange it is that my hand has still the same acute sensation, it still is the whole of me. My body is numb, I am trying to turn around, and I see my husband, half-raised on his elbow, watching me. "Won't you tell me what has happened to you?" he asks.

I have been married thirty-eight years. I have been a good housewife. Our relation is perfect. I stretch my hand to hold my husband's. "Shame on me," I thought. Why should I think of all these things after so many years? Where is that Mircea? Just as I thought it, a sigh heaved up from the bottomless depth of my soul, as if it said—"Here I am. I have entered into the breath of your life. Why did you forget for so long? Why? Why? Why?"

Since a few days some trouble was brewing in our family—my aunt had brought into our home a young girl— her name was, let us say, Aradhana. She was six years older than me but we were friends. Aradhana was very pretty. A young boy, whose name was Jatin, lived in their house. He came from a poor family. an orphan with a village background. But he was good at studies, and handsome too. Jatin was very devoted to Aradhana's father, who was his patron, protector and mentor. So Aradhana's father decided that he would marry her to Jatin. When Aradhana was only twelve years old this marriage was settled though it was decided that they would wait a few years till she came of age. They lived in the same house, so they met often. But Aradhana disliked Jatin almost to the point of hatred. If Jatin entered the room, Aradhana would leave it. If Jatin wrote her a letter she would tear it to shreds without even glancing at it. At that time no girl or boy dared to discuss their marriage, or proffered any views regarding it to their parents. Yet she had often told her parents and her elder sisters, begging them piteously not to marry her to Jatin. "I will never marry him, ma," she had said again and again, sobbing, "I cannot stand him." "But why?" her elder sister had asked, shocked at her impudence.

"He is such a promising boy why don't you like him, especially
when he likes you so much? What do you think of yourself, you
impertinent, fussy, spoilt child; why should we turn down an
offer that has come from the bridegroom's side?" So at the
age of fourteen Aradhana had been married to Jatin. She
was now twentythree years old and had a son. Her husband
always tried to flatter her and keep her in good humour. His
was an abject idolatry, servile and pretentious. Yet Aradhana
said her life was nothing but a large dose of quinine mixture;
it left an after-taste of bitterness in the mouth. "Dear Ru,
I cannot tell you how I suffer to live with that man, what
agony it is "
    "Why?  Jatin-uncle loves you very much."
    "Nonsense," she spoke vehemently. "All sham mockery."
    One day the bitter taste of quinine-mixture was washed
out and her mouth tasted the sweetness of honey. A young
professor came to live next to their house. He was about her
age. They came to know each other and Aradhana realised
for whom she had been waiting so long—the meaning of her
existence, quinine-mixture notwithstanding. But that young
professor, let us say his name was Soumen—he was also born
of an Indian woman—like my mother his mother also taught
him what was virtue and vice, dharma and adharma, according
to the age-old traditions of this country. All these restrictions
were never meant for men in ancient and ageless India, and
Soumen was not an Indian only, he was also a modern man.
So he made no difference between man and woman. His love
was stronger and deeper than Aradhana's. Yet he had told
her that they should not meet any more. He did not wish
that Aradhana should fail in her duty towards her husband.
There was no divorce then among Hindus, therefore their love
had no future at all. But Aradhana was not such a moralist.
She said, "Why shouldn't we meet? If Draupadi could have
five husbands, why can't I have two?" She was joking, of
course. Soumen became desperate, not knowing how to
control himself or to decide what his duty was. Eventually

he wrote a letter to Aradhana, extolling the merits of fidelity
and asked her to be faithful to her husband, and went to a
Christian monastery for atonement.  He imprisoned himself,
as it were.  But Aradhana was determined to make him break
his vow.  One day she came to me: "Dear Ru, you write so
nicely.  Please write a love letter for me, with as many
quotations of poetry as possible."

"How will you send it to that monastery?"

"I know a way.  Please do as I say.  You know Soumen
is a pundit: he gets so annoyed if there is any spelling mistake.
So I ask your help—otherwise can't I write it myself?"  I felt
very inspired.  This was the time I got an opportunity to
write a love letter.  Aradhana had brought down from the
shelf a collection of Rabindranath's poems—*Chayanika*.  The
main snag about Rabi Thakur's poems is   it is difficult
to distinguish between the devotional poems and the love
poems.  However she had selected two, "Secret Love" and
"Love Revealed".  She asked me to insert in the letter a line
that said "Why did you give me love in my heart, Lord, when
you denied me beauty?"  I said, "You are so goodlooking,
this line won't do at all."  Disappointed Aradhana began to
grumble, "But that line is so beautiful."  After much hard
work we put together a twenty-eight-page love letter, sprinkled
with poetry.  It made an unerring hit.  Pierced to his heart
by this arrow, Soumen broke his self-inflicted imprisonment
and met her.  I cannot of course claim that this was due to
the magic quality of the love letter.  He was waiting for a
pretext.  Ultimately they eloped.  My worry then was what
would happen next.  Eloping with another's wife, has a
special word in Bengali.  Unless one knows it, one cannot
gauge how wicked such an act is—"to bring out a wife from
the home."  I have been hearing constantly that Soumen had
committed this great sin—as if Aradhana had not!  I know
well that it was Aradhana who coaxed Soumen out of the
monastery.  Jatin had written to say that he was completely
out of his mind.  So Aradhana's father went to recover his

daughter.  He had accomplished that task.  Now they were
all planning how best to punish the foolish and irresponsible
young couple.  If my father wrote to the University, Soumen
would surely lose his job.  My concern was that love-letter.
If by any chance it leaked out that I wrote that historic letter,
what a catastrophe!  I could not even imagine what mother
would do.  She would weep and exclaim, "So my daughter
also does such awful things!  Is this what I have taught you,
Ru?  My head is lowered in shame."  It was quite possible
that she would jump down from the verandah and kill herself.
And father?  What would he do?  I daren't even think of his
reaction.  I froze at the thought of his thundering voice,
"Hmm!  So that's all you know of grammar!  What's
happened to your declensions and conjugations?  You don't
even know the proper use of dental cerebral 'n' and you go
and write a twenty-eight page love letter!"  He would fume
and shout so much that the doors and windows would
rattle—who knows, the Bakul Bagan Road house might become
a heap of rubble!  For two days I was mortally afraid.
My only hope was that Aradhana would have pride enough
not to admit that her love-letter was written by someone else.

   We have not been doing our cataloguing these few days.
I do not know what Mircea might be feeling.  I clearly see
that he has no faith in me.  For example, I told him the
other day that I had sent my poem on the *chatim* tree to a
well known magazine, *Kallol,* and one of its organisers, one
Sri A., who was also a poet, had written me a charming letter.
Mircea was clearly displeased.  But why?  Can't one poet
write a letter to another poet?  I know why Mircea is so full
of doubt.  I have never told him that I love him, though he
has repeatedly told me so.  But how could I!  I am never sure
that this painful bliss, this constant desire to be near him is
love.  I must find out what it is.  I have not even told my
dearest friend Milu about it.  What's the use?  How can she
know?  She has never been in love.  She will just say something
to please me.  I can tell only one person—because only he is my

friend—it is not age alone that determines friendship—father
says the definition of a friend in Sanskrit is—"One from whom
separation is not bearable." I cannot bear to be separated
from him. No, that is not true. For how many days I have
not seen him, yet I do not feel like going to him. Why? Why?
Because I do not want to leave Mircea even for a day.
Suddenly I felt a yearning to see him and I began to cry.
"You are my companion forever in life and in death."

Milu entered. "Ru, Mircea asks if you will come down
for cataloguing?" "Yes, yes." I get up. I arrange my hair,
I put a vermillion mark on my forehead. We did not have
many cosmetics in those days. We did not even use perfume,
because all cosmetics were foreign made. So we used rose
water or *keora* water. Mother said I did not need to use
perfume at all, I was a "lotus girl," my blouse became fragrant
by itself. Why then am I putting rose water on my hair?
As if I don't know! I am cheating Mircea. Poor man, he
thinks I don't care for him, but it is not true. I want him,
I do want him.

As I come down, I feel a tingling sensation in my body
—I do not remember whether it happened exactly that day
—because I kept no journal—I am writing something that
happened forty-two years ago, neither from a diary nor
from exact memory—so I do not know whether the sequence
of events is correct—sequence, that means one after the
other,   that is, what was *then* before or after, as *now* it
has no before nor after. Now those events are all present
simultaneously; I do not know whether I am being explicit
enough, but it should not be too difficult an idea to grasp
either; when Krishna opened his mouth Arjuna got a darshan
of the whole universe, past and present, all together, as it were,
the whole of time and space in its completeness. That's what
I see to-day. Past and present have fused. Yes, my dear
friends, Parvati and Gautami, you will have to believe me—
intermittently I enter into 1930. So I wrote :

A life that is lost forever
beyond the seas of time—
if it does return again
        in totality
within the heart
in the form of light,
and sits down
beside the moon and stars . . .
that manifested sun
will reveal to me
the universal form . . .
Then there will be no other way,
I will surrender myself, O lord,
and seek your benediction

However painful, I will not close my eyes in fear like
Arjuna. I want to see him again, I want to hold him in my
arms. A faith in the supernatural is working a psychic
disorder in me; so I pray—if there is a Being who wields
the destiny of man, then let him take me across these
forty-two years. I cannot make out the lines of his face.
I can see nothing except his bright and intent eyes. I see
only a portion of his fair, white throat and a part of his
chest through the little opening of his shirt. I want to place
my ear there and listen—if deep down somewhere that
beautiful music is still playing a tune, that first foot-fall of
light, the murmur of first love.

We are arranging the books—we are writing titles in
the cards and dropping them into the box—we are working
silently—occasionally I watch him from the corners of my
eyes—his hands are shaking a little—who knows what is going
on in his mind—exactly what happened, and when, I cannot
say—where did it happen? In his room or in the library?
I cannot see. I see only a big window and suddenly I find
myself in his embrace and his face coming down on mine.
I am trying to escape, I am fighting him, but why? Why am I
doing it? I don't know. Maybe I want to be defeated—I
certainly am not trying to preserve my virtue. I was

defeated—Mircea planted his lips on mine—at a tender
touch my mouth opened and I felt his mouth on mine. My
whole body began to sing. Yet tears rolled down my cheeks—
that is how I am—I cannot differentiate between sorrow and
happiness. I don't see from where Mircea can bring so
much joy. What a wonder it is—it is much better than
anything I have known so long. One can can learn nothing
second-hand, neither can one get at reality from books—all
these thoughts were passing through my mind, my mind was
full to the brim. I feel no sense of sin—and why should I?
I committed no sin. I tried to stop him, didn't I? Let him
commit the sin—but this is not considered a sin in their
country—so I have presumed from all the stories he told me.
He releases me—I arrange my hair, and as I drape my sari
properly, a song began to murmur in me, "There is nectar
in my heart—do you want it?"

"Ru, Ru, Ru," someone calls.

"Coming, mother." My body has become light—I
cannot walk, I am soaring—on both sides of my shoulders
tresses of hair are blowing in the wind—they have become
wings—the peacock has spread its plume and is dancing in
me—I am floating up the stairs. "Clumps of reeds rustle,
mad with mirth—on the trembling new leaves the zephyr
plants a kiss." Suddenly I look up and see, holding the
banister, Shanti staring down at me from above the staircase.
In her eyes I see no jealousy, nor disapproval, only a question—
just a little thirst for knowledge! Yet a sudden flash of fear
makes me sweat. "The trembling new leaves" turn into
stone and the kiss of the zephyr wafts away to some unknown
destination. Of course I know I need courage—fear is
dangerous—so I say a little belligerently, "What are *you*
goggling at?"

"What am *I* goggling at?" she asks, piqued. "Where
were *you* so long?" Offence is the best defence, I thought
—so, with a proud gesture I said, "Don't you know where
I was? Aren't we cataloguing?" Shanti did not reply. She

stood there, absentminded, with a far-away look; did I suspect
tear drops gather in the corners of her eyes?

Shanti was five years older than me. I would soon be
seventeen, she twenty-two. She resembled her brother Khoka
a lot—she was no beauty—but the two shapely eyebrows,
arched like bows over her two bright eyes, were splendid. She
was a bright, sprightly girl bubbling with life. Poor all along,
she and her brother stayed with us. She had no formal
education, but she could, of course, read and write—but that
was all.

When Shanti was nine years, she was married to a boy of
nineteen. His name was Ramen. Two more years made
the boy twenty one, but Shanti could be just eleven, still a
child. Uncle Mantu used to say that Ramen thought that,
on waking up one morning, he would find a full-sized young
woman, but Shanti could not fulfil his expectations and remained
a child; that certainly was her fault and so, to punish her for
that great crime, Ramen sought out a full-sized woman and
married her. That girl was not only mature but goodlooking
too. So in her own house Shanti became a slave overnight.
Her only duty was to serve them or stand waiting for their
orders. She had to come away from her husband's bed and
sleep on the floor while the new wife slept with him. They
slept on the bed, covered with a mosquito-curtain, and Shanti
had to sit outside and massage their feet. Shanti did not mind
doing that. She said, "It did not matter that I massaged my
husband's feet, what really mattered were the mosquitoes of
Faridpur village." If the massaging was not satisfactory, he
would kick her. How long can a person suffer all this?
Ultimately she took poison to kill herself. But she did not
die; they pumped out the opium. Her husband got frightened
and wrote to her parents. Khoka was sent to fetch her here.
Shanti's mother had eighteen children. She wanted to send
her back to her heartless husband. She said "However a
woman may suffer, her husband's home is the only place for
her." Hearing her views my mother had quickly brought

Shanti away from her. Shanti's mother said, "*Bowdidi*, why are
you not allowing her to go to her husband? How can a young
girl live alone? Who will look after her or bear her costs?"
My mother had told her not to worry on those accounts—
she would stay at our house and would get training in
nursing—mother would make her independent.   In matters of
helping people in trouble, mother was quite an institution.
There was no count of how many persons she had helped in
life.   Khoka also had joined a typing school.   But Shanti and
Khoka were not the same.   Shanti paid off her debt to mother
by her labour.   She worked from morning till night.
Everyone ordered her about—even I did so.   No one hesitated
to yell out to her for a glass of water.   And Khoka? He could
only make people laugh; he had no other gift.   He would not
lift his little finger to help in the house work, or any work.
Father thoroughly disliked him.   So Khoka evaded him.
Father would have turned him out of the house if mother did
not intevene.   Mother would not turn anyone out of the house.
And she certainly was the mistress of the house.

     Poor Shanti had to live the life of a widow even though
her husband was alive.   Mother was deeply sorry for her.
Of couse her plight certainly was much better than that
of a widow's—she could at least wear the vermillion mark
between her parted hair.   She could wear coloured saris
with borders, she could take rice twice daily and also was
allowed to eat fish or flesh.   But she could not marry again.
No Hindu girl can marry twice, even if her husband dies,
and Shanti's husband was alive.   But mother would marry
her off if it was possible at all.   After all, she said, she is
as good as unmarried, since she is a virgin.   But there was
no way out—for if she tried to marry her to someone it would
be illegal, and Ramen would come and create hell.   He would
shout and scream and go to the police and turn the Bakul Bagan
home into a little inferno.   He was capable of anything.
Shanti loved someone—he lived near her parents' house—
Shanti remained ever eager to hear his footsteps.   But he

never came. He was married. And mother would never
allow such illegal love. There was no solution to this problem
in Shanti's life.

So, I wondered—why the tears in her eyes? She has
suffered so much that all her tears should have dried up by
this time. A spark of fear trembled in my heart—and at
once the song whispered, "My mind is fearful, if the lotus
stalk breaks"—well, how did Rabi Thakur ever know all
this? Such an experience must have happened to him also
—but his feelings must have been like Mircea's, not mine.
I am a women—this is a woman's song, "Her shy, red
blushes reveal a secret dream" . . . this is a girl's affair,
not a man's. Some girl must have told him—who could
that girl be? I shall have to look for her in his writings.
But why do I think of all this? One must never be
disrespectful to one's elders. I should be ashamed of myself.

I stood before the mirror—the free end of my sari has
slipped from my shoulder and is sweeping the floor. I feel
like dancing—so I clap my hands and go round and round
singing, "On the lake of youth sways the lotus of love"—
*tup-tup-tup-tup* . . . I was spinning like a top as I drummed
my feet.

Months earlier, I had heard this song at the Presidency
College. A student of my father sang it. Many times
I thought I would like to hear it again. But how could
I tell father? "I want to hear that song again from your
student." Had I said that, what would have happened?
Nothing at all. Father would have proudly told him—
"Susil, my daughter wants you to sing that song again for
her." But I never asked. To be truthful, I never understood
the song properly. But I understand it now. Every day
a poem or a song is becoming meaningful to my mind and
body. Can a body realise the significance of a song? Of
course it can. This particular song is becoming meaningful
in my whole being—that's why I am dancing—*tup-tup-tup-tup*.
Shanti entered—a vermilion spot ablaze between her curved

eye brows. I felt like putting vermilion on the line of my
parted hair. I cupped her face in both my palms and sang,
"In the fragrant pollen of the lotus a drop of tear trembles,"
and asked: "Do you understand this song—'On the lake of
youth sways the lotus of love'?"

"Have you gone crazy?" Shanti asked, though not much
surprised at my poetic mood.

"Shanti, I want to learn dancing—at Santiniketan Rabi
Thakur gives dancing lessons to the girls."

"Why don't you go and join?"

"Don't you know why? Will father allow me? He will
not let me move out a step. I am a prisoner here. Of
course I am a prisoner of his love for me. But imprisonment
can never be a happy state. Once Rabi Thakur wanted me
to act the role of Malini, the heroine, a highly spiritual girl
in one of his plays. He told me, 'I'll borrow you from your
father for a few days, to play the role of Malini. I feel you,
like Malini, also have a sky in your mind.'

"A sky in my mind? Never heard of such an expression
before. Till then the sky was above and my mind was in its
place, but no sooner had he said that than the sky descended
and spread over my mind all its intense blue. What ineffable
bliss filled me! He was a magician with words. He could
gather clouds and bring down the Alakananda from the
heavens by words alone. But did father permit me to go?
He told me, 'Do you want to spend your life doing drama?
Attend to your studies—the tapasya of a student is to study.'

"Dear Shanti, when I am married and I am free—I will
take Sabi to my home and I will teach her dancing. No one
will be able to stop me." I used to think that a girl became
free after marriage. But of course it won't be so if the
marriage was like Shanti's. Which woman is free? Is my
mother free? No, she is not. To whom shall I be married?
Mircea? Mircea? Never, never—it will never be—the stalk of
the lotus will break. Embracing Shanti, I kept my face on
her shoulder and began to weep. She was surprised: "Why

do you weep? What good is there in learning to dance?"
      "Not that, not that," I sobbed.   "I am just feeling sad."

      The standing lamp, with its huge white dome aglow. I am
sitting, reclining on a cane sofa.   On the opposite side Mircea
sits on his bed.   There is a  writing table between us.   He
has spread out his feet.   When I remember him now, I
always see him like this.   I am watching him.   He looks
absent-minded.   What is he thinking? If he wants to read
Whitman to me, I will never agree.   The other day he almost
forced me to listen to three poems.   They were not poems,
but three pieces of log.   No, Mircea is not concentrating on
literature today—he does not even wish to study Bengali.
Extinguishing the cigarette butt in the standing ash tray he
looks at me with unblinking eyes.   Then he takes out his
spectacles and begins to wipe the glasses—I can see his eyes
without the glasses.   I feel very scared when he takes them off.
"Why can't I bear to look at you, Mircea, when you take off
the spectacles?" I ask.
      "Because of my myopia."
      I am very fearful about his eyes.   I am afraid he may go
blind.   He says with serious face, almost bereft of emotion,
"I want to ask you something, will you marry me?" A little
ripple of laughter begins to gurgle in my throat.   I control
myself and think, 'This is how they propose, just as I have read
in English novels.   But it is never done like this, no one
proposes from such a distance.   The boy comes near the girl,
kneels down, then holding her hand he proposes marriage."
I feel cheated.   Nothing turns out properly for me.   Sitting
two yards away, he asks, "Will you marry me?"
      The only door of this room opens into the passage that is
the entrance to the house.   So people are constantly moving
in and out—there is something of a curtain hanging on the
door, but it is a useless decoration—so what else could he do?
I look at the photograph on the piano—his sister's—she is a
pretty girl—I want to make friends with her.   Mircea loves

his sister most. He says again, "I have written to my mother
and sister all about you. They will be very happy to meet
you—you will have no difficulty in our home." Now my heart
begins to pound. There is paper and a pencil on the table, I
pick up the pencil and begin to doodle. What can I say?

"Why are you silent, Amrita, tell me if you have any
objection to marrying me?"

"It is useless for me to say anything, Mircea. Father will
never agree," I say candidly.

He is surprised. "They will not agree? Your parents?
But they wish it."

"How do you know?"

"They love me so much. They have accepted me as
one of them . . ."

"Yes, but so what? That does not mean they will marry
me to you."

"Amrita, speak for yourself. We will discuss them
later. I want to know what your views are." I sit silent
and say to myself, *See how he mistrusts me—but please,
Mircea, have faith in me, at least at this moment.* But I am
unable to talk at all. I go on scribbling on the paper.

"Listen, Amrita, I am telling you, I will not take you
away from your dear ones. I will stay here and take a
lectureship at the university; at a hundred and fifty rupees
a month. What more do we need? That will be enough."
He speaks earnestly, his voice now mellowed with emotion.

"Mircea, I tell you my father will never agree. Never,
never."

"But, why not? Because my complexion is white?
Because I am a Christian?"

"I do not know exactly why, but certainly because you are
a foreigner."

"Do you want to say that the professor is in favour of
the caste system? Is there any difference between a Hindu,
a Muslim, a Christian or a Buddhist to a philosopher?"

' Of course there is"—I am scribbling on the paper—

"why did you come so near, Mircea, why, why?"   My lines
are going awry and my spellings are impossible.

He goes on talking.   "If what you say is true, then
why did they allow you to be with me so much?   We are
almost always together."

"I don't know.   Can't we love each other like brother
and sister?"

Mircea is shocked and hurt, as if he could not dream of
such a possibility.   "I your brother?"   I am feeling confused
and a little annoyed too.   To allow two people to catalogue
together is not to permit their betrothal; what was wrong
in letting me mix with him?   He continues to ask the
same question again and again—whether I love anyone else,
or whom did I love first.   I find no other words to reassure
him—I say, "I told you I loved a tree—a *chatim* tree."   His
face breaks into a confused smile.   He does not grasp
all this poetry.   Both of us sit in silence.   The scrap of paper
in my hand is now full of scribbles—the book *Mahua* was
on the table and I was copying the writer's name, Rabindranath
Thakur.   His calligraphy was beautiful.   It was then our habit
to copy it.   Some could copy his signature as perfectly as
the original.   Agitated, Mircea stands up and his gaze falls
on the paper.   "Why do you write his name here?   You need
his views?   You need to get somebody else's permission
to love me?"

"Mircea, you are wrong, the whole country imitates
his handwriting—that does not mean a thing."   I am ready
to leave.   I feel a longing to go near him and put my head
on his shoulder.   If I could do that I would be sure that the
little cloud of sorrow that is gathering in his mind this
moment would blow away—but that can not be, so I go
to the door.   I can feel his eager eyes following me, "Amrita,
listen to me.   Will you do one thing for me?"

"What?"

"Forget Rabi Thakur."

"The things you say, Mircea!   Can one forget the sun?"

"The sun! How can a human being be compared to
the sun?"

"When you learn Bengali—then you will also know
whether a human being can be like the sun."

I tell myself—I shall one day surely show you the
sun—and then both of us together will be sun-worshippers.

We were busy with two important events. Mantu was
getting married and my book was getting ready for press.
Mantu was eager to marry and he liked the girl the moment
he saw her. From this time Mircea began to wear
Bengali-style *dhuti* and *panjabi*. He looked charming in our
dress. But I never told him so. Why should I? Did he not
tell me that he could not make out whether I was beautiful or
not? But that was absurd, because I had enough proof with
me. For instance, a few days before Mircea came to live
with us, my cousin Sita's marriage was settled with a
Zamindar's son. Their family came to our house to see the
girl. The near relatives of the bridegroom inspected Sita
with an absolute thoroughness—they made us untie her hair,
they examined its length, they made her walk to see her gait,
and they also asked her to sing.

Though they really should have decamped after listening
to her singing off-key, unharmonious on the harmonium,
they did not do so. They liked her  They said, "Since
everything now is settled, let the bridegroom come and see
the girl himself. The boy was "modern", so he wanted to
meet the girl. The would-be bride's mother was modern too,
so she also said, "Let him come and meet us all—he must see
what a cultured family we are." So he came. His name was
Mriganka. Mriganka was very fair, plump and glossy—his
rubicund face had a perpetual benign smile. He looked very
much like a zamindar' son—that is, a bit of a dandy. My
mother said that Ru should not come out. But Sita's mother
said, 'What nonsense! Now that the marriage is settled—
where's the fun if he does not meet his would-be sisters-in-law?"'

My mother could not very well say, "Your daughter is
not as goodlooking as mine and Mriganka might change his
mind." So Mriganka came—more than once—there was
feasting and fun. One day Mriganka invited us all to a
bioscope. I assumed that Sita was already married to him,
so I behaved just as a younger sister-in-law should, that is,
I joked and made him laugh. Then suddenly Mriganka
disappeared. They enquired at the boarding house where he
was staying and got the information that he had left for his
country estate. His father wrote from there that Mriganka
had changed his mind and would not say why. He was
leaving for England, where he would study law, he was
awfully sorry, and so on and so forth. For a few days
our family met in sessions to guess the reason of his sudden
change of mind. Sita's mother said. "It was a blessing that
she did not get married to such a whimsical person."

Then I heard that he had written a letter from England
to my father, asking for my hand in marriage. My parents
were very unhappy about it. My mother said, "I warned
*didi* not to allow Ru to come out, but she wouldn't listen to
me. Is it good that such things should come about among
relatives?" Father said, "Such things happen when one is
over-zealous to be modern." And Sita's *didima* who is also
mine, that is, my mother's mother, pronouced a maxim, "Any
man who, while getting betrothed to one girl, looks at another
lustfully, is an immoral person. There can be no question of
Ru getting married to him." That ended the episode.

But if I tell this story to Mircea now, what will happen?
Ha-ha! What will happen! What fun! I can start like this,
with a serious face, "Now, Mircea, you cannot decide whether
I am beautiful." I know, as soon as I say this, he will look
at me plaintively, because I have noticed that since a few
days he has been trying to take back his words, but I won't
allow it. Once you have given your views, well, it's over.
Then I can continue. "But Mriganka can see." Don't
I know what will happen to him if I tell him the story?

Well, you never told me anything about this person".

"What is there to say?"

"What bioscope did you see?" I shall answer carelessly,
"O, I don't remember all the details." Ha, ha! Great fun!
I like his jealousy—it's adorable. But jealousy is not a thing
to adore; it's demeaning.

"Jealousy moves like a viper with raised crest" or "One
goes green with jealousy"— because it is poisonous. How
silly! It is not that kind of jealousy—it is love—it is love—that
tiny bird of jealousy is waking me from my slumber. That
little lark is frolicking from one branch to another and from
one day to another and is calling me: "Awake, *sakhi*, awake.
As the song says, "In the bower of my youth the bird sings."

Can any one tell me why I am not jealous? He says
so many things—specially his experiences at Ripon Street.
All the girls there fell for him—they were constantly after
him—someone threw a pillow at him—and many other
stories—but these never impress me. As the proverb says,
"They run in through one ear and run out by the other."
I never even cared to ask. But, to be quite candid, why should
I feel jealous? He hates those girls. That's why he has run
away from them. So, it is not actually noble-mindedness on
my part: I am surprised to hear all that he has to say about
the Anglo-Indians. They all think themselves as pure
descendants of the British and so much above the Bengalis!
They hate Mahatma Gandhi whom they mention as "Gandy";
and though they themselves are uneducated and narrow-minded,
they consider us uncivilized. Mircea suffered much in their
company; for him it was a nauseating experience.

Strange, is it not, that we know nothing about these
people? Where and how they live, their customs and manners;
we are not even aware of their presence in the country.

We live in the same country and shall continue to do
so for ever and ever, yet we shall never come to know each
other. They have such muddleheaded and wrong ideas
about us. And we? For myself I never cared to have any

opinion about them.   If I did not hear from Mircea I wouldn't
have known that there existed such a community as Anglo-
Indians.   We meet them only in the stations because most of
them are railway employees; we also see their living quarters
from the speeding train.   I like to watch their houses becauses
they know how to hang a curtain properly, they tend to their
flower pots carefully.   Bengalis are very slovenly in these
matters.   But I know that they hate us because they won't
travel in the same compartment with us, for they feel they
belong to a superior race, the British.   But, let's be truthful,
don't we also hate them?   We call them "crossbreeds".   Is
that a decent word?   But I know that we hate each other only
because we don't know each other.   If I could mix with those
girls, they could never hate me.   No one up to now has shown
hatred towards me.   If I try to make friends with the dark
young man who comes to Mircea, will he hate me?   Impossible.
I'll tell Mircea: why not introduce me to your friend?   I'll
try an experiment.   Then I'll see how long he can retain his
prejudice.   What will happen then?   Ha, ha!   The bird will
sing again, "In the bower of my youth the bird sings."
        Mircea wears a *dhuti* every afternoon.   I hear he wants to
embrace Hinduism.   He will be an Arya and a Hindu.   He is
studying Hindu scriptures but that does not necessitate a
a change of religion.   I do not know why he wants to be a
Hindu.   Mantu is very excited about it.   Is it possible that he
thinks that father will easily agree if he becomes a Hindu?
He does not know our world at all.   Our social customs are
quite beyond his grasp.   Doesn't father know that among his
students Mircea is certainly the best?   But he belongs to another
religion.   Even if it were not so, if he were a Hindu Bengali,
he would not be eligible—he would have to be of the same
caste, but of a different clan.   If the clan names are the same,
it would mean that probably many thousands of years ago
they were of the same parents so it would be incest if they
married—therefore two persons having the same clan name
can not be married lawfully.   He can not get into the heart of

all this complexity, though he constantly enquires about our
customs and social injunctions. He does not know how much
even our family is bound by these irrational rules. And father,
who is so learned, who knows so much, does not know that
happiness never depends on a person's caste or clan name.
And me? I don't care about these things. Never, never will
I enter into the prison house of prejudice. Even if I am not
married to him I will prove with my life that I don't care for
these silly customs. I don't care for anything in Hindu
society. I don't even like idolatry or icon worship the way
Hindus do it. What happened during the pujas? We went to
our country house in East Bengal with father about two years
ago. In that joint family seventy persons lived together.
They were all cousin-brothers and their children. Apart from
the family members about twenty students lived in the house.
They studied in the Sanskrit school attached to the house.
Such schools were called *Tols*, the medium of teaching was
Sanskrit, and subjects varied from high philosophy to practical
medical training. Indigenous drugs were manufactured in our
home. Such schools were scattered all over the country
to facilitate the progress of education by private efforts.
Sometimes they were subsidised by the Government. The
students lived like one of the family, completely free of any
expense. As my eldest uncle would say, "We don't sell
learning." The head of the family was an elderly man, a
medical practitioner; he was the eldest cousin and chief earner.
The whole family depended on his income. He was the
almighty boss. He had two wives. He married a handsome
young girl because his first wife was childless. For this my
mother and uncle Mantu were decidedly against him. But
many in the family approved of it. Even if they did not, they
had no courage to dissent.

During the Durga Puja we went to visit our village home.
We lived in the big city of Calcutta, our father was both
prosperous and famous, so we were made much fuss of. In a
well-to-do house in East Bengal the arrangements for puja

were elaborate indeed.   In the yard under the arcade the image
was being modelled from clay.   The process went on for days
and days.   Coconut candies were made and heaped into
baskets.   Rice was fried over hot sand and little white flowers
popped up emanating a savoury flavour.   I had never been in
a village before.   So I enjoyed it hugely.   And all my cousins
were pleased and proud of me.   We were a large group of
teenagers, we loafed about aimlessly in a holiday mood.   We
hired a few sailboats and went punting in the canals of East
Bengal's delightful waterways.

In those parts these canals served as roads.   On both
sides on the bank huge clumps of bamboo bushes stooped
down, almost touching the water below, making it dark with
shadow.   Sometimes the enormous banyan trees sent down
their serial roots as if eager to touch the rushing water with
their elongated fingers.   This was the first time I experienced
a Durga Puja at such close quarters.   I knew nothing about
puja, but I vastly enjoyed the preparation.   The whole
atmosphere was filled with a festive mood.   One occurrence
not only shocked me but made me very unhappy.   On the
varandah they were all sitting, the elders of the villages.   One
of them was an old gentleman, serene-looking, wearing a
white flowing beard.   I was doing *pranam* to the elders one
by one as was our custom, but when I came near him and
stopped to touch his feet he jumped up saving, "Oh no no,
no."   My uncles were also flustered, "No, no, Ru."   The
eldest uncle said, "You must not do that to him, he is a
Muslim."   He apologised for my fault and kept on repeating,
"She does not know.   She is only a child."   I was astounded.
How could anybody be so frightfully rude?   I felt
disappointed that father did not say anything to support me.
I told him that when I met him alone.   "You are right,"
he said.   "You were showing respect to your elders—caste
does not matter."   "Why did you keep silent then?"   I asked,
"How can I do otherwise?   Elder cousin was there.   How
can I contradict him?"   Now more than ever when I think

of Mircea I remember all these details. Even if father is
himself willing, he will never be able to give me away in
marriage to a foreigner. All these relatives who are really
nobody to us, who do not understand half of what we say,
are invincible. My second uncle would hurry down to
Calcutta and advise, "O Naren, do not commit such a sin.
Do not send our forefathers to eternal damnation."

One of my cousins, Nasu, was a painter. He painted the
background of the image. One day I found him tying a
buffalo to a tree. Though I could guess what that buffalo was
meant for, still I asked him, "What are you going to do with
it?" My heart wrung with pain at the possible fate of the
animal. "It will be sacrificed before Goddess Durga the
mother, on the eighth day of the lunar month—eight goats
and one buffalo." "Who is going to do the act of sacrifice?"
I asked uneasily. "Me" Nasu declared proudly. "Who else
can decapitate a buffalo at one stroke?" "Nasu, aren't you
ashamed to brag about it—what great bravery is there
to kill an helpless innocent animal? Can this ever be a part of
religion?" Nasu raised his eyebrows, quite appalled. "What
are you saying, Ru? How can one worship Goddess Durga
without animal sacrifice?" Then I began to deliver a fiery
lecture, giving all my arguments against this barbaric ritual.
A whole crowd of teenagers surrounded me. They were
my great admirers. So they paid heed to all I said and felt
sympathetic, perhaps more to me than to the buffalo. All of
us trooped to second uncle. He was of medium height with
a round face and large smiling eyes. He was capable of
immense affection: if for no other reason he could agree
to stop this ritual just to please me. I liked him greatly,
especially for one reason—when the students sat at their meals
he would come with a hookah in hand puffing tobacco every
minute to watch the women of the house serve them. They
were guests; they must be fed well. He had a fear that the
serving mothers might tuck away the better pieces of fish for
their own sons. None else in that house was so particular

about other people's comfort. But he refused to enter into
any theological discussion with me and told me plainly, "I am
not the head of the family. Neither is your father the head.
Go and appeal to the chief. Whatever his orders are, they
will be obeyed." So all of us moved towards his room but as
I reached the door I turned back to find myself alone, all my
faithful cousin devotees having deserted me. However,
I entered that fierce battlefield all by myself and without
trepidation. The almighty chief was a skinny small man of
about sixty. He squatted on the bed, hookah in hand, and
intermittently pressed his lips to it and inhaled the smoke.
His young w.fe sat on a mat, nursing her new-born child.
I gave him a complete logical statement against animal
sacrifice, and appealed that all the goats and buffaloes
purchased for this purpose should be returned. He went on
puffing, then without even looking at me said, "It's all
symbolic. We sacrifice all that is evil in us—and the animal
reaches heaven when it is sacrificed before the Goddess."
I was a great arguer. I placed before him the arguments of
atheists who told the Brahmins performing animal sacrifice
at a Yajna, "If that animal goes straight to heaven because
of the sacrifices, why don't you get your old father and sacrifice
him, since that is probably the only way for him to reach
heaven?" But the old man remained unshaken in his views.
I heard later that he had told others, "That daughter of Naren
is a sophist." Then I told my devoted cousins "Let's boycott
this puja. And for the three main days of the festival let's
not stay at home." Early in the morning we packed dry
food, coconut candy, various sweetmeats, flattened rice and
banana, sugar-cane and oranges and went out in the sail boats.
The whole day we moved through the canals under the blue
autumn sky, and over the gurgling whirling muddy water.
From the distant villages sounds of drums conveyed to us the
message of an unseen festival—but we were not unhappy.
We enjoyed the boating, the fleeting fragrance of the *sephali*
flowers, and the sensation of absolute independence. It was

a grand picnic also.   We returned every day in the evening
and hopped straight to bed.   I particularly refused to talk to
the elders.   But our aunts and grand-aunts felt very mortified
that the children did not join the festival.   All the three days
I prayed earnestly that if there really existed any supernatural
power, let it work a miracle and save the poor buffalo. But
my ardent prayers remained unheeded.   The beast's blood
flooded the sacrificial post.   In this matter father did not
interfere.   He allowed me to go my way.   I think he was
happy to see my strength of mind, my firm determination to
achieve something.   Probably he thought this was the first
step to becoming a Sarojini Naidu.   But would he support
me in Mircea's affair?   No, never, And would I be able to
be so firm?   No, it is one thing to do something determinedly
to help others, be it a buffalo or a human being, but quite
another to speak out regarding my own matters—shame,
hesitancy and a sense of guilt would seal my mouth—particularly
in this matter it was impossible to speak out—it would be
immodest.   I am a prisoner.   Who will free me?   I thought,
Do not become a Hindu, Mircea.   Hinduism will take you
nowhere.   Look at me, what have I gained by remaining a
Hindu?   It will not give you strength; it will take it away.

From the bower of my youth the cuckoo calls me over
and over again, "Awake, O woman, fearful of first love. . ."
I am standing in his room facing the window.   I am trying
to voice that song but some expectation makes me tremble
inside.   He is standing behind me, very near.   One hand is
round my waist and another hangs from my shoulder in front
of me like an unfinished necklace.   His face is near my ear—it
is touching my cheek—he is whispering something into my ear.
   "Mircea, I am afraid.   I am very afraid."
   "Why?   Why are you afraid?"   I am trembling—I know
what will happen now—just what I read in that disgusting
book *Hunger.*   He has made me sit on the big cane chair.
My body is numb—it is afternoon now—the whole house is

quiet in a lazy siesta. I came downstairs to look for letters
in the letter box. I know I must get up and go—yet I see
I have kept my hand on his neck in a fond embrace—I have
no power to move it away—and on my uncovered breast
he has lowered his face. My body is so frail—I have no power
to exert my will—the perfume of his hair has filled my breath—
he is murmuring something, maybe "goddess", and I am
whispering, "It is a sin, Mircea, it is a sin." A few seconds
passed—then a big bang, somebody opened a door—he freed
me and moved away in an instant. I have straightened
myself in the cane chair and am arranging the free end of my
sari. It cannot be more than three minutes, yet within this
flicker of time the world has changed for me. I could have
never dreamt that such a thing could happen to me. I keep
repeating "it is a sin" but I have really no sense of sin or even
of repentance. Fingering my loose hair he says, "I am telling
you, Amrita—there is no sin in it—because it is love, and
God is love." I see Jharu has come to the yard—he is
entering the kitchen—he has not noticed anything. We are
now at least a foot and half away. I am at ease now. I call
out to him, "Jharu, make tea." Well, this is pretence—I am
putting on a false attitude—is this not bad? What does the
song say, "Even if you burn with sorrow, do not do a false
deed, even if you face punishment do not utter a lie. All
glory to truth." So? Am I not doing something false?
But it's no use telling all this to Mircea. It's good that he
does not consider it a sin—would it be nice if he thought
so and went away? I also want him—if he again draws me
to him, I certainly will yield. I watch him—his lips are
pressed—his hands are trembling, it seems he is impatient—
why is he impatient? Is he angry because I talked of sin?
Shall I draw nearer to him and embrace him? How can I?
Jharu is alert. Then my other mind begins to frown fiercely
at me. "No, no, no, you mustn't stay here another moment.
Get away, get away, run—" I get up and, without once turning
back to look at him, I run up the stairs with quick, uncertain

steps.

That night there was no sleep for me. For a long time
his touch lingered in my body. It is difficult for me to
conceal such an experience and yet behave with ease. I am
not accustomed to conceal things. Is that why I am feeling
so impatient? Or have I any other expectation? What
expectation? My own eyes are peering down into that
unknown abysmal depth in me with severe disapproval.

Today I am lying on the floor on a mat. The cool stony
floor. I am turning over and thinking, "Can I write about
such an experience in a poem?" How? Yet many writers
do write. Even Rabi Thakur wrote one. Whenever I come
across that poem, I dislike it. I don't read it. Why did the
great poet write on such a theme? Those few minutes are
returning to me, accompanied with a little shiver of panic.
I am gradually getting into a stupor—I don't know the source
of this feeling in me—is it in the body or in the mind? I
remember another of my loved poets.

> Words are but loads of chain
> in my flight of fire—
> I pant, I sink, I tremble, I expire—

"Flight of fire", "flight of fire"—that line of the poem
begins to whirl in my head—and I go down and down. My
mat turns into a bed of feathers!

I was entering through the passage with a whole heap
of parcels, all purchased for Mantu's marriage, when Mircea
spotted me and stretched out his hand and took the parcels
to help me. I was relieved of the burden. This is their
custom. I like it. Look at Mantu, how swiftly he dashed
up the stairs, leaving the whole lot of packages for me to
carry. And Khoka? Even if I carry bricks, he won't lift his
little finger to help me. Getting up to greet a woman,
drawing the curtain, and not sitting till she sits—all these are
European customs. Ladies of our family are tremendously
impressed. Even the aunt who scolded me the other day
because I was laughing with him has changed her views.

I heard her telling mother, "What a good boy this Sahib is—
how nicely he mixes *dal* and rice with his fingers and eats the
plate clean, who would think him to be a European—he is
just like one of our own boys." I smothered a giggle. *Then
why were you so angry?* I thought. My mother replied, "He
is an excellent boy– he is good at his studies and obedient –
I like so much to hear him call me 'ma'." Shanti took it
up, "And when he wears *dhuti* and *panjabi* he looks like
Gouranga himself."

He had ordered many exquisite art objects for Mantu's
bride—beautifully embroidered clothes and wood carvings.
I felt envious. It is true that they were getting married so the
presents should naturally be for them, but he could at least
give me *something*, even a handkerchief. He never gives me
any presents—well, no, for he gives me books. Only the
other day he presented me two volumes of Goethe's biography.
He gave it to me the day after the earthquake. That was a
beautiful night! At midnight the earth shook. We all hurried
down to the street. The tremor did not last very long.
Then we all came inside and sat on the stairs leading to the
yard. Mircea made coffee. It was a star-dusted night.
I had never before nor after seen him so late at night, so that
night for a long time pervaded my mind like a fragrance.
The night has its own beauty, and it gives a special vision
to one's eyes. He made the memory of this meeting at night
permanent by presenting that book to me next day. He
wrote my name on it, adding "as a token of friendship
after the earthquake of 28th July 1930". He told me that
it was their custom to present something to a friend after
an earthquake. This is the only reminder of his stay with us
that I have had with me all my life.
He had read out to me portions of the book and also
talked to me about the life of Goethe, the poet who asked for
light. "Light, more light!" he exclaimed on his death bed.
I realised this was not merely a craving for sunlight for his

death-dimmed eyes, it was just speaking through symbols, as
we speak of the light of intelligence, the light of knowledge . . .
Our poet also has written, "Where is light, where is light—
light it up with the fire of *viraha*". What is *viraha*? The
exquisite sorrow of separation from a loved one. But how
can such a thing throw up any glow? Can't the happiness of
union become a light? Why in all the literatures of the world
is separated love extolled? Laila and Majnu, Romeo and
Juliet, Radha and Krishna, even Rama and Sita. . . . I don't
understand all these things. When I am upstairs and he is in
his room, I constantly feel a yearning that is painful enough;
but if he goes away, never to return, that will be terrible. I do
not think such a state could give any light, it would lead me
only to unthinkable and impenetrable darkness. So the
Yaksha of *Meghdoot* put out the light of *viraha* and dreamt of
the heaven of union. My mind cheered up as I thought of
*Meghdoot*. I leapt up the stairs reciting the poem. How was
that heaven? "Where there are no tears except tears of joy,
where there is no separation except the love quarrel and no
age except youth. . . ." Father came from the sitting room and
said happily. "Reciting *Meghdoot*? Pronounce Sanskrit
properly! It is 'y' not 'j'—why do you have the tongue of
a Sudra?"

"How could you hear me?" I asked.

"If Sanskrit is uttered within the radius of my ears, can
I ever miss it?"

I am uneasy about Sabi. She won't leave us alone for a
minute. For the last few days she is saying she will teach
Mircea Bengali. Mircea also considers it a good idea because
I am teaching him as much Bengali as he is teaching me French.
There is little hope that the two of us will ever be proficient
in these two languages. The trouble is, Mircea feels that Sabi
does not understand a thing about what is going on between
us—so we can do a little bit of wooing and cooing in front of
her, he can hold my hand. . . . But this is a mistake. I will

be seventeen soon, and she complete eleven years. She is not
such a child. Yet she talks like a child. It is a kind of pose.
When she was only six years old, a Brahmo relative of ours
tried to obtain a divorce from her husband. The impact
of that unusual incident shook educated Bengal. Heated
discussions went on for and against such an outrageous act.
Whenever ladies met, this was the only topic they could
concentrate on—Was it good to leave one's husband or was it
contemptible? One day when my mother and aunts sat down
for an argument, they asked us to leave the room. Sabi was
reluctant to leave, so she said, "Why don't you carry on? I am
a little girl, I won't follow what you say." Everyone laughed.
True, she would not have understood then, but she certainly
understands now. Actually she understands more than I did
at her age—I always pretend that I understand many things
even if I don't, but she does quite the opposite—oh, both of
us are good at pretending. Apart from this I have been noticing
a strange change in her. That father makes such a lot of
fuss over me, that Rabi Thakur loves me so much or, to be
exact, that I love him and can go to him any time, that such
an illustrious man has become so strangely attached to me,
but she cannot reach him—this troubles her. She is suffering,
and the pain is acute and sharp. But I must not blame her.
If one has to witness someone else getting so much of
something that remains beyond one's reach, it cannot be a
very satisfying state of affairs. She is not old enough to
realise that she is not ready yet for everything. So she pouts
and whimpers, "Everyone loves *didi*. Nobody loves me!"
People laugh at this coming from a sweet little girl, but that
does not take away her sorrow. When I went to Delhi,
she told the famous editor Ramananda Chatterjee, "You never
feel like coming to our house when *didi* is away!" Now
she is watching Mircea—she has understood that we have
formed a very special kind of friendship—I know she has
understood much. She is unhappy that this man also has
been attracted to *didi*. I am unable to discuss this with

anyone. Who can I talk to? I am especially afraid because
Mircea seems not to sense the danger. He may one day
expose himself. Sabi asked me once, "What were you talking
with your eyes?" When I told Mircea this, he thought it very
poetic, "To talk with the eyes! A good expression, let us try it
again!"

The more I watch Sabi, the more scared I get. Will she
destroy this heaven? Not purposely but by the secret heat
that is gathering in her. "No," I console myself, "she is a little
child, what can she do?" Yet I have no peace. I know Shanti
knows everything. So does Khoka, but they will never betray
us. Possibly Kakima, Mantu's wife, also knows, but she
won't go against me, we are now good friends. So I am
scared only of that wisp of a girl! I laugh at myself—needless
alarm! Then I remember the poem:

Fear keeps a constant vigil, over the bed of love.
Amidst the heart of the joy of union, keeping beat with the
pulsating ecstasy, trembles the wrathful God of pain.

The poem is terrifying, almost eerie, or so I thought.

Every day we go out for a drive in our Chevrolet.
Sometimes we speed through Jessore Road, sometimes by the
lonely Tollygunge Circular Road that holds south Calcutta
in a half circle. We all go—*baba*, *ma*, Sabi, Mircea, and my
two very young brothers. Mircea sits in front. This little
time we come close to nature. I long to walk alone with him
in between the shrubs and trees, on some full moon night
bathed in light or in the glow of stars. I have read so much
about what lovers should do, but nothing turns out properly
for us.

Prafulla Ghosh was a professor of English, his fame
resting on his being an authority on Shakespeare. Father
often invited him to read Shakespeare. Once he invited him
to dinner. We waited and waited, but he did not turn up.
Dinner time was long past. We got sleepy, annoyed and
exhausted with waiting. Finally he arrived, ate a satisfying

dinner and then, as he was washing his fingers, he said, "You
know, Naren-Babu, to-day I behaved truly like a professor.
I forgot all about your invitation and ate my dinner at home
and then while washing my hands I remembered! Like that
story of the two sisters-in-law—a young wife with her husband's
sister went to the river to wash the dishes, a crocodile came
and snatched the sister away.   Returning home she forgot to
tell her mother-in-law her daughter's fate.   After taking her
meal, when she went back to wash again, she remembered and
said, 'I remember while washing my face that a crocodile took
away the sister-in-law, merrily dancing on the waves'—shows
how much love there was between the in-laws."   As he talked
he mimicked the prancing motion with his bulky body.   The
room rang with peals of laughter.   I remember that day
because strange thoughts came to my mind on that occasion.
He was reading *The Merchant of Venice* and recited the lines
which Lorenzo says to Jessica while sauntering in the garden:
"The moon shines bright. . . . On such a night as this, when
the sweet wind did gently kiss the trees. . . ."

There are so many people in the room.   We exchange
glances and often his lips broaden into a gentle smile, and I
realise it is possible to be alone in a crowd.   But of course it
is much better to be like Jessica and Lorenzo.   For us that
will never be.   If on a moon-bathed night or on an evening
quivering with the trembling light of the glow-worm, we move
away together from the crowd, Sabi will not leave us.   She
will run to catch up.   I say to myself, *Such distance can come
between two, even when walking side by side!* But I have never
discussed all this with him—not even how much I love him,
because I am not sure of myself, I do not know whether this
constant longing to see him, to be near him is really love—
who can assure me on that point?   Moreover, he will then
become complacent—the bird of jealousy will fly away—
I don't want that—I like it more than anything else.   So
sometimes I purposely create a situation that will make him

sick with jealousy. For instance, the other day the writer
Sri A. was sitting in his room—I began to chat with him—
I started in English but quickly switched to Bengali—why
need we talk in English just because of Mircea—it is not
our language. I didn't even look at him—how his face
looked that day—just like a July morning overcast with
cloud! . . .

He becomes a little cruel when he is jealous and that's
what enchants me. Strange. How can my attitude be
described—is it coquetry? I shall have to look it up in the
dictionary.

Gradually he has begun to boss-over me. He thinks I am
his property. He thinks that my parents and other members
of the family all know and acquiesce. I have been suffering
from beriberi, so my feet are always swollen. I have to rub
in an oil made from indigenous herbs, I think there is tiger's
fat in it—it smells awful. But that does not mean that
I should not be allowed to walk barefoot. I like the feel
of my feet on the cool marble floor, but he starts arguing
and orders me to put on slippers. Green chillies are not
forbidden, it is really the bad mustard oil, the cooking medium,
that causes beriberi—but he has his own views, and he orders
me not to take green pepper. One day after the meal,
Kakima, Mircea, and I sat talking. He was angry with me,
so he said to Kakima, "Kakima, you are newly married,
you need to be sweet, so you should never take hot green
pepper. Let peppery girls do as they like." I retorted,
"As for nice and sugary boys, pepper's bad for their
sweetness."

"What do you mean?" he stared at me angrily. "I
can't eat green chilli because it is hot? Watch!" He picked
up a plate full of green chillis from the middle of the table
and, selecting a big one, began to chew it raw. A terrible
character really!

"Throw it away, throw it away," I shrieked and tried to
jump up, but couldn't because he kept me in my place by

imprisoning my feet under the table.  He had much more
strength than me and I could not struggle to free myself for
fear of Kakima, so he went on munching hot chillies one by
one.  In the meantime his lips became swollen and red right
up to the chin.  Red patches appeared on his white face, but
he remained unshaken.  Kakima was unconcerned.  She fell
in a fit of giggles on the table.  I tried to snatch the plate
out of his hand.  Kakima had no idea that a man was about
to commit suicide in front of her.  But Sabi understood.
After all, she was my sister, our minds were made of the same
mettle.  She shouted, "Ma, ma, ma, Euclid-da and *didi* are
fighting." Mother came running from the kitchen.  In an
instant Mircea released me and stood up.  Mother stood
transfixed, motionless like a picture—Why did that quiet boy
do such a frightful thing? As if in answer to her unspoken
thought Kakima said, "That's because Ru didn't listen to him."
"Just because Ru didn't listen to him?" she repeated
absentmindedly  That is the first time I saw a shadow of
suspicion darken her eyes.  She scooped up some butter from
the pot and, stretching out her hand, commanded him, "Eat it."
Mircea took the butter pot and left for his room, his head bent.

Mother fumed, "You finished your meal a long time
back, what are you all doing sitting here?  Have you nothing
to do?"  Though terrified inside, I pretended to be normal,
and casually said, "Ma, I just said it needs courage to eat
chillies, so he began to show his courage.  Isn't that it,
Kakima?"  I turned to mother.  "Utter dunce.  Yes, that's
what he is."  My voice was calm, it betrayed nothing, so
mother trusted my words, the cloud of suspicion blew away
early, because my mother wanted it to blow it away.  She
did not want to entertain any mistrust about the persons
she loved.  Mother hadn't the courage to face unpleasant
truths.  It is not that she was like that only then—all through
her life she remained the same, obtusely unobservant, because
she did not want to observe.  So when a woman was stealing
her husband away from her influence, she thought it would

all pass off if she overlooked it. For ten years this went on.
Mother never became alert to the danger. She realised it
suddenly only after she was denuded of everything. Her idea
was, should one be cheated because of one's trust? Is it a
fault to trust? That afternoon a sixteen-year old girl also
cheated her. Though I remained panicky for long, I said to
myself, *I am shrewd, aren't I?* It is only for Mircea that I am
turning into a liar. Oh no. What did Dusyanta say? To
lie is an instinct with women. Mother is walking up the
stairs. If she has any trace of doubt left in her mind. I must
try and efface it. I shall go up and nestle with her in bed.
So I told Kakima, "I am going up to mother, please go to
Mircea's room and find out what has happened to him."
She winked at me and said, "What do I care!"

Mother could not know my thoughts when I lay in bed
beside her. I put my arms round her. However one may
love another person, how easily one can cheat, because nobody
unless told can know another's mind. If he could? Then
all the preciousnesses of life like love, respect, and trust would
be in shambles in a second. I tried to guess why Mircea
did such an awful thing. Is it because I was disobedient or
was it to display his "valour" or was it something else? Was
he hurt? Did he want to take revenge? I couldn't make
head or tail of it. I could have never done a thing like that.
Can one inflict so much suffering on oneself? Many people
can. My Thakurma could. Her thirsty lips refused water
even on her death bed because the nurse was of another caste.
She could do without food for two or three days with ease;
but these had a reason—she did it to acquire piety. He also
might have his reasons. He was probably testing himself.
How much suffering he can go through for me! I felt very
small, indeed, at his capacity for self-mortification. He has
much more strength of mind than I have. I shall never tease
him again. Now I will tell him my mind. I will tell him
everything, not in the manner he did, but sitting near him and
touching his feet—not with my foot but with my hand—what

harm is there if I touch his feet?  After all, he is superior
to me not only in age but in learning and also in strength
of mind.  I felt defeated and crushed—but I was happy.
I was happy that he had grown taller than me by manifesting
his power of self-mortification.

Father's rising blood pressure has put the whole household
in a tumult.  Some ruptured vessels have created blood clots
that obstruct his vision.  This is a serious ailment, but even
if it were not serious mother would consider it so.  It is not
only in our house but in every household where the master
of the house is the most important.  He is ninety five percent,
and all the others together make up five percent only.  That
means that his wish, his convenience are more important;
others hardly matter.  In our family this attitude is stronger
than in other families; the master of the house is also the
ruling deity.  When he is ill there can be no other thought
in our minds, especially in mother's.  Mother must sit up
night after night attending on him without showing fatigue —of
course father accepts this untiring service as his due.  This is
the attitude of all Indian men; the wife probably is rewarded
by the work itself, by her pleasure of serving her husband,
and also maybe by the virtue she will acquire; but on the
husband's part there is no need even to be grateful.  This
lack of gratitude is not considered a lapse on his part.  Even
if he is not ill, the best food in the house is put away for him.
When he is asleep, the whole house must be stifled into
stillness; but he can shout or thunder when others are resting.
Even those who were considered extraordinarily civilised men
also behaved in the same way.  They never suffered from
any sting of conscience, nor would others expect them to be
different.  The master of the house is the bread-earner, so
he also had absolute right to dismiss all other views and lead
every member of the family according to his own views.
Maybe this is a necessary and useful custom to maintain
discipline in a large joint-family, but it invariably turns the
ruler into an arrogant and selfish person.  He considers

himself to be a god ruling over that particular household.
But actually he is no god; he is just a human being full of
weaknesses and bound down by the pleasures and sorrows
of life like any other insignificant member of the family.
Just as an omnipotent king is for a country, so is the master
of a household for its members, supervising the destiny of
their inferiors.   Especially if that man is a man of qualities—
his power becomes absolute.   My father's talents are varied,
his qualities are immeasurable.   There is no one to equal him
in erudition.   Impenetrable Sanskrit texts he deciphers and
interprets in a minute.   He has never needed help to go into
the depth of abstruse philosophy written in archaic Sanskrit.
His memory is sharp.   He has read all the books in his library,
some six or seven thousand volumes.   His powerful personality
awes even learned pandits—he can defeat anyone in argument,
he can prove to any man that that man does not know even
the proper use of dental and cerebral "n".

 We never thought that our father could have any fault.
For us he was flawless, as pure as a god.   Mother was at the
root of building up this image.   She never realised the danger
of it.   She thought children should never even in mind
criticize their father.   After all, the age-old maxim said,
"Father is heaven, father represents virtue, father is our
greatest penance.   The gods are pleased if father is pleased."
At that time the grip of this ideal was loosening in many
families, but it was intact in ours because of my father's
extraordinary qualities.   Yet gradually I began to feel a little
resentment.   I was growing a bit critical.   I was ashamed
of my attitude, but I could not check myself.   The first day
I had the audacity to argue with my father was when he was
ill.   My Thakurma in her time had brought into the household
a young girl deserted by her husband.   She stayed with us
all her life.   Though she came from a low caste and was
actually a maidservant, we looked upon her as our own.
All the children loved her very much, I specially.   She suffered
from chronic asthma and eczema.   I noticed father never

cared to get a good doctor for her or buy medicine for her.
Mother tried her best to give her as much treatment as she
could, but the money of course was in father's hands.   One
day I discovered her writhing in agony.   I marched straight
to father and said peremptorily, "*Baba,* you are always calling
doctors for yourself and getting medicine, why don't doctors
come to see Chapa-didi?"   Father was astounded at my
audacity.   He just said, "Why are doctors coming for me and
not for Chapa-didi?"   There was surprise in his counter-question,
as if he could not believe his ears—how could I make no
difference between him and the maidservant?

I went away thoroughly ashamed of my impertinence.
How could I have uttered such a thing, I asked myself.

But I know I am gradually growing rebellious.   No one
in this house can go against father's will.   So is there any
point in my wishing something?   Father is like an Emperor
who could order anyone crushed under the feet of an elephant
or behead anyone, as he thought best.   Of course he won't be
able to decree physical punishment—but what about the mind?
He holds unchallenged sway over our minds.   If by any
chance he comes to know of what is going on, he will do the
same thing that the Great Mogul Emperor Akbar did—not
in body but in mind—he will roll a boulder down on this
Anarkali of love.

One day Mircea asked me, "Have you seen the statues
at the Konark temple?"

"I have never even been there.   Why do you ask?"

"I used to think no human being could possibly resemble
them."

"I haven't been to Konark but I have been to the temple
of Bhubaneswar and also the temple of Jagannath at Puri."
I told myself, he might visit Konark, because actually it was
a ruin ; but he would not be allowed into a  real temple, like
at Puri or at Bhubaneswar.   What a godforsaken country
this is—where men are afraid to touch men!

We are standing in the ground floor verandah, I with
my back to the railing, supporting myself against the wall.
Behind me the *madhavi* creeper, covered with bunches
of flowers, is swinging in a gentle breeze.   Off and on the
flowers brush my left cheek.   He is standing in front of me,
a little distance away, and watching me with a serene look.
Suddenly he speaks as if in a whisper, "You look like a statue
on the facade of a temple."   This is the first time he has said
something admiring my looks—well, I am not sure if it is
admiration or what—who knows whether it is good to look
like a statue?   I want to hear a better description of my
beauty.   But what others say so nicely, he does not.   Maybe,
in their country they do no know how to describe beauty, as
we easily do   Like Kashiramdas describing Draupadi: "Her
nose surpasses the beauty of *til* flowers, her voice is like nectar,
her waist shames the waist of a lioness, her eye-brows form
the arch of Kama's bow, and her hair is like deep, inky
clouds."   Can't he say something like that?   Just "You look
like a statue!"   What a let-down!   Nothing turns out right
for me.

My book is almost ready.   Father has decided it will
come out on my birthday—the day I complete my sixteenth
year.   All the littérateurs, artists and poets of Calcutta will be
invited.   Father is preparing a grand show.   Just as in
England, when a girl comes of age she is presented to the
court with great pomp, so will father introduce the new poet
to the society of scholars.   Preparations for a very big event
are going on for days, centring on me.   My parents are both
so engrossed with their first child that others recede into the
background.   My two brothers are too young to feel it.
But Sabi?   She feels neglected.   She is continuously pouting
her pretty lips.   As a matter of fact her illness, which is
growing rapidly, is more mental than physical.   It was severe
the day we went to see Uday Shankar's dance at the New
Empire.

Two years back Anna Pavlova had come to Calcutta.

My parents went to see the performance.   The elite of
Calcutta buzzed with comments about it, good and bad.
That was the first time my mother saw a woman on the stage.
I was not taken as I was not considered adult enough for
this.   But I heard all the remarks that mother went on making
before the other grown-ups.   Mother was no connoisseur
of dance but her artistic sense and feeling of beauty was
subtler than father's.   The elysian dance, *The Death of a
Swan*, kept mother bewitched for some days.   But she had
reservations.   Pavlova did not dance with her gown flowing
down to the heels.   She had really very few clothes on.   Her
thighs were bare and when she whirled like a top, her frock
flew up and revealed her small underwear.   According to
mother, this might be necessary for art, but it was certainly
not good for social hygiene.   When they were coming out
of the theatre-hall, mother saw her nephew D. at a distance.
D. was not a child.   He was doing his Masters at the
University.   But mother was worried that even he had seen
such a dance.   And D  was also no less worried that his aunt
had spotted him in a forbidden place!

In 1930 Uday Shankar gave his first performance
in Calcutta.   Pavlova's Indian disciple!   The whole of Calcutta
buzzed with the news.   Our country was not used to such
performances in those times.   A few very specially privileged
westernised persons might have seen some ballet, but Indian
dance could only be seen in temples, where the Devadasis,
the slave-girls of the gods, performed.   They could never
marry, because they were married to the god of the temple—
though actually to the priests.   I had seen their dancing
in the temple—these dances were traditional, but performed
by uneducated girls, who were more or less outcastes.   We
had also heard about *baijees*, who were the degenerate
descendants of the court dancers of kings.   People from
"good" families did not even know where they lived.   It was
only the fat-bellied lecherous landlords who produced them,
like a conjurer's trick, in their garden houses, from some

unseen quarters. The very word *baijee*, that is, a "nautch girl", was never mentioned in good society. Who else did dance in India? The tribals—they had their dances, on festivals religious and social, and also for recreation. But that men or women from "good" society should display themselves on the stage, was an abhorrent idea. Since 1926, Rabi Thakur had introduced dancing on the stage. When he was visiting the north-eastern region of the Himalayas, he was taken to the district of Manipur, where he saw the lyrical Manipuri dance. On a moon-lit night, young and old danced in the open air, in their gorgeous tribal dance costumes, following the theme of Radha-Krishna. Rabi Thakur was enthralled and decided to introduce dancing in "decent" society. In 1926—in a play with a Buddhist theme—a girl from his Santiniketan school danced. The play was especially written for this purpose. The girl danced before the image of the Buddha—her dance was her worship. This was more or less a rebellious act, no less strong than a political one. The message of the play was so captivating that it silenced the wagging tongues of the critics. I had not seen it because I was not old enough. Just as Sabi was not old enough to go to the dance performance of Uday Shankar. I found her standing in a corner covering her face with her two soft palms tapered like lotus buds and whimpering, "Everybody loves you, nobody loves me."

Father phoned from the College to say that there was not a single seat available at the theatre hall. So we had to get a box. It would be just right for the four of us, father, mother, Mircea, and I. It was expensive to reserve box seats, but Mircea was ready to share the cost. Mother wore an Egyptian scarf studed with silver tinsels, and she looked like a queen. Mircea wore *dhuti* and *panjabi*. Calcutta's high society was fully represented there. In this top circle there was a large group, belonging to the Brahmo sect, who suffered from a superiority complex. Not everyone, but decidedly some. They never regarded us as sufficiently civilized. It was

long before we were given a passage to this high society.
Our pedigree was questionable, since we were "backward"
Hindus.   So they did not usually recognise us.   But that day
quite a few from this group of the specially superior elite
discarded their superciliousness and, during the interval, came,
stood under our box, in batches, and began conversation.
Father's attitude was no less overbearing.   He was after all
accompanied by an exquisitely beautiful wife, a moderately
pretty (the views of Mircea notwithstanding) poetess-daughter,
and a foreign disciple in Indian dress, and added to all that
was the box.   Altogether it was an immense affair that reduced
the pride of the Brahmos to rubble.

Uday Shankar was magnificent.   The shadow on the
screen, dancing in the background, keeping rhythm with the
movement of his statue-like figure, created a celestial world.
His outstretched arms vibrated like the ripples of a stream.
His velvety body was as supple as liquid in a bowl.   We had
never seen anything like it before.   Mircea was thoroughly
overcome and remained speechless.   That whole night he
played the piano, he could not sleep, and his music floated up
to my room and kept me awake as well.   Since then I have
witnessed a variety of dances performed in various countries
of the world, but nothing ever compared with that experience.
Both of us were emotionally ready for it, and the pain of
creation, manifested in the artist's body, filled our beings with
a beatitude.   Mircea kept on saying, "India! This is India!"

If anyone asks me now, how long he stayed with us, how
many years, months or days, I won't be able to answer.   In
my fifty-eight years of life I have truly lived for six or seven
years—the rest have been only repetitions.   If among those,
Mircea's stay with us was one year, then that was not just an
addition of three hundred and sixtyfive days.   They were not
rotating on the axis of the earth, they remained steadfast at
one point.   Those moments with all their beauty remain fixed
into my consciousness.   My mother was a great scholar of
Vaisnava literature.   So I once asked her about the meaning

of a poem, where Radha says, "I have been watching your
beauty throughout my life, yet my eyes are not satiated. I
have kept my heart on yours for millions of years yet it is not
soothed." I said "Why are these lines quoted so often? It is
not a perfect piece of poetry, as there is so much exaggeration.
No one can live for millions of years." "How can I explain
it?" she sai smiling. "No, it is not exaggeration. There are
experiences that cannot be measured by time. The bliss and
pain that sprouts from an eternal source, and is never
exhausted— this poem tells of that." I sat thinking, "millions
of years"; that's infinity. The joy that is never content—who
can tell me whether it is good or bad? My eyes filled with
tears thinking of an eternally unsatiated desire.

Sabi's illness grows. Uncle K is physician—he uses herbs
and indigenous drugs. She raves much of the time—she
speaks incoherently pointing to the photograph of Rabi
Thakur. She will not let Mircea out of her sight. He will
have to sit beside her and hold her hand. This makes me
happy, because he then has to stay mostly in my room, beside
Sabi's sick-bed. So many people come into the room, but he
sits quietly near her bed and smoothes her hair. He couldn't
have done it if I were ill. But he can with Sabi, since she is
a child. I feel a strange satisfaction that he has become one
of us. I remember the day when uncle K. was explaining to
mother about some medicine. He was sitting near Sabi and
I was standing at a distance, near my bed. Suddenly he
looked up at me and smiled. That smile sent through me a
queer sensation that ran up the spinal cord. I sat down on
the bed to steady myself. I was the "big uncle", so it was
my habit to analyse everything. This odd feeling filled me
with innumerable questions. How could it happen? It is
certainly an affair of the body, not of the mind. But the body
is not touched so it is not a sensory act. Then what is it?
Whom can I ask? Never will I ask him, because he will then
puff up like a balloon about his ethereal influence over me.

Moreover, how would he know, he was not a doctor. Suppose I ask uncle K. "Uncle, you are a physician. Can you tell me why I sometimes get this queer sensation, looking at Mircea? What happens then?" What happens? Hah! Then I shall be laid in another bed beside Sabi and they will shave off the hair from the top of my head and rub it with an oil meant for lunatics, or they will pack me off to the asylum.

One day Mircea said, "I would like to know something about the newly-weds of your country."

"I don't understand."

"For instance, Mantu and his wife—I don't notice any exuberance in them."

"Why should they display it to you?"

"In our country it is noticeable. I try to scrutinize your aunt's face, but find nothing."

"What impudence!" I was scandalized, "Why should you scrutinize her face? This is very wrong."

"Oh, no. Not like that. They are newly-married, but I notice no visible marks on her face "

"I am amazed, Mircea. Marriage is not chicken pox. why should she have any special marks?"

Trying to control a grin, he said, "But in our country they do. Would you like to see what kind of marks?"

"Yes."

He caught me with both hands and I felt a pressure on my lips, sharp and delicious.

"Look in the mirror," he said, releasing me abruptly.

I was startled to see my face in the mirror. There was a small round mark on the lower lip, clear and fierce. I remained immobile before the mirror, my eyes staring out in utter panic. "What shall I do, Mircea? What shall I do?" He kept a calm face. He had a journal in his hand, he casually turned over a page.

"Mother will know, won't she, Mircea? Tell me, please tell me."

"Very likely she will."

"O, what will I tell her?"

"How do I know what you will tell your mother?"

"Why did you do such a thing? Why?"

"But you asked me to."

I began to sob.

Going through the book with great attention, he said without even looking at me, "If you start crying I will make another mark."

I walk up the stairs; my hands and feet are shaking. Fear, an all-encompassing fear has gripped me. I have no idea what the fear of death is like. But if at that moment God appeared before me and asked, "Do you want to die now, or meet your mother upstairs?" I certainly would have preferred the former. But who knows where God is? He paid no heed to the prayer of a terror-stricken child, and I had to face mother within a few minutes. Mother was startled to see me. She looked at me with a fixed stare and fumed, "Ru, how did you get that ugly mark on your lip?"

"What mark?" I spoke calmly, in a smooth voice.

"Go and look in the mirror."

"O yes, I hit against the door."

"Which door?"

"Which door? Er . . . er . . . I don't exactly remember, maybe, maybe the library door."

"Maybe? You've got hurt and you don't remember where you got hurt? Tell me the truth."

"No, ma, I was not hurt so badly. O yes, now I remember. I bit my under lip accidentally."

"Why didn't you say so? One can never get marked that way by hitting against a door. It's a tooth mark. Now go and cover it with a little cream."

Good-natured, completely artless, and trustful, she was relieved to believe my words.

My birthday is approaching   The house is bubbling

with enthusiasm, as the preparations for the celebration
advance.   All the top literary personalities have been invited.
The ceremony will be according to ancient Indian tradition.
The seniormost man will set free a white dove, as a symbol
of emancipation.   As the preparations progress, Sabi gets
more and more ill.   She babbles disjointedly.   Maybe it is not
really disjointed to her troubled mind, but who is going to
care about that?   In those days, our guardians did what they
wished.   They seldom thought or their children's psychological
needs.   On the birthday evening, when the house was full of
guests, she tried to jump down from the first floor verandah.
This was certainly more to attract attention than to commit
suicide; it was impossible to do that in front of a full house.
The bacillus of her disease was a sharp-pointed poisonous
suspicion: "Everyone loves *didi*, no one loves me."

Our relatives were also critical.   They began to remark,
"Naren-babu really makes too much fuss about his eldest
daughter.   It will certainly turn her head."   My friends were
fearful that I might become too "big" for them.   Even Mircea,
who was so long certain that my parents had finally decided
to marry me to him, suddenly told me, "If we can't get
married, then I shall want to see you three times in the future.
Once when you have become a mother; the second time,
when you are old; and a third, when you are on your death
bed."   Though I know he was just being poetic like me, and
saying things whose meaning transcends the literal words
used, yet I resented his fancful statement.   What could be
its inner meaning—does he want to be like the Buddha who
saw the four stages of life?

Almost all the leading writers turned up, but Rabi Thakur
did not come, because he was out of Calcutta.   I cannot go
into the details about those who were present and what they
talked about, but one incident made a deep impression on me.
A young poetess suddenly attacked a senior poet saying that
the elders had all become backdated and their poems were
no more readable.   My mother resented this arrogance.   She

told me later, "Won't this young lady herself ever get old?
Does a poem lose its value simply because it was written in
the past?"

She quoted Rabi Thakur who had once remarked that
all young writers are like adolescent boys, who constantly
stand before the mirror, inspecting their non-existent
moustaches. I also never liked this idea of "oldness". What
grows old—human beings or their ideas? In that part of a
man's being which is immortal, lies the source of literature
and art. So, what once was good, if it was really good, can
it become not good just because time has passed?

However, that day I was the youngest of all the writers
who were there to celebrate my birthday. None of them
was too high for me, none ignored me. They stretched their
hands out and lifted me into their boat. Overnight I became
the contemporary of Sarat Chandra, Kamini Roy, Priyambada
Devi and others! We had for long been bubbling over with
enthusiasm about Uday Shankar. So father invited him also.
I wanted to talk to him a little, alone. I chose a corner in
the verandah and brought his tea there. Mircea arrived,
stumbling a little over his flowing *dhuti* that trailed on the floor.
He was even more of a fan of the dancer than I. He could
have sat down, or taken him downstairs to his room, if he
wanted to talk alone. Instead, he looked around with a
woebegone face and went away. I was a little disappointed
with Uday Shankar. Speech was clearly not his medium of
expression; the person who on the stage sometimes resembled
the mountain peak and sometimes a supple wave, appeared
now as only a plain human being.

We used to go out for long drives, all of us together.
But since father was ill, neither he nor mother went with us.
So Sabi and my two young brothers, myself and Mircea went
out to the Lakes for an evening stroll. Sometimes Shanti,
sometimes a maid-servant, accompanied us. At that time
the Dhakuria Lake was just being dug out—the bigger one
was ready, but work was going on for the smaller one. It

was at that time not such a crowded place as it is now. A
pointer to Calcutta's population then was that Southern
Avenue was a wilderness—jackals howled in the evening and
probably just one car passed each hour. To the younger
people in the house our affair was an open secret. No one
objected. Shanti, of course, was more or less an ally. During
the evening stroll, she purposely shepherded the children
away from us and left us alone.

Since the last few days I have been afflicted by a thought
that he will soon have to go home to attend his sister's
marriage. What will I do then? I am more or less certain
that our marriage is impossible. I am also certain that I
won't be able to bear separation from him. What to do then?
I do not know. I am not mature enough to chalk out my
future action.

One day as I sat pondering as hard as I could, masses
of inky clouds gathered, and it began to rain. I came running
down to enjoy a shower in the yard, when he called. He was
standing near the door, supporting himself on the door frame.
He called out to me, "Amrita, come here." As I moved
towards him he took me in his arms. I tried my best to free
myself. "Why are you pushing me away, Amrita?"

"I am afraid, Mircea. I am afraid."

"Afraid, or jealous?"

"Who should I be jealous of?" I was surprised.

"Are you jealous of yourself? Do you think I love your
body more than yourself? But that's not true. It is not
that, Amrita, not that. I am searching for that you which is
your soul. But you are in your body. That you, which
cannot be touched or seen, that you, which is beyond your
body, I am trying to touch that spirit in you." He looked
intently into my eyes. A shaft of light peeped through the
massive clouds and it fell on a side of his thick spectacles and
glittered. I closed my eyes. "I don't understand, Mircea;
I am afraid."

The story of 1930 is nearing its end. My formidably

erudite father and experienced mother remained obtusely
unaware of all that was going on between the two young
persons. No suspicion ever crossed their minds. They had
to be informed by an eleven-year old slip of a girl.

Sabi's sickness was strange. Sometimes she frolicked
about happy like a butterfly in spring. Sometimes she
became incoherent and went into hysterics. That evening
all of us were strolling near the Lakes. Shanti shepherded
the children a little ahead of us. We sat down behind a bush.
The evening was maturing. We sat close to each other—a
profound silence encircled us. On the tranquil, dark water
before us fell our twin shadow, elongated by the dim lamp
that had just flickered up. Like nature outside, my mind was
tranquil, entranced by a glow of peace. But he was restless,
impatient—he had put his arm round me. As if that was not
enough—he touched my thigh. "No, no, Mircea, no."

"Why not? Will you never be mine? You don't
like me?

"Believe me, it will never be. They will not agree."

"But why? They have almost given you to me."

Poor fellow, he did not understand our society, our faith
and our customs, in spite of his study. "Let me go. I am
afraid." I tried to wriggle out of his embrace. "Never,
never in this life will I let you go." Just at that moment
there were shouts and screams. Shanti called out, "Ru, Ru!
Look what Sabi is doing!" We ran together and found Sabi
wallowing on the ground and muttering incoherently. Mircea
picked her up and laid her on a bench by the side of the water.
I smoothed her hair and tried to pacify her. The moon began
to rise slowly and steadily, unconcerned as ever about all that
it witnessed. Shanti took the children away to the car. Sabi
tossed about and screamed, "Euclid-da, come near me—caress
me, kiss me, please." Mircea stooped down and planted
a small kiss on her forehead and said, "What has happened,
Sabi, what is your trouble?" She began to scream—"Caress
*didi*, caress her, do, do, do," she prattled. "What nonsense are

you talking, Sabi," I tried to stop her.   The more I tried to
pacify her, the more wild she grew, insisting on that one point.
Mircea was only too glad to comply.   "Yes, yes, I must also
kiss *didi*," he said and became effusive in his caress.   Instantly
I pushed him back.   "Move away," I said angrily.   In a flash
she cried again, "What have you done?"   "No, no. Sabi.
He has done nothing—he is standing near you—let's go to
the car."   I tried to calm her, though my nerves became
taut with tension.   As I tried to talk to her, a terrifying
presentiment of the impending disaster gripped my heart.
The joy of love dwindled into insignificance as fear spread
through my veins.   Fear, like a viper, inserted its fangs in me.
My mouth tasted bitter.   We got into the car.   Shanti was
waiting.   Mircea felt no foreboding.   Whistling and happy,
he sat beside the driver.   Sabi kept quiet in the car.   I was
hoping against hope: "She will forget, after all she is only
a sick child."   Reaching home, he went to his room and I
to mine.   My parents' voices coming from different directions
sent a shiver through me.

Afterwards, whenever I remembered that evening, I
throught of the fear that remained interwoven with the
experience of a tender love.   Was it a crime for a sixteen-year
old girl and a twenty-three year old boy to be in love?   Where
else would God's greatest gift descend on the earth, how else
would love be born?   What a threatening and frowning society
we lived in!

Less than an hour passed, and mother entered my room.
"Ru, let's go to the terrace."   Mother's face was solemn and
her voice quivered.   We went to the roof—it was a cool night,
illuminated with stars.   Fear subsided.   I was at peace with
myself.   Yes, I would surely be able to face mother.

"What is Sabi saying, Ru?   I can't believe my ears."

There was a wooden bedstead on the terrace.   Mother sat
on it with her arms round her knees and her feet joined together.
Her long hair hung loose, forming a background for her
straight and beautifully chiselled body: moonbeams shone on

her face. She looked like an icon on a pedestal, lit up by the
lamp of worship. My mother was only sixteen years older
than me. We had gradually become friends.

"Tell me everything, Ru." I stooped and laid my head
on her feet.

"Ma, ma, ma."

"Tell me, Ru, do you want to marry him?" It was my
nature that, even during serious moments, un-serious matters
flashed into my mind. I smothered a giggle as I thought
of Thakurma—what would she say if she was here? "You
shameless girl," she w uld have snapped at me. "Discussing
your own marriage!" Mother repeated kindly, "Tell me,
Ru, do you really want to marry him? —Then I will certainly
arrange it. I will not allow my girl to be unchaste even in
mind." With my head still resting on her soft feet. I
whispered "Ma, ma, ma, yes, I want it. I won't live without
him." "Is that so?" she heaved a sigh. "All right then.
I shall see to it." I lay on mother's lap for long—the cool
night encircled me like my mother's affection and soothed
my troubled mind. The world seemed serene and tranquil.
In a moment all my fears disappeared. I should have told
her earlier. I had completely misunderstood her. My mother
d d not say it was wrong of me to love him, or it was a sin
to touch him. After some time she told me to go to my
room. "Stay there—don't come to the dining room. I'll
bring your food to your room." I did not meet him that
night. Nor d d he play the piano. When he played his piano
downstairs and the music floated up to me, as I sat listening
deep into the night, I could feel in my body and mind, in a
different level of my consciousness, a strange sense of union.

I lay thinking. I had told him so many times about my
apprehensions, but I cannot tell him now that there is no
fear. Probably mother will tell him tomorrow. With
sleepless eyes I remained engrossed in day-dreaming . . . .
I see him standing on a painted wooden seat, wearing a silk
*dhuti* and a scarf thrown loosely over his white body, with

sandal-paste decorations on his forehead, like Sri Krishna
himself.   Oh no, Sri Krishna was dark: however beautiful
Sri Krishna might be, it is better to be white.   Will they put
a sacred thread round his neck?   Oh, no, that was impossible.
And dur ng the moment of "auspicious vision", when they
throw the scarf over our heads, to hide from others the first
moment of "meeting of glances", will Malabika, or Mala for
short, die of jealousy?   Is she dying even now because she
has already teased me by saying "How is the play-acting of
Kacha and Devayani going on?" . . . Will she say, "Why, the
'over-forward' girl has already accomplished the ceremony of
'auspicious glance'."   And Runu?   My school mate will look
at me wide-eyed: "Hmm.   So you headed for a love-marriage!
You certainly have courage!"   What will Milu say, Aradhana,
or Didima?   I am sure they will all be happy.   No one will
speak ill of me.   As I lie thinking all this, his sleeping face
constantly comes before my eyes, like cotton clouds in the
blue sky of autumn.   Poor man, he does not know that his
wish has been granted.   He wants me so much, but I can
never be close to him for more than a few minutes.   Now
his trouble will be over.   But for me, will it be bearable to
be separated from my parents?   Of course, there is no need
for that.   He has told me he will live here.   Well, that won't
be proper, will it?   I shall have to visit his country as well;
must I not meet his mother, his sister?   Thinking of his
country, I remember the wharf at Princep Ghat.   We went
to see off Rabi Thakur when he was going to Europe.   What
a great big ship it was!   Now that my fear is gone, a strange
shyness makes my blood rush to my face.   Now he will have
to be told.   Who will tell him?   Who else?   I must tell him
myself.   But when?   When he comes to Calcutta.   It is one
full year that he has gone out of the country.   Night deepens;
I lie half asleep and half awake.   I watch between the two
shores, while on a narrow waterway, the ship *Strathaird* glides
along.   This is the Suez Canal and beyond it is the blue
Mediterranean.   As the ship moves on, breasting the heaving

clear waters, it changes into a "peacock-barge" of fairyland.

Next morning as my mother entered the room my heart began to pound. Her eyes were swollen, voice stern. Has she had a sleepless night? "Ru, you mustn't come down to-day. Stay here. Don't speak with anyone, neither Shanti nor Chutki. I'll soon come back." I stood paralysed. What could have happened? Then my knees began to sag—I lay back on the ruffled bed where I had slept last night. After a little while, mother came with a glass of milk. "Drink it. I have much to say to you". I never liked milk but now I made no fuss. Mother sat beside me and spoke in a stern voice, "Ru, your father has told me to enquire into it fully— tell me, how far have you gone?" I lay speechless. I was wondering who had lied. Shanti often fabricated a story, but she wouldn't go against me. Sabi would never lie. We almost never lied. Mother has told us repeatedly, "Even if you have to bear punishment you should not utter a false word." My voice quivered: "We did not go very far. We went near the Lakes; you may ask Shanti." Mother realised I had not understood the significance of her question. She felt relieved. Both of us remained silent. I could hear the children downstairs—an open tap was running—Jharu was shooing off an obstinate crow. In the freshly awakened household everyday life had started. But just at that moment mother and I had gone faraway into some other world in some other time. She exhaled a deep sigh and said, "Ru, tell me the truth, what has Euclid done to you?" I dug my face in the pillow; I will not answer these questions—or tell a lie. How can I tell the truth? Then all will be his fault. Is it only his fault? My guilt is no less. He has no one here, no relatives, no friends. My father is everything he has; now if father also goes against him on my account, that will be terrible for him. Mother repeated, "Ru, get up, look at me." It is impossible to tell a lie in front of her searching gaze. My lips are parched. Why do I need to bend so low to get such a wonderful thing, I thought.

"Why are you not answering me, why are you not looking at me?" mother continued. Then very resolutely she added, "Why has your face gone blue? Where is my spirited daughter who never compromises with principles? Why is she in such a state today? Ru, your head is hanging down in shame, you are crushed by guilt. What a calamity that I have to witness this!" Mother's voice got choked with emotion. I know her reproaches are correct. Yet, however wrong it may be, I will lie. I will not get him into trouble. Well, what harm is there if I take all the blame? "Tell me, Ru," mother persisted, "did he kiss you?

"Yes."

"Where?"

Now I shall have to think out a safe spot. I knew lips won't do.

"On my forehead."

"Is that all?"

"Yes."

"Have you gone into anything like Gandharva-vivaha?"

"Like what?" I asked, surprised beyond measure.

"Why, don't you know what it is? Like exchanging of garlands?"

"No such thing ever crossed my mind." I later realised mother was looking for an excuse. Had we done anything like that, it would have been easier for her to help us.

"Now, Ru, I must tell you I couldn't do what I promised you I would. Your father is adamant. '

I began to shiver. She kept her hand on me.

"Be quiet."

"Why, ma, why?"

"Your father says we know nothing about him—his lineage—who knows he may have some foul disease."

I am astounded. What does she mean? "He has been with us for nearly a year, and never even run a temperature—why should he be ill?" I asked.

"Oh no, not that kind of illness. Your father says he

knows all the bad places of Paris. You don't have to try to
understand. You don't know how bad the French are. They
are uncivilized."

"But he is not French."

"It comes to the same thing. They have borrowed
French culture."

"But why should French culture be bad? The whole of
Europe follows them."

"Has it improved by doing so?"

"Hasn't Europe improved?"

"Not that, Ru. You know nothing about their society.
When you grow up and read the stories of Maupassant, you
will know. Husband and wife are constantly unfaithful to
each other. One cheats another shamelessly, they marry one
person and run after another. You will never be able to llve
in an awful society like that."

"I have read Maupassant's *Necklace*. There is nothing
wrong in it."

"No, no, Ru, there are awful stories also. What your
father says makes me shrink in fear. This can never be good
for you."

"Ma, ma, ma dear . . ."

"What can I do, Ru? He says if I insist, he will die. Do
you want to kill your father? You don't love your father.
Is that boy dearer to you than us?"

I am shocked to discover that I feel no concern for
father's illness. On the contrary I am angry with him. He
constantly keeps mother intimidated by the threat of his
blood pressure   and makes her bend to his will—so I begin
to pray—why don't I have blood-pressure, O God—strike
me with blood-pressure right at this moment! Mother went
on, "Ru, if you press too much then he might get a stroke,
do you want that? Control yourself, my precious, can we
ever get all that we ask for?"

I don't know how my hours and minutes passed. At
midday mother came. "Get up, Ru, Mircea is going away.

He says he wants to see you once before he leaves for ever."
I cannot get up—my bones are being pulverised—how shall
I stand up?

"Get up, Ru, get up—he is standing in the blazing sun,
on the street, you will stand in the verandah—your father
has agreed—he can see you once."

When in 1972 I entered 1930 again, I reached the same
state in which I was on that 18th of September. Again my
bones began to creak and my heart rang—what a wonder, I
did not even know that a part of me remained steady in the
same spot—it is that part in me which is unborn, imperishable,
everlasting and uncreated, that which does not die when the
body dies. I have not the same body today but it is the
same being, the same undying Amrita.

I am standing on the middle opening of the verandah.
He is down on the street, the swinging *mahavi* creeper casts
a quivering shadow, protecting him from the fierce sunlight.
He lifts his face upward towards me, a face writhing in agony.
It seems as if someone is piercing him with a hot iron spike.
Upto now I have never seen a face seething with misery like
that. Then he folds his palms and does *namaskar* to me.
"Goodbye." At that moment I realise my mistake. I have
never told him that I also love him. I thought of saying it
but I put it off. Now it will never be said. I gasped, "Oh
no, no, Mircea, no!". And then everything went blank. I
heard later that I fell flat on the floor. Not unlikely because
the strength went out from my legs. I woke up to find
myself lying on the passage and my mother splashing water
on my face—she was muttering "Durga! Srihari! What shall
I do now, what shall I do," as tears streamed down her cheeks.

Mircea was gone, who knows where he went. Who
will tell me? I do not meet anyone. Mother wants to
hide me from curious eyes. People will laugh at me. I
take no food other than cold drinks. It is impossible to eat.

My mother is quite a doctor; she does not force food on
me.   She says during such emotional disturbances as sorrow,
bereavement, and anger, the body secretes poison—then
one needs only liquid to wash it out.

I sometimes wonder if I should ask Sabi if he has told
her anything—but then I control myself.   She is a little girl.
It is bad enough that she had to witness all this.   It has been
all my fault.   I heard later that he told her, "What have
you done, Sabi, what have you done?"   And the poor child,
she wept too.   "I did not know, Euclid-da, that *didi* will
suffer so much and so will you."

I cannot tell how, many days later, I see just an evening.
There is still a little glow of sunlight in the sky outside,
inside the room is mildly lit by a blue lamp in the corner.
Suddenly someone enters.   I cannot see her face but I
remember her words.   I see her legs draped by the sari
steadily approaching.   Who is she? Kakima, Shanti or
Chapadidi? She stands by my side and then advises, ' Do
not try to run away, Ru.   That will never do.   You are a
minor—if you do that you will at once be brought back.
You won't suffer any more, but he will be jailed—not the
kind of jail where they put our boys in every day—but he
will have to live with criminals—they will make him wear a
'halfpant' and break stones."

I dig my face in the pillow.   "Why are you threatening
me?" I sob.   How helpless I am, how helpless! "I am not
going anywhere—I am suffering here alone," I say.

"I am not threatening you; only warning, in case . . ."

Two or three days passed.   I suffered specially because
I could not tell him anything or bid a proper goodbye.

It is early morning.   The door opened, Khoka entered,
and in his usual jocular way began play-acting: "Why all
these tears?   Shame on you, from where did you come,
O cruel traveller?"   He recited Devayani's speech to Kacha,
then suddenly becoming serious: "Mircea wants a book
of yours; he has none with him."

"Do you know where he has gone?"

"Of course.  To that Ripon Street house."

"In the house of those Anglo-Indians?  O God, but he loathes going there.  Those girls are bad, Khoka."

"But where else can he go?  Where can a foreigner go if he is turned out at a moment's notice?"

"O Khoka, dear brother Khoka, what will I do?"

"Sh-sh-sh!"  He put his forefinger on his lips.  Then he spun on his heel.  "There are spies everywhere—go, get the book, quick."  I brought the book out, and it was then that I thought of warning him—I wrote at the back of the book—my hand was shaking so the letters began a strange waltz—I did not realise that at that very moment I made a lie immortal with the strength of my love.  "Mircea, Mircea, Mircea, I had told my mother that you have kissed me only on my forehead."

I have given the book to Khoka.  I am feeling better. Now I have a contact.  "Khoka, I'll write a letter- you must get me the reply."

"Alright, be quick."  I took a small sheet of paper and began to write.  I have so many things to say - but all my thoughts are running away, escaping like steam from a boiling kettle.  I remember only two points—I shall keep these two promises—I wrote "I shall never forget you" and then on the other side, "I shall wait for you, wait for you, wait for you." I repeated these two lines over and over again and then I gave the sheet to Khoka, "Give it to him."  Something must be done afterwards.  I have long hair; in these few days it's got all matted.  I have not allowed mother to comb it.  I am always fretting.  She tolerates my rudeness in silence.  After giving the letter I again lie on my bed and throw my long mass of hair over the pillow and cover my eyes with my arm ; then I take a vow, "I shall not forget, no, I shall not—father has no control over my mind."  Then, that vow begins to move in my sleep; in silent footsteps it starts to descend carefully step by step and goes down to that bottomless depth of my

mind where the clamour of the world does not reach,
nor can day and night, where the sun or the moon does not
rise nor do stars twinkle; entering that cavern it falls asleep
in a yogic slumber.  Who could have guessed that after forty
two years it would wake up again?

Days pass but Khoka does not appear.  At last I catch
him one day.  "What's the news?  Did you give him my
book and letter?"

"Certainly."

"Well?"

"Nothing."

"What do you mean, 'nothing'?  Didn't he send any
message?"

"No."

"Why 'no'?  Find him right now and tell him I want
an answer."

"But he is not there, he can not be traced.  They say
he is gone."

"Oh what do you say, Khoka, why did you not tell me
this so long?"

"What would you have done even if had?  Even if he
drowns himself can you do anything?"

"Oh Khoka, do something, my good brother, I beg of you,
get me his news."

"Yes, yes."  Khoka bolted.

Morning and night are racing after each other.  What
an infallible law determines the movement of the wheel.
That revolving wheel continuously cleanses our experiences
of joy, sorrow, bereavement and happiness and transforms
one substance into another, like a centrifugal machine that
squeezes out the superflous water and condenses the matter.
Mother says the burning torment of bereavement lasts for
three days—then gradually the flames tend to subside.  A
mother recovers from the loss of her son and a widow learns
to be on her own.  Every day there is loss and every day we
receive compensation.  All this is well known.  Some know

it secondhand from reading books or from others' experience,
but I through direct experience of it.  I thought I would cut
my hair, I have not done it, now I don't even wish to.  My
other mind is saying what good will come by cutting off
your hair—you will look ugly.  This lust for life—I can
recognise it.

Mother has started gossiping as a diversion.  Mantu is
extremely rude with her; his wife is a shrew.  She is talking
against us to her parents—even against me.  But I am not
attentive to mother's comments.  Let them go to hell if they
like—what do I care?

Mother was fingering my matted hair trying to free the
knots and make a long braid.  She spoke slowly, "You know,
Ru, sorrow also has a value.  All the thinkers of the world
say so.  Pray to God—He will calm your mind.  It is only
suffering that makes a person seek Him."  Then she quoted
a song, "One who is shot by an arrow, falls at your feet."
Switching off the light, mother left me to sleep.  The lines
of the song keep on repeating in my head but my listless,
drowsy mind can grasp nothing.  "One whom you hit with
a flower, whose wound is concealed by comfort, whose
ill-fame is like a perfume, one who has not seen the blessedness
of your fierce face—such a one, O God, does not know your
glory."  What does this song mean, I ask myself—have
I got any ill-fame?  Yes, of course, our neighbour B. B. has
said, "What a nasty affair is this?  Why invite a Christian
in one's home?"  Father says we will move house—we need
not stay in this loathsome locality.  Everyone is talking.
Gradually a strange stupor encompasses me, yet the song
remains whirling in my head, . . . "falls at your feet, O God,
falls at your feet . . ."  The lines become arrows and go on
hitting my head with a continuous twanging.  I am rolling
on the bed; suddenly I fall down.

When I woke up I found the whole house in my room.
Even father.  This is the first time I saw him after Mircea's
departure.  I heard him telling mother mother, "Give her

a little brandy with milk.  You should call the doctor
tomorrow." Then uncle Mantu spoke with asperity to father
and left the room.  I was surprised at his impertinence—this is
the first time I saw him get angry with father.  I watch them
wide-eyed and speechless.  Two strong lights are burning,
yet the figures are like shadows—I saw father; no, not he,
but his silhouette moves towards my bookshelf, father is
looking for some books.  He picks up a book on Japanese
mythology, bound in blue silk with a figure embossed in
gold.  Father opens it and tears off the first page—Mircea
presented this to me.  Then one by one he gets out all the
books and tears off the pages where the two names are
written—the giver and the taker of the gift.  He could not
find that page in *Goethe's Life*—it remained stuck to the
cover—so that's all that remained as Mircea's memento.
Father slowly tears the papers into shreds and flings them
out the window.  In any other house the books would have
been destroyed.  But that cannot be in our house.  We also
have a Genghis Khan.  Only he does not burn books.  He
can burn human beings but not books.  The book is his God.

Father's friend with his family is going to Madhupur
during the vacation.  Father said we would all go together
and live in the same house.  The change in the environment,
specially to be in the midst of nature, will heal my wound.
But I knew there was very little chance of that.  One question
like a sharp knife is constantly pricking my heart and has
made it raw—why doesn't he reply to my letter?  How can I
contact him?  I know where Ripon Street is but who will
take me there?  I cannot go alone.  I could have gone with
the driver but I don't trust him—he scares me.  He has
been watching us with the eyes of a hyena.  Khoka has
disappeared.  The day we were to leave for Madhupur
Khoka came to the station.  I took him aside and asked,
"Why don't you come, Khoka?" He kept silent.  "Tell me,
why don't you?"

"I can't bear to see you suffer so much, Ru, there is a limit to human endurance."

"But don't you realise I am dying to know everything about him? What is he doing now?"

"He is not here. He has gone to the Himalayas."

"The Himalayas? Why don't you say to Darjeeling?"

"No, not to Darjeeling, to the forests – he has become a sannyasi."

"Sannyasi! Why should he do that? Is that why he does not reply to my letter?"

On the train I covered myself up with a sheet and began to think. This strange news perplexed me. Has this man gone out of his senses? He should be contacting me and sorting it out—instead he runs off to the Himalayas! Fat lot of good will come of it! I began to cry. My parents noticed that I was crying, They talked in whispers. Mother has to feed the children, make the bed, she has to do everything. Who is there to help her?

1 am sinking in my grief. Father is a child in these matters. He has never poured himself even a glass of water.

Gradually my tears dried—the intensity of my agony began to get blurred—whisked by the speed, the world seemed transitory, ephemeral. My senses were getting dimmed by the unearthly glow of suffering. In that half-asleep world I heard father's voice, "Pull down the shutters on her side. She might jump through the window." I said to myself I would never do such a thing. Life is beautiful; so is my sorrow. This life will burn like a lamp—"Kindle it with the light of *viraha*, the pain of separation." I understood the song then.

The house in Madhupur is lovely. Nature round us nurses my wounds—the azure sky and the waving paddy fields enter into me and release the heat. Nature is like mother. I have also my mother with me. But he has no one—he must be terribly alone in the forests. One day, sitting on the steps of the pond, mother said, "Now be strong, Ru, you will never see him in this life."

"Why, ma, why?"

"Your cruel father has made him take a vow that he
will never contact you."

"Why should he keep that vow? Is he a monk?" I flared
up. But mother's voice "You shall never see him in this
life" began to spin like a top in me, it squeezed out a sigh
which was almost a wail.

During our stay at Madhupur the armoury at Chittagong
was raided by teenagers. It was a daring deed. The place
and the persons involved in it were familiar to us. I had
played with them as a child. Naturally we felt very proud
of them. So when father said, "This is all childish madness",
we argued a lot. Maybe it will not help much to attain
freedom—but the act of sacrificing everything for one's
country is satisfying enough. If I could go in for such work
I certainly could have got cured of all that was ailing me.
But I am helpless. I have no way to wield my own destiny.
I know they want to rid the country of the British. I don't
know exactly what the British are doing to us—but can they
tell me who will free us--can human beings? As I lay awake
night after night gazing at the cheerless moon I resolved
often: "If I ever get a chance I shall fight against our narrow
social customs—against caste, against silly prejudices. Of
course I am a minor, but my mother is not –still, can she
use her judgement? Is she free? Has she any right over her
own daughter?" I know mother is suffering too. She
respects this love—but she is helpless even more than I, as
she cannot even express her dissent.

When I think of 1930 I can mark the year only because
I know it. Otherwise the date is meaningless. The sky has
no sides; we mark east or west by our little earth; so all the
experiences that have entered Mahakal or Infinite Time
cannot be specified by any date. By its depth and expanse
it surpasses its presence in time, and then it is both far and near —

it is moving and not moving.  So I cannot tell when it
happened, before our Madhupur trip or after.  I am turning
the page of a book already read, and what I thought was on
the right side I find is on the left.

I am in bed.  Mother is talking.  The main topic of her
discussion is father's illness.  By telling me of its seriousness
she is trying to make me soften towards him.  I have not
lost my regard for father, nor has my love towards him waned.
But I am turning into a critic, and I am becoming impatient.
I am thinking that when father gets ill she is anxious as much
as he is.  But if mother is ill, nobody is anxious.  So I don't
support her.  Mother understands my silence and feels
helpless.  Suddenly I hear father's footsteps—he comes and
stands before the door.  Father has large eyes, an acquiline
nose, his complexion is like bright copper.  When he is angry,
it gets redder.  Now father's face is red.  "What good is
lying and crying like this?  Won't she sit for her examinations?
Even Chutki is sitting for them. What need is there for so
much mourning?'' he thunders. Mother gets up and pulls
him away from the open door—but I can hear everything
because I am now all ears.

Mother whispers, "You can't press things too far.
There is a limit to coercion."

"But how can we allow her to spoil her life and career
like this?  Will she not appear at the examinations?"

"Had you considered examinations that important, why
did you take her out of the school?  She would have finished
in the usual course."

"Phew!  They teach nothing in the school.  Had she
been attending regular school, could she have read so much
literature?  All the best poems of Rabi Thakur she has
by heart.  Even boys doing M.A. have not read so much.
What can those half-literate teachers teach?  They write
remarks with red pencil on the homework—'good', 'bad'—
all bogus."

"Well then, you have got what you wanted—she has

learnt much – why worry about examinations? She could do
them later."

"Oh no, no, no! She must sit for her examinations—
my daughter must get her degrees. What a disaster! I was
moulding her so nicely. Everything got spoilt. She will
write poetry no more - she will not study—all my hopes are
shattered. Well then, find a suitable family and get her
married," father groaned.

Mother spoke as if trying to pacify a child in its tantrums.
"Give me a little time, I will need a little time, then I will
make everything all right for you."

"But you are not moving in the right direction. You
must turn her mind against him. Tell her these men are the
skilled hunters of Europe. Good at games . . ."

"I shall do nothing of that kind," mother retorted.
"Poor boy, he's gone and become a sannyasi and he's roaming
in the forest. If I can't help him, at least I won't slander him."

"But what difference will it make to him? He will never
even know. I am not asking you to be harsh with him. You
need tactics if you want to win a war—sentimentality is hardly
enough!" Then he uttered the age-old maxim: "All's fair
in love and war."

Mother flared up, "That is not my view. My intellect
will never go against my conscience."

Mother is strong in her stand. She always is. She has
her own views, but she can't implement them. She gets
defeated by her love and consideration for others. I listen
to their arguments but my mind, dizzy with distress, accepts
father's words. So it was a game indeed! Or why doesn't
he write to me? The game is over!

Next day I told mother, "Ma, tell father I will sit for the
examinations. We have three months yet to go, ask him to
get me the syllabus, there is enough time."

"Of course there is, Ru. It won't take you long if you
put your mind to it." Mother is very pleased, she is trying
to placate me. "Your father says, with what expectations

I named her Amrita—she will drink the nectar of knowledge.
She will become a Brahmavadini. Try to fulfiil his aspirations
a little, my pet; don't ruin yourself over a trifling matter."

The experience of the first day when I sat down with
father to study was sad indeed. Father asked me to write
some derivations, and analyse the suffix. I could hardly
concentrate. Father took a round and came back. Looking
at me sitting with an empty paper and a far-away look, he
flew into a rage. So he is not able to control this wisp of
a girl! "What has happened? Has everything gone out
of your head? Why aren't you writing? Write!" he
ordered. My fingers remained as inert as ever. Then
suddenly he slapped me hard. Strangely I felt no pain.
Mother came running. "What is all this? You shouldn't
hit a grown-up girl!"
Father got up. "Impossible, impossible. She is just being
obstinate."

Mother stood speechless. That day I was angry not
with father but with my mother. Because father at least
was doing what he thought right; but mother could not
stick to her own principles; she constantly gave in to pressure.
Later she had to pay heavily for this weakness. As I came out
of the room, I found Shanti standing on the landing. She
looked up at me with sad eyes. "I won't live here any more,"
she said in a disturbed voice.

No one's health improved in Madhupur. Sabi lay ill.
And just at that time she had to go through a torment all
for me. My young brother was also running a high
temperature and, above all, I was causing mother so much
distress. When the whole household was so disturbed,
Father decided to have himself thoroughly examined in the
Medical College. So he went to the hospital. They allowed
me to stay the whole day and attend to him. This I did
dutifully. In the evening his colleagues, students, and friends
came and the hospital cabin became a place for social
chit-chat.

One day father asked me, "Ru, won't you write poetry
any more?"    I did not answer.   I want to write but whatever
I write becomes much too "open".   It cannot be published
or shown.   To transform personal into impersonal is the work
of a writer; what was mine only becomes everyone's.   But
all I wrote at that time was becoming obviously personal.
I wrote a poem on Shakespeare asking the Bard where he was
when we were bidding goodbye.   It was not the window of a
rich man's manor, but does it matter, I asked.   And there were
no flowers on that dirty street of Calcutta but surely that
cannot make the event less important?   "O great poet,
I thought you·were standing behind me encircling me like the
painted background behind an idol—I hoped you would give
life to my wounded love.   Can a golden image make Juliet
immortal?   It is *I* who have made her so.   Sing my praise,
O poet."    All these poems I threw into the flames after a year
or two.   But I know now that had I shown them to father
he wouldn't have been angry.   If anything written down
reaches a standard, at once it gets transformed divinely.
He would not be bothered with such unimportant details as
who wrote it or why.   He would have told me, "Good to have
a variety of experience—it's all *maya*—this world of karma is
an illusion but you have to walk through it all to drink the
nectar of pure knowledge."   Ever eager for that supreme
knowledge, father cared little for the people who endure their
petty sorrow-cum-happiness in this world of karma.   The
message that man is greater than all else was never acceptable
to him.

In the hospital I was kept busy with various tasks, specially
reading out books to father and taking down dictation for
the book he was writing then.   On the surface I was normal,
but an uncontrollable throbbing agitated my heart all the
time.   Whenever I thought of him walking alone in a forest,
tears welled up and I burnt with a sense of guilt.   I thought
of snakes and shudder ed, "How can he live in a forest—he
is a Sahib, isn't he? They are used to good living."

Father used to say, "Ru, you must change the table
cloth oftener—you see, it shouldn't get soiled with grease—
they in Europe live spick and span." I bled inside when I
thought of this, but I kept a cool face. I was ashamed to
show my suffering in front of them. Yet one day I swooned
at the hospital. I don't remember what the immediate cause
was—maybe there was no cause—I was exhausted, that's all.
The doctor said it might be something like a nervous
breakdown. Mother was greatly upset but father said,
"She can get well if she tries, if she uses a little will power—
but she won't . . . ." Had the doctor been anyone else then
father would have challenged his knowledge in medical
science and with question and counter-question would have
convinced him of his ignorance in the subject, but the doctor
was none else than Sir Nil Ratan Sircar. He could
"sniff-diagnose" a typhoid fever from pneumonia. With
his arrival courage returned to a death-gripped person. That
was the doctor, a friend and well-wisher, who cured me.
I recovered fully within seven or eight months. In between
this time I sat for my examinations, and the results were
good. I was really sorry to get cured. I felt my best
weapon had gone blunt: how would I fight any more?

Nine or ten months have passed. I have not heard
about him any more. Khoka has left the house: so has
Shanti. A sister has been born to us. Mantu and his wife
have gone to live separately. This was not a smooth break.
Mantu was angry with father who lacked the guts to face
him. So father quarrelled with mother instead. I was angry
with Mantu. How dare he go and defy father? Was it
not father who had so long taken care of him, fed and
educated him? I used to love him so much but now I have
decided I will never see his face again. Mother said, "Now
my home is breaking up." Her home, so long full of
relatives, dependents and guests, echoed with laughter, music,
discussions, and recitations. It was bubbling over with life.
Her happy home was her little world, gay and illuminated,

where she was the queen.   But one by one the lights were
going out.

   One day as I was standing on the stairs, father called me
from the back and said, "Yesterday Mircea came."   I began
to shiver.   O God what would I hear next!   "He has grown
a beard!   He has become a sannyasi—I could not recognise
him at first—ha-ha-ha-ha!"   I did not reply nor turn to face
him.   As I stood with my back towards him I began to
descend without replying.   Father called out,   "Ru, Ru, he
is going home.   Put in the car all the antiques he left behind."
These were some Tibetan curios that he had purchased in
Darjeeling.   They were left here on the staircase and reminded
me of him.   Now I put them into the car myself.   I did not
regret it because I was never an idolator.   For me no object
can be a symbol of an idea.   I am not sorry that I don't
have a photograph of him.   What is the need?   A photograph
is no substitute for a person.

   I was surprised at father: Why was he running him down
for his beard?   Is it easy to roam about in the forests?   He
has purposely added physical suffering to mental.   But he is
matchless in self-mortification.   I know it is all pointless to
do that, maybe foolish also, yet one respects it.   There is
nothing so horrible as the act of *sāti*.   Yet when Thakuma
talked about someone in their family several generations
earlier committing *sati* her face lit up with pride. Widowhood,
shorn of all pleasure, and lean with fasting, is not a matter
for ridicule.   As I was packing the antiques, I pondered:
Will father ever be able to deprive himself or inflict the least
suffering on himself?   Why then did he mock him?   In answer,
the third eye of William Shakespeare opened in me: "He
jests at scars who never felt a wound."

   None of us are improving in health.   So it is decided
to go to Benaras during the vacation.   I feel I have completely
recovered from my mental disorder.   Mental disorder? What
else? All this talk about love etcetea is rubbish.   But mother
has no peace, she is worried on one point: How will she get

me married? Will I be able to love anyone else; will that
be proper?

Love is not an object which you have to steal from one
person to give to another.  Many do not realise this truth.
Individuals do, but society does not.  One gloomy evening,
sitting in an almost empty house from which all the gaiety
and laughter had been squeezed out, mother looked pathetically
at me, "Tell me, Ru, did you ever utter any *mantra* of marriage
or do any little ritual?"

"Ma!" I flared up.  "You asked me this question before.
Didn't I tell you then such an idea never crossed our minds?"

"Well then, why did you mutter a marriage vow—when
you fell at the hospital?"

"What vow?  *Om mama vrate te hridayam dadhatu?*
'Let your heart hold me firm in my vow'?"

"No, something in English."

"Have I ever seen any foreign marriage?  How should
I know?  Why are you accusing me for no reason?"

"No, I am not accusing you.  In case you have said
something, why don't you tell ma?"

"What is it I am supposed to have said?" I asked
confusedly.  Mother tried to remember, then haltingly, "It
doesn't sound like any marriage hymn to me, but since your
father says so. . . . I recollect only some words—In sickness
and in health."  "I have never heard anything like this—I
couldn't have said it," I spoke with conviction.  Mother
heaved a sigh.  Later I remembered.  I saw a bioscope,
where I read those lines.  In those days the movies were
silent; the words were: "For richer or for poorer, for better
or for worse, in sickness and in health I take thee till death
do us part . . ."

This was nothing serious, but mother was seeking
support.  If there was a ritual then that would be inviolable.
The sufferings of two human beings, though, are not as
important.  Social injunctions, customs, and rituals are
supreme.  This not only *was* our country, it still is.  It

would of course be unfair to say that mother also valued
ritual over-much or was bigoted in any sense of the term.
She was even more rational in her outlook than father—
but in this particular instance she was looking for a plea.
In support of my mother I will narrate a strange incident that
occurred when I was only seven years old and Sabi was two.
My mother, Thakurma, Chapadidi, and we two sisters lived
in Puri—a great place of pilgrimage. The main deity is
Jagannath. One day we were all standing near the inner chamber
of the temple—it was an auspicious day—the crowd was
enormous. Suddenly, wearing a borderless pure white sari,
a widow approached us, followed by a young boy of about
sixteen. He came straight towards us, gave a sweetmeat
to Sabi and throwing a garland round my neck, said, "I give
you the garland. Lord Jagannath is my witness." And in a
second mother and son melted in the crowd.

"Who was that?" shouted my Thakurma and ran after
them. Mother snatched the garland from my neck and threw
it away. She did the same to poor Sabi's sweetmeat. Then,
holding my hand and picking up Sabi, she walked towards
home. After a little while Thakurma came up helter-skelter.
"Oh *Bouma*!" she called out to mother. "He did say 'Lord
Jagannath is my witness,.''

"Stop it!" mother warned her. "Jagannath does not pay
any heed to ravings." Thakurma rubbed her forehead:
"O dear me, today is the fifth of the lunar month." My
mother was severe, she told her sternly, "If you utter another
word on this topic I shall leave you here and go away to
Calcutta by the next train." This silenced Thakurma. Later
mother told me that probably he had taken some kind of a
vow that on such a date he would garland a virgin in front
of the Lord Jagannath. It is a strange country with stranger
customs that can make dupes out of sensible persons.

With relatives, children, and servants, a big group went
off to Benaras. From there my parents, I and my three-months

old sister were to visit Hrishikesh and Lachman Jhola, two
places of pilgrimage in the Himalayas.  I was overjoyed to
hear this because those were the places where Mircea had
stayed as a hermit.  Though there was no reason to be elated—
I knew well he had left for his country.  Then why was
I happy?  This is one of those feelings which are beyond
reasoning and which play hide-and-seek with us.  I will not
go into all the details of our travels in Delhi, Agra and other
places because that would put my story out of focus.  I start
straight from Haridwar, where we managed to secure a guide
and a car and moved further up towards Swargadwar.  This
was the first time I had taken refuge in the Himalayas—it was
like taking refuge among the gods, it was so quiet and without
care.  I know the sea breeze has a grip on the human spirit,
but nothing is like the hills.  I have never before seen such
trees, tall and erect, wielding an overpowering influence, nor
have I seen such swift-rushing streams and felt such a
salubrious breeze.  The cool air entered me and blew away
one by one the little sparks of grief.  I was sure the fire of
torment burning so long would soon be extinguished.  He did
well by coming here.  Is it only because the air is fresh or is
there anything else?  What is it?  How can I know the full
glory of the Himalayas, the king of the mountains, the abode
of the gods?  We are passing over flat ground—the thatch
forests are dense, they canopy the car fully—we see nothing
but sleek greying thatch, moving like waves.  The child began
to cry—and mother and I became busy with the wailing infant.
Suddenly we heard the guide's remark: "There are tigers in
the thatch forest."  Father shouted, "What!  Tigers!  Why did
you bring us here, you fool?"  The more angry father grows,
the more placid the guide becomes.  "Nothing to fear," he says
calmly.  "Tigers also fear for their lives.  As soon as we blow
the horn they will slink away."

I felt troubled again.  Oh God!  How must it feel to trek
around here all by oneself—not a matter to joke about.

Reaching Swargadwar, we crossed the river by boat.

This is the first time I have crossed a mountain stream,
rushing and gurgling with a fierce loveliness.  Later I spent
my life on the banks of such rivers.  It lashes down the slopes,
slapping against the boulders its transparent water; sometimes
it spins in a frenzy, sometimes gushing upward it sprays
around, twinkling like pulverised glass.  It wets our faces
like a drizzle.  Father leaned from the boat and scooped up
some cool water in his palm and drank it.  So did we, it was
delicious—we had never before tasted water so exquisitely
soothing—well, this is the Alakananda, the part of the sacred
Ganga near its source—we have almost reached heaven—this
is Swargadwar, the door to heaven—we are now crossing the
door—so, closing my eyes and clasping my palms together
in reverence to the state of grace to which the nature around
has taken me, I recited an ode to the Ganga : "O redeemer
of gods and men, purifier of sins, O deliverer of the impious,
O sacred Ganga on your way to the sea . . ."

Father was overjoyed to hear me recite a poem with
spontaneous effusiveness.  "Go on," he urged, "say the whole
of it."

We reach the other side.  We are walking on the
foot track flanked by mountain on one side and dense
foliage on the other.  Alternately mother and I carry the
infant.  There are little caves on the facade of the hills.  The
guide said the Sadhus sit there in meditation.  Each one has a
cave for himself.  They sit in different yogic postures, mainly
in the lotus position.  Some have long matted hair and are
smeared with ash.  Some of them are strolling up and down the
track with a *Kamandalu* and a trident in hand.  They get their
food from the welfare organisation of Kali Kamliwalla.  This
rich man, eager to acquire piety, has arranged free food
distribution for these hermits.  Some of them don't even move
out of the caves where they sit, engrossed in meditation.  The
food arrives on time.  Suddenly the guide pointed to an empty
cave and said, "Here lived a Sahib for some months: he has
gone away now."

Father began to grumble, "Must be him. The fellow came to study but instead loafed around in the forest and went back—such a waste . . ." Father kept on muttering as he walked ahead of me. I realised he felt sad. He certainly loved his student, as much as it was possible for him. Who ruined him but I? Indeed! Who started the game? I am trying to plead for myself. But I am not sure how it began. I only know how it ended. Or do I?

We are walking in a line on the narrow track, cool under the trees; spotted with light peeping through the leaves, all of us are covered as if with a blanket of lace. My wound has begun to bleed again: as I walked stumbling over the road uneven with scattered pebbles, I felt I was following his spoors. On the next cave we saw a sannyasi sitting cross-legged, resting his chin on a stick. He has large eyes: they are fixed at a distance. One could make out    he is remarkably different from the others we had been meeting for so long. The guide said, "Two years ago he worked as a judge, but after listening to the call of the Supreme Being he has renounced the world. He doesn't go anywhere. He eats only once every alternate day and moves out of the cave only to ease himself occasionally. No one has seen him sleep or speak. He sits like that gazing into the blue, steadfast in his resolve." I am always humbled before the power of self-mortification. I began to wonder whether this hermit will tell me if the Sahib in the adjacent cave was really he. After all, it isn't that there are hundreds of Sahibs loafing around in the forest of Swargadwar. So in front of the cave of the judge hermit I stumbled over a stone. I told father, "You walk ahead if you like. I'll wait here, I've hurt my toe." As their figures receded, almost vanished round the corner, I went near the hermit and said, "I know, Sir, you don't talk. But you are a hermit, it is also your task to relieve the world of its sufferings. Will you tell me something about the Sahib hermit of that cave? Was his name Mircea?" Not a flicker on that impenetrable face: no expression visible in those

unblinking eyes gazing towards the distance. I began to cry,
"Why don't you speak, O Sadhu, why don't you speak?
I need to know it. Will all the fruits of your penance be
ruined if you utter a word?" No result. He sat as immobile
as ever. By this time another stranger had appeared on the
scene. He is watching us wide-eyed. He certainly felt
touched by the sight of a pretty young girl crying her eyes out,
in a lonely forest, at the feet of an apathetic Sadhu. He
probably had not acquired enough virtue to become completely
callous to human suffering. He spoke to me with sympathy,
"Don't cry, please don't cry. No matter how much you
entreat him, he will not speak. Tell me, what is it you want
to know, ma?"

"What is the name of the Sahib who lived in that cave?"

"I don't know his name. Who can enquire about the
name of a Sadhu as it was in his former state?"

"Have you seen him?"

"Yes."

"What did he look like?"

"Like a Sahib."

"What does that mean?"

"Well, fair."

"What was his height? Did he wear spectacles?"

He indicated his height with a gesture of his hand but
could not remember about the spectacles. Then I entered
the cave. I searched the walls for his name, and also if he
has left any message. As I searched carefully, straining my
eyes, my heart began to pound as if to see his name would be
seeing him. I search for it like one demented. I have to be
quick, my parents will return any moment. But there is
nothing written on the wall. Only some sums done in Bengali
script. Suddenly my two minds began to fight. The foolish
one says, "This has been purposely done to torment you.
What was wrong in just writing a name? Father wouldn't
even have known. What was the harm? Who will tell
me?" And my sane mind answered, "How would he have

known that you will come here on his trail? So why are you
so distracted or angry?" But I am not able to chastise the
surging ocean of my grief and grievance. What power have
I or what self-control have I practised to gain strength enough
to win over my stupid self now distraught in agony. I am
convinced that the name was not written there purposely--to
sever all connections with me. Nothing else, nothing else . . . .

In the distance their voices became audible. I came out
of that cave and ran to the judge-hermit. It is good that
this man is so obstinately mute—otherwise he certainly would
have blurted it out to father. We began to walk back towards
the river. The boat is crowded. One has to hold on to a
rope because it is very unsteady on the whirling sream. Only
a few days earlier, a boat collided with a boulder and turned
turtle. We were told about thirty persons lost their lives.
There is no way to escape in this river—the current is so
strong that one would be dashed to pulp against the boulders
that stick out from under the water. I am sitting on the right
side of the boat—I touch the water with my hand—and
just then an idea buzzes like a bee in my head—this is the
opportunity to teach him a lesson for not writing his name
on the walls of the cave. If I fall here everything will be
finished instantly. I am not the type who can bear much
physical suffering—why not try once the maximum of
suffering? That is the only way to punish him. Oh but how?
He won't even know, or will he? The letter that he will
receive from father will make him sit up in 1 Melody Street.
Father will write, "I trusted you, I gave you refuge, food and
education and in return you have given me death. Perhaps my
affection towards you was an impiety that has brought disaster
in its wake."

And as for my parents? Both of them will be served
right! An elation of vengeance began to goad me.
Suddenly mother said, "Ru, move inside, why are you leaning
out?" I began to think of Milu—how she will cry! I
remembered Didima, Shanti, Khoka, everyone. Thakuma

used to say that at the time of death all the events of one's life
pass before one's eyes in a procession. It must be that—that's
why I am recollecting everyone I know. Is that so? Only
then I thought of not a human being but a photograph hanging
in my room in Bhawanipore—the photograph where two eyes
from a face with a velvet cap follow you in whichever direction
you move. I saw that gaze go piercing through me while
telling me, "So that's all you are? You got defeated so
easily? Then my songs are not for you." I woke up from
a stupor—as if from the darkness of a moonless night I saw
the dawn. How near the edge I am sitting! I got scared and
moved towards father. Father stretched his hand out to me.
"Move inside, don't lean out, Ru." And I who had been
thinking to jump out to punish him kept my head on his breast
and putting my arms round him began to weep. Mother got
anxious. "Why is she crying again?" "It is because of the
beauty around us," father tried to make the matter light.
"She always feels that way when she is in the midst of nature."
Impossible; it was becoming impossible for them also to
bear this burden of mourning.

We returned to Haridwar. At night I sat alone in the
verandah of the bungalow. It was a dark night. The forests
on the other side of the bank became incandescent with the
minute lights of myriads of fireflies. I could hear the
rumbling of the river below repeating itself in the echo—
this river, the life stream of our country, the Ganga with its
sacred water washed me clean with her invisible hands. I
lay on the chair with my eyes closed in a state of complete
serenity and realised the meaning of the song—"I have made
you the polestar of my life—I shall never again lose my way
in this marine journey."

# Book Two

IN OUR YOUNG DAYS, THAT IS UP TO THE TIME OF HIS DEATH, Rabindranath was addressed by his compatriots young and old as Rabi-babu or Rabi Thakur. In foreign countries his name was Anglicised into Tagore. Nowadays we find even Bengalis distorting it as "Tyagore". Nothing can be more disagreeable to the ear. Rabi Thakur or Rabi-babu is not a suitable form of address either, but that was how it was. The famous editor Ramananda Chatterjee used to say "The Poet". Later I picked it up from him. I have never addressed him as Gurudev. The students of Santiniketan addressed him so not as a preacher shepherding people into the fold of religion but as a teacher. He never considered himself as a religious preceptor but only as a poet. For all of 1930 he was out of India. At the end of his travels he went to the Soviet Union. I think the Russian scholar Bogdanov visited father sometimes and commented adversely on his visit to that curtained country. Father also received an invitation, but the Government refused him permission. He was very put out, and wondered which country was more curtained. He used to tell us often about a Russian high official he met in 1922 when he was in England. This man gave him expensive dinners—father smelt that something was in the offing. Then one day after a sumptuous meal he requested father to put him in touch with the freedom fighters of India, as his country was eager to help the movement. In answer, father said that that was a splendid idea if he would kindly answer one question: after driving the British out with their help, with whose help would we oust *them*? Needless to say, after this retort the hospitable

Russian disappeared.   Father recounted this incident with
glee.   He had no desire to get mixed up with political or
social movements; his single unwavering aim was to cultivate
pure knowledge.   He was remarkable in his fixity of purpose.
When Rabindranath returned from his European tour eight
to nine months back, I met him once or twice but had no
opportunity to have a private conversation, as he was always
in company.   On my return from Hrishikesh I wrote him a
letter.   I don't remember the contents fully, but I gave him to
understand a little of the agony I was passing through.   I felt
shy to write all, I was not brave enough either.   There was
some chance of father wanting to see his reply.   My father
was a great admirer of the Poet and was attracted by his
charisma, yet he also felt a certain resentment, because
the two of them had totally opposite personalities.   The poet
also greatly admired his erudition, but I must admit that his
openheartedness shrank before him.   It is understandable
where I stood in such a situation.   Father knew that I could
reach him easily and he was gracious to me, so whenever.
I wrote, father wanted to make me write all that father had
to say.   He would tell me what to write, then correct my
language and spelling, and add ideas which I would rewrite
again before posting.   So I could never get to write my own
letter.   This was another torture that I had been going through
from childhood.   The Poet once told me laughingly : "I would
like it far better if you write simply to me whatever you feel
rather than high philosophy." . . . I knew he would even have
appreciated a few spelling mistakes.   He was playing with
a little girl and did not particularly relish pretentious
high-flown philosophy coming from her.   I was never as
free as his other admirers.   But this time I wrote him a letter
myself.   I reproduce some portions from the answer I
received almost immediately—

*To the fortune-favoured girl :*

The agony expressed in your letter made me suffer
intensely.   If there is a conflict between the person and the
family, it is not easy to quietly bear it and steadily build up
harmony at your age and experience.   I don't know how
to advise you.   I remember my youth, when my days were
thorny with acute suffering.   I did not know if these would
ever pass away: I thought the road would be endless and
impassable.   But the fulfilment of life comes not by forgetting
suffering, but by daily turning sorrow into understanding,
turning cruel into tender, and sour into sweet.   I don't think
this would be impossible for you because you have the power
of imagination, which is the same as creative power.   You
will not abandon yourself to the hands of circumstances.
You will create your own destiny.   I know how difficult it
is in our country for women to exert their full strength.
They do not get a fair chance in the world outside and little
help to expand their mental world.   Yet I ask you to have
faith in yourself.   Let your glory transcend your destiny.   If
I had power to soothe your agony,   I would have tried, but
I can do nothing but wish you well with all my heart.   If
any meanness of others is oppressing you,   I bid you not
to bend before it.   August 1931.

*Affectionately yours ...*

A year before I received this letter, in the month of
September, which according to the Hindu calendar is the
month of Bhadra, Mircea went away.   According to our
custom in the month of Bhadra even an animal is not turned
out of a home, let alone a human being; but we were a
modern family and paid no heed to such superstitions.

I read the letter many times.   I liked it, but it could not
cure my depression.   It could not touch me to the depths.
After coming back from Haridwar I behaved normally and
father was satisfied.   My examination results were good
indeed.

Mother is more alert now. The house is now empty.
Shanti and Khoka have left; so have Mantu and his wife.
One day as I sat alone in my room with the letter in my hand,
mother came in and I gave her the letter to read. We two
then sat for a long time in an intimate speechless companionship.
Slowly and steadily the darkness deepened and filled us with a
strange emptiness. I suddenly spoke, my voice hardly audible,
"Ma, will you let me go to Santiniketan once?" Mother said,
"For some time I have been thinking of telling you myself to
go." My mother had the gift of speech. I had met many
scholars, many Ph.D.s, but few could speak so well or had
so much understanding. Taking me in her arms, my mother
went on to say, "Ru, you have received a gift. How many
are fortunate like you? Such respect, reverence and love as
have no connection with worldly affairs, completely selfless
and unrelated to the phenomenal world—how many are
fortunate to see that aspect of celestial love? It seems
you were prepared for it even before you were old enough
to know it, just as a flower passes the night not knowing
it is waiting for the light. And then, day in and day out,
his poems. songs, thoughts and reflections have lifted you
upwards. Do not allow yourself to get crushed, do not make
this invaluable good fortune fruitless. Go to him. Do not
hesitate to tell him everything. This is not good, especially
when you are lucky to have someone to whom you can make
a complete self-surrender. Confess everything to him and
get purified—he will show you the right path."

"Ma, I want to go alone."

She took the hint and said emphatically, "O yes, I will
see to that."

But I could not follow mother's advice. I can not
remember what day or what time I reached Santiniketan.
When I entered the room he was sitting in an arm chair—
his paintings lay strewn all over the floor—that was the
period of painting. He was not surprised to find me
appearing without previous intimation, as I was in the habit

of paying surprise visits. He simply said, "There is no one
in the house, so for hospitality one will have to depend
on the cook Ganapati."

I dropped on the floor near his feet.

"Have you read ghost literature?" he asked. Meaning
the game of planchette that was popular at that time. But
I was not interested in ghosts or the past. I was more
oppressed by the present and the living. "I have come to
tell you something," I began, as my heart started thumping.

"Yes, I have received both your letters. What has
happened, Amrita?"

I sat silently, my head bent, holding on to the leg of
the chair. What shall I say, or how shall I begin, and what is
the use either? Why need I bring him into this— would
I like to have him in disagreement with father? That will be
the ruin of me.

He held my hand, trying to help me and said, "Tell me,
Amrita, what has happened?"

"It is about the young man who lived with us."

"Which young man?"

"You saw him . . ."

"Did I? Where?"

"We came here."

"When was that? Are you talking of your uncle Mantu?"

"No—no, my father's student."

"Which one, a member of the Rabindra Society?"

"No, no, let me tell you—remember you saw us near
the tennis court?"

"Oh, yes, that Sahib? What happened to him?"

I did not reply to his question but simply said, "Why
did you go away for so long?"

He smiled tenderly. He knew well how to answer
such questions. With just a twist of a word he could uncork
the vessel of nectar. He knew how to develop a human
relation to its fullest beauty, without shattering anyone,
keeping everyone in his or her own place—he could take what

belonged to him and pay the giver the fullest price.    This was
an art.    Loving him no one was destroyed or harmed, but
the light of their lives shone brighter.

"Why did I go away?    To show my paintings.    In
Europe they know how to see a painting—here no one knows—
but had you asked me not to go then maybe I woudn't have!"
He shook my head a little, his eyes twinkling in mirth.
I knew he was joking but it was sweet to hear him say so.

"Now tell me . . what happened to the Sahib?"

"He's gone."    I could say no more.    I got up to my feet
and dragged myself to the western door and then, falling
on the floor, I began to cry.

"Come to me, Amrita, come here.    Tell me everything."
I hear his voice.    But I have no strength to get up or even
to speak.    I am tossed by a storm; how can I walk back
this distance of three of four yards?    Impossible; I can't
follow mother's advice.    How shall I begin?    Whose fault
was it, his or mine?    I know I am being disobedient but
I won't be able to pass this test.    If it were possible I would
fly out of this window and go to mother.    Suddenly I feel
that he has come up to me and is sitting beside me on a cane
stool.    "Get up, Amrita, be calm."    I get up, he helps me
to sit up, supporting my back on the door.

"Are you finding it difficult to tell me all?"

"Yes."

"Well then, don't try to say anything    There's no need
to.    Only calm yourself."

I try to control my sobs.

"You don't have to say anything, Amrita.    But only
tell me, should I do anything for you?    Do you need my help?"

Usually while speaking with someone he rarely looked
at the person.    He had a habit of fixing his gaze at a distance
or keeping his eyelids lowered.    He was addressing humanity,
not that particular person in front, whose problem is a human
problem.    I now realise the significance of it.    I could not
then.    I used to feel a little offended.    But I know each

person for him was a representative of humanity, who came
to him with love and joy, sorrow and happiness, and a heartful
of questions.  I now realise that had he not had this
detachment his highly sensitive mind could never have
achieved as much as he did—it would have battered itself to
pieces in the action and reaction of worldly affairs.  But that
day I am sure he was talking to me, "Tell me, Amrita,
tell me."  He looked into my eyes.  "I will do whatever you
want me to."

"I will do whatever you want me to."  The words began
to dance, beating rhythm with the waves of the seven seas.
He repeated tenderly, "Speak out what you want."  My body
and mind are soothed, I smell the perfume of sandal paste
as if I am on the threshhold of a temple.  What more is
there to ask for?  I whisper, my eyes closed: "Allow me
to stay near you."

' Oh, certainly.  It's no problem.  Why don't you get
admission here?  Then at dawn when I sit on the verandah
waiting for the sun, my namesake, to appear, you will come
with *gandharaj* flowers and sit beside me.  In the evening
we will read poems together.  But you must not talk while
I write."

My mind is full of peace now.  I feel he is describing
heaven.  But this will never be.  Father won't allow me
to get admitted here.

Afterwards he told me, "I cannot let you go like this—
think it over tonight and tell me in the morning whether
I can help you.  Such problems are not solved in one minute."

That was a sleepless night.  I was alone in the ground
floor, as the house was empty.  As long as the servants were
awake I heard muffled sounds, snatches of Saktipada and
Ganapati's voices floating to me.  Now  it was completely
quiet.  Lying in bed I began to argue with myself.  What
shall I tell him?  Can he help?  Why can't he?  He can tell
Andrews Sahib, "If you please take this girl to Europe that
will be doing me a favour."  Andrews Sahib will certainly

comply; he may be a *sannyasi* but he has feeling for others.
But can they really do it without father's consent? If the
Poet and Ramananda Chatterjee both say, "Look, Naren
babu, what you have done is not right"—then? Then he
will be ablaze with anger. He will say, "Rabi-babu, when
you married off your daughter, did you consult me? I know
you write very good poetry but my family problems are *my*
problems." Why should I bring him into all this and get
him insulted? Moreover, where shall I go? To whom? It's
nearly a year I have not heard from him. After that terrible
midday when he left, there is no trace of him. He could at
least write a letter to Khoka. He has not done so. Why
should I go on seeking him? No woman should take the
lead; that is absolutely shameless. Shame on me that I still
think of him. Skilled hunter of Europe. I shall pluck out
your poisoned arrow. I shall forget you, forget you. I will
tell the Poet to-morrow I don't need his help—I need nothing.
Now my mind is at peace. The Poet had once taught me a
hymn. Whenever your mind is troubled chant this, he told
me: *Anandamparam nandam paramasukham param tripti:*
Bliss, supreme bliss, perfect happiness and complete
satisfaction. I went on repeating the Sanskrit lines. Again
the fragrance of sandalpaste filled the cool night air, as if it
smeared the raw wound like a balm, the wound that has not
healed one bit for a year. Through the open window the
sky is visible; gazing at it I thought how easy it is to forget.
One day in a half-conscious state I swore not to forget but
today fully awake I firmly promise I must forget. A bright
star is watching me—it has got eyes—those eyes smile at me
as they watch with pity my unstable mind

We shifted from our Bhowanipur house in 1931. Our
happy home is gradually breaking up. All the old people
gone, now a new one has come. She is slowly tearing asunder
the ties of love and affection that kept this family together.
Let us presume her name is Rama. She is not pretty. Her
face is round like a wheel—her eyes are large and protruding—

they goggle at you—nose a little roundish and very small
compared to her large face.   She is very short.   But her voice
is sweet.   She is soft-spoken, quiet and gentle, not boisterous
like us.   I am fond of her.   It is pleasant to talk to her.   She
is a good scholar.   Scholar in the sense that her examination
results have been good, but she has no understanding of poetry.
She has so far written nothing.   There is no depth in her
conversation, but one thing she certainly has, and that is
perseverance: it was revealed later after it took her ten years
to get her Ph.D.   I could never have waited all that long.
Gradually she is becoming one of us.   Mother attends to her
needs as she does to ours.   Rama is helping father in his
work and remains always with him.   I am not averse to her
close attachment to father, only I feel that gradually mother's
place in this house is getting disturbed.   I worry a lot about
this.   Father now scolds mother all the time as if her faults
are increasing daily in geometrical progression.

Before, mother was in full command of the house; now
her voice is ignored.   Mother is suffering, so she tries to
placate them.   I feel ashamed of her weakness.

If there is one person in this world who knows, then that
certainly is me, that there is no need to have a social relation
in order to love a person or be loved.   I also know that true
love is like light that brightens up the whole environs.   Love
is not an object, not a gold ornament that you have to snatch
away from one to give to another.   I also know that when
you love someone truly, then everything related to that person
becomes dear to you.   You even come to like the servants
of that house.   But what do I see now?   She is trying to
increase her influence over our family affairs and also discredit
mother.   What is unbearable to me is the falsehood.   Why
don't they admit the truth?   However I may suffer, I am
prepared to face the truth, but I cannot keep my eyes shut
like mother.   So each day grows more intolerable than the
other.   Father also is no more as full of me as he used to be.
I heard that he was unwilling to marry me off to someone

from a faraway country because he would not have been able
to bear my absence, but now I feel his concern for me and
my studies is fast waning.

I have joined a college. No one can see the crosscurrent
that flows underneath. Mother tries to hide it. She makes
a great show of affection towards Rama, but she has lost her
sense of security. So mother feels that she should marry me
off. Exactly my view also. I have no desire to live here.
I want to escape. I am burning inside with anger because
I have to compromise with falsehood. I pretend not to know
what I know well, and not to see what I see.

Years roll by. Every day mother's life grows steadily
more unpleasant and she has to face humiliation. Mother
suffers most when outsiders talk against father and Rama.
People's tongues are wagging; they enjoy slander.

I know that Rama's love is not pure—in the gold of
love there often is the alloy of selfishness. Otherwise can
one humiliate a person one loves or bring disorder in his
family? In our country slander is an institution; now this
institution gets busy. Never mind how much mother wants
to hide it by saying "She is like a daughter to us—" the lashing
tongues do not stop.

However, I am not writing my mother's life so I need
not elaborate on this issue. Only I have fully realised that
there are two different kinds of love which look very similar
from the outside, though they are really opposed—one kind
can lift a person so high that from there all smallness and
selfishness disappear—it fills one's world with light and
fragrance and makes dear all that was unpleasant before—by
its light the usual things appear extraordinary, and dearer—
this love does not make you greedy or provoke you to
persecute your rival. But there is another kind of love: its
appearance is the same, but it deftly puts a noose around
the other's neck—or chains one down. It demands: Where
is your provident fund? Why not make me the assignee
of your life insurance? What about the house? You must

disinherit your children and write a testament for the copyright
of your books.    And what about your name and fame?
I want people to know that all this belongs to me.    And
your wife?    Send her with the children to your village home.
They will be looked after well there by your relatives, and
that is all she deserves.    After all, she is not educated enough
to be your companion.

Human beings walk on the tightrope or on the razor's
edge, you may say.    If one knows the trick one will reach
the destination, otherwise one falls midway and breaks
one's neck.

Mother is restless.    So am I.    My one thought is how
to leave this house.    And then I hesitate.    In whose care
shall I leave dear mother?    Now father looks out for a
pretext to scold me, because he can read in my eyes silent
censure.    In 1934 I was in college doing my B.A.    I went
to the zoo with my girl friends, no very derogatory act,
but father rebuked me with such vehemence that it became
obvious that he had other reasons for doing so.    Mother
knew, but she was pretending not to know.    She was too
afraid to face the truth.

I cannot forget the day when the funeral procession of
martyr Jatin Das, who died fasting in jail, was taken out on
Russa Road.    I went to a friend's house on that road to
watch the great spectacle.    An enthusiasm, a patriotic zeal
moved through our frames; it gave us a strange sense of
elation.    It was not death, it was life.    I was not mourning,
it was a festival!    Subhas Bose was standing in an open car.
Millions were walking barefoot; it was a sea of humanity
rolling down the street.    Intermittently various slogans rose
in a crescendo and pierced the sky.    The sound of the
slogans was like some mysterious chant that overpowered us.
We felt like going down to the crowd and joining it.    Many
banners flew over the mass of heads and placards with various
writings were waved.

I read two lines by Rabindranath:

> At the time of sunrise
> Whose message do we hear—
> It says, do not fear, do not fear,
> One who gives his life fully
> Has no death, has no death.

The poetry goes to my blood instantly and makes me ecstatic. I began to recite from the balcony the lines that come after—

> O fierce God, how shall I sing your praise,
> Tell me, O lord.
> Keeping rhythm with the dance of death
> I shall beat the drum of my heart.
> With terrible sorrow I shall fill the basket of my
>     offering.

I got bewitched by my own voice as I kept on reciting loudly. "Chutku, let us go and join the procession."

"Let's," she said enthusiastically, and then, after second thoughts, "But your father will scold you."

"Let him."

We went down and mingled in the ocean of men. I had never seen such a crowd before. I have of course pulled the chariot of Jagannath at Puri. That is the greatest concourse that people witness once every year, but this was even bigger. Suddenly a British police sergeant riding on a white horse galloped into the crowd; whip in hand, he began to slash around like one demented. We also got hit a bit. When I returned home my sari was crumpled and torn, I was dishevelled and covered with mud. I planned to lie, but could not; at that moment my mind was on such a high level of emotion that I thought it would be insulting to the great death we witnessed today. So I spoke the truth. Father scolded me so much that it seemed my brain disintegrated.

I constantly ask myself, How can I be free? Mother was never properly free, she had to steal money or persuade father for her constant need of helping poor relatives. But she used to have sufficient influence over father and could persuade him in many matters. I used to wonder how those who love freedom could want to keep other in chains. But

reason does not play a great part either in family life or in
politics. The British say, "Rule, Britannia, Rule the waves,
Britons never will be slaves"—but look at what they have
done to others and then that is also their pride—"The sun never
sets on the British Empire." Logic is seldom used.

Mother is searching earnestly for a good match. She
has now an exercise book where she jots down systematically
names of potential bridegrooms, their qualifications, and
other particulars. A boy who has all the required
qualifications, that is, a good government job, inherited
property and a university degree, is always difficult to get hold
of. It was more so then, because jobs were limited indeed.
So mothers of unmarried daughters spread their nets around
to ensnare any available suitable groom.

Then slander became active and one would vie with
another to break the match, so my mother remained
intimidated, as all our relatives knew about Mircea and also
about what father was doing now. In beauty and glamour
and related matters I was not really a nonentity, so why worry?

From this time I began to think more about the country
than about myself. The worst thing here is the caste laws,
the prejudices. I must work against this. But how can I?
Who is going to listen to me, except myself? So I told father,
"Why don't you marry me to someone from another caste?"

"Why?" His large eyes widened in surprise. "What's
wrong with our caste?"

"Well, then we achieve two things together, get married
and also break caste."

"Two birds at one stroke? I have nothing to do with
such reformatory marriage experiments."

Information arrives about a prospective bridegroom of
extraordinary suitability. He is a doctor. He holds a big
position. But we Bengalis are no less prejudiced against
dark skin than Europeans. So mother spoke with melancholy,
"What shall I do, Ru, the boy is very dark." I really enjoy

the fun. Should I say, "But you don't like a fair skin, either do
you?" No, I must never bring all that up again. The doctor's
old father grew fond of me but the doctor did not. He was
worried about the physique of the Bengali race. He is only
five feet four or so, he wants a girl to be at least five feet seven.
For if a short boy is married to a short girl, what would
happen to the future of the race? I am only five feet two—
so he refused the proposal. I could not blame him of course:
just as I want to use the opportunity to improve the moral
side of the nation, he is trying to improve the biological.
Both of us at least have one thing in common: we are
patriotic! He was of course invited to visit many other
houses where other girls were shown to him. As he belonged
to our caste, some of the girls were our relatives. In one
house he was enchanted to meet one of our grannies who was
nearly a sixfooter. "You are wonderfully tall," he remarkd.
Granny moved her long stick-like hand which swayed like a
branch and said, "But you cannot marry me."

I have heard he never married. He couldn't get a girl
the proper height.

At last the marriage is settled. What a relief both for
mother and me. Mother has decided to have it over with
quickly, before the tongues begin to wag. The would-be
bridegroom satisfies father's specifications: he has a doctorate
degree in science and a couple of gold medals. Father said
proudly, "He got the doctorate in just five years." Mother
said pointedly, "And what about your students? They go on
struggling for years."

"Science and arts subjects are not the same," father
snapped back, taking the hint. The groom-to-be was invited
to come and meet me over a cup of tea. But he did not
come. Later he gave me the reason. He had heard that the
girl was very pretty. So there was every chance of his
failing in love with her after meeting her and there was far
more chance of her rejecting him. What then? Better not
meet. This was probably the first and last time that he

indulged in deceit in his whole life.

The arrangements for the wedding proceeded, though
not many relatives came.   How could they?   It was all to
be finished within just five days.   Mother was not in good
health.   She was suffering from gastric ulcer—mainly because
of her worries—it was a psychosomatic disease.   She was very
unhappy.   After all, her daughter was not brought up in the
villages of East Bengal—after so much literature, poetry and
all that, how could she have such a "rustic" marriage without
even meeting the man once!   She began to grumble;
ultimately she told me, "I must go and persuade him to come
and meet you.   Won't you like to?   How can you get
married without seeing him even once?"

"No need, ma."

"No need?   You don't want to meet him?"

"Are you not ashamed, ma, to tell me this?   Why
should I see him?   Suppose I say I won't marry him, I don't
like him, I would rather marry Mr. K., he is of another caste
but never mind, I like him, will you then listen to me?   You
will begin to argue, won't you?"

"Well, why won't you like him?   Looks are not everything
in a man, there are many handsome nitwits."

"Stop talking nonsense, ma.   You are all the same.
You have no courage to face the truth and specially you,
you are to be blamed more than anybody else.   You keep
your eyes shut."

My cruel words made mother weep.   "The harder I
work to please you, the more you scold me, all of you."

It was true.   I really made mother suffer.   Sabi went
to the bridegroom's house.   Returning, she fell on my neck
and began to cry.   "O *didi*, I beg you not to marry here—
run away, *didi*—I did not like him at all."

I smiled and thought, *But you drive away whomever
I like;* but I said nothing.   She must have forgotten
everything; after all, she was a kid.   Such a nasty affair
should not have happened in front of her.   The trouble is

that you cannot erase anything from life.   The picture that
is once painted can never be wiped out.   In literature the
writer can, like the artist, erase portions that are not in
harmony; but life preserves all, one cannot rub out a line;
if one could I would have rubbed out 1930 from my life with
all my energy.   From the branch of my ever-green life let
1930 drop off like a dry leaf and be gone, just as my love for
Mircea is gone.   I do not remember his face; even if I do,
I feel no pleasure nor pain.

I began to cry from the time of the blessing ceremony.
I wept incessantly; uncontrollable tears, like rain—but I
didn't know why I wept.   Suppose someone said, you need
not marry.   Would I agree?   Certainly not, at least I have
reached the door through which I can escape from this house.
I will be free from now on.   At least I will be able to go to
Santiniketan whenever I wish.   Yet I am crying, God knows
why.   People think a devoted daughter is unhappy to leave
her parents.   Just the opposite.   But none can guess my
thoughts.

On the wedding day the *shehnāi* flute began to play
from dawn when I ate curd.   *Shehnai* makes one's heart ache,
it's the music of separation.   One of my Brahmo uncles used
to sing devotional songs.   I was fond of this uncle of mine;
he had an inner life.   I begged him to come after the
wedding and sing something to me.

At this time the Poet was in Ceylon.   A telegram was
sent seeking his blessings; and the blessing arrived by
telegram.   On the day of my wedding I realised that
everything might not be all right.   I wondered whether I
had thrown myself out of balance, whether I would be able
to go through with it.

I got married in the evening.   As we sat in our nuptial
chamber surrounded by friends and relatives who were
helping us with the customary shell game and everybody
became hilarious as the bridegroom fished out the little shell
from the heap of rice, I saw my Brahmo uncle pass by the door.

I left the room, to the amazement of my friends.   I was
in need of a song much more than the cowry game.   Uncle
could not believe that I could do such a thing.   But he was
pleased with me.   We sat in a corner of the verandah.
I was surprised to see the *krishnachura* tree in front decorated
with coloured lights.   Then I closed my eyes in prayer and
joined uncle in his song:

> We begin our journey.   Pilot, I salute you!
> Storm or tempest, we will not turn back.

He blessed me.   "Go to your room, ma, may your life's
journey be smooth."

After blessing us both and wishing us well, my parents
close the door behind them as they leave us.   My husband
is thirty-four years old; he is fourteen years older than me.
We gaze at each other.   He is not a good-looking man;
there are other defects; but I can see he is a good man, an
essentially good man.   I am not afraid nor am I embarrassed.
I am wearing a sari with green stripes, on my forehead are
the sandalpaste decorations of the bride but no vermillion
line marks the parting of my hair.   The marriage is not
complete, because we have not performed Kushandika,
that is, the final fire oblation done together, which is the
ceremony consummating a Hindu marriage.   Generally
bride and bridegroom are not left alone at night before
that ceremony.   Some younger people stay in the room as
chaperones; but ours is a modern family and we don't worry
much about such orthodox details.

How can I sleep in the same bed with a man whom
I have never seen before, I wondered.   I am not scared; only
uncomfortable.   I said, "I will lie on the carpet." He said
"O no, let me do that."

We argued for a little while.   Then I gave up.   I cannot
ask him to sleep on the floor; after all, he is our guest.

"All right, then I will sleep on the bed," I agreed
reluctantly.   It is not good to be disobedient the very first
night.   I could not find anything to talk about.   He is not

one to talk either.  However, his silence did not appear
strange to me.  As I lay, turning my back towards him and
covering myself with a sheet, I said, "I want to get up at five
in the morning when uncle comes to sing.  If you are up
earlier, will you kindly wake me up?"

Then we put out the light and lay in silence.  It is then
that it happened  I saw Mircea whom I had not seen for the
last four years; crossing a continent and the Indian Ocean,
he suddenly entered through our locked door.  When he was
staying with us I had never seen him at night except on the
night of the earthquake, or sat on the same bed with him.
But today he came and sat on my nuptial bed.  I am amazed
to see him.  "Mircea, why did not you come in the morning?
I had forgotten you but today I was thinking a good deal
about you."

"What were you thinking?"

"Well, I was wondering since you became a hermit and
sat in penance in the Himalayas you might have acquired
supernatural powers.  I thought you would come and  persuade
father.  But you didn't turn up."

"Here I am."

"But it's too late now."

"For what?  What is before and what is after?  What is
late and what is early?"  Saying this he put his face on my
heart.  It is from there the blood-carrying arteries and  veins
run—crushed by his kiss, blood oozed out from them, and
drop by drop it ran down the leg of the bed, then after
forming a pool on the floor it moved in a stream and
crossing the verandah the stream poured out on the street.
Then it began to look for the Ganga - O sacred sea-seeking
Ganga, make my blood-stream your tributary and take it
to the sea.  Let all blood flow out from my body; there will be
fresh blood, fresh life.  Tomorrow morning I will wake up
into a new beginning.

Opening my eyes in the morning I realised my husband
has awakened me.  He said, "You said you wanted to

get up at five—it is now five in the morning." I was
astounded. I realised this man had had a sleepless night.

"Have you not slept all night?"

He smiled meekly. "Yes, you told me to wake you up
at five—so I kept awake for fear I oversleep."

This is my husband. Many years have passed since
that day but he has remained the same—keeping an unwavering
vigil over my well-being.

Next day father gave me a letter. This letter was written
to me by my husband a few days before but out of excessive
politeness he had sent it to father to give to me if he wished.
The purpose of this letter was to introduce himself before
the marriage to give me a glimpse of his personality.

*Mademoiselle,*

Understanding that you are going to choose a partner
in life I beg to offer myself as a candidate for the vacancy.
As regards my qualifications, I am neither married nor am I
a widower; I am in fact the genuine article—a bachelor,
being one of long standing. I should in fairness refer also
to my disqualifications. I frankly confess that I am quite
new to the job and I cannot boast of any previous experience
in this line, never having had occasion before to enter into
such partnership with anyone. My want of experience is
likely, I am afraid, to be regarded as a handicap and
disqualification. May I point out however that though
"want of experience" is a disqualification in other avenues
of life, this particular line is the only one where it is desirable
in every way. A more serious handicap is the fact that I am
an old bachelor with confirmed bachelor habits. For further
particulars I beg you to approach your mother who studied me
the other day with an amount of curiosity and interest that
would have done credit even to an egyptologist examining a
rare mummy. In fine, permit to assure you that it will be my
constant endeavour to give you every satisfaction. I have the
honour to be, mademoiselle,

*Your most obedient servant . . .*

The letter cheered me up. It fell like a shower of
sunshine over a gloomy storm. Nothing can heal one's wound
more than hearty laughter. Laughing, I returned the letter
to ma. "Have you read it?"

"Yes, your father was. . ."

"Why didn't you give it to me yesterday?" I asked
mystified.

"Well, we were not sure who wrote it."

"Why? The name is there." I was sorry that I didn't
get it before last night. Then we could have had something
nice to talk about. At least I could have said, "You are
certainly a humorous person"—but I missed the chance.

From this house I will go to my in-laws and then to a
distant hill in an unknown solitary place where my husband's
work takes him. I stand before the big wall map of India
and look for the place where I am destined to live my life—
but the name is nowhere. What an un-mapped godforsaken
country I am being banishod to, I muse.

At the time of parting father began to cry like a child.
So did I. All my resentment against my parents vanished.
I had completely misunderstood them—whatever they did
was for my good. My heart ached also for Rama - poor
thing, she did work hard during the wedding preparations.

A few days after the wedding the Poet returned from
Ceylon. We planned to go to meet him. But I am not
willing to go accompanied by father. But I am not willing
to go accompanied by father. So I bravely said, "You go
before me; I will go alone later."

"All right," he said gravely ; I am taking my son-in-law
in the morning. You better go in the afternoon."

I decided to go alone, but Rama followed me. I was
surprised to find her get into the car. However, I was in no
mood to ask her questions. An intense emotion is rippling
through my frame ; I am not sure why I am so restless and
flurried. I climb up the spiral staircase, I am wearing a

Benaras silk sari, its free end is slipping off. Rama helps to
fix it. I have bangles, earrings, and *sinthi* on my forehead,
anklets ringing, and vermillion smudged on my parted hair.
My bride's dress is typical.

　　　The Poet was waiting for me. Seeing me he stretched out
his arms. "Come, Amrita." I fell on his lap and began
to sob. I could hear him speak to Rama, "Would you be
so good as to go and wait in the other room? I have
something to say to her." Rama went away. He gave me
a little time and then said, "Sit up, Amrita." I obeyed.
Then he began to speak, his voice mellowed with emotion
and eyes lowered, "You know, I never like to sermonise.
I do not relish rolling boulders of big advice on a distressed
mind. Yet I will have to talk to you today." He stopped
a little to give me time and then went on in his inimitable
sweet voice pouring out a tenderness that could soothe the
deepest wound, "Your father came to see me with your
husband. I did not find much to talk to him. Only pundits
can be so ruthless. But you need not be hard on yourself
because someone else was hard on you. One has no control
over others, Amrita, but one shonld have control over oneself.
I do not know anything about the person you are married to—
how he is, whether the environment will suit you—yet I hope
that whatever be your destiny, you will grow bigger than it.
I know you have power to make others happy but what
I ask you is to be happy yourself. If you are unhappy,
if you get defeated by unfavourable cirumstances, then
I shall take it as my defeat. But I know that will never be.
You will certainly succeed. If you can build a beautiful nest—
your happy home where everyone is happy—then I promise
you I will visit your joyful home." With deep affection
he stroked my head. I bent low and touched his feet with
my head. I kissed the soft smooth feet and said in a tear-
choked voice, "I will do as you say."

　　　On returning home Rama reported to father secretly.
I cannot imagine what she might have said; she could have

heard nothing unless she was eavesdropping.  Nothing
blameworthy happened.  I did not complain, but if my tears
were an unspoken complaint then it couldn't be helped.  But
father began to scold his married daughter with uncomparable
vehemence that day—it rose up and up in a crescendo and
I thought it would never stop.

That was a queer time—our elders thought they could
dry a tear with reproaches, whiplash one to laughter, and
stop one from loving or make one love by scolding.  Now
the order was: "Love your husband."  Anyway, that day
I decided that I would never come back to this house, now
that I had an opportunity to leave it.  But that was just a
passing thought of an anguished mind.  From my solitary
banishment I have come regularly once every two months,
incurring expenses that were beyond our means, mainly to see
father.  People nowadays would not believe how much our
elders depended on the efficacy of a rebuke.  The few days
we were in Calcutta after marriage, mother wanted detailed
information regarding our progress in conjugal life.  When
she thought the speed was slow, she would feel frustrated and
get angry with me.  She need not have got upset.  My
husband was totally an introvert, but slowly and steadily
we became good friends.

The rains had set in when we reached that lonely spot.
It poured in an incessant splatter as our car wound round
the corkscrew bends.  Driving through miles of primal forest
we at last reached a clearing and coming down the slope
arrived right in front of a lovely red-roofed bungalow, dressed
in honeysuckle and blooming rose creepers.  The neat little
house smiled at me.  The quiet lonely forest lay in front
and on the bluish horizon a white line of eternal snow threw
an unexpected brilliance.  Entering the house I found it clean
and well decorated.  The servants were in spotless white
uniform, turbaned and barefooted.  I did not come into a
slovenly bachelor's quarters.  Though we were better off than
my husband's family, I must admit I had never lived in such

comfort before.

Yet our relatives were not satisfied, they kept sniping.
According to them it was an unequal match.  Specially those
who were of my age—they were false-sympathetic —"So
it has come to nothing more than this!"  I used to get angry
at such remarks.  I quarrelled with Gopal and we separated
for good.  Eventually they all agreed that since I was happy
they had nothing to say.  "Yet what a choice!" I argued
with them neither for show nor for prestige.  I was pleasantly
surprised to know the men folk of my husband's family.
They never lorded it over others, women were the real
mistresses of their homes.  I had noticed in many other families
that all the best things were reserved for the master of the
house.  This could never happen here: the men would take
no advantage over the women.  On the contrary, when the
wife was cooking the husband tried to fan her in spite of
her embarrassed protests! In fact I had never before seen so
many good people in one family.

I am not going into all the details of my life.  This is
not my biography, this is just a story in which Mircea is the
hero.  But in order to complete the story I have to say
something about my husband too, because I am incomplete
without him.  A great part of me has blended with his
personality.  The home life we have built up for the last
thirty-eight years has been smooth.  We have seldom disagreed.
From house décor to children's education, we have always
been of one mind.  Our children, though not highly talented,
possess human dignity and integrity.

The emptiness I felt at the time of my marriage did not
disrupt my world.  My desire to be free had been fulfilled.
The moment I entered my husband's home, my shackles fell
off.  I realise that from then I would be able to do what
I felt was right.  Freedom of course does not correspond to
irresponsibility.  I hope I have never used my unlimited
freedom in a way that is unworthy of me.

A few days after I settled down in my new home I thought

I should tell my husband about Mircea. So one day I began
like this, "Once a foreign student lived in our house for some
time, he wanted to marry me, father objected, so he went
away to the Himalayas." That is how I prefaced the story.
My husband replied, "Is that so?" No more questioning, no
curiosity. The less he has to say, the happier he is. He would
like to end all discussions by putting in one or two humorous
remarks, so since he went to the Himalayas, the drop scene
fell after that—that must be "The End." I could not continue
the story. But my conscience remained uneasy. After a few
days I began again, this time I firmly decided I must tell him
even if he was not interested. "Well, that night in *basar
ghar*—when I lay shrouding myself with a bed sheet—what
did you think?" No answer.

"You must tell me what your thoughts were. Did you
feel hurt?" Silence—impenetrable silence. But I also was
determined I must tell him that day, tell him all. After much
provocation he replied, "One is naturally not comfortable,
sleeping in the same bed with a stranger. One may not
like it."

"Did you feel uncomfortable—did you dislike it?"
"Not at all."
"Did you like it?"
"O yes, certainly, I was impressed."
"Didn't my behaviour strike you as awkward?"
Under pressure of my unceasing questioning he gave way.
"I thought about my friend Bhupesh. Maybe something
like that is going to happen to me, I told myself." The story
of Bhupesh runs like this—Bhupesh's marriage was arranged
by his elders. He had never met the girl until his wedding
night. In the *basar ghar* when they were alone the girl said,
"I cannot be your wife. I have chosen someone else as my
husband. He also loves me. But my father did not agree
and turned him out ruthlessly and forcibly married me to you.
What shall I do now?" She began to weep. "You should
also not marry me," she said. Bhupesh wanted the name and

address of her disappointed lover.   Still in his bridegroom's
dress, he left his flower-bedecked *basar ghar* and went in
search of that man at dead of night.   The marriage was not
complete yet—the consummation of marriage is doing a *yajna*
together, when husband and wife offer an oblation of clarified
butter in the sacred fire, and walk seven steps together.   This
part of the marriage is done the next morning.   On the
wedding night the bride's father with various articles makes a
"present" of the bride, bedecked with ornaments, to the
bridegroom.   In Bhupesh's case the girl had been given to
him by her father, that is, property had changed hands,
that's all.   The real marriage would be completed the next
day.   The girl of course by then had become Bhupesh's
property.   Arriving at the right address, Bhupesh called the
man out.   "What a man you are! Sitting and mourning! Have
you no duties to perform?"   Bhupesh returned accompanied
by him, and woke the girl's father up.   "You have committed
a sin, but since you have given your daughter to me you have
no right over her any more.   I will now give her in marriage
to the person she loves."

"Really?   What happened next?"

"They got married."

I thought: Ah well, she was certainly a brave girl.

"Is there any sequel?"   I asked.

"Yes, there is. . ."

"Bhupesh fell in love with that girl on that fateful
wedding night of his.   Gradually he changed.   Lack-lustre
and anguished, he often visited the married couple.   Then
one day he died.   There was a kerosene burner in his room;
he fell over it from the bed and was burnt to death.   Some
say he committed suicide."

"Of course it was suicide," I emphasised.

How terrible! There is no beauty in this horrid end of
an unrequited love.   Love would be an emptiness if beauty
went from it.   In my mind I began to see a scorched torso.
The flesh on it was raw.   I saw the head too with hair burnt

and a roasted face that was groaning. How horrible! If anyone
has to suffer like this by loving me, then that would be the
undoing of me also. A shiver ran through me—if his friend
was like this, certainly he also would be the same. No need
to go into the past any more. I will never be able to hurt
my husband. If at this moment Mircea appears and asks
me to go with him, can I follow him? Never, never! Which
heaven of happiness can I aspire to reach by making this
gentle soul unhappy? I am now old enough to realise that
happiness does not reside in an event or object outside one's
mind. It can swell up by some touch from outside only if
inwardly we are prepared for it. If I continuously get burnt
by the fire of conscience, if those wounds are lapped by
slanderous vulgar tongues and pricked by social censure,
then can I be happy by just falling into Mircea's arms?
Impossible. It is not the body that can create happiness—
it is the mind which is eternal source of joy. I know
my mind will never be able to enjoy anything by hurting
others.

It is not possible to be happy by making others unhappy.
This is a very simple statement. It has been repeated over
and over again. But is it really so? Then why even now is
Rama burning my mother in a slow fire? Well, let it be—
I cannot help it. I know only that I shall never make this
good man suffer. Is this only duty on my part? Am I being
only a dutiful wife? No, I love my husband. I have truly
begun to love him deeply. It became clear to me the
other day when the servant boy told me at about eight o'clock
in the evening that *Sahib* might lose his way in the forest.
Had he gone to his place of duty on a pony, the pony would
have brought him back safely home but . . . It was a
moonless night and rain poured in sheets. There was no
trace of any living person on the road. They were talking:
"Wild bears abound in that part of the forest." I became
so distraught with fear and anxiety that had they not taken
out a search party I would myself have put on a mackintosh

and gumboots and walked out, not fearing bears or tigers.
Is not that love?   Yet, sitting in this beautiful home basking
in the sunshine of my husband's love, can anyone tell me why
my soul feels so forlorn?   "I wander with empty hands
from street to street, O Lord."

   Our married life moves smoothly.   The relatives may
insinuate or friends make caustic remarks, but we are happy
indeed.   In one point we are like-minded.   He has no
prejudice.   He also is against all caste taboos.   He is critical
of our social customs and rational in his attitude.   I was
surprised to hear that the first day he took meat it was beef.
Even I was startled to hear it.   He was not a meat eater
but the day he reached this place to join his post he was invited
to an Englishman's house.   The lady of the house was a
miser.   She usually kept one piece of fish fry on the table and
urged her guests, "You must eat at least one fry", but that day
she had no fry, she offered beefsteak intead.

   "Why did you eat?   It was insolence to invite a Hindu
and offer beef," I asked.

   "But there was nothing else.   They would have been
embarrassed.   If one has to eat meat, what difference is
there between a goat and a cow?   A cow is better because
by taking one life you get more meat.   In that sense
an elephant is the best."   What an invincible argument,
I thought.   In those days it was an act of great valour for a
person coming from a middleclass Hindu family to eat beef.
But for him it was a simple act of following reason—he was
not rebellious—not like me—I am consciously and purposely
eager to break all these foolish customs, especially caste.   But
he is just acknowledging truth simply and naturally.

   When Rabindranath came to know him well, he wrote
a poem called "The Good Man."   This verse depicts my
husband :

    Maniram is really clever.
    No jolt can shake him.
    He is eager not to show off.
    He keeps under cover his competence.

He is at ease only when he can hide himself in a corner.
He shuns that assembly
Where he is honoured.
He never says "Give me more"
And would not step on anyone even given the chance.
If he notices that the food is not enough
He says "Well, I am full today."
If there is no salt in the curry,
No one can guess it from his face.
If his friends deceive him
He says, "It's just a mistake."
When the debtor remains silent
He says "I have no urgency."
If he is beaten up
He says "The fault must have been mine!"

The essence and message of this poem is the message
of the Gita : "He who is unperturbed at the time of trouble
and unattached to the pleasures of life is a yogi."

My husband has all the qualities necessary for an ideal
person as described in the Gita.  But he has not had to sit
in penance to acquire these.  These were gifts of God.
I want to acquire these qualities—I have read the Gita many
times more than he has; but I have acquired nothing.  I am
anxious, perturbed, impatient, and I possess all the defects
that one should try to rise above.  Like a pond full of fish
all the faults continuously wriggle inside me.  So I constantly
suffer from a sense of desolation.  A sense of nothingness
overpowers me.  For instance, the other day I sat thinking
how many words have I spoken through the day—I counted
and found it could not be more than seven or eight sentences:
"Why are you half an hour late today?"  "Are you going
to play tennis?"  "Will the Osbornes come to dinner on
Sunday?"  That would be about all.  What more is there
to talk about?  We two belong to two different worlds.  What
he has read I have not.  But that should not matter.  I am
ready to read even chemistry if he will teach me.  I can enjoy
any subject.  My unsatiated thirst for knowledge can be
whetted even by unfamiliar subjects if someone helps.  But
he cannot do that; he is an introvert and most unwilling to

talk.  Of course what I have read he has not.  Barring the
few poems he had to read in his school books, he has not
read a line of poetry.  But I can read some poetry to him,
can't I?  No, poetry cannot be thrust upon anyone.  It is
not a bullet one shoots, it can touch the chord inside only if
one is in tune.  Yet I know that had I read poems to him
he would have listened patiently.  He would never have
behaved like my friend's husband.  My friend who was a
connoisseur of poetry wanted to read some poems from *Mahua*
to her husband during their honeymoon.  The husband also
had shown a good deal of interest, but before she could
begin to read he stretched out his hand and said, "Let me see
the poem you are going to read."  After taking a look he
returned the book to his wife.  "What did you want to see?"
the wife asked, a little astonished.  "I just wanted to find
out how long it is."

My husband would never do a thing like that.  If I read
to him volumes and volumes of poetry he would listen patiently
and say "Very nice."

Some days, not some but nearly every day,  I am
oppressed by loneliness.  I was never one for an afternoon
nap but—what shall I read?  There is no library in this
wilderness.  The few books we have I have read over and
over again.  It is only when I go to Calcutta that I procure
some books.  All my ties with the literary world have snapped.
My husband, even though he never cares to talk, also suffers
from loneliness.  Once when I was away he wrote, "For the
last fifteen days I have not seen a civilized person except in
the mirror."  The profound quiet of the evening is strange.
You feel as if you are in another world.  We sit together
in the verandah, I try to open up a conversation, just one or
two words trickle out, and then they get lost in the desert
land of silence.  In which language shall we speak?  We use
different languages.  So we remain silent.  In this solitary
land all sounds tend to increase the quietude.  From the
dark deep forest a night bird rends the air with a shrill

whistle, sometime a bat falls with a thud, crickets chirp
incessantly in a brassy din—si, si, si, si,—the running brook
by the side of the lawn never for a moment ceases its
interminable splash—it keeps on falling and falling.   These
sounds are no companion for a human being.   They
continuously remind one, "You are alone."   I can feel every
day that I have lost my world.   I am not keen on writing any
more.   What shall I write?   My pen has lost its way in this
wilderness.   Many of us think that natural beauty inspires
a writer—the poems improve in quality if the poet writes
sitting surrounded by a rose garden—the guide now in
Santiniketan points out to the visitors the tree under which
Rabindranath wrote his immortal poems.   Nothing could
be more ridiculous than this.   The Poet invited the world
to the lonely expanse of Santiniketan to satisfy his own need
of inspiration.

Constant human contact, being tossed by joy and
anguish, churned by the conflict of good and evil, is the life
that a writer needs.   The unruffled calm and inexorable
loneliness of a forest may help hermits but not me.   This
beautiful nature around me is not giving me life but is taking
it away.   A person needs another person; at least I do.
Would a flowering tree have been better than Mircea?   I
remembered something: "Whom did you love first, tell me.
O tell me."   "A tree.   I loved a tree"—now hang on to a
tree, I said to myself.

Of the twenty-two years of my solitary confinement in
a forest life, only three years have I lived fully.   The rest of
the days are only repetitions.   I have written about this
period elsewhere.   It can't be dealt with here.

As far as I can remember that was in 1938.   Father
told me in Calcutta,   "Mircea has dedicated a book to you
and he has sought your forgiveness in the dedication."

The news was so unexpected that my heart began to
beat faster and went almost out of control.   I stood speechless,
turned into a statue.   After a few minutes he said, "He has

been jailed for writing pornography." My English was poor,
I did not know what the word pornography meant. I had
no desire to ask father. I knew it could not be anything
excellent if it had sent the writer to prison. I walked away
silently. I was astounded to look up the meaning in the
dictionary—how ugly—perverse—is the book he dedicated
to me the same one? Why did he have to do a thing like
that? What was the need to dedicate a book to me or to
seek forgiveness, I asked myself. I felt no curiosity about
the book because my mind shrank in disgust. I shivered to
think that at one time I had come so close to such an awful
man. I tried to forget the whole affair. With a firm
determination I rolled down a boulder of repugnance and
closed the opening of that cave which lay in abysmal depth,
illuminated by the colours of memory. It would be wrong
to say I did it. It just happened that way.

The days roll by from morning to night according to
schedule. Sometimes I feel that it was unfair to both of us
that we were married so hastily by our elders. Whenever
such ideas cross my mind I feel ashamed. Am I being
disloyal to my husband, I ask myself. No, that question does
not arise. In spite of his greatness there is no doubt that
the two of us belong to two different "castes". Whether
this "caste" difference makes my husband also suffer I cannot
tell, because he gives no expression to it; if he did, the question
of caste would not arise at all. I can certainly feel the depth
of his love and concern towards me. Everyone knows it.
If I go away for a fortnight he falls ill. I also never stay away
long. 1 suffer, I feel anxious for his well-being. Yet . . . yet
those empty days in the hills hang like a load on my neck,
because I cannot talk. I have much need to express myself.
I sometimes question myself why I am disturbed about the
difference in "caste". Is there any way out? If I had not
been suddenly married to this person but got married to
that dark-complexioned medical man, what would have

happened? Would we have been of the same "caste"? Oh,
wasn't he terrible? A person who does not wish to see the
face, the mind or the personality but only cares for the height!
We could never have achieved ideal companionship. So why
worry? Yet . . . that "yet" lingers on. People might ask,
What have you not received—husband's love, respect in your
father-in-law's house, freedom? I must admit I have no
complaints. If I say I am sad because I could not discuss
the poem of Rabindranath which came out in the last issue
of *Prabasi* nor read out a poem to anyone for one full month,
will anyone sympathise with me or weep over my fanciful
sorrow? People will laugh at me.

Yet, I need so much what others don't want at all.
There are some persons who are never satiated with worldly
goods, whose aspirations never end, who are continuously
searching for some fine gossamer uncatchable things that
have no worldly value

Who fashioned our minds in this way, so that we have
become so different from so many? Rabindranath Thakur,
who else? We who have seen this world through his songs
and those who have not are strangers to each other. Our
worlds do not move in the same rhythm.

Though I am living in the mountains, the current of my
life is not forceful as a mountain brook. It does not gush
forward and·hit against rocks. It has become the calm
stagnant water of a pond. I have no connection with
the greater world outside my limits. I sit absent-minded,
floating on the insignificant boat of everyday life. How lonely
I am, how miserably alone. Sometimes I recall that he gave
me his word that he would come to my home. Will he keep
his promise?

I love my home enormously. I always love to keep it
neat. In mother's house it was an irksome task. There
were too many people and mother was also a bit disorganised.
If someone scribbled on the wall or threw papers in the yard,
she did not care. Any village Sanskrit pandit could come

and squat on the sofa and stain the upholstery and then
the very next day a primly dressed European scholar would
be visiting father. I used to get exhausted cleaning and
rearranging the house. Here I get full scope. My house
sparkles like an ornament. I polish the wooden floor with
scented wax: it dazzles and catches my shadow. I clean the
glass, polish the door knobs, the curios. I paint the flower
pots red once a month. In my kitchen all the pots and
jars are well arranged, spotless. Everything is in its place.
In my ten-acre compound every plant is trimmed. On the
dining table the polished cutlery dazzles. In the morning
the bearer knocks at our door with a tea tray. For breakfast
he plugs the coffee percolater and the aroma fills the house.
The old *mali* with one tooth missing gives me a smile when
he enters with heaps of flowers for the vases—there are at
least twenty vases to be arranged. Sometimes I go to
the garden myself and select the flowers; his large cutter snaps
the stalks from the tree. I never liked Japanese flower
decoration—it is artificial, it is like a toy. And we Bengalees
have little idea of flower arrangement—look how they tie
a bouquet with wire at Bowbazar. Horrible!

How long can a delicate flower stand such tyranny?
Or they stick a variety of flowers in a rickety vase. I was
amazed to see a flower arrangement by an English lady: she
put almost a whole branch in one corner. I watch and I learn.
I have learnt many things in the Thakur household; I now
learn much from the British ladies. I use the plural but
actually among the four families of officers living in that
lonely spot there is only one who is a proper housewife.
I need not speak about the rest. They kill their time over
tennis, bridge, drinking, dancing, and intermittent flirtation
with each other's husbands. They care for nothing else.
Their menfolk are ignorant and drunkards. Maybe in their
inner self they are as human as we are but I have not the
eye to see it, nor sensitivity enough to feel it. My mind has
become too fine; it shrinks in their company. I know this

is a fault.  Of course they see this fault from another point
of view—they are British, we are despicable natives—they
condescend to mix with us, invite us to balls and bridge—
this should be enough to gratify us.  Instead of that I resent
almost every overture.  Is it immoral to play bridge?  Of course
not, but it is certainly wasting one's time.  I crave for the
company of someone with whom I can exchange my views.
That part of my mind where I need a comrade is as bleak
as a stretch of desert.  And now I ponder if I mix too much
with these people, my personality may change.  I know
I feel attracted by their exuberance.  If there are five persons
together, they can grow riotous in revelry.  Their life attracts
me: that is precisely the reason why I must never be over-
friendly with them.  I know my overwhelming emptiness
is a potential danger so I hold the helm strongly and steer
myself on the correct path.  I know no one can harm my
husband, but I can be harmed.  I have many weaknesses,
so I post a sentry in me who keeps vigil.

A clash is imminent over the issue of drinking alcohol.
I am not going to be defeated.  I am not the person to yield
to pressure and gradually follow in their footsteps.  They
say a person is known by the company he keeps.  I am a
different bird; I will not flock with them.  This will certainly
be considered bigotry now-a-days.  It was even then, but
I did spend a lot of energy to stop the inflow of alcohol into
my home.  Had I not been so insistent, my husband, who
might or might not himself abstain, would have arranged for
hospitality.  He had already stored a few bottles and was
hesitating—but I put my foot down firmly.  Even for our
wedding not a single foreign item was bought   Not even
a mosquito net or a fountain pen.  We struggled with a
Guptoo fountain pen and would not touch a Parker and
now, "Should we indulge in drinking revelry with foreign
liquor?" I asked.  My husband laughed at my vehemence.
"Otherwise they will think us niggardly."

"Why?  We can serve *sandesh*."

"They don't touch *sandesh* in the evening."

But I was determined not to yield. I did not know what I was in for, because I was flouting the British. They were the superiors, our rulers. Even a friend gets annoyed if someone stands away from the group. He might take it as an aspersion on himself. Everyone, in whatever he does, secretly seeks the approval of others.

I told the servant boy to bring out the bottles from the cupboard and throw them in the running brook. He looked at me wide-eyed. Waste this dazzling brilliant liquor in the water! Gurkhas, both men and women, have an unsatiable thirst for strong spirits. Next day the women from the plantation came to cut grass and, hidden between the tall reeds, sunk in the clay, they found a most unexpected treasure. The Gurkhas have a wonderful trait—they are intrinsically honest. They won't touch a thing that does not belong to them. You could leave your house unlocked for days together. No one will slip in and remove any thing. I was really mistaken in thinking I was alone—it took me a long time to know these people. These honest hard-working simple folk were like trees to me, because I was a prisoner myself. Prisoner of my philosophy, and a host of other things. It took time to get my eyes trained to watch the meaningful panorama of human life that was so vibrant around me. With eyes inverted I lived a life of my own. The table boy asked, "You have thrown away the bottles, madam, can they have them?" Then with my expressed consent they gulped the scotch whisky neat, bottle after bottle. The undiluted liquor did what it was meant to do. They had to be carried to hospital, the whole lot of them! My ill fame as a prude travelled fast.

For their dinner parties robust British planters with a a cockney twang come from various plantations, sometimes driving thirty-odd miles. As the night deepened I watched them change. Downing glass after glass of frothy sparkling liquid they went into a state of stupor—their personality

changed—some who had no voice began to sing in husky
off-key—some sat nodding drowsily—some went and perched
jovially on the arm of a chair where a woman was sitting,
some suddenly squatted at my feet and with voice choked
with emotion declared "I will be your dear," punning on
"deer" because I had a pet.  I could never fathom why
mature men decide to turn insane wilfully.  All this made
me unhappy—I was thrown into a world where I did not
belong.  I watched them just as a clean person watches
the unclean, the awakened the sleeping, and the emancipated
the person in bondage.

       After dinner, past midnight, we two, husband and wife,
return home.  The servant boy walks ahead of us with a
hurricane lamp and a stick    There is other noise except
our footfalls; dry leaves crackle as they get crushed.  In that
calm wilderness that sound alone strikes the hillside, and
deepens the sense of forlornness.  Over our heads between
the small opening of the canopy of thick foliage moonbeams
fall on the road below, making a mosaic of light and shade.
I know exactly what flowers and trees are in which bend —
where snatches of fragrance float in or where the glow
worms kept a bit of forest ablaze.  They say some snakes
also have a fragrance akin to that of new rice.  Snakes
abound in this region.  We are no more afraid of them.
They sneak away as soon as they sense our presence.
Of course the python does not flee: it is too slow to move.
Unless you tread on it a python will not stretch out to attack
anyone but it will widen its eyes.  That's why that man
died—the man who stumbled on the coiled serpent under the
tree.  He began to run helter-skelter in the opposite direction.
Actually, attracted by its magnetic gaze, he should have turned
immobile or gone towards it.  Luckily he could run away,
and running two miles up the hill, he fell dead at my door step.
He died of sheer fright.  Bears seldom come out on our way,
because they are scared of us.  But the "bread man" who
walks eighteen miles through the dense forest on a steep

narrow foot track, to bring supplies from the town, often
meets one.   He devises many tricks to drive away the fierce
animals.   One day as he was walking bent under the load
of stores in the basket at his back taped to his head, he
saw a dark figure looming among the foliage.   Sensing
danger he threw the basket down the slope.   The bear ran
after the moving object, leaving the static one behind!   The
"bread man" was saved—but not the bread!   We call him
"bread man" but he brings everything from the town
eighteen miles away, as nothing is available here—neither
fish, meat nor medicine.   The place is like a leaf from a
children's story book.   I was specially fascinated by the
terrible owl *kiorala* with wide, round eyes; it can kill and
eat up a big live cat in minutes, and also the flying squirrel
with its soft downy bat-like wings.   How different is the
world into which I have stepped from the populous city and
its urban pleasures.

I am gradually becoming one with the surroundings: the
primal forest and the primitive tribal man are entering slowly
into my consciousness.   The progress is slow, because we
don't know how to enjoy ourselves like the Europeans.
They are agile; we are sedate.   On a holiday they casually
sling a gun over their backs or take a fishing rod and go out
for game, their servants following them with basket loads of
food and drink.   They eat and drink to the full, and this
man flirts with that man's wife behind the bush.   Oh, they
miss nothing here.   Even in this godforsaken place they
know how to enjoy themselves.

Can we two pandits fall into this pattern?   We suffer
to see a meek beautiful deer riddled with bullets.   Yet
slowly we begin to learn from them.   Indeed there is much
to learn.   They have a great quality, a great ability to adjust
themselves to the most unfavourable circumstances.

Barring alcohol and deer hunting, I began to enjoy the
wild life.   On every off-day I would collect a group and go
out on a picnic.   Riding miles on the forest track, we go

further and further away to the bank of some lonely spring
or near some mountain stream.   The trees in this forest
stand erect and vie with each other to get a glimpse of the
sun.   They want to outgrow the hills that have imprisoned
them and seem to rest their heads on the blue sky.   As I move
on through the forest fragrant with a musty smell of wet
moss that hangs from the branches like the matted hair of
some lonely maiden, I feel a strange detachment—like that
of the ascetic prince Buddha who left his kingdom.   "Riding
on a lone horse," he said, "I shall enter the deep forest."

Where am I going, I ask myself, and who are these
people? They are all shadow figures.   Did I ever seek this
life? God, even the insects get companions, but you have
denied me one!

My fatigue disappears as, turning the bend, I suddenly
meet the gurgling mountain brook, flowing on pebbles.   Its
rushing water gets blocked by large boulders here and forms
in pools.   We splash in these cool clear pools and bathe.

There is a plant called *titapati*, the "bitter leaf"; we
crush the fragrant leaves and throw the pulp in the water.
The fish get tipsy with the fragrant spicy water and behave
erratically like any human animal and become our easy prey.
We light a fire with dry branches and fry the fish on an
improvised stove.   Large boulders like little hillocks stand
in the middle of the gushing river, the water whirls round them
frothy and white.   Sitting on a boulder I feel like reciting a
poem: *Sagarika*, "Daughter of the Ocean", written by
Rabindranath, addressing the spirit of the East Indies, specially
Java.   "Bathing in the ocean with your wet hair flowing,
you sit on the pebble-strewn shore."

"Jack do you know there is a country called Java?"

"Of course I do.   There are large tea plantations there."

"Oh! That's why you know.   Do you know Indian
civilisation travelled there thousands of years ago? It also
reached Siam."

"Never heard of such a thing.   Was there anything like

civilization in India before the British came?"

Now, what conversation can one expect to have with these people! My husband would not easily open his mouth nor would he enter into an argument, but even he got exasperated sometimes and blurted out one or two home-truths.

Jack said, "You two are educated intelligent people—why don't you get converted? How will you be saved if you don't become Christians?"

My husband replied, "We do not want to be in the minority."

"Meaning?"

"Do you know the population of the world?"

"No, how much?"

"Two thousand million. Do you know how many are Christians?"

Jack remained puzzled. My husband said, "May be six hundred million. Is it not better to be with the majority?"

Gradually people began to visit us. Responding to my invitations, relatives came during the vacations. Whoever visits this side of the world has to come to us because of my solicitude. My husband's work is also expanding, and our guests are pleased to visit us though the market is eighteen miles away. I keep my cupboard full. I love to treat my guests to a variety of food which I cook myself. I have made cooking a hobby now. My guests enjoy their stay. They get tea in fancy pots by their bed, shoes by the door polished, and clean garments, washed and ironed every day. I cover their beds with silk sheets and sprinkle lavender. I try to make a good impression on my guests so that once they are here they may never forget the experience. For the first few days everyone is elated—"How lavishly you live—a Class One hotel"—"What scenic beauty!" But after a week they feel the weight of loneliness bearing down on them. Then they seek the least pretext to leave.

My unending energy cannot be fully used up in house-work alone. So I am learning to rear chicken. A new

method of poultry farming had just been introduced. I watch
with trepidation the combs of leghorns, the plumes of the
fat Rhode Island Red. I am also trying to run an apiary.
I prefer to read the fascinating "biography" of honey bees
over and over again; I care less to handle them for fear of
getting stung.

There are so many varieties of insects in this forest land.
They are nothing to us human beings, but their lives are no
less important in the pattern of things. Sometimes I sit for
hours in the garden just watching an active coloured beetle
or a caterpillar in an unending search for some unknown
wealth. There are some plants here which are phosphorescent
and throw a glow around them. Once father told me he had
read in the *Puranas* about glowing plants. He said, "Search
for these." I have seen these incandescent heavenly plants.
There are some creatures that carry lights, one row of ten
on the spine and two rows on the two sides. Unbelievably
strange creatures! How many multicoloured multisized
butterflies flutter around! They blow around in the cool breeze
like little petals from my rose garden. There is another little
object as gay who romps around trying to catch the winged
creatures: she is my little daughter who arrived in 1936.
She gives life to the song, "With what joy you have spread
your wings, O little firefly."

My main activity here is farming. I grow vegetables.
I have with great care cultivated potatoes for six years; my
yield was twenty times more than the seeds put in. I used
to get really puffed up at my success with potatoes. Some
may consider this a let-down. But I am convinced that
even a poet can go into ecstasies over potato-growing. A
tiny seed is planted. We never know what is happening
inside the ground. We only raise the earth round it, water
it, watch its green foliage; but when in due time, removing
the soil, we see the shrunk little seed still there, surrounded
by so many round robust fruits which have taken life from
it, we remain amazed by the wonder of the sight. I remove

the earth slowly and one by one the potatoes slide down—the
whole afternoon I stand with the gardener and collect potatoes.
When he pours out the little round objects with his big sinewy
hands and they fall over my delicate tender cupped palms, what
a picture it makes—van Gogh should have painted *Potato
Collectors*.

I remain surprised, eternally amazed. One can find joy
everywhere in every act. Watch that little creature, an exact
replica of a dahlia leaf—no one would guess that it is not a
leaf till it moves. But if there is the slightest stir it will at
once become still, in an effort of self-preservation. Unless
one sees, one would never believe that an insect can be made
as an exact imitation of a leaf. Strangely enough, when it
dies, it withers like a leaf. Nature's mimicry is marvellous.
That insect alone is a wonder that makes me sit for hours
thinking over the eternal enigma. My eyes and mind are
getting gradually trained to watch nature around me, so rich
with colour, fragrance, and form, and throbbing with life.

Yet—that "yet" will never leave me. Sometimes at
midnight leaving my warm bed beside my husband I come
out and sit in the verandah. I think of others. Most of the
people I know seem to be happy with their lot, why can't
I be? I have everything that one can seek or expect. Why
this interminable emptiness—as if I could not perform what
I was to perform, as if I could not speak what I wanted to
speak, as if I could not get what I was aspiring for.

This unspecified desire remains ever elusive and
unsatiated. This is certainly not a normal state. It brings
in a whiff of despair from one knows not where. Yet I am
like that. I once read a poem which describes my state of
mind at that time. "Listen, if the stars twinkle in the sky
then there must be someone who wants to see them. There
must be someone who says 'Let them burn'. Someone who
says 'What is that small point, is it a jewel?' Attacked by
the dust storm of hot mid-day he kisses the outstretched hand
of God and says, 'I shall not live without a star'.

In the solitude of the cool night I stand alone, and
raising my face upward, I search for my star.

If anyone presumes that my feelings now have any
connection with the incident I began this story with, he will
be completely wrong.   My feeling of desolation had nothing
to do with the Mircea affair.   I was not seeking anyone but
myself—that part of me which could not express itself used
to wring my heart with an unnamed anguish, whereas the
other part of me was happily engaged in its circle of daily
life.   In the evening the servant boy would pull the shutters
down and draw the curtains.   He would light a fire in the
fireplace with big round logs.   We two would sit facing the
fire sniffing the spicy scent of resin emitted by the burning
pine wood.   I sat with my knitting and my husband sat
fingering a magazine or the two days' stale newspaper.
At that time I never thought of anything fine or poetic, nor
was I then grieving for any person.   My thoughts were
centred generally round such matters as my husband's
promotion, injustices done by his boss, my little girl's
steadfast refusal to take food, and so on.   Or I would think
of some new recipe or a new design for a piece of furniture.

As I try to write the story of my life I can very well see
that there is no story at all.   How can there be? Stories
emerge from contact with life.   The contact and conflict of
human experience and variety of efforts give colour to our
life's picture.   What story can nature evolve? Many incidents
occur that are fierce but one cannot make stories out of them.
For instance, every year forest fires rage.   One usually hears
about forest fires but how many have seen them? In summer
the leaves dry up and become ready fuel, they brush against
each other and kindle a fire.   Or some unmindful forester
drops a spark—the dry leaves catch it—they begin to
smoulder, then suddenly leap into flame.   When the whole
hillside becomes a huge firework, it can be seen from a great
distance.   The bamboos crack, making a vicious clatter, and
the angry fire-god jumps from one branch to another.   Death

cries of trapped animals rend the air. Once the forest catches
fire it cannot be extinguished. One has to clear the forest
around it to check its onslaught. My husband fights fires
—it can't be done by the illiterate—it needs intelligent effort.
Every day we hear of some events arising out of ignorance.
Of these, one stirred me deeply. Two men were cutting
the steep side of a hill to widen the road. They dug and
dug, making the ground loose under a huge jutting boulder
looming over them. Eventually it tumbled down and the
two were buried alive under it. My husband told me later
that he could see only one hand sticking out from under
that stony grave. I did not see it, yet the picture of a lone
dead hand haunted me for long.

I have mentioned the primal forest, the forest that was
never planted. The same trees or their progeny thrived
here from time immemorial. We have plants here which
were found during the "coal age"—the leaves look like ferns
but they are trees—on a single trunk the leaves spread out
like an umbrella. There are such dense forests here that
no human being has ever set foot inside. We are now
approaching one: the trees will be felled to reclaim the land
needed for a new plantation. They go in search of land on
elephants. Elephants are faultless climbers, they don't need
a track like ponies do. Now the trees are being hacked.
Huge treess felled with an ordinary axe. Often serious
accidents occur. But the stamina of these hill tribes is
invulnerable. They can bear, without a twitch, their bones
sawed without anaesthesia. From the fancy sophisticated
atmosphere of a great city I have come to spend my best days
in their company.

In this godforsaken place there is no telephone, not
even a telegraph office. Telegrams arrive on a pony from
the railway station in the valley six miles away. There is
a thatch-roofed hut to serve as a hospital where a quack
presides.

To reach this place one has to drive up on a narrow

steep road winding in hair-pin bends for six miles.  The car sometimes becomes perpendicular and on some very narrow turns one has not more than two inches space on the slope side.

Still I am courageous.  It is the courage of inexperience which makes a fool rush, so I am inviting Rabindranath Thakur to come to my home.  He begins to form an idea from my letters that I have kept my promise; now he will have to keep his.  Mother's letter has made me even more enthusiastic.  She wrote to say, "We went to see the drama *Chandalika*.  After the play was over, when we went to meet the Poet he asked me, 'Where did you send her away, Sudha? Amrita can't see anything like this any more'."  Mother had added, "I felt that seeing us he was sad and missed you."

After receiving this letter I wrote to him again.  I don't write to him regularly.  He is already over-worked and he cannot, however busy he may be, refrain from replying to letters.  He has to write so many unnecessary letters for the sake of courtesy and kindness.  I don't want to add to his troubles.  But now I am writing such letters as would make him feel that I am the happiest person in the world.

During the two or three months' wait after the date of his arrival was fixed, a tide of joy billowed around us. Our relatives and friends were astounded at my good fortune. Some of our relatives wanted to join us now; they would like to push in and if possible oust me!  But I was firm. At last, at long last, I am going to be rewarded for the penance I have been going through from time unknown. I will not get jostled out by spurious elements.  The son and daughter-in-law of the Poet have written to say, "We are sending father to you.  We are not coming.  You have wholesale and exclusive rights."

Yes, I do want exclusive rights!  We re-do the already decorated house.  Brushing and scrubbing; flowering shrubs pruned, each little weed froked out from the grass, the lawn mower whining away,  We change the curtains, paint the doors.  "In my golden temple I have spread out a lotus

seat." All my fatigue of loneliness has vanished. That
brook over there which with its continuous splash used to
make me jittery—its nagging noise has become a sweet
murmur now. And that rasping cicada which with its
continuous drone used to drive a screwdriver in my head
suddenly produces a melodious chirrup. The breeze that
used to blow through the silver fir trees bringing in the
mournful sighs of the lonely forest has now begun to play
the golden vina: "Come, O come to my heart, O master of my
heart."

From 1938 to 1940 was the light-year, the timeless years
of my life. I will not write now about that period. I am
tracing the line of the internal current of my life. I realise
the relativity of time in my experience. In these three years,
the time between his arrival, departure, and arrival again,
remains continuous. It is an unbroken time which remains
steadfast, pouring nectar over my everunsatiated life and
making my insignificant existence meaningful and sublime.

He enjoys our household. I get up early and get ready.
He sits facing the east waiting for the sun, his namesake, to
come up. Sitting on the floor besides his chair I join him in
silent contemplation. Thus begins my day. It ends after
I have tucked him to bed and drawn the mosquito net.

With him in our house every day is like a festival. In
this unapproachable place a car-load of people may arrive
any moment without previous notice. How can they
intimate beforehand? There is no telephone or telegraph
office. So I have to arrange their meals quickly. The
loneliness has blown away from this mountain village—as
if a musical soirée is going on in the house all the time—
not only for me but for every one. My husband has also
opened up a great deal more than before. His jovial punning
comments are more frequent. The air round us has become
salubriant with the ozone of happiness. We walk a little
above the ground, almost like levitation.

I do his work for him: I copy his writings, dust his

furniture, do his bed. I polish his silver plate and brush
his slippers. The hordes of servants, specially those who
have accompanied him, are scandalized. They have not seen
a demented person like me!

On the back of his working room, is his bath-room,
attached to the bed room. Once I was washing his clothes
in the bathroom, facing the open door towards the garden.
Sri A., his secretary, saw me and and approached me, "What is
this? Why are you washing the clothes yourself? Where are
the servants?" Greatly embarrassed, I tried to speed up
my work. Saying "Stop it, stop it", he called out,
"Where are you all?"

"Please go away. I do it every day. I will do in now,"
I said.

"Every day you do his washing?" he asked, wide-eyed.

"Yes, does that hurt you?"

"He will be annoyed if he comes to know of it."

"But how will he know?"

"Because I will tell him." Saying this, he opened the
door towards the working room. "Look, Sir, Amrita Devi
is washing your clothes and won't listen to me."

I stood up, leaving my work, flushing up to the ears,
feeling like a culprit who has been caught red-handed.
Reclining on an easy chair, he was engrossed in a book.
At this sudden disturbance he removed the book kept it
turned up on his lap and smiled tenderly   "A, what do
you know of all this? Shut the door." To me he said,
"Carry on your work, Amrita. Now I know why my clothes
are so spotless these days!"

I am sure it was quite the opposite. I couldn't have
washed better than the servants, but that was how he
rewarded me.

He came to our home four times in three years. The
fullness of the gift that these three years brought swept away
all my sense of loss. I did not at that time fully realise the
value of this gift. It was not an easy job to come to this

unapproachable place at the age of seventy-nine ignoring
the hazards of a dangerous journey. Our near relatives, even
much younger than him, had not dared do it. But the ever-
young poet ignored the physical impediments. Into this
primordial forest-land the world entered with the "poet of
the world." I came in close company with illustrious men,
I listened to the fascinating stories of different continents
and men. Bergson, whose system of philosopy I had read,
but never realised that he was a living talking human being,
began to talk with me. Bernard Shaw with his mischievous
sneer, Romain Rolland with his grave deepset eyes—all the
faces from the covers of books became my friends. I saw
scenes from an unknown world. I used to hear most about
Russia. He had an insatiable curiosity to know more about
the experiment that was going on there. I saw the paper
*Moscow News* for the first time and was surprised to find
him so patient and eager about a country much criticised
by others. He made me translate three articles from *Moscow
News* regarding the advancement of women, and these
appeared in different journals. A sense of fulfilment
elated me.

My husband now talked much more than before. Once
I asked him, "Are you not jealous that I am so absorbed
in him? Please tell me. You should be."

"Should I? You are what you are. Why should I like
you to change?"

"Still, that would only be usual."

He made a pun on the word and said, "What 'use' would
that be? Would I have been jealous if you were Mirabai?"

The Poet his fascinated by our home. He calls my
husband "the perfect gentleman". The serene nature outside
and friendship in the home—the two together completed
a circle.

One morning as he was sitting stooped over his writing
table I came and stood behind him. After my bath my hair
was loose and wet. The spicy cool air was stirring the single

stalk of a hollyhock that danced in the sparkling morning
sun.  A little distance away, bordering the fish pool where
I was cultivating a new hobby, was a row of bright yellow
tiger lily.  He gazed at that colourful line.  Suddenly he
said, "You know, Amrita, you have built up a wonderful
home.  I knew you would.  When I decided to come here
many wondered whether it would suit me.  I knew it would;
otherwise why should she call me, I thought.  It's a beautiful
home, flowing with ease like that singing brook.  Do you
know what I like most here?  That you two never quarrel.
This peaceful understanding between you two is very beautiful.
How I watch R and P when they start fighting.  They go on
and on eventually P gets defeated and becomes silent, but R
won't stop.  She comes back again and again like a snake
attacking its victim."

"Why don't you scold them?"

"I do.  But with no results.  To make a beautiful home
is a work of art—it's a kind of poem.  In this land of flowers,
with a flower-like little girl, you have made a happy home.
I am very pleased to see it, Amrita, very pleased."  Holding
the back of his chair, I stood breathless.  I must tell him the
truth, here and now.

"It is not true.  I have been cheating you."

"What did you say?"  Putting his hand back he pulled
me in front.  "What did you say?  Young lady, whom are
you cheating?"

"Everyone.  I have achieved nothing.  Half of it is
just sham show.  I have no companion in my empty nights."

"Why this self-mortification?"  He spoke tenderly.  "How
much one can give oneself is limited by space, time, and the
person concerned.  What one could not get, the unfulfilled,
one should not keep on regretting that—what is in one's hand
is enough."  Then he stretched out his hand, pointed to the
row of lilies, and said, "That you have done this is enough.
Madam, I am grateful to you for this, very grateful."  In
spite of all this sagacious talk, in his heart of hearts he fully

realised how heavily loneliness here could hang on a person.

He told me something that evening which I have ever since preserved as a precious jewel in my heart.  We were sitting in the verandah.  The tall dark trees on the hillside were standing like ghosts, getting blacker every minute by sucking the darkness of the deepening evening.  Everyone else had gone out for an evening stroll, so the stillness was even more deep.  Suddenly he spoke: "I want to tell you something, Amrita, if it is any consolation to you.  I would like to say, in my long life I have received many gifts, yet the gift of respect, worship, and love all mixed together that you have offered me is something that is rare for me.  I also needed it before my final goodbye from this world, otherwise I wouldn't have come so many times."

Work is the best companion of man.  That's what the Poet used to tell me.  But to create one's own field of work is not easy.  Once the Poet was watching the labourers going up and down the road with loaded ponies.  Suddenly he enquired about the number of coolies working in the plantation.  I told him about five to six thousand.

"Why are you lonely then?"  he said.  "Call them to your home, go near them, solve their problems, they certainly need friends—be their friend."

We arranged a grand "function" on his birthday and invited illiterate labourers to our home.  This probably was a unique event in those days, when such mixing among the "superiors" and the "inferiors" in an industrial area or plantation was unthinkable.  In all the tea plantations, the labourers, that is the coolies, could not enter the compound of an officer with shoes on.  If a coolie was riding a pony, he had to get down respectfully as soon as he noticed the topi of a sahib.  Richard once whipped a person because he did not dismount.  In this society I found a new job, a new direction to seek deliverance.

A fight ensued with the Britishers who were never happy with us.  As the Freedom Movement proceeded they grew

more and more sullen and stiff.  A silent battle raged between
us.  Once my husband's boss asked him, "Have you noticed
that your wife is getting rather friendly with the coolies?"

"Yes."

"What do you propose to do about it?"

"Nothing; she is a free person."

"What about discipline?"

"I have noticed no indiscipline."

"Then I must talk to her."

"I would rather not, Sir.  The reaction might be sharp."

I am not going into the details of the price we had to pay
for all this.  I am only mentioning my gain.  At that time,
in this desolate little village barring the days of the disastrous
famine of 1941, there was never any dearth of food.  But
men have other needs.  I began to cater to these.  Our doors
opened wider and wider for festivals, "functions", dance and
music.  The next fourteen years of my stay there became
meaningful.

I came to realise that even among the illiterate and
the shabby and the poor there are people who have fine
sensibility and deep understanding, who are involved in the
search for the unknown.  There are, among the lowest class,
people who have music in their throats and poetry in their
mind.  Whenever I noticed the spark hidden beneath the ash,
my mind filled up with an unearthly joy.  I still preserve
an art object made by one of these men who used to put in
eight hours of hard manual labour.  Actually I came near
the source wherein is born what we call folk-art, folk-song,
folk-culture—the untutored, pure creative spirit.

Being a globe-trotter I have since seen many nations
and races, but in innocence and faithfulness that hill-tribe
surpasses many.  At least that's my feeling    I have noticed
an excellence of human qualities among them which one
rarely comes across among the sophisticated.

When I went to make my home on a tiny hill perched
on an arm of the mightly Himalayas I came with a sense of

emptiness in me, but when I left the place after twenty two years, that emptiness was gone. I came back with a full life—full of affection, love and friendship. The strong Gurkhas who can endure their bones sawed without anaesthesia made our departure glorious by their touching tears.

Exactly eleven years after Rama came to us, that is twelve years after Mircea's departure, my mother's life became a shambles. The decay that started ten years ago slowly and steadily undermined the edifice on which a family is built. Suspicion lurked; fidelity and trust were gone. Mother struggled pathetically for ten years to keep up father's image as one almost as faultless as a god—but people talked. Innuendoes, and sometimes pointed and direct attacks, were directed at our vulnerable position. Mother bore with patience the immense anguish that constantly made her heart bleed. Her children were all on her side but no one could share her suffering. In spite of her unwavering loyalty to her husband, her constant endeavour to cover up his faults, she could only postpone the ultimate collapse that happened in 1941. Father left her with her four minor children to fend for herself. Our beautiful home that had floated on the crest of poetry and philosophy crashed on the rugged rocks of a mundane world. With only the residential house to lean upon, she had to face a merciless world. The depth of cruelty that a broken home has to suffer is immeasurable. Even her right to the house was challenged. Can vindictiveness have its roots in something that was once love, I used to ask myself. However, I was never as soft as mother was, or as kind. I rode on a lion and spreading my ten arms I defended her right to have the house. Strangely, our so-called sympathisers, who so long used to push wedges to split up the family by their gossip and scandal-mongering, now began to wag their tongues again. This time they sang a different tune. Certainly the wife was no match for such an erudite

person.   He needed a proper companion.   The avaricious
wife and her daughters are fighting for the house!   Lashing
fiery remarks blew about, making the atmosphere murky and
sooty.   Very few realised that the minors were being deprived
of their rightful inheritance and no arrangements were made
for even their sustenance.   Mother was the weaker party.
She had neither money nor fame or scholarship.   Her only
support was her grown-up daughters, so they also became the
targets of attack.

 Those who have gone through the different tests that
life is cruel enough to hold out for some all too often, know
that there are events which are not as they appear to be.
The same love that can be an act of worship and elevate one
spiritually has another diabolic counterpart which can crush
the altar on which all that is best in man is placed.   Both
look exactly the same, from the outside, as if they are twins,
but one gives life, another takes it away.

 My father, immensely talented and universally respected
for his scholarship, could have risen higher and higher.
Instead, he lost his family, peace of mind, prestige and respect.
After ten years of separation from his devoted wife and
six children, estranged from friends and relations, his
personality mutilated, he died in disgrace.   We have heard
that before his death he told several persons secretly that
he wanted to come back to mother to seek her forgiveness.
The news reached us too late.   That was the final tragedy
of my greatly talented father and virtuous mother.

 The little boat of my life is floating on strong currents,
knocking against many events.   I am no more a little girl—
I face the world with as much strength as it demands of me.
I have hardened.   The tender skin that could feel the finest
touch has now, by continuous friction, become rough.   I am
now a person of action, and worldly-wise.   Yet even now
I am not satiated by my housework or by tending to the
family-affairs alone.   Sometimes I am seized with an intense
melancholy.   My old dissatisfaction comes back.   I am now

far removed from the world of letters. There is an
over-crowding there. I get no opportunities to write. I have
come back from my secluded world after twenty-two years
to find all roads blocked. So I pick up any work that seems
worthwhile. The ill fame and insult that I had to suffer get
fully compensated by the respect and honour that I receive.
So all in all a harmony is achieved.

In 1953 I went to Europe with my husband, who was
on a mission and I on a pleasure trip. For the last twenty
years I had not thought about Mircea at all. Maybe
sometimes a self censure passed through my mind—my life
would have been cleaner had not such a thing happened. But
can that trivial affair of my childhood affect a mature person
like me? I had often consoled myself with such thoughts.

I met father's student Hiranmoy in England. He had
settled there with his English wife. I could not recognise
him, he looked so European. Suddenly, he asked me,
"Do you remember Mircea Euclid?" I remained silent. I
wondered what was the need of asking such a strange
question. He continued, "He was dedicated a book to you."

"How many children do you have?" I countered. That
ended the discussion. It made no impression on me.

We were touring Europe, speedily moving from place
to place. We met a professor and his wife at Paris. His
name was Nicholi Stanescu. I cannot remember where
I met them first. I can only recall a somewhat large sitting
room, almost bare, with three couches in one corner. They
had invited us to tea. We sat taking about their country
which was also Mircea's. They were exiles. Paris is full of
such refugees from eastern Europe. They were talking
about their difficulties. The sufferings of these exiles were
limitless. As I sat listening to the atrocities of a war-mad
Europe, I kept thinking about Mircea. Who knows whether
he was dead or alive—dead in a concentration camp,
butchered or starved. Should I ask them, I thought; then
I checked myself. Why should I care if he is dead or alive.

Yet I didn't want him dead. In this wide world I still hoped
to meet him once, if only to ask him why he had deceived me.

But did he really deceive? One part of my mind said,
"Father turned him out, what could he have done?" Did I
not see his face seething with agony when he said "good-bye"?
But the other part that remained murky with suspicion
replied, "The hunter of Europe, could he not write even a
letter?" "But," the soliloquy went on, "what need was there
then to roam about in the forests and go through so much
suffering?" All through my life such arguments went on
often in my mind for and against him. There is solace in
trust and anguish in suspicion. I did not want to go through
it all over again. Picking up a sandwich I casually asked
Mrs. Stanescu, "Do you know a writer named Euclid?"

"Certainly. He has written many books on Indian
philosophy."

"Is that so? Can you show me one?"

"Yes, of course." She rose and brought out a fairly
large book on "Yoga". Leafing through the book I was
shocked to see the dedication. It was dedicated to my
father. "To my revered guru Narendranath Sen". Well
then, had he contacts with father after all that happened?
Isn't he really a Kacha once again? A careerist like Kacha
himself. I realised then why he did not write to me. It was
more necessary to write the book on Yoga. It was necessary
to become a specialist in Indian philosophy. "Greed of fame
and erudition," I told myself. After ages my heart began
to burn again. My lips quivered. I pressed them with my
teeth; blood made my mouth salty. Suddenly looking up
I found Madame Stanescu watching me intently with
inquisitive eyes. She asked, "Is your name Amrita?"

"Yes, why?"

"Well, then we know you. You are Euclid's first flame!"
The lady began to laugh. I flushed with rage. I said to
myself, "Not flame, but ash." I threw a glance at my
husband who sat talking with the professor. I could not

guess whether he had heard us. Nor did I feel like pursuing
the topic. Enough is enough, I said, his name is not fit to
be uttered. A selfish insincere cad! After twenty years I
came to know of him but, the knowledge began to gnaw
at my heart.

We went on a sightseeing tour in Italy. Making a hectic
trip around Rome, Florence and Venice, we returned to the
south of France. What a wonderful country! We two,
husband and wife, were enjoying the trip immensely—only
sometimes I felt sad about the little boy I had left behind.

Coming back to Paris we booked a hotel near the
Champs Elysées. After a week when the bill was brought to
us my eyes popped out. ' Oh, this is beyond our means!"
So we changed over to a hotel in the the Latin Quarter. We
stayed there for ten days. A man lived next to our room
whom I often encountered on the stairs and we exchanged
greetings by nodding. In these ten days we hardly talked,
through we could have. Had we talked then, who knows
this story might have turned out differently.

The day we were leaving for England I was sitting on a
large sofa kept on the landing near the Reception. Our
baggage was being brought out and heaped in a corner. My
husband was settling the bill at the counter, when that man,
on his way out, suddenly stopped near the luggage. I
watched him; it seemed he was reading my name on the box.
Then he came near me and after hesitating a little said, "I
am Ion Popescu. Are you Amrita?"

I was startled. My heart began to hammer almost
audibly. "Why do you ask?" I replied.

"I pay you my homage," he said and lifting up my hand
planted a kiss on it. Then I knew to which country he
belonged.

In a moment my world began to whirl. "Can you tell
me," I asked abruptly, "where does the writer of that book
live?"

"Here in Paris, only two blocks away from this place."

"Only two blocks?" "Yes." His lips broke into a grin.
"O God," I said to myself. "Can I now go and catch him?
can I tell him, 'perfidious man, you have purchased learning
at the cost of truth. You may have become a pundit but
you are not wise. You are like a wooden ladle that, though it
remains soaked in honey, does not taste it.' I can tell him.
'Mircea, you are saved. Because you have no truth in you,
you don't have to suffer but why does not my truth die?'

The man stood staring at me. "Would you like to
come with me and meet him?"

"No, but if I write a letter will you please . . ."

"Oh yes, I certainly will." Enthusiastically he ran to get
some paper. I wrote a short letter which ran somewhat like
this—"Mircea, after many years I heard about you. How
are you? Have you married? I am touring Europe with my
husband. I have a daughter and a son. I would be extremely
happy to meet you. But we are leaving Paris now—in a little
time we shall reach Dover. I am giving you my London
address. I shall be glad if you come. Come, please."
My husband approached me with some problem he was
having at the counter. I gave him the letter and said, "Do
you remember I once spoke to you about a foreign student
of my father? He is here, so I am inviting him to London."
He glanced through the letter and said, "It will be nice if he
comes." Then he went back. Popescu was standing behind
me. He placed his hand on my shoulder tenderly. "Write a
good letter, madam. You are trembling all over."

"I am not trembling—I am shivering—it's a cold day
today." I folded the letter and, as I was sealing it, he said,
"Why didn't you write a good letter, madam? I don't
understand why your letter needs to be censored."

"Oh, no, not that. I wanted my husband to check my
English. You know my appropriate prepositions are never
appropriate."

"Is that so?" he winked. "Why not do something
inappropriate for once?"

We left for London. No reply came. I waited for a
week, then I gave up. For a few days my tears rolled down,
uncontrollable. My husband thought I was missing my son.
Then I forgot the incident.

We left our forest resort for good in 1954 and came
back to Calcutta. When I left this city twenty-two years ago
the ethos of the literary world was different. There was no
overcrowding as there is now. Talent was encouraged and
respected. No writer had to sell his soul to get an opportunity
to see his name in print, or to take a job in a publishing
house; nor did women-writers have to go and visit the bosses
at the journal's office, or be chummy with them. There
was no rush in the field of art, literature, or music. So talent
was free to pursue its natural course. In these twenty-two
years an intrinsic change has come in the world of letters.

As equality grows, quality diminishes. In the field of
learning, literature, art, and politics people are rushing in
like a river in spate. Persons who have no background,
who have not learnt to respect scholarship or art for their
own sake, persons who do not feel poetry but write for
showmanship, or for the benefit of the "masses," are crowding
this world. I feel estranged, I am a stranger here. Yet
people know me, respect me. My work and life are steadily
expanding, in spite of obstacles.

In 1956 I went to Europe again. This was the last time
I heard of him. In a large auditorium, when I was coming
down from the rostrum, a sprightly young girl, her face
framed with golden curls, approached me. "Are you Amrita?"

"You pronounce my name well," I said, surprised.

"Well, I know you."

Oh, do you? Then as if it spurted out from the deepest
subconscious, I heard myself saying, "Do you know Mircea
Euclid? Can you tell me where he is?"

The girl hesitated. "No, I know nobody of that name."
Then after a little time. "Yes, he is dead."

Sometimes the dead can give more solace than the living.

There is a kind of peace in death. It soothes all aches. Yet
the wound began to bleed again. So he is dead. The end.
Finality. Nothing remains after death. I have lost all
opportunities now to challenge him for his treachery. I had
thought so long that one day I would catch hold of him!

Whenever I think of him my mind splits into several
sections and a debate starts. The worldly mind where
the intellect is alert, the mind that deals with the problems
of the everyday world, says, "Certainly it was treachery. At one
snubbing from father he ran away with his tail between
his legs. He was no man. Who cares for his scholarship?
Character is greater than books." But the other mind
in me keeps on repeating, "Why are you so angry? Maybe
he has written but his letters have not reached you, or maybe
your letters have not reached him." There is still a third
mind in me which lies deep down; no arguments, no logic
can ever reach it. It says, "Can everything be explained only
by events and facts; can truth be realised by arguments?
Listen to the message that emanates from the soul, listen
in silence. Not through the ears, nor by the intellect, but
by the heart you will hear the echo of truth. He has not
deceived you."

Vera was watching me. I looked up, a little embarrassed
and asked, "When did he die and how?"

Vera said, "Oh, no. He has not actually died, but he is
dead to us. He has gone over to the fascists."

"Has he?" I chuckled. I could see him standing there,
with a butterfly moustache like Hilter's, opening the gas-chamber.
It suited him well. He is certainly competent in the job.
Has he not sent me there repeatedly by refusing steadfastly
to respond to my call?

After that I did not hear his name for two years. In
1958 I was doing some research work in a university. The
work was good for me. I feel fatigued if I am not occupied
and harnessed; I don't know then from where a devastating
feeling of emptiness attacks me. So I pick up any work

available.  The best was writing.  My mother lived nearby.
I was to stay with her till my work was done.

   One day, as I sat engrossed in my study, Satyen-babu
came in and sat down, reclining against a large cushion.
He began to talk about the time he had met me in Paris.
After a little scrappy conversation he suddenly blurted out,
"I read Euclid's book."  I remained silent.  I turned into
stone.  It happens like that whenever someone mentions his
name.  Has anyone abserved a stick insect?  It's a strange
creature.  It looks like a moving stem—it walks in long
strides on its elongated stick-like four feet, but if there is a
slight tremor anywhere, or if you touch it, it at once becomes
stiff and drops down like a dry branch.  Exactly that happens
to me when his name is mentioned.  My body of flesh and
blood changes into dead wood.  So it happened: I turned
into a wooden doll.  Satyen-babu continued, "Reading his
book I realised you loved Rabindranath."  His remark did
not pierce my impenetrable silence, so he asked a question,
"Why were you so angry with your father then?"

   Closing the book I rose to my feet.  "Well, Satyen-babu,
you are a very learned man; may be for that reason it pleases
you to embarrass others."  Without giving him a chance for
further conversation I abruptly left him.

   I rode a cycle-ricksaws home.  It was a little more than
a two-miles ride.  The evening fell gradually; the grey sky
grew darker;  the stars began to appear.  I tried to remember
the past but everything seemed hazy.  Have I not almost
reached my destination, I thought.  Why should I look back?
Let my road ahead become wider and wider.  The few years
that are left, I shall make them fruitful.  I want to do so much
but I am denied all opportunity, there are so many obstacles.
So much needs to be done, yet the path is thorny.  I will not
allow the imperfections of my past to hinder my forward
march.  Reaching home, I found mother waiting for me
at the gate.  Seeing her, anger flared up in me.  This lady is
the cause of all our suffering.  She spoilt my life in order to

please "him". Whenever "he" demanded must be fulfilled.
The "child" must be pacified. Other people's sufferings
did not matter. The whole world must revolve round "him",
but what was the gain? She deluded herself for ten years,
dreaming all would end well. It was she who ruined us all—
father, herself, and me too. Now she boasts of having me
married off so well. "Well" indeed! If it has turned out well,
that is not her credit  Just to please her husband she did
something which she knew was not right. They married
me to someone fourteen years older than me and banished
me to solitary imprisonment. They did their best to kill my
soul. Now she claims credit. She often says, "Well, my
son-in-law is Mahadev himself. It is your good karma of a
previous life that you have a husband like him. How dare
you grumble?"

It is certainly true that he is Mahadev himself—a yogi.
All the qualities that others have to strive hard to achieve
are inborn in him. But did I want a follower of the Gita,
a yogi? Oh, no, I wanted a human being made of flesh
and blood.

Mother asked, "Why so late?"

I snapped back an answer angrily. Poor mother, offended
by my unexpected rudeness, spoke with dismay, "Why flare up
unnecessarily? All of you wreak your vengeance on me!"
At night we slept side by side in two cots. It was winter.
Shrouding ourselves in blankets we lay inside mosquito-curtains.
Both of us were sleepless. Mortified, mother was very quiet.
Suddenly she spoke anxiously, "Are you crying, Ru?" I did
not answer. But my frame convulsed in uncontrollable pain.
Mother lifted her mosquito-net and, walking a few paces,
came to me. "What has happened, Ru? What have I done
to hurt you so much?"

"Satyen-babu has humiliated me."

"Heavens! What did he do? Is he getting senile?"

"No, no. Not that. He told me that he has read
Euclid's book and he has gathered from it that I used to

love Rabindranath."

"Splendid!" Mother said, irked. "The more they read, the more stupid they grow. Why did he have to read Euclid's book to know that?"

Mother put her hand on my head, trying to soothe my distress.

"Do you know, ma, what else he said? 'Why were you so angry with your father then'?"

"Is that so?" Mother gave a start. "Some of them really get dulled with too much reading. Your Thakurma used to call your father an 'erudite goat'. What a comparison to make! Are all loves the same? Have you ruined anyone's family, have you deprived anyone of his rightful inheritance, have you appropriated anyone's property, have you dragged anyone down to shame and ignominy? The love that transcends the affairs of this world is a purifier. If that were not so, could you have built up such a beautiful home? Oh God, how people talk! They have no sense." Mother embraced me. "But why must you suffer, Ru, at this silly talk? You should know the difference, yourself."

"Ma, I am not crying over that. Let them say whatever they like regarding the Poet. I am not ashamed of it. That is something beyond praise or shame."

"Absolutely. Then why do you cry?"

It was then, after twenty-eight long years, that I uttered a name in front of mother. Lifting my head from the pillow I raised my face upwards and called out, "Mircea, Mircea, Mircea."

Taken aback, mother said, "What is it, what is it?" Perhaps it took her some time before she could remember his first name—for he was usually referred to as Euclid in our family. Mother caressed me tenderly. "Ru, have you met him in Europe? Surely you met him in one of your visits?"

"No, ma, no. That mid-day when he left us was the last I saw of him."

"Then you are in correspondence. Surely you write to

each other. Tell me the truth."

"No, ma. I wrote him a letter but he has not replied."

"All this trouble was because of your father." Mother sighed. "Why did he have to have a Frenchman in the house!"

I smiled at mother's fixation about Frenchmen.

"When did you write, Ru?"

"In nineteen-fiftythree, in Paris."

"Why did he not reply?"

"Would it have been right, ma? Would you object?"

"Oh, no." Mother heaved a sigh and spoke with distress. "Nothing can be wrong now. Yet perhaps it was better not to keep any contact. He did it for your good. He did not want to disturb your life. After all, though he was French, he was intrinsically a good boy." Then she carried on her soliloquy. "For no fault of yours, you had to go through this trial. It's all your father's fault. And then, who knows how the wheel of karma turns? From the very next year after we turned out that poor boy, our family began to disintegrate."

Seven years after this conversation, crushed in body and mind, mother left us.

# Book Three

ANOTHER ELEVEN YEARS HAVE PASSED AFTER MOTHER'S DEATH.
In this period I have visited Europe twice, but I have not
heard of him any more. Nor have I thought of him. I have
taken some special responsibilities and I am engrossed in
work. I am reaching old age; my health is failing. I have
a happy home with children and grandchildren, but I also
have a wider home that encompasses my friends and colleagues.
It is possible that I have been able to build up an image
of mine for them. As far as I can guess, that image is like
this: I am strict person, especially rigid regarding matters
of love that have no social sanction, so my friends try to hide
carefully from me any secret affairs that happen among them.
My views regarding good and evil are unyielding, almost
ruthless. I react sharply to any lapses, and I am supremely
practical.

I must have built up an image of myself to myself
I never compromise with anything I consider wrong. I like
sobriety and dislike lack of restraint. I think that each
person has a duty towards society. No one can shirk it,
neither for the sake of personal inclinations nor for an
artistic urge. If anyone does, I do not approve of him. In
fact, I have acquired all the qualities, good and bad, that
a leader should have! For my social service, though
sometimes ridiculed, I have received recognition—as much
as I deserved. So the two circles of the home and the world
are now complete. There is no more any regret or unfulfilled
aspiration.

At this time, suddenly, in 1971, I heard of him again.
One evening, in Srimati Parvati's parlour, when our

colleagues and friends were in a jovial mood, Parvati suddenly remarked, laughing, "In the city of—lives a professor, an admirer of Amrita Devi."

Everyone became enthusiastic. "Is that so, is that so?"

In my long life I have received as much censure as admiration, so there was nothing strange in this piece of news.

"What is his name?" I asked casually.

"Mircea Euclid."

Blood began to throb in my veins.

"Well," I told myself, "I always thought that Parvati loves and respects me. Now look, how she is insulting me! I must remain as unconcerned as possible." But Parvati continued, "Two years ago J. met him. He was tired that day, perhaps ill too. Meeting a Bengali from Calcutta, he began to talk about Calcutta. He told J. that everybody runs down Calcutta, but the Calcutta he knew, forty years ago, was wonderful. For him it is a sacred place—especially the women there were the sweetest, they knew how to maintain dignity and yet be friendly – they always recited Tagore's poems, and so on. Listening to his enthusiastic remarks, clever J. realised that all that meant something more than what was actually said. So he asked, 'Sir, when talking about Calcutta, are you talking about a place or a person?'

"Professor Euclid said, 'Let us go and sit somewhere.' Then relaxing in a cosy corner he asked J, 'Do you know Amrita? How is she?'"

"Then he handed J. a book written by him many years ago—the book is titled *Amrita* and on the dedication page, is written in Bengali, 'Do you rememeber me, Amrita? If you do, then can you forgive?, But J. does not know that language, so he did not bring the book."

Someone asked, "Why didn't he bring it? Some of us could have read it."

There were many persons in the room. Everyone was laughing. They were having fun at my expense! Everyone whether friend or foe enjoys persecuting others. I was

shocked at the cruelty of my friends. My head began to reel.
After these forty long years I heard of someone who met him
and to whom he mentioned me. I can see them getting more
and more merry. Someone said, "Amrita-di, why don't you
write a letter to him? We shall get his address from J.
You must write, it will be great fun."

I felt as if my sari had caught fire—the fire will spread
and engulf me. I must get away from here.

As the days passed the idea began to work its way in me.
Like an ant it began to gnaw continuously. At last I have
his correct address. Why can't I write? He has not
forgotten me. What's the harm in exchanging letters?
After all, both of us are two old people. What harm if I ask,
"How are you?"

At this time we were very busy. There was a war on.
The whole of West Bengal was bubbling with activity.
Everyone was involved in some work or other. In all this
confusion, I forgot that evening. Compared to other people's
extreme adversity and misery, my own fanciful sorrows
appeared meaningless.

Thousands of men, women and children were crossing
the border seeking refuge. They were homeless and destitute.
The hot flame of their anguish was blowing over us also like a
desert wind.

We go to the frontier every day. An epidemic has broken
out among the refugees. We are getting accustomed to
seeing dead bodies strewn on the streets near the camps.
Once as I was passing a camp-site, I saw the death-bed of
an elderly woman of about my age, at the road side. She
lay on a dirty, tattered rag, under the shade of a tree. Her
body, otherwise still, broke into sporadic convulsions.
It was evening and the western sky lined with bright hues
was changing colour moment to moment. The world
ot beauty around us remained complacent and quiet, regardless
of human suffering. A life is ebbing. The taper will soon
blow out. Tomorrow there will be no trace of it left. Who

will remember that she was once alive—that she once loved, or was loved? What can be the significance of it all? Standing near a dying person, I saw my own death bed. I don't think I will die on the street. May be I will wait for death on a bedstead, surrounded by relatives: and after that? Her body and mine are the same. There will be no trace of either her or me. A strange sense of detachment overpowered me; and tears welled up in my eyes. Everyone thought they were tears of pity. "Take Auntie away from here. Go to the city, Auntie," Rashid said, while administering saline. He didn't know that I was only mourning my own death. I will end like this—all that I have received and all that I have not, will become the same—the dirt and the gold are the same. In the few days that we live—how we make others suffer! We can cause a little happiness, intead we inflict unending suffering. Standing beside my own death bed I suddenly saw him. In that strange circumstance his memory began to haunt me. Sitting in the speeding jeep I got engrossed in one thought. Now that I can get his address, why not write him a letter? Can't one write a letter to an old friend? But how will I collect the address from Srimati Parvati? What will she think? Let her think what she pleases; what do I care? As if facing an imminent death, all my old values appeared pointless. I did not care for either praise or blame.

Next day I wrote: "Dear Parvati, kindly let me have Professor Euclid's address." Along with the address Parvati wrote back some more details. "He has a worldwide fame and he dwells in India, in his mind "

I am not impressed by worldwide fame, especially if it is built on erudition. Learning devoid of human understanding has no value for me. Is it not the greed for such things that made him . . . Oh, never mind. Let me write a letter and see whether he replies. So I wrote: "Mircea Euclid, I heard from J. that you have enquired about me. I want to know whether you are the same person

whom I knew forty years ago.   If that is so, kindly reply
to this letter."

No reply.   I waited and waited.   Then I brushed it
away from my mind.   There are so many things to do, so much
to perform—no need to worry about a trivial matter.

In 1971, again I heard his name.   Many persons were
coming from Europe to offer help in the acute distress of
the millions of homeless people who trekked into our country.
We met a couple who had volunteered to help.   The wife
knew many languages.   Once we sat in a field, resting,
when suddenly she asked me, "I have read a book where a
name, identical to yours, is mentioned.   Is that your name?"

I quickly glanced around, fearful of someone overhearieg
us, but made no reply to her query.   She also did not pursue
it further.

We were getting more and more involved in different
activities.   We were meeting new people every day.   Our
home and the world had met.   I had never lived so fully,
like this, before.

From this time, that is from the end of 1971, a strange
feeling began to grow in me.   I felt a yearning to go
somewhere.   I repeated to people, especially to foreigners,
"I will soon visit your country."   "Is that so?"   they would
ask.   "When?"

"I am not sure when, but soon."

This strange longing gathered momentum every day
and made me unsettled and restless.   "I am restless.   I
aspire for faraway things; I forget, I ever forget that I have
no wings."   That was my state of mind.

In 1972 Sergui Sebastian visited Calcutta.   I mentioned
that at the beginning of this story.   When I went to meet
him, on my birthday morning, I went with a little curiosity.
But I was shocked to hear what he had to say.   I was always
sceptical about Mircea, but I never knew that he was such
a liar.   "What shameful lies, Sergui, your friend has written,
and you are praising him!"

"He is not my friend, but my Guru. I am not his equal."

"Well, a nice Guru you have selected! Because of his own guilt, he has taken revenge on me and disgraced me."

"You don't know about his suffering. He only tried to escape it by taking refuge in fantasy."

"None of these explanations is enough for me to forgive him, Sergui. He has given me nothing in life, he has only heaped indignity on me."

Sergui sat with his head bent, unable to answer my allegations.

"What shall I do, Sergui? The world is coming nearer —I have my family, my good name. . . ."

"It's only a story—one has to use imagination to write a story—though I know India is very much the same, as it always was, in these matters," he said.

"Tell me, why did he write such lies? Was it for money? Why did he use my first name? It's libel."

"You misunderstand him. Have you forgotten his love? In every book that he has written there is some mention of his life here. Is it not for you that he turned into an Indian?— he couldn't untie the bond of your name."

"Why doesn't he reply to my letters then, if he was really so much in love?"

"Doesn't he?" Sergui was surprised. "You wrote to him and he has not answered? How many letters have you written?"

"I wrote him three letters altogether. I have reminded him of my existence every twenty years."

"He works against his heart, believe me," Sergui pleaded. "His nature is to inflict pain on himself. I am sure he did not write because he felt *too* eager to write."

Both of us sat wordless for some time. I remembered this trait of his character. Self-mortification was a passion with him. A mysterious person indeed! He has loved me so much, has introduced me to every person in his country. But why did he portray me as something that I was not?

On one side I feel angry, and on the other I remember him. Memory, acute and keen, fills my puzzled mind.

"Sergui, is it not possible to meet him just once? Tell me, will he see me if I go to him?"

"Why not? He lives in his mind, here, in this city."

As I sat talking to Sergui I realised what is meant by an astral body. My astral body had come out of my fleshly one. I was not here, I could see myself clearly in two parts, as I have described earlier.

Since that morning I constantly returned to the past. I re-lived each day, each event of 1930. Each incident came back as direct experience. This was not an easy feeling. I have no language to express the acute anguish I felt to live at two different times simultaneously. On the one side my present life, with all its demands, and on the other my former self, like a ghost from the tomb, looming over me and touching the flowing stream of life. My mind has turned into a string instrument. At the sightest touch it begins to trill; gradually the past comes to the front and the present recedes. I am not certain how the days are turning to nights. But the nights are terrible—terrible. Unbearable is the flame of anger burning within me. I resolve that I must avenge myself. I will not, even though many years have passed, accept the injustice done to me. I think of all this consciously, but a metamorphosis is going on in me that is of a different nature.

A friend of mine has been residing in his country for many years. I wrote to her: "Sumita, you must have read Euclid's book. It's a shame that you have not told me anything so long. I have now heard everything from Sergui. That man lived in our house, as my father's student, and was much benefited by us. He has repaid it by taking revenge. You must write and contradict him. It is your duty to uphold the dignity of Indian womanhood."

Sumita wrote back: "Amrita-di, you have in your letter mentioned something which is as painful to me as it is

embarrassing. I repeatedly requested Sergui not to mention
the book to you, but he is a person of fixed ideas. I have
not been able to convince him, either before he met you
or after, that the subject will be most unpleasant to you.
Whatever Sergui may think, I have discussed the matter
with quite a few literary persons here, who agree with me
that it was very wrong of him to disclose your identity. . . .
But please don't worry, forty years have passed. No one
remembers it any more. There is no chance of any of your
family members coming to know of it."

As I sat thinking over Sumita's letter I realised that she
had tried to console me. The book is alive. I can see that
it has an unusual longevity. Sumita also wrote, "If we
bring up this point afresh, it will amount to mud-slinging."
But what mud? In the innocent heart of a little girl there
was no dirt. The filth has been created by that man in his
imagination.

I tell my friends, "Look at the prank fate has played on
me. The family I have raised, the events of my long life,
my husband and children—they will be wiped away in time.
This, my real life, will become a shadow, but someone who
is nobody to me, whom I met for a brief while in the long
journey of life, he will remain—someone who is nowhere in
my life—my name shall remain tied with that total stranger,
even after death. Social relations, even blood relations end
with death, but the tie he has created is unbreakable. What
shall I do, Parvati?"

Day after day passes. I keep awake night after night.
I cannot think of any way to clear my name of the indignity
that he has heaped on me. I had to tell my friends all. It
was too great a load to bear alone, and it was only then that
I realised how the world had changed. My friends did not
despise me for my unconventional and untimely mental urge.
In our times this could not have happened. We did not know
how to see or accept truth. What would have happened
to me if I were born in the times of Bankim Chandra? He

would surely have consigned me to an inferno.

I am restless.  No one can help me—and that inscrutable man forever remains inside a shell, hands and feet drawn in like a tortoise.  As ill luck would have it, just at this time a near relative of mine visited their country.  He was hugely shocked.  No gentleman should do a thing like that.  Why need he write such a book on a trifling matter that concerned a teenager?  The more I hear, the more I realise that the book is not dead.  It has been alive for forty years and now that the world is contracting, who knows—it will gradually become stronger and more virile.  I feel angry with myself.  Why have I never enquired, or taken notice of the book?  I have been hearing of it for so long, yet I behaved like an ostrich.

I am very conscious of my name and fame.  If someone tells me, "I read a report of your speech," I at once get the paper to have a look at it.  If any paper criticises me, I am very upset.  Yet I never wanted to see a whole book written on me.  If father was alive I would have taught that man a lesson.  A libel—absolutely a libel!  Father knew it, yet did nothing.  I began to cry to father, "Look, *baba*, what your beloved student has done to me.  You tried to save me from his hands, but could you really?  Sergui has told me that because he could give me nothing in life he tried to immortalise me through art.  Can a lie be immortal?  No good can come out of untruth."

Look at that treacherous man   I said to myself—whose memory I have preserved in the depth of my heart as a sacred trust, whose name I have never uttered.  He has been, for the last forty years, selling my flesh for a price.  This is the Western world!

How can I explain to you, Parvati and Gautami, that this fear and disgust dwell in one stratum of my mind, but there is another stratum deep down, where the workings are different.

On sleepless nights, the fire of anger burns within me

but with it burn my pride, prejudice, and all that I thought
valuable so long.   A taper of fear is coming up from within
and is burning everything in its course.   I am melting like
a candle, and its light is spreading all over.   Drop by drop
the hard straight candle is slipping like liquid, melting my
vanity, my sense of prestige.   Everything is falling in that
fire.   My ego built through the prejudice of the ages was
unbending like that candle.   But today the fire of fear has
made it tender.   Is it out of fear? Am I afraid of scandal or
disgrace? Am I suffering only for that? When at midnight
I stand watching the stars I realise it is not so.   One who
was growing larger behind the fear has destroyed it also.   It
is love, indestructible, deathless love.   It is the fire of love
that destroyed everything else and began to emanate light.
The light entered into the depth of my being, in every corner
of my heart, and all the blind alleys began to brighten up.
All my pretensions, all my self-deceptions are evaporating
eroding; I am starting to see the full image of truth.   My
life is becoming meaningful in a new sense.   I remember
him, his half-forgotten face, his voice, his inscrutable ways,
his anger, jealousy and, above all, his love.   Gradually I
am being lifted up into another dimension.   It is another
existence from where the good and bad, the truth and untruth,
the fact and fantasy of this world appear meaningless.   The
shell of this outer world begins to peel off from me—mind
says, praise or blame, all are the same—there are things
truer than these.

I lay wondering why he destroyed this love, a gift of
God.   What did it matter if he had to go?   If in ten years
we could have exchanged even a single letter, that would
have been enough.   With that one letter we would have
bridged the oceans and continents of separation and could
have become "*ardhanariswar.*"   Our two-selves could have
acquired a completeness.   But do Westerners understand
all this?   For them the fulfilment of love must be in bed.
Yet *he* knew, certainly he did.   I can see myself again in his

arms, framed within a door.  He is whispering, "Not your
body, Amrita.  I want to touch your soul."

This is the truth, truly the truth.  The body perishes,
the soul is immortal.  It cannot be killed by killing the body.
Where is that body of mine?  The bower of my youth?
In this old decrepit body, my hair is greying and my face is
lined, but the soul is the same, uncorroded by time.

None has succeeded in destroying it, neither my father
nor Mircea; neither time, my own pride, nor the rich
experiences of my life.  A feeling of immortality is entering
in me—I am touching the infinite.  "One who thinks, I am
killing, or one who thinks, I am being killed—both do not
know that no one kills or gets killed."  The truth that
no scriptures could teach is now becoming self-evident.
Love is deathless.  My soul, held by him in that Bhowanipur
house, still remains so fixed.  The infinite is flowing through
the finite—the limitless is held in the limits of my body—
I am far and I am also near, I am here and also not here.

I am an agnostic, maybe an atheist.  But the change in
me is shaking my disbelief.  Let someone tell me, who I am,
what I am.  Where did the sixteen-year old bodiless self of
mine exist so long?

I do not know how to deal with myself.  Sometimes
I get embarrassed.  One day my husband and I were going
to my place of work.  It was a long drive.  Usually when
we are together, I do all the talking and he replies.  That
day, preoccupied with my own thoughts, I sat silent.  He
tried to open a conversation, but without success.  For
two hours we sat together in the speeding car, totally silent.
Reaching the destination I realised how odd it must have
appeared.  So I said, "For so long you seldom spoke, now
it is my turn to be silent."  He smiled, "You have beaten me
in the competition."

I wrote to Sumita, "You won't have to write anything
contradicting the book.  To me all these small truths and
untruths are now the same.  I want nothing else but to see

him once again. . . ."

The fear is gone, but I am suffering from fatigue, as if my whole life has slipped from my hands. I wrote to Sergui, "I am like someone waiting at the shore, embarkation card in hand, but the ship does not come. I must meet him once more before I die."

Sumita wrote back, "We were overwhelmed to read your letter. I told Sergui that the maxim, 'Truth is stranger than fiction', is proved. When that novel was written, did the writer ever imagine that the events of the future will by far supersede the present? The last part of that novel is tragic, but the present tragedy is much greater than that. The artist of life writes better than us."

Sometimes I talk with Sergui at night: "Really, Sergui, you have made my world turn upside down. The wound that remained sealed for forty years—you have opened it again. Now it has begun to bleed—the blood can't be staunched." My pillow gets wet with blood. The sky of my sleepless night is red—opering my eyes I see my husband sitting on the bed—watching me.

"Won't you tell me what has happened to you?" he pleads with tears in his eyes. I know I must tell him. My friends have also asked me to. They all respect my husband and care for him. They tell me he will soothe my anguish with his kind sympathy. Yet till now I have been reticent. What right have I to hurt his feelings? Is it possible not to hurt? In these thirty-eight years of our life together. someone whose existence was never felt, whose name he has not heard—will that unknown person suddenly appear out of nowhere, like the genie of a fairy-tale, as if, as soon as the bottle was opened, emerging in clouds of smoke and turning into a looming giant.

Someone who had no contact with our world—whose whereabouts were not known, on whom I have not set my eyes for the last fortytwo years—is it possible that a lost memory of childhood can make this living world of his

an illusion, a shadow-play?  Will he be able to bear it?
All these thoughts made me hesitate, otherwise I was in
no mood to hide—the reality had become a mirage to me.

I sat up and looking straight at him I said, "I wanted
to tell you all the time, but I also wanted to spare you."

"I am so unhappy to see you suffer."

Then I told him the strange story.

He sat stupefied.  "What did you say?  We have been
so close for thirty-eight years and I have known nothing.
Why didn't you tell me in the very beginning?  There was
no need to go through all this."

My heart began to ache at his words.  Has anyone
been put to such a test?  He has done so much for me, he
loves me so dearly, my happiness is his happiness, I am his
all-in-all.  Now, at this age, I am taking him to the brink.
One who has given his all, will he find that he was not repaid?

"Oh, no, no," I sobbed.  "Believe me, I have not
cheated you."

"No need for you to assure me.  I have never felt that
there could be anything more than what I received.  You
have fulfilled me.  What I have received from you is
incomparable—I have no regrets.  Only I am sorry that
you have suffered.  And I am sorry for that gentleman.
What a pity."

"Don't talk of him," I snapped.  "A betrayer—he was
served right."

"How can you have peace if you think like that?  You
were in your home, with your parents, and that poor young
boy, in a foreign country, was turned out in an hour's
notice . . . Really, your father cannot be forgiven. . . . '

He made me lie down. I could feel he was mothering
me. I was surprised to see that he felt no loss.  But has
he really suffered a loss?

"Believe me," I entreated.  "I have never suffered.
Otherwise wouldn't you have known?"

"Yes, I never saw you suffer."

"If I were unhappy, could you have been happy?"

"You are right.   So after half a century you are now
missing him?   What strange things you say!"

"I know.   I am also no less surprised.   Sometimes
I wonder if I am going insane.   It is disgraceful of me.
I am committing a sin, am I not?"   I began to weep
inconsolably.   I felt greatly relieved after opening my heart to
my husband, as if I was inhalling fresh air after being near
suffocation.   My tears now bring my emancipation.   My
husband smiled, "What can I tell you? Sin or virtue, have
I ever come across such a thing like this or even heard of it?
Who am I to sit in judgment over you?   I am unhappy that
I have nothing in my power to relieve your distress.   Yet,
you know, I somehow feel that this suffering will do good to
you.   I have noticed that there is a purpose working through
your life."

We sat together, an old mature couple, bewildered and
sleepless, waiting for the dawn.

It is very difficult to write about those days: nothing
was happening.   There were no incidents to write about.
The yearning can be expressed only in poems.   So I began
writing poetry after many years.   At midnight, when the
whole house was asleep I would leave my bed and sit writing
poems.   I remember the poems that I destroyed once.   I
*will* write now.   I will now accept the truth.   All debts must
be cleared.

I receive a letter from Sergui.   He writes:

"Dear Amrita Devi:

Your confidence moved me beyond expression and I
am asking myself whether I am worthy of it . . . The most
prominent and touching fact I experienced in India is that
of having met you; it can be connected by threads of my
destiny with what happened to me when I was a teenager.
At that time I read two books—*Amrita* and *Sadhana*.   Both
of these impressed me to the highest degree and I became

fascinated by the Indian world for the rest of my life. . . .
Finally I was able to visit your country. There I had the
opportunity to learn from your distress what the soul is—
what we are all.

"I was aware as I told you at that time that time and
oblivion are touching only the surface of our consciousness,
that our active memory is in fact absolute and thus we
are in a way immortal. This was my strong conviction, but
as a human being I need to find new evidences in order to
support it. You gave me, I can say, the most tremendous
proof of our atemporality, that in fact our consciousness is
only apparently dominated by time and that we are able to
get rid of it. The real death is oblivion and our only chance
to become immortals is to repress it to become an Amrita.

"However great your suffering might seem you have to
realise that after having fulfilled your terrestrial duties you
are now in a condition of grace which is beyond happiness
and unhappiness. . . . Only love can defeat time and oblivion,
and one decays and is in their power by being unable to love
or by drawing it back to unconsciousness. . . ."

Sergui's letter makes me think: What is truth? What is
immortality? I am getting the taste of immortality because
I can touch again the living presence of what was once dead.
Watch that man entering this room with a bundle of papers—
is he more true than those two stooping figures over the
wooden box, dropping cards for making a catalogue? Is the
past unreal, not the present? Has it gone away anywhere or
is it fixed somewhere? The lid has been taken off—one by
one the shadow figures are emerging and making their
existence felt.

Sometimes I am afraid of my own emotion. It is like a
hot spring that spurts up from the depths of the earth and
sprays the ground. So from an unknown depth springs
this burning flame of love. I feel scared. Oh God, will it
dry up the garden around me?

Sometimes 1972 blends with 1930 in such a way that I

do not know how to cope with it. I cannot express the exact
quality of this feeling. Maybe such an experience is so rare
that no language is adequate to convey it. Had it not
happened to me I would not have believed it. Yet I am
trying to convey it so that, if some day this story is published,
psychologists will probably be able to find out the reason
and the source of it all.

The night is deep. I hear the clock chime ding-dong.
It is two o'clock. I can see Shanti lying beside me. I can
hear the music floating up from the piano downstairs.

I feel restless on the bed. "Shanti, I can't sleep."
"Nor can I. Euclid-da is playing the piano non-stop."

"This is really bad." I sit up on the bed, "I must go
down and tell him to stop it."

Shanti says, "No, no, not now. Tell him to-morrow."

I am already on my feet. I am drawn by a strange
inexplicable attraction towards him—the music is like an
invocation—I am spellbound. I must go to him now, I must
go to him now, I really must. He is calling me. I approach
the door.

Shanti also gets out of bed. "What are you doing, Ru?"
"I am going down to tell him to stop playing."

"Are you crazy? Look at the time—it is two o'clock--
does anyone go to anyone so late at night?"

"If one can go at eight o'clock, why not at two o'clock?"

"No, it's not done. One never goes to a man's room
at night."

"But you do."

"What nonsense! Where do I go?"

"To every room—to father's room, to Mantu's room."

"At two o'clock? Never! Besides, we are relatives."

I am angry. Pushing her aside, I approach the door.
I must go. I shall not enter his room. Standing outside,
I shall only request him not to play. What harm will come
of it? Shanti is getting insolent; she is trying to boss over

me.  Shanti stands with her back to the door.

"Who do you think yourself to be, Shanti, how dare
you stop me ?"

"You will presently see what I think of myself—shall I
call auntie?"

The magic worked.  The roaring lioness turned into a
mouse.  Burying my head in the pillow, I began to weep.

"Dear Shanti, you know what is going on between us
—is it a sin?"

Shanti sat resting her cheek on her palm, meditatively,
and then gave her considered view; "Oh, yes, certainly it
is a sin."

"But who is committing the sin, he or I?"

Shanti kept on thinking.  "I think," she spoke dejectedly,
"both of you are equally involved."

"Certainly not.  I am not doing anything wrong.  And
I ask him not to."

"Then don't go to his room any more."  Shanti spoke
firmly.  Then, watching my face, she melted in pity.  "Why
do you think of sin? Do as you please.  I shall never tell
anyone."

This is January 1973.  The clock is chiming one, two.
I am sitting on the bed.  I feel I shall have to get down
quickly, or Shanti will stop me.  I am trying to get to my
feet.  Someone says, "Where are you going?"

"Downstairs."

"Where? It's two o'clock, long past midnight."

"What is the difference, two o'clock or eight o'clock?"

Shanti catches me from the back and immediately I
realise it is not Shanti, it is my husband who is holding me.
I begin to tremble, I tremble in fear, abject fear.  What has
happened to me? I have become "timeless".  I fall on my
husband's chest and putting my hands round his neck I
begin to sob, "Save me.  Oh save me! Who can save me but
you? It is wicked of me to cause you so much distress."

He soothes me like a mother and tries to put me to
sleep. "I have no distress, none at all. My only worry is
that I have nothing in my power to lessen your misery. But
I shall do what I can. You must certainly go and meet him."
"What will happen if people come to know of it?"
"Why should they?"
"Maybe I will tell, it will slip out from me." I can
remember nothing, nothing at all. Tell me who is calling
me. Can he be a person whom I have not met for forty-two
years, who is a stranger to me? Mircea is just a tool,
it is someone else who is using his name, changing my
whole personality, my inner being. He is constantly saying,
"Learn to see the truth." I know this experience will not
last long. I will return to my ordinary self, but just now,
believe me, a change is going on in me. I have even
forgiven Rama. I feel no repulsion towards her any more.
I am thinking of the days when she was a young girl. She
was sweet-natured and full of humility. She has broken
up our home. She has caused mother immense suffering, yet
she has also suffered. She could not get the real thing, see
got only the skin instead of the fruit. So she is continuously
trying to bask in the glory of father's scholarship—his
name and fame. By some pretext or other she includes
her name in each of father's books, like one demented. A
person who had a devoted wife and six vigorous children
like us, how little of him could she have had! Besides,
father had no capacity for selfless love. Now, as the bygone
days are coming back, I think of all this. Maybe I can
love Rama now. Believe me, I love her as I used to, at one
time. Once I told her, "Can anyone cause humiliation to
a person one loves?" But to-day I feel, may be Rama was
also just a tool. It is someone else's game we are playing.
We are marionettes in his hands. Maybe what appeared
as loss from the outside was actually father's gain from another
aspect. Sadhu Bijoykrishna Goswami had told father that
he would have a fall. Father had the seed of it in him from

birth. It was his immense "ego", and we have all of us
tried to preserve that ego. We regretted that father could
not be President of our country. Did he not deserve it, we
said. It was only for her that he lost everything, power and
prestige, and died in indignity while living in the ignominy
of her "protection."

　. . . But today I see differently. Would it have been a
great gain to be the President? Maybe he achieved better.
Maybe, before leaving this world, he became completely
egoless and gained the peace of humility. Losing all worldly
benefits, maybe his inner being received a fullness　The loss
was turned into a gain. The little flaw that he had, along
with his genius, maybe that was washed out by the tears
of humiliation, and before he left this world, he achieved a
perfection of soul, a purification, and for this Rama was
the cause, not we. Today I realise that this world is not as
we see it. So I say, "Uncover your face, O Truth, I want to
meet you "

　Will anyone believe that month after month I remained
sleepless? I am seeing him, talking to him and quarrelling
with him. The reason of my quarrel is—Rina is now
reading his book to me, and it is just a basket full of lies.
I tell him, "Don't you think that your book revives my
memory?" I am reading it because my memory was already
revived, otherwise I would not have cared. I did not care
all this time. I knew the book was there but I never felt
like touching it. This book really has no quality to revive
memory, on the other hand it hurts. It wears a mask of
truth—it is the work of a delirious mind. It seems he was
certain that both my parents and I had spread a snare to
catch him, an eligible bridegroom! Because of this
preconceived notion he failed to understand me　He never
grasped my thoughts. I too, of course, gave him little
chance　I never opened my mind to him—there was no
time. Exactly for that reason, in his book he puts in my
mouth absurd confessions. It seems his unsatiated desire

made him indulge in a strange fantasy. A kind of self-
deception I suppose that in the science of psychology
this mental state must have a name. I do not know it,
I am not proficient in that science. I think it requires colossal
daring to try to navigate the inexhaustible, mysterious ocean
of the human mind. So I do not judge him. I try only to
uuderstand It seems it is different in quality from mine.
Can anyone ever reach truth through the door of untruth?
The face of knowledge and truth remains covered by the
rubbish-heap of untruth. That must be removed—that is
why I am taking up my pen. The more I read the book
the more critical I become. I know he had reason to be
angry with my father, even to hate him, but I do not
understand how he can berate the same person whom he has
acknowledged as his revered Guru. Why did he use his
name if he hated him so? I cannot fathom such a complex
mind. I sharpen all these criticisms like little poisoned
arrows and throw them at him, but strangely, they vanish no
sooner than they leave the bow-string, and do not reach the
target. My angry thoughts are like little round pebbles
on the waves of my heart. I can't use them to hit him;
from moment to moment they slip from my hand, roll off,
move away and get lost.

There is a conspiracy of destiny of which for so many
decades I knew nothing. Fate has conspired to tell me all
now. So many people are giving me information about
him. Is it accidental? Is any event accidental, or is each
event connected with another by a causal link? Do we
ourselves do anything or are we all puppets tied to strings?
One who had no trace in my life for so long, how could
he loom so large now and engulf my present existence?
And strangely enough, I get plentiful news of him now.
A professor told me that he had met him two years ago.
"Professor Euclid is remarkable. He was in Calcutta forty
years ago, but he remembers even the roads. He asked me
if I knew where Bakul Bagan Road was."

He also tells me that Professor Euclid lives in a strange
world of fantasy—he leads a detached life and India is his
dream-land.  In his writings, specially his fiction, he deals
more with the fantastic than the real.

The more I hear of him the more restless I grow.  I am
now convinced that my angush will not abate till I meet
him.  Yet I wonder: Whom shall I see?  Where is that
twenty-three year old boy?  Or, whom will *he* see?  Where is
that sixteen year old girl?  As he does not want to see me,
I don't worry about his problem.  But my problem is: Where
will I find the person whom I want to meet?  Do I want to
meet a twenty-three year old boy—almost a child?  A child?
What else?  At my age he would be almost like a grandson.
If by any chance I can meet that Mircea, we can't be friends,
can we?  Yet the person whom I shall meet now is an old
man who is an absolute stranger.  What solace can he be to
me?  "How can it be," I ask myself, "that a completely alien
person attracts me now so much that all the strong ties of my
present world are becoming loose?"

Is it intelligible that this mysterious passion of my
sleepless nights, that constantly yearns to set off on an
unknown journey, is for meeting an alien, a stranger living
in some strange city?  Can he be the reason for it all, or is it
some other power, from some other place who is moving me
towards an unknown destiny?  Can there be someone who is
the source of all knowledge and all love, and the message is
coming from that direction?  My agnostic mind does not
like to admit it, but the doubt is never eased.  In the evening of
my life I am basking in morning light.  Morning and
evening have blended.  Time is instantaneous.

Sometimes I think of Sergui; is this a taste of immortality?
I remember the lines I wrote in my young days: "When time
will lose its minutes and moments."  I am now held in the
embrace of that unmarked, perpetual time.  Is this, can this be
deathlessness?  If so, then why this affliction?  Why do my
tears flow so incessantly?  But is it really an affliction?

Should I not try to escape it then?   Do I want to escape?
Would I like these months to vanish like a mirage and myself
to go back to my mundane daily duties, get immersed in my
housework and financial problems?   Can any person of my
age imagine that while living in the material world, encircled
by children and grandchildren, one can float away to a dream
land?

Constant friction with the material world makes us
tough and worldly.   We then become careful and calculating.
I was like that too.   Wasn't I counting my annas so long?
And today?   If someone says, Come with me leaving
everything behind, I will show him to you, shall I not go?
If someone asks me, Do you want to own a four-storey house
on Theatre Road or do you want to see him—is there any
doubt what I shall prefer?   I am not unhappy at this change
that has come inside me.   It is a blessing to feel the excruciating
emotions of youth at my age, so I write:

> I do not know whose gift this is,
> Who preserves an unending wealth.
> On the slush after the ebb-tide
> Who is it that makes the water murmur a song?
> What a blessing—a blessing indeed!
> That call comes from the unknown confluence.

Gazing at that "unknown confluence" I am not helping
anyone else, but gaining a fulfilment myself.   As the sage
Yajnavalkya said, "One can only gain oneself and none else—
the son is dear to me not for the sake of the son but for
myself—the husband is dear to me not for the sake of the
husband but for myself."   They are filling up my soul.
By remembering Mircea I have not given anything to anyone
else—it is only I who have gained a third eye to see the world.

Some tell me why need I dig up an old memory which
I forgot so long ago and got busy performing my terrestrial
duties so fruitfully.   Why am I not exerting myself to get
over it?   I do not know the answer.   I feel only that this
abstract formless love is playing an exquisite music in my
body and mind that I have not experienced before.   Sergui

is right: there is a message of immortality in it.  The
endlessness that is felt in the tears wrung out by music, the
insatiety that dwells in love,—it is the same message that
I am receiving, transmitted by some cosmic magician.  I am
not prepared to mock it.

Besides, let other people say what they like, my husband
does not mind.  He was telling me the other day, "The same
event does not repeat itself.  One has to judge each incident
separately, on its own merit.  It is a fact that our lives do
not and can not coincide totally.  Some parts of your mind
are unknown to me.  When you write poetry I do not know
what you think.  I am not acquainted fully with your literary
world.  So it is another expression of your mind.  It does
not worry me."

I am surprised to notice that he feels neither loss nor
hurt.  Had he done so, I would have been in abject misery.
I could never have thought of going to meet Mircea.  I cannot
aspire for any happiness by hurting my husband—it will then
lose all value.  Then love itself will be humiliated.  There
is no greater sin than that.  Can I go on a pilgrimage with a
load of impiety upon me?

Day by day I am reaching such a state that it is becoming
impossible to carry on my daily duties.  How can I converse
on worldly topics?  When I visit a government office, I am
fearful of what the deputy secretary will think if tears begin
to roll down my cheeks.  I try hard to control myself but
without success.  I sit in my parlour reclining on a chair
half-dazed, oblivious of my surroundings.  The servants are
puzzled    At my age the usual reason for shedding tears would
be a strong difference of opinion with the daughter-in-law.
For the elderly ladies of Bengal that is a common pastime.
The servants have not noticed anything like that, and if
there is trouble in the family it is expected that others will
also be affected by it.  But normal life is moving placidly;
only they find me in an inexplicable state.  I am ashamed.
I realise my foolishness, but my mind is out of gear.  While

in a car I watch the speeding car in front and feel an urge
to get down.   If I hear of someone going to any foreign
country, a sense of desperation overpowers me.   I fear that
this unbearable poignancy may prove too much for my old
body.   If I fall ill, I won't be able to go to him.   But,
strangely, my health has improved.   These past few months
my heart has given me no trouble and my blood pressure is
normal.

I continuously argue silently with those who tell me to
exert myself to reject this attack of memory.   Actually I
argue with myself.   They say the more you think about it,
the more obsessed you will get.   This wise advice proclaimed
by the unwise may be partly true but never wholly.

An event that has not troubled me for forty-two years
—the memory that had moved away in my young days,
like a shadow, and had not held me in its grip—why is it
now worrying me so?   For instance, in Paris could I not
have gone with Popescu?   Who knows what might have
happened then?   Even then I used to think myself as an
elderly person (as we Indian women are prone to think).
But how old was I really?   Only forty-two.   Now reaching
sixty, I know I was not all that old    Why did I not
feel so strongly then and why now, with one foot in the
grave?   In the grave?   I just say this, I don't feel it.   I am
not feeling my age.   The shell of age has dropped off me
and the flame of the ageless soul is burning.   Can anyone
just wish oneself into such a state or move away from it?
Are these things in our hand?   That afternoon, when father
introduced me to Euclid, was it he who caused it?

And did I call Sergui Sebastian on the 1st of September
1972?   What is it but a conspiracy of time immemorial?
These events are connected with the first beginning, when
this earth was nebulous gas, as it is said in the poem *De
Profundis*: "Where all that was to be in all that was."

Some console me: "There is no harm in reviving old
memories, but where will you go and why?"   Others say,

"It will do you good. You will be set free as soon as you
see an old man—you will feel ashamed—'Whom have
I come to see?' " My mind at the surface agrees with
them. But the deeper mind says, That will never be. The
person you want to see has not aged, as you have not
aged. Age is just a cover—it can be removed   Some do
so by constant endeavour, some gain their soul as a gift, as
a boon, as a gift of mercy. Whose mercy? I don't know.
I don't know whether God exists, but I now know the nature
of our inner being. All my doubts are vanishing like a
moving mirage. This experience cannot be transmitted to
others just as light cannot be shown to a blind man. It is
an experience that is beyond argument, beyond intellect,
which cannot be learnt in books and scriptures. I now
realise this timeless, indestructible love will never get
crushed by wordly affairs—it will flow from moment to
moment and carry me away from the profane state, like the
river that grows in speed as it approaches the confluence
of the sea.

I must go to that distant land. Easier said than
arranged. The problems are many. I do not want to
intimate this to him beforehand, as there is every chance
that he will run away. I feel he does not intend to meet
me, or won't be able to. Why? Is he suffering from a sense
of guilt after writing that incredible romance about me?
I don't think so. I don't think he he has realised how much
he has harmed me. Just as Sergui also has not.

Slowly all the preparations are progressing, about my
journey. Foreign travel is complicated; there is no end of
bureaucratic paraphernalia. During daytime I work hard to
arrange things, but at night I feel diffident. I am not so
young. If I fall ill in a foreign country, who will look after
me?

Pravati's husband also says, "How can you allow
Amrita to go alone in her state of health? And that
strange man—who knows how he might offend her?"

They are worried. Only my husband is not. Usually he
is very much concerned about my health. But now he
consoles me, "There will be no trouble. No one will offend
you. You will never fall ill. All the arrangements will be
made. You will safely return home." I am surprised at
him. If I hesitate, he enthuses me. We are surprised at
his ease and optimism. "You will certainly go and end
this fairy tale of yours!"

I am in doubt whether I can secure an invitation. I am
hoping to influence those with whom I am connected
in my work. But I shall get a chance only if there is a
conference. There are still many hurdles to cross.

As I sat musing a gentleman came to see me. He is
working out an extensive scheme to build up an educational
institution. He suddenly told me, "I am optimistic about
the future of my work because my astrologer has told me so."

I am surprised. I have seen quite a few of these,
they are all fakes. So I said, "Do you believe in those
charlatans?"

"There are many cheats, but not everyone is a cheat."

"Will you take me to him?" I asked. I am horrified
at my degradation. I know it is a weakness. I have lost
faith in myself, so I am looking for a miracle.

I went to the astrologer. The old man was sitting
perched on a bed. I did not disclose my identity, actually
I was ashamed of my weakness. The astrologer was looking
thoughtfully at the signs of the Zodiac. I was smiling.
I know I will fool him. How can anyone know what is going
on in my mind?

My age is my armour. Peering over his spectacles the
astrologer asked me, "What do you want to know?"

"Tell me something about my future. I don't need to
hear about the past. I don't have much future left though."

"No, no, you will live long. And very soon, before the
eleventh of April next, you will cross the seas. Take note
of the date," he emphasised.

"How will I go? I have no money."

"You will get an invitation.  Money will come.  But you must try."

I am amazed.  He knows nothing about me—how can he guess so much?

"Tell me, astrologer, what good will come of it?  What will happen there?"

"There you will meet a man whom you have been wanting to meet all your life."

I tried to remain calm and spoke gravely: "Who is that man?"

"A *mlechcha*."  I gave a start.

"What kind of meeting will that be?" I cautiously asked. It is then that he used an English word.  "Romantic."

I laughed.  "Dear astrologer, to whom are you talking? Look at my hair—snow all over."

Irritated by my insolent laughter he said, "I look at no one's hair, tooth, or nail.  I look at one's stars."

There is no doubt it is a conspiracy of eternal time, that after forty-two years Amrita will meet Mircea Euclid. Have I any power to fathom this mystery?  How can I, this little insignificant I, understand it all?

"Astrologer, you have predicted something awful," I said lightly.  "Suppose anything like that really happens, will I be censured?"

"No, certainly not.  Why should you be blamed?"

"Why not?  Is it good to have romantic encounters at this age?"

"Why not, why not?"  the old man grumbled angrily. "How can there be defamation, if the stars combine favourably?"

My invitation arrived.  Money was arranged.  One by one all the difficult knots are being untied.  Amazing.  Who is moving me to an unknown future as if holding my hand? How is it possible that, while living in a middle-class Bengali home, my life is entering into such a colourful and unique

expeience? My friends ask me to write it all, to finish that
unfinished, fantastical tale of Mircea—specially when I am
going to end in life the story that began in 1930. Why should
I also not do so in literature? Now has come "the last of
life for which the first was made."

Is it not queer that of whom I have known nothing for
so long I am now coming to know much since the last few
months? I hear that he is married but has no children. He
keeps himself buried in books and seldom moves out of his
library. I am unhappy to hear this. I hear that his wife
keeps a vigil over him and that she opens all his letters.
Some say he probably received no letter from me. But I do
not believe it. There was nothing in my letter that might
be regarded as objectionable, and why should she be jealous
of me? I am only a shadow of the past. I have received
no news of him after that fateful afternoon of 1st September.
That is why I doubted his sincerity and why the poisonous
cloud of suspicion suffocated my love. And now, after so
many decades I hear he had told someone, "I sent her a
photograph of mine, from Svargadvar, through Khoka. I
was wearing a beard then—she told Khoka to ask me to
trim it." I was astounded at this news. When the incidents
of 1930 are passing before my eyes, as picures in a film show,
I can see each incident. I can see exactly where father was
standing when he said to me "Ha-ha, he's grown a beard!"
But I can't see where Khoka was when he showed me the
picture. I don't remember the scene. And could I be so
heartless as just to say, Ask him to trim it? I would
plead, "Oh, Khoka, can't you take me to him?" But I
remember nothing like this. I think hard. With the
photograph he must have also written a letter. But I have
seen no such letter. I know now that Khoka used to go to
him sometimes and borrow money. Khoka had told him
awful blood-curdling stories about the persecution that I was
supposed to be going through, that my mother had whipped
me, and so on; just to make him suffer.

So I decided to go to Khoka. There was no shame
now in talking about something so distant in the past. One
evening I went to Khoka's house. He is still as poor—no
wonder, because he has a dozen children! They are all grown
up now, yet his is a hereditary poverty running through three
generations I found the house completely dark. They
lived in a good locality of Calcutta. All the houses around
were bright with light, only this one had the appearance of a
haunted house. I went on knocking at the door. After
a little while Khoka came out. It was after many years that
I saw him. His ugly face looked uglier with age; the loose
skin on his face was lined. He said, "Who are you?" Then
he studied me for a while in the dark. "Oh, it is Ru. It's
long since I have seen you. What is it that brings you to a
poor man's door?"

"Why no lights?"

"Easy to explain—I could not pay the bill—so they
disconnected the line. Won't you come in? Let me go and
fetch a candle."

Khoka came back with the candle and holding it up
gazed at my face, "You are still quite beautiful, Ru these
days the girls have no grace. . . ."

"Is that so? Nice to hear it. Tell me, Khoka, where
are those letters that Mircea wrote to you? Give them to me."

The trick worked. "Mircea's letters! You have
remembered him after all these years!"

"I am writing my autobiography. Shouldn't I write a
little about him?"

"You will if you have courage. If you want to pose as
a woman of great virtue, you won't."

"I have decided to write fully about him."

"Good, good. I am happy to hear it. Everyone says
you are a person of immense courage. It shouldn't be difficult
for you. . . . How nice those days were, Ru. . . how wonderfully
sweet and what a good boy was Mircea." Khoka began to
ruminate on old memories. "To turn him out at a moment's

notice. . . . Uncle had no sense of justice.  To believe a silly
child!"  Khoka rambled on. . . .

"Khoka, please give me the letters.  I remember nothing.
Perhaps those letters will remind me.  Tell me, how many
letters did he write?"  I was calculating how many he could
have written in ten months.  Maybe two each month . . . .

"Oh quite a few, but I have destroyed them all."

"Why?"

"I wanted to be discreet."

"Khoka, give me his photograph—the one with the
beard.  There was no need to destroy that."

"I gave it to you."

"Never.  I have not even seen it.  Had I seen it, I
wouldn't have forgotten.  Khoka, please give me the
photograph.  And there certainly are at least some letters
—give them to me, please."  I spoke urgently.

"You *are* funny.  Do I carry forty-year old letters
in my pocket?  Let me look for them.  Come after a week."

After a few days he sent for me.  Some letters had
been found.  Khoka slowly came down from upstairs.  He
was wearing a *lungi* and his hairy body was bare.  I saw
the letters tucked at his waist.  The sight of these stuck to
his obese body, moist with perspiration, sent a cold shiver
through me.  I stretched out my hand, "Give them to me."
He gave three letters to me and said, "After a good deal of
searching I have discovered these—may be there are more.
I'll look for them again."  I began to read immediately.
Khoka continued, "Read them at home, Ru.  Let us talk a
little about the old days.  Do you know  I saw your
shadow on the glass door from the other side of the partition.
I told Mircea, Come and sit in this chair and watch the door.
Then I stood where both of you were a little while ago.  You
see, when I told him,  I have seen your shadow—the poor
fellow gave a start."  Ignoring his prattle I began to read the
letters.  They revealed a European mind opening up to the
touch of the magic wand of ancient India, and burning with

the fire of love.    The first one was written on the 10th
of November.    He left us on the 18th September so there
must have been more.    The letter runs, in shaky English:

*Svarga Ashram*
*Risikesh*
10th Nov. 1930.

*My dear Coca*

I came back in the ashram yesterday night, after many
days of solitude at Brahmapuri forest, and I got your letter.
Misunderstanding between you and me!    Certainly not.
There were some details unknown to you and for this reason
I have explained them to you.    Let the people call me
Srichaitanya, this cheap taunt does not trouble me.    I am
glad that my two friends (you and A) do not believe them.

When you judge my *vairagya*, do not judge it like an
European, be an Indian.    You will understand better than
me why Jesus had to go through twenty years of hard
preparations in the desert before sending his message.
Mind you, Jesus has preached only 18 months and has
changed the world—and I know many good brains of our
time who preach all their lives without changing even their
own soul.    I am not in a hurry to return to the world.
The world came to Sri Ramakrishna after his realisation and
Swami Vivekananda travelled all the world but could
convert none.    Too much talk, too much talk.    *Sadhana*
does not mean going about, lecturing, writing books, boxing
the ears and teaching the asses without number of our time.
At least my *sadhana* means something else and something
more.

My father mother and sister are expecting me home so
I have not received any letter from them for a long time.
. . . The manuscript of my book "The Light Which Failed"
. . . has been received by my friend on "that" very day,
that is 18th September.    Is it not strange?    . . . The society
of literary women "Femina" has chosen my last novel for

the prize of 1930 . . . And all this and that and that one and
this one are rubbish, senseless and lies . . .

Kindly show this letter to A.

Yours friendly<br>
*Mircea*

Reading this letter I realised how his resentment against
my father was growing.  He did not care for his lecture-tours
or teaching of philosophy any more.  But it was apparent
that he held him in so high an esteem that he was comparing
him with the greatest men of the world and getting
disappointed.  It was the tragedy of my father's life that
all his dear ones wanted to see him greater than he really
was.  The next two letters:

*Svarga Ashram*<br>
25 November 1930

*My dear Coca*

I was waiting for your letter and I read in haste.  Why
do I not write home about my ill fate?  I have written
something to my sister.  They all know very little about
myself and about my thoughts as to understand me by letters.
They know that I was intending to marry a Hindu girl and
I was to stay in India 5 more years.  It is my fault that they
only know this much.  But about my soul I am always
taciturn with everybody. . . However, I will tell them everything
but not just now.  I wait now for my dawn   Do you think
it will take long time to come?

See that rubbish about my literary fame, it could not
help me a bit in my suffering so I care little about literature
and distinction.  I am reading now day and night the
Upanishads and parts of the Vedas.  I went to *Gurukul*
Hardwar the famous College of the Arya Samaj and I was
invited to lecture on comparative religions.  I accepted in
principle, because in *Gurukul* I will have the opportunity to
talk in Sanskrit.  There the boys live in a magnificent spirit

of ancient Aryans, in a wonderful purity under the trees, in the open air. This is the only life which I can stand now.

You ask me why I am not going for a short journey at home? Because they will not allow me to come back. They will read in my eyes what India taught me. They will be afraid and will manage to keep me in Europe. Europe is for me the continent of dreams. There I was free and young—there I was indifferent to life and happy in my ignorance. All this is a dream for me now, the shores of Sicily and the ruins of Rome, the blue dark sky of Florence and the solitude of Switzerland I will never see again. I have to fight here in India with India. India gave me the bondage, India will give me the freedom . . . . I am not playing the fool, not with myself nor with my country. So what is the good to go back and to talk lies about my spirituality and my wonderful studies in Yoga when the truth is . . . agony.

I beg from you a more sympathetic understanding, you do not know yet what a disaster has befell me, what a complete disaster. I am going to stay here. I work as a mad man in Sanskrit and Indian philosophy. I got now a lamp. I work deep into night. It is a very cold and lonely place. I am a Hindu now.

Please show to A this photo and this letter of mine. She knows how much I suffer because I am not allowed to present her a copy.

How is Sabi and the boys.

> With love
> *Mircea.*

> *Svarga Ashram*
> 5 Dec. 1930.

*My dear Coca*

I read your letter. Why to forgive you? You did the right thing by telling your friend about the financial difficulties which are "drowning" you. It is my fault that I am unable to help you. So do not worry and be Coca again! I am

working as a mad man.  I have translated *Katha Upanishad*
into our language and I have completed my long paper on
the philosophy of the *Upanishad* . . . . I can say about the
*Upanishad*—"it has been the solace of my life—it will be
the solace of my death."

When I am tired and over-worked I write literature . . .
the writing is my only afternoon rest . . .

I have to ask you now something—have you shown my
photo to A? What is she doing now? What is her plan? You
are writing in every letter that she is still "passing through
a crisis" but this word is after all only a word.  You
understand I hope that I am so eager to know everything
about her.  I know she is doing and will also do in future
the right thing but I would like to hear more about her.  Why
are you not showing my letters to her when she is alone—
and give me indirectly some details about the actual state
of her mind? No necessity to say that "she cannot forget
the past" because "the past" is only a word.  Do you see
what I mean . . .? The mad experience (you may call it love)
which has excruciated me for the last three months begins
now to show its positive concrete and everlasting aspect.
She has changed my life but making it a thousand time
better.  The awakening is magnificent as a sunrise.  I have
seen the Real—and I have seen all the dirt of the intellectual
and social world too.  Everything is dirty and cowardice.
And I feel an inexpressible volatile joy to know myself pure
and strong among these worms eating their fetid happiness
in the name of law, social norms etc.  More lies I discover
more I feel consoled that I am not destined to enjoy this
life.  I shall not enjoy anything, I shall renounce everything.
Show this letter to A please . . .

Your friend
*Mircea.*

As I stood reading the letters, I thought Mircea had
strewn pearls before a swine.  He took a vow under duress

that he would not contact me, so he was writing to Khoka.
He was sure that Khoka would show them to me and that
I would do the right thing, at the right time.  He had
complete faith in my ability to do the right thing.  He trusted
me, and what did I do?  All my life I imagined that he had
deceived me.  Actually I could have done much.  This
was my country.  I had many friends and some of them
were illustrious men.  Was there no one to support me?
Why did I not seek help?  Just because I had a preconceived
notion that in these matters the man should take the lead
and not the woman.  It would be a shameless act on the
part of woman to take the initiative.  This was a kind of
prejudice and also vanity.  I was a foolish, vain and
worthless girl.  I should have realised that as a foreigner
his position was vulnerable.  Of course I never knew at
that time that father did send the police to warn him.  Father
told him that if ever he tried to contact me he would
immediately be repatriated.  Father wrote to him, "You
have sullied my home.  You were like a snake under the
grass, and when the snake raises its head, it is time to strike—
so I have struck."

Naturally he had no alternative, yet all my life I had
been blaming him . . . . On the other hand, Khoka had been
telling him lies.  He surely told him that he had shown me
his letters, since he has told him so about the photograph
and fabricated my remark about my asking him to trim the
beard.  Is it then impossible that he also suspected me of
deception?  He might have thought I purposely avoided
to do "the right time thing at the right time," that I had no
truth in me.

These letters were kept within two miles of my house
all these years and I discovered them now, after four
decades!  This is Karma, this is destiny!

Khoka's interminable chatter went on . . . .

"Why not read them later?  Let us talk about our
childhood, Ru. . . ."

I said, "Swine." I was trembling in rage.

He was startled to hear such a vulgar word come from so sophisticated a person.

"What are you saying, Ru?"

"Nothing. I just named an animal."

"But who do you mean?"

"Just that animal. But, Khoka, tell me—why did you not show me these letters?"

"I did show them to you."

"Liar. Tell me why you betrayed his trust."

"What could you have done even if I showed them to you? Had you any strength to do anything?"

I watched him intently. Perspiration was glistening on his crude face. In the dim light of the candle he appeared to me like some primitive animal in a cave. Why did this man behave so hypocritically? There are no answers to these questions; and what is the use anyway? And I am being unnecessarily rude. The poor fellow understood little of all these thoughts.

"Anyway, I am going, Khoka. I am thankful that you preserved these letters for so long." I opened my hand bag and was about to push in the brittle papers, yellow with age. Khoka said, "You know, Ru, how prices are soaring these days—for long I've had no job—if you give me a few rupees I could buy this week's ration."

I took a few rupees from my bag and throwing them towards him came away with quick steps. I felt a sort of nausea. Khoka called me from behind, "Do you know where he is?

"Yes."

"Where? Tell me."

"Where he always was."

Khoka was surprised. "What kind of address is that?"

"That's the only address I know, Khoka."

It is amazing inded that 1930 conspired to prevent our union and 1972 conspired that we should meet. My confidence is growing.  I may be able to reach my destination.

I am unable to understand how a person who wrote such beautiful and sensitive letters in 1930 could write that obnoxious book in 1933    I found no depth of thought in it.  Now I am afraid whether the tender and beautiful mind that is expressed in every line of these letters is still alive; or has it dried out under the pressure of pedantry?  The more I hear about his famed scholarship, the more apprehensive I grow.  I know the soul gets crushed under the load of learning.  My father used to say, "Many of us are bent with the burden of learning and move like an animal weighed down by the load on its back.  Only for Rabindranath is it different.  It goes into his blood and what is a weight for us turns into wings for him and makes him soar high up in the sky."

As the time of departure comes near and all the obstacles melt away, I am puzzled to think from where this whirlwind blew and changed the course of my life—and what will be the culmination.

My husband of course is continuously assuring me, "Be sure some good will come out of it.  I am certain all this has a purpose.  Suffering is never fruitless.  Both of us will profit by it."

"But how can *you* profit by it?" I ask.

"Oh, I will," he assures me.

I know he is gaining much.  All of us now know his mettle more than we ever did.  We respect him more.  He himself is discovering his own worth.  As if he is passing, with honours, a test of patience, love and selflessness.

He is crossing all the hurdles of life effortlessly.  I sometimes wonder whether that mute judge-sadhu of Hrishikesh could ever attain the height my husband has reached, living in our ordinary, mundane household.

I am busy writing my lectures and attending to various other details.  Yet I am moving in a dream—my mind is unattached and overpowered by a strange nameless emotion.

I have taken up my pen to write about this strange and
unusual phenomenon, and not really about what happened
in 1930.

The story of two young people. The sudden and abrupt
ending of an early love is a common occurrence. Such
episodes are aplenty. They have happened in the past and
will happen in the future. Many writers have written about
the sad endings of first love, with pens much more powerful
than mine. I am writing to record the episode that happened
forty-two years later, because it is astounding and probably
without precedence. And it is precisely for that reason that
I find it extremely difficult to express things—there is no
language to convey my state of mind of this period. It
seems words have become lifeless shadows—they have no
strength to catch my ideas.

Since some months before I remembered Mircea again
—quite a few months before Sergui came—I used to feel
a mysterious yearning in me, of which I have written. I
cannot describe the acuteness of that feeling. I continuously
hummed those lines—"I am restless, I aspire for far-away
things—I forget, I always forget that I have no wings."
My feelings at this time can be expressesd only through
music.

We had a colleague, a padre who had many foreign
contacts. Off and on I asked him: "Can you arrange for
me to go to some far-away place?"

"Where do you want to go?"

"Anywhere, outside this country."

"What's wrong with this country?"

I would sulk. This man won't help.

"Well—we will do something, but tell me where you
want to go."

"Anywhere—Japan, England, America."

"Anywhere?" He scrutinized me. "You are an
amazing woman."

This yearning was like the dawn before sunrise, as

if some unknown power was calling me from some
unknown place and freeing me of all my shackles.  It was
like a message of spring that comes unseen and makes the
seed sprout, opening the prison door of the earth.  It was
destined that the walls of my prison would fall apart.
Mircea was only a tool.  What prison is this?  It is the
prison of a blind faith in this world, the world that I have
known only through my five senses and considered as
final.  I know this state of my mind can only be temporary;
it won't last long.  Yet for a little while, the door of
the prison house opened for me.  I could view the
infinite.  I was lifted to some other dimension from where
I realised that what we think of as past is not past.  Time
does not go away anywhere; it has no beginning, no end.
Like Arjuna, I had a darshan of the Universal Form.  But
what did I gain by it?  Bewildered, I beseech: God, tell
me how did I profit by it?  But do I not know the answer
myself?  The question of loss and gain does not arise;
there are certain events which have no purpose in the
world of everyday life; but those unreal, purposeless and
superfluous things build the human world, so different
from that of the animals.  At least for these eight months
I realised I was not a biped only; I was a human being with
a seed of immortality in me, with the right to view reality
from another perspective.

The Infinite has picked me up from the world below.
Holding me in its lap, it is dancing—its loosened hair has
covered my eyes, face and whole body.  The front and the
back have blended; east and west, far and near are the
same.  My prison is broken.  I am emancipated from
shame, fear, and all social ties.  Only love, unconquered by
time, burns like a pole star on the corner of that limitless
expanse.  It is guiding me, it will pilot me over the ocean.

Reaching the airport, I want to do *pranam* to my
husband.  His tender love, like a cool breeze, soothes my
body and mind.  But I cannot touch his feet here.  He will

be embarrassed, so I whisper, "You have always given me so much freedom." He smiles, "Why should I keep your freedom in my pocket and dole it out occasionally? Your freedom is your birthright."

# Book Four

AS OUR CAR SPED OVER THE HIGHWAY OF THE GREAT CITY,
I told John, "When we get to Wood Land you must tell me."
I have his address. I have collected the home address and
telephone with difficulty. There was no need to. But I
made it a ritual. I must have the right address. So long I
have been wandering on the wrong path.

The car is moving. . . new country, new city, unknown
faces are around me; I but proceed towards a destination
forever known. My mind is dazed, as if I am in a trance,
as if the person sitting with the address in hand, is a
different one from myself, from this body that has passed
through a long life. It is very difficult to keep these two
identities together. It is a hard task to remember who I am.

John said, "We are in Wood Land."

Wood Land— a wide forest on both sides, or large
houses of a populous city? I don't know. I can see big
houses with small gardens in front and sometimes a woodland
shaded by the foliage of spreading tall trees. Which one is
real? Who knows? One scene is outside, another is
inside. The scene inside   is  truer because it is the mind
that sees. Mind is the seer. The world I am living in at
present is the world of the mind. On how many sleepless
nights I have thought about this road—a path twisting
its way under the shade of tress—that thought is there even
if there are no trees.

The car stopped. Molly introduced Shirley and said,
"This girl will take you wherever you want to go."

"Did you ring up the professor? Do you know if he is
going to be in?" I asked.

"Yes, I did.   But his secretary said he has no fixed
times."

Shirley is a young girl.   She is a student of this
University.   We went to a cafetaria for some food.   She
brought the tray in, but I could not identify the items; the
fork slipped from my unsteady hands intermittently.   Shirley
must have been surprised.   Coming out on the street, I
asked, "Do you know where the theological college is?"

"Just after two blocks," she replied, pointing ahead.

"Can I walk it?"

"Why not?   It is just two blocks away."

We were walking side by side.   I tried to talk casually.

"Are you going to meet someone there?"   she asked.

'Yes, I have a friend there."

"Does he know you are coming?"

"No."

"When did you last meet him?"

"Fortytwo years ago."

"Heavens!   You have never met in these forty-two
years!   Then you won't even recognise each other."

"I think we will.   Forty-two years is not all that long
a time.   How old is this earth?   Who knows when the sun
was born?"   Suddenly I thought I should not have spoken
out this soliloquy aloud.   She might be puzzled.   Shirley
of course was surprised for a different reason.   She said,
"I wonder how it feels to meet a friend after forty years!
I can't even imagine it."

"You will in time."

"Must be dramatic."

"Everyone says life itself is a drama."

Shirley slowed her pace.   "Here we are."

Suddenly, as if from nowhere, by the touch of a
magician's wand, a signboard appeared on the lawn at the
side.   Can a signboard be so meaningful?   Am I seeing
the Holy Grail?   I floated up to the front door, walking
as if on air.   Shirley opened the large front door.   On the

right side is a large board, a series of names on it.   She
asked, "Whom do you want to see?"

I was breathless—it was impossible to talk—so I
pointed out the name.

"Oh, he?   A great man, very distinguished."

Shirley is holding me, supporting me, to help me on
the steps, why?   Am I an octogenarian?

I asked, "Why is he so famous?"

"He is a great scholar."

A great scholar!   My mind shrank back.   Whom had
I come to see?   So I asked: "Shirley, tell me whether he is
only a pundit, or is he wise."

Shirley was puzzled.   "I don't know really, I am not
acquainted with him.   I am only a student."

We have come near the lift.   Somebody was operating
it; it was a private lift.   Outsiders have to use the stairs; it's
only three stories.   I heard Shirley speak strongly "Open,
the door.   She arrived only yesterday, crossing thousands
of miles.   She won't be able to walk up one step."

I thought, Why is she saying this?   Am I trembling?
Shirley supports me in the lift.   Who knows why, in this
strange land, this unknown young girl is mothering me?

The lift stopped on the third floor.   We entered a
library.   As if I woke up from a dream—so this is a
library.   A good beginning indeed – we crossed the library
and entered a corridor.   Rooms on both sides.   Shirley
said, "There's the professor."

I entered the room.   At once the old man made a
sound, "Ohh!", and sprang to his feet.   Then he sat down
and got up again and then turned his back towards me.
What is this—I said to myself—has he recognised me?
How could he?   He has not looked at me—is it possible
that he can recognise my footfall?   Impossible.   In any
case this farce should not upset Shirley.   Coming back to
the door, I found Shirley standing wide-eyed and immobile,
like a picture.   The only witness of this strange meeting

between two old people.  I said, "Shirley, please leave us.
I will come to you after a little while."

My mind is now at peace—no excitement any more.
All that was to be done has been done.

"It is your first day today," Shirley said.  "In this great
city, you might lose your way."

"No, I won't."  I have been able to come so far,
crossing the ocean of time; I will not lose my way any more,
I told myself.

I find it difficult to come to Mircea from the door.
The distance is hazardous because of the books strewn all
over the floor—the books are heaped like rocky mountains
that reach up to the roof.  I have an eerie feeling—I am
shivering not because of cold but in fear.  I have heard
that, pressed by hard boulders, delicate animals are crushed
into fossil.  Has something like that happened to him?  I am
watching him . . . he has no hair on the top of the head;
only at the temples and at the back there is some white
hair.  He is as slim as ever and as restless.  He picks up
papers from the table and throws them back on it.

"Mircea, why are you standing with your back towards
me?"

"I will not see you.  I am waiting for someone else."

"Who are you waiting for, Mircea?"

"For an Income-Tax Officer."

"Income-Tax Officer!"

"Yes, yes, yes."

"Don't be a fool.  Do you know who I am?"

Without waiting for his answer, I heard myself repeating,
"Have you recognised me?  Do you know who I am?"

"Certainly, certainly," he tilted his head.

Oh, this is the same Mircea—the same indeed—
that twenty-three year old boy is visible in this sixty-six
year old man.  He used to tell me, You use the word
"*beeshan*" ("terribly") too often   Everything is "terrible"
for you.  So many people have told me that.  Maybe I

also used that word now, for he shakes his head saying,
"Certainly, certainly."

What a mystery! What an endless mystery!

I could recognise him so easily with my whole being.
This is he, and no one else.  And me? Who am I? I am
also the same me.   Indestructible is her sixteen-year old
mind.  You could seek her even now.  I said, "Tell me
who I am."

"You are Amrita. The moment you set your foot in
this country, I knew."

"How?" No answer.  "Tell me."  I repeated the
question.  "Why don't you speak?"

"Ed told me."

"But Ed did not know the date; how could he tell you?"

"Well, I knew."

' Turn around, dearest Mircea.  I have come from far
to see you   Won't you look at me?"

"Listen, Amrita."   He is holding the book-rack for
support, as if otherwise he might fall   "Let me tell you: I
have viewed this whole affair differently.  I am not saying
I am right.  Maybe you are right.  Why maybe—certainly
you are right."

"Why didn't you reply to my letter? Did you get it?"

"Yes, very short, two or three lines."  He made a sign
with his fingers.

"Why didn't you reply, small or big   where were your
manners?"

"Who was thinking of manners?" Then after a while.
"I am telling you, that experience was so—so sacred that I
never thought I could touch it again.  So I put you out of
time and space."

"The truth is, you thought I forgot you in my new life."

"No, no, Amrita.  Never for a moment did I think you
could forget me."  He got out a book from the shelf.  "Only
I never knew that you wanted to see me."

"Why?"

"There are so many beautiful things—the mount Sumeru, the snow-capped Himalayas—can you reach them? We know they belong to us, but can you have them? Yet that is not forgetting. They remain like the most beautiful dream caught in the innermost being of a person's private universe."

"But you see, I can reach it, here I am."

"That's because you are Amrita, indestructible Amrita. Can I do what you can? Your culture is many thousand years old—your background and mine are not the same. You are the daughter of immortal India. . . ."

"Is that so? I was told you are also an Indian."

"Oh yes, that's what I tell everyone I call myself an Indian."

"I don't want to listen to all this chatter. Turn around, Mircea, I want to see you."

He is standing but unsteady—there is about three yards space between us—so I raise my voice. We are quite old, maybe our hearing is weak.

He appears confused. "How can I see you? Did Dante ever think he would see his Beatrice with eyes of flesh?"

I am trembling. I am angry at his confusion. This man really lives in an unreal world of fantasy. From where does he bring in Dante and Beatrice?

"Why do you speak of putting me beyond time and space? Have I become a ghost? In what dream world, in what obscure heaven do you live, Mircea? I belong to this real world. I am the Amrita of flesh and blood standing in your study—this is the truth. You will have to admit it. Get rid of your escapist mentality."

"What shall I do, Amrita? You have a husband and I have a wife. What can I say now?"

I am shocked beyond measure. I stand speechless. What is this man saying? "Mircea, you have read so much, but you have acquired no wisdom! You don't speak like a wise man. Is love a material object that can be snatched away from one and given to another? Is it a property or an

ornament? It is a light, Mircea, a light—like the light of
intelligence, like the light of knowledge, is the light of love.
The light of intelligence has a limit—it works only in one
sphere, but the light of love is more lustrous—it shows
everything in its true form.   Once this light is lit, the whole
world gets filled with love.   Even unpleasant things appear
pleasant.   Believe me, Mircea, my husband has become
dearer to me after I remembered you.   I never loved him
so much before.   Will you believe that?"

He nodded his head in affirmation.   "Certainly, certainly.
True indeed."

"What is true?"

"All you say is true—you always speak the truth."

"Yes.   I have offered myself to truth and truth alone.
So I have come to recognise a supreme truth.   It has not
been an easy task, ignoring the frowns of society round
me.   Before my family, relatives and even before my own
children, I have fallen from the high pedestal of honour.
Some must think me senile.   What will people think if they
come to know of this?   You know our country—they will
spit at me.   Is it easy to come to see you after forty-two
years?"

"Not at all.   I could have never done it.   How many
times have I had invitations from my dreamland India, but
I have never gone.   How can I go there again?"

"Why?   Because I am there?"

He nodded his head.   "Yes."

"But I came because you are here.   Do you know who
gave me such courage?"

"That's what I am wondering—who made you so brave?"

"Mahatma Gandhi.   Have you read his *Experiment
with Truth?*   He opened his life before all.   So I told
myself: I talk so much of him at his birth and death
anniversaries, why can't I do what he could?   Otherwise
what's the sense in delivering talks on him?   You know
I do a good deal of lecturing."

"Did Gandhi become so great?"

"Oh yes, he grew taller. He became a much greater man than what he was when you saw him, in 1930—he dedicated his life to humanity—he was not a bookworm. . . . So I am asking you—look at the picture of me you have drawn in your book! I see no resemblance with my character—it is not me."

"Fantasy. Fantasy. I wanted to make you a mysterious being, a goddess—like Kali."

"Nonsense. Don't compare me with Kali. I am not that dark. . . you always belittle my looks."

"All right, all right, like Durga who can perform impossible things—an inscrutable being—who strikes with one hand and rescues with another—an enigma—the enigma that you were."

"Mircea, I am telling you, fantasy is beautiful and truth is more beautiful, but half-truth is terrible. Your book is a nightmare for me  I was a simple little girl who sometimes played the philosopher. I was no enigma. The mystery is your creation. You love the fantastic and unreal. But now I have really come, to perform an impossible deed." He was still standing with his head turned away from me. I stretched out my right arm towards him. My mind is lucid and steady. I will free him from his world of fantasy. We will see each other in this real world. "Awake, dearest, awake."

Mircea did not turn—his head is bent low—he is determined not to turn—"What do you want from me?"

"Peace, I want peace from you."

"Ha, ha," he threw his head back. "How can I give you peace, when I have no peace in me?" He laughed.

I am afraid. Fear grips my heart. Has he gone insane? Why can't he touch the true, the beautiful and the good? I suddenly asked, "You used to play the piano wonderfully well—do you still play?"

"No. I gave it up a long time ago"

"Why?"

"What's the use? Waste of time—"

I thought, How can he play music? His fingers have
become hard like book covers—all the blood vessels there
have dried up. . . . No, it can not be brought to life again—
that melody will not fall like the shower of rain any more.
"Mircea, here I am standing in your room, a human being
made of flesh and blood, not a symbol, not a myth. Is
this nothing to you? Beatrice went to heaven and met
Dante there. She must have been a ghost then, but is it
nothing at all that I have come to you in real life?"

He spoke without turning, with little gasping sounds.
"Wonder! What a wonder it is! So I tell the pessimists;
who knows what may be the possibilities of life? Who
can say what may happen or what may not? I never thought
there was any chance of meeting you."

"Well, turn around then."

He turned towards me, but his head was bent. He
was not looking up—he was still not prepared to meet me.
I plead, "Why are you not looking up, Mircea? You have
written in your book that if you meet me you will look
straight into my eyes. Have you forgotten that?"

"Oh that was a long time back—forty years! *Hai!*
Forty years!"

"You know people ask me how long you lived with us.
How long did you, Mircea? I cannot remember."

"A thousand years!"

"Well? Do you then not know who you are, who
we are all? I have come to see that you whom weapon
cannot pierce, fire cannot burn."

He spoke in Sanskrit: "*na hanyate hanymāné sharíre*
—it does not die, when the body dies "

"Well, what then? That you who has no beginning,
no middle, no end—I have come to see that being in
you. If you look at me, believe me, in a moment I shall take
you across the forty years, exactly to that spot where we

first met."

Mircea raised his face. His eyes were glazed. Oh no, my worst fears are true—his eyes have turned into stone. He will never see me again. What shall I do? I shall not be able to put light into those eyes—I have no lamp in my hand—walking across this long way, who knows when its oil dried out and the taper burnt off? Fear changed me— I am no more Amrita. I turned into just a mortal and I thought like him—forty years, forty years! It is too late indeed. I turned back—I must reach that door, move that brass handle and open the door; then I will slip out to the street and walk up to Shirley. From the depth of my being a sigh heaved up and it whirled in the room. I walked towards the door, crossing over the little hillocks of books, when I heard Mircea's voice from the back, "Amrita, wait a little. Why are you breaking down now, when you were so brave for so many years. I promise you I shall come to you, and there on the shores of the Ganga, I will show you my real self."

I am not a pessimist. Inside my broken heart a tiny bird of hope was in its death throes but no sooner Mircea's words reached me, than that little bird revived and turned into a phoenix. Has anyone seen a phoenix? It looks exactly like an albatross. The huge bird flapped its great wings and then, picking me up, it rose higher and higher as the roof of Mircea's study opened like Pandora's box and the walls disappeared—all the stony books turned into ripples—I heard the gurgle of flowing water.

That great bird, built with the illusion of hope, whispered to me, as we moved towards an unknown continent, crossing Lake Michigan, "Do not be disheartened, Amrita, you will put light in his eyes."

"When?" I asked eagerly.

"When you meet him in the Milky Way—that day is not very far now," it replied.

# GLOSSARY

*Akas Ganga* : Milky Way or Chayapath.

*Alta* : a red colour used for decorating the soles of the feet.

*Anadi Dastidar* : A well-known singer and teacher of Rabindranath's songs.

*Anarkali* : Sixteen-year old slave girl whom Emperor Akbar buried alive.

*Andrews Sahib* : The missionary C. F. Andrews, a friend of Rabindranath and Gandhi.

*Ardhanariswar* : Siva and his consort in one body—a deity that is half man and half woman.

*Arya Samaj* : A religious reformist movement in Hinduism.

*Ashtanga Yoga* : Eight forms of yoga.

*Bankim* : The well-known Bengali novelist Bankim Chandra Chatterjee, whose *Krishnakanta's Will* is available in paperback.

*Bāsarghar* : The nuptial chamber.

*Brahmo* : A unitarian sect, which intended to reform Hindu society and was strictly against all forms of idolatry.

*Brahmavadini* : Any woman-sage who speaks about the supreme being, the Absolute.

*Balaka* : A book of verse by Rabindranath.

*Amrita* : The feminine noun suggests one who has become immortal by drinking the nectar of immortality *(amrita)*.

*Bijoykrishna Goswami* : A well-known religious preceptor of 19th century Bengal.

*Bowdidi* : A form of address for an elder brother's wife ; literally, "wife-sister,"

*Bauls* : A sect of folk singers who follow a special humanist
  philosophy, combining idealistic Hindu and Muslim
  beliefs.

*Chatim* : Horse-chestnut.

*Chandsi* : Ointment—a *hakimi* medicine made by traditional
  Arabic physicians.

*Darshan* : Blessing consisting in viewing of eminent person.

*Dhuti* : A long piece of cloth, tucked at the waist—a man's
  dress.

*Didi* : Elder sister.   According to Indian custom, elder sisters,
  brothers or cousins are respectfully addressed as *didi* and
  *dada* (or *di* and *da* used as suffix with the name.)

*Didima* : Mother's mother.

*Draupadi* : Wife of the five Pandava brothers in the epic
  *Mahabharata.*

*Durga* : The saviour deity of the good and destroyer of evil.
  She rides a lion, has ten hands; with a lance in one of
  these she slays the buffalo-demon.

*Dushyanta* : A king who betrayed his wife Sakuntala, a hermit's
  daughter and, when accusing her of falsely incriminating
  him, said, "With women lying is instinctive."

*Gandharva vivaha* : The system of marriage prevalent among
  the Gandharvas, who were celestial musicians   It is an
  accepted form of marriage in which girl and boy can marry
  of their own choice without rites, and in secret.

*Gouranga* : Founder of the Vaisnava sect.   A religious
  reformer.

*Gurkhas* : A martial people who reside in the Himalayan
  region.

*Gurukul* : A university in the Himalayas, where education is
  imparted in Sanskrit and in the ancient Indian methods.

*Haramjada* : Son of a swine.

*Indrapuri* : Indra is king of the gods ; "puri" (a place, a house)
  —the palace of Indra.

*Jatin Das* : A patriot who died fasting in jail.

*Jivatma and Paramatma* : Jivatma is the sentient soul

incorporated in the human body; Paramatma is the
supreme spirit.

*Kacha and Devayani* : The story of Kacha and Devayani
describes how Kacha was sent by the *suras* (gods) to learn
the hidden art of bringing the dead back to life. The
priest Sukra, though it was against his interest, accepted
Kacha as a disciple seeking knowledge. Kacha stayed
with him and Devayani, the daughter of the priest. They
fell in love, but, after acquiring the knowledge, Kacha
went back to heaven saying that his work was more
important than love.

*Kalidas* : Famous Sanskrit dramatist (circa 4th century A.D.)

*Kalidas Nag* : A famous professor and historian : a friend of
Romain Rolland, and close associate of Rabindranath.

*Kama* : Cupid in the Hindu pantheon.

*Kamandalu* : A special water jug used by hermits.

*Kamini Roy* : A famous poetess.

*Karma* : The Hindu theory of action-reaction and birth-rebirth.

*Keora* : Water-made with *keora* perfume.

*Kesava-Krishna* : Who holds in his four hands four emblems—
conch shell, chakra, mace, and lotus.

*Kashiram Das* : The translator of the *Mahabharata* in Bengali
verse.

*Konarak* : Sun Temple of Orissa famous for its erotic carvings.

*Kshitimohan Sen* : A distinguished professor in Rabindranath's
institution at Santiniketan; author of the Penguln book
on Hinduism.

*Kushandika* : The performance of joint religious rites by bride
and bridegroom.

*Lathi* : Baton.

*Lungi* : A poor man's dress, somewhat like a sarong.

*Ma* : In India women are universally addressed as "ma" or
mother, sometimes to show respect, sometimes out of
affection.

*Madhusudan Dutt* : Nineteenth-century poet who introduced
blank verse in Bengali and is referred to as the "Milton

of Bengal".

*Mahadev* : An appellation of Siva.

*Mahakal* : Infinite time; an appellation of Siva, the
   destroyer-aspect of the Hindu trinity.

*Maharshi* : "great sage"; honorific of Maharshi Devendranath
   Thakur, father of Rabindranath.

*"Mahua"* : A book of verse by Rabindranath.

*Mali* : Gardener.

*Mantra* : Hymn or esoteric sacred formula.

*Mankumari Basu* : Child-widow, and well-known poetess; she
   was Madhusudan Dutt's neice.

*Maya* : illusion.

*Meghaduta* : "Cloud Messenger", a lyric poem by Kalidas
   where the separated husband asks the cloud to carry his
   message of love to his wife.

*Mirabai* : A woman saint-singer of the 16th century.

*Mlechcha* : A foreigner.

*Nagrai* : Indian-style hand-made decorative shoes.

*Namaskar* : A form of greeting one's equals by pressing one's
   palms together.

*Nataraj* : The dancing Siva.

*Nilambari* : A blue sari specially meant as Radha's dress.

*Pan* : Betel nut leaf chewed for digestive purposes, generally
   after meals.

*Panjabi* : A loose shirt; men's wear.

*Puranas* : Hindu texts of mythology.

*Priyamvada Devi* : A lyric poetess.

*Punthi* : Ancient manuscript written by hand on leaf or
   bark-paper.

*Purdah* : "Curtain"; orthodox women usually remained,
   unseen by strangers, behind the curtain.

*Pranam* : A form of greeting one's elders.

*Rabindranath* : See Rabi Thakur.

*Rabindrik* : Tagorean.

*Rabi Thakur* : Rabindranath Thakur (Tagore).   Rabindra
   means the "great sun".

*Radha* : Krishna's consort.

*Raga* : Raga has many meanings—anger, love, music, colour, etc. Here he puns on the word, meaning not anger but love.

*Ramananda Chatterjee* : Distinguished editor of three monthly magazines, and close associate of Rabindranath.

*Ramen Chakraborty* : An artist of repute. Later principal of the Art College, Calcutta.

*Sadhana* : A book by Rabindranath.

*Sadhana* : Penance.

*Sahib and mem* : European man and woman. Sahib is also used to mean anyone in high office.

*Sakhi* : A loving address meaning friend; closer to "darling"— extensively used in Vaisnava literature. Radha's friends were her sakhis; they were sakhis of Krishna also.

*Sakuntala* : A drama by Kalidas.

*Sala* : "brother-in-law"; but meant as abuse when used for others.

*Sandesh* : A kind of sweet.

*Sankara* : The great philosopher who propounded the theory of illusion or the relative reality of the world (maya).

*Sannyasi* : Sadhu, one who has renounced the world.

*Santiniketan* : "abode of peace"—name of the school founded by Rabindranath.

*Sarat Chandra* : A Bengali novelist of repute.

*Sarojini Naidu* : A poet and politician of repute; she wrote her poetry in English.

*Sati* : Self-immolation of a woman on her husband's funeral pyre.

*Shehnai* : A special kind of flute.

*Somapayee* : One who drinks the juice of the *soma* creeper. This intoxicating drink was taken by the sages of India for inducing transcendental meditation. Soma also means moon—the soma creeper waxed and waned with the moon.

*Srichaitanya* : Same as Gouranga—founder of a reformist religious sect, four hundred years ago.

*Subhas Bose* : Subhas Ch. Bose, a great nationalist leader.

*Sudra* : The lowest of the castes.

*Svayamvara* : A girl who chooses her own husband.   In
    ancient India girls of high families chose their own
    husbands from gatherings specially arranged for this
    purpose.